Praise for bestselling author Debra Webb

"Brims with tightly woven suspense around every corner, and twists and turns abound. Webb moves effortlessly between two very diverse romances and masterfully keeps the reader on the edge until the last page."
—*RT Book Reviews* on *Striking Distance*

"Debra Webb is endowed with an incredible imagination and an impressive ability to create multidimensional, realistic characters."
—*The Romance Reader.com*

Praise for bestselling author Julie Miller

"Another excellent book from Julie Miller!"
—*Romance Reviews Today* on *Forbidden Captor*

"[Miller] writes some of the most intense story lines, and her latest entry is a smooth, nonstop ride."
—*RT Book Reviews* on *Nanny 911*

DEBRA WEBB

Debra Webb wrote her first story at age nine and her first romance at thirteen. It wasn't until she spent three years working for the military behind the Iron Curtain and within the confining political walls of Berlin, Germany, that she realized her true calling. A five-year stint with NASA on the space shuttle program reinforced her love of the endless possibilities within her grasp as a storyteller. A collision course between suspense and romance was set. Debra has been writing romance, suspense and action-packed romance thrillers since.

Visit her at www.debrawebb.com or write to her at P.O. Box 4889, Huntsville, AL 35815.

JULIE MILLER

Julie Miller attributes her passion for writing romance to all those fairy tales she read growing up, and to shyness. Encouragement from her family to write down those feelings she couldn't express became a love for the written word. She gets continued support from her fellow members of the Prairieland Romance Writers, where she serves as the resident "grammar goddess." This award-winning author and teacher has published several paranormal romances. Inspired by the likes of Agatha Christie and Encyclopedia Brown, Ms. Miller believes the only thing better than a good mystery is a good romance.

Born and raised in Missouri, she now lives in Nebraska with her husband, son and smiling guard dog, Maxie. Write to Julie at P.O. Box 5162, Grand Island, NE 68802-5162.

BESTSELLING AUTHOR COLLECTION

DEBRA WEBB

Striking Distance

HARLEQUIN®
entertain, enrich, inspire™

Recycling programs for this product may not exist in your area.

ISBN-13: 978-0-373-18066-0

STRIKING DISTANCE
Copyright © 2012 by Harlequin Books S.A.

The publisher acknowledges the copyright holders of the individual works as follows:

STRIKING DISTANCE
Copyright © 2004 by Debra Webb

FORBIDDEN CAPTOR
Copyright © 2005 by Harlequin Books S.A.

CONTENTS

STRIKING DISTANCE   7
Debra Webb

FORBIDDEN CAPTOR   323
Julie Miller

Dear Reader,

Thank you so much for purchasing *Striking Distance*. This is a very important story in my long-running Colby Agency series. Just a couple of months ago the fiftieth book in the Colby Agency series was released. If you're new to the series I hope you will be intrigued by this story and want to read more.

Victoria Colby is one of my favorite characters. Her journey through tragedy and triumph has made her one of my readers' most beloved characters, as well. This story in particular reveals so very much about Victoria, past, present and future.

Hold on to your heart—you're in for an emotional and action-packed ride! Be sure to visit my website, www.debrawebb.com, for news about upcoming books!

Enjoy!

Debra Webb

Debra Webb
STRIKING DISTANCE

Special thanks to Denise Zaza, the absolute best editor on the planet. Thanks so very much for your trust and your encouragement. It was only with your unerring guidance that this dream came true.

This book is dedicated to one of the finest men I have had the personal and professional pleasure of knowing. He is definitely one heck of a good man. This one is for you, Ebb Deason.

Chapter 1

No matter the legacy a man left behind, ultimately it was his death that defined him.

Chicago's Rosehill Cemetery was something of a tourist attraction with its medieval castle-like entrance of Joliet limestone and dozens of brooding mausoleums ranging in architectural styles from Egyptian to Gothic. The inhabitants, Civil War generals and soldiers as well as vice presidents, all lay in perpetual slumber in a place so blatantly filled with pomp and circumstance that even the soft tread of footsteps seemed an intrusion.

However well landscaped and adorned with lush shrubbery and graceful trees, this city of the dead with its foreboding Celtic cross and shimmering lake was still just a cemetery. Row after row of markers, whether mere headstones or more elaborate structures, represented lives that existed no longer.

His seeking gaze settled on one plot in particular where a woman stood quietly, probably reminiscing about the life long since laid to rest there.

The date of death engraved on the cold granite head-stone indicated little about the man interred...but the name inscribed on that same glossy black surface said all that one needed to know.

James Colby.

Beloved husband and father.

Another epitaph should have been added: Ruthless butcher and marauder.

The great James Colby had been shot down and killed like the worthless bastard he was and not a minute too soon. But, even in death, his presence still lingered among the living. His essence kept alive...his work continued by a woman who was no better than he had been. Though she'd been warned, she persisted in her self-ordained, lofty endeavors. Just like her husband, nothing would stop her.

Except death.

And now her time was close at hand.

From his vantage point fifty meters away, well within striking distance, he read her every expression, watched her every movement through the crosshairs of his high-powered tactical scope. It was a face he had come to know intimately with the use of advanced technology and un-ending patience.

Looking weary and resigned the woman peered down at the elegant headstone as she no doubt struggled with the overwhelming silence around her...felt dizzy with the stifled senses of the dead and buried. The smell of damp earth would fill her nostrils with each breath she drew into her lungs, a sickening reminder that the rich, sodden soil perpetually cloaked her long-dead husband in its cold, relentless embrace.

Nothing could change the past.

Victoria Colby, he knew, had slowly come to realize

that only she had the power to change the future. He'd waited a very long time for her to come to that understanding.

And yet she was powerless to deter him from his course.

She would die.

Soon.

The decision had been made long ago. His mission sanctioned even before he became a man.

He zeroed in to where her black heart beat beneath the tailored navy suit she wore. His finger curled around the trigger as his respiration ceased entirely. The bipod held the rifle steady, its precision aim a work of master craftsmanship.

He could kill her now...this instant...and nothing or no one could stop him.

Certainly not the crippled excuse for a man who stood a few meters to her left, watching, his senses so keen, his internal alarm so sensitive that he recognized some unknown threat even now. Smelled the danger in the very air. His rigid posture broadcasted a status of elevated alert.

But Lucas Camp had nothing to fear today.

The venerable Victoria Colby remained safe for the moment.

Oh, she would die.

But only one knew the day and the hour that death would come.

And it damn sure wasn't God.

Chapter 2

Victoria Colby knelt before her late husband's headstone, uncaring that the waning October sun had yet to dry the morning's heavy dew from the grass. She traced the deeply gouged lines in the sleek surface that formed the letters of his name...the date of his passing. A heavy breath caught in her throat before it raggedly slipped past her trembling lips. How she missed him still.

Fifteen years had passed since she'd watched his body lowered into this grave. Since then the life she had once known had ground to a sudden and vicious halt. Without the help of her dedicated friends and colleagues at the Colby Agency, the private investigations firm her husband had nurtured like a child during his final days on this earth, she would surely not have survived his murder.

Her friends had gathered around her, united in strength and loyalty by the heinous tragedy, and held her up when she would otherwise have fallen. With their help she had risen from the ashes of devastation and forged ahead with her husband's dream, making the Colby Agency the very best in the business of private investigations. She had reached that goal, surpassed it, even. James would be very proud. The Colby Agency employed only the finest in the fields of investigation and security. The reputation she had garnered with the help of her outstanding staff was unparalleled.

As proud of that accomplishment as she was, fifteen years was a very long time to devote oneself to nothing but work. In a few months she would turn fifty. That milestone would be reached with nothing to show for her half century on this earth other than her esteemed agency. For some that might be enough, but not for her. She needed...wanted...

She glanced at the man who respectfully waited a short distance away. His presence made her all the more aware of how much more she wanted. *He* had been there for her through it all. Had waited patiently for his time to come.

Lucas Camp had served the United States government in one capacity or another for his entire adult life. Most of that dedicated duty had been spent working covert operations that only the president and God knew about. Not once had he hesitated, not even when his own life was at grave risk, when assigned a mission. It was that same man's selflessness that had saved James Colby's life in Vietnam and had shored up her resolve on too many occasions to name when she had felt ready to give up...to crumble beneath the weight of seemingly perpetual agonies. He had showered her with an unending source of friendship and kindness, of encouragement and belief in her ability to go on.

For some time now she had known that Lucas was in love with her. Admittedly, what she felt for him could be called nothing else. She knew without reservation that

James would want her to be happy, would want no less for her than the kind of man Lucas Camp epitomized.

And still she had hesitated to allow their close relationship to evolve naturally.

The past had haunted her for far too long.

Victoria stared down at her left hand and the narrow gold band that had resided there for twenty-seven years. It was time she moved forward with her personal life. She slipped the band from her finger, held it tightly for one more moment, then pressed it gently into the soft soil at the base of the headstone. "Thank you for all that you gave me, James," she whispered. "You'll always be in my heart."

She swiped away a lone tear that trekked down her cheek and drew in a deep breath of much-needed resolve. It was time to move on, to look to the future rather than the past. She braced a hand on the cool surface of the granite and pushed to her feet.

She had waited long enough.

So had Lucas.

If only she knew the right words to say to thank him for his patience and unending devotion. But there were no words to accurately describe her feelings. Actions spoke louder than words. She'd asked him to bring her here today to show him her intentions.

She smiled when he joined her. "Thank you for giving me a moment."

Those gray eyes searched hers with a kind of uncertainty she would never have associated with the man she knew so well. "You're sure about this?" He glanced at her left hand and its bare ring finger.

Victoria nodded. "Yes. It's time I paid attention to what's important *now*."

An emotion she couldn't quite define replaced the uncertainty in his eyes. The ferocity of it made her pulse rush with anticipation. "We'll take this slow, Victoria. One step at a time. There's no need to hurry."

Warmth spread through her at his words. He'd stood vigil so very long and still he wouldn't make a single move without considering her feelings first and foremost.

"We'll take it slow in the beginning," she allowed, wanting him to hear in her voice the warmth that his nearness generated inside her.

A tiny smile quirked the corners of his mouth. "You're the boss." He gently folded his arm around her. "Let me take you to lunch," he suggested, that ever-watchful gaze doing a quick, covert—but not quite covert enough—area sweep. "The wind is brisk out here, don't you think?"

She kept her smile firmly in place and resisted the urge to look around the cemetery, brutally squashed the little shiver that threatened to scurry up her spine. Something had put Lucas on guard. He wanted to get her out of here in a hurry but without alarming her in any way. He didn't want to ruin the moment that he knew had been a long time in coming for her—for them.

She trusted his instincts too much to ignore his assessment. Though she hated even the suggestion of running from a threat, she wasn't a fool. Fate had been cruel to her, she'd lost her child and her husband in the space of three years. There had been a time when death would have been a blessed relief. Even now, at times, she wondered how she had survived the utter devastation. If the threat involved only her, she might choose to ignore it... but that was not the case. She'd come too close to losing Lucas only a few months ago on that godforsaken island to think for one second that he was as untouchable as he'd like her to believe.

She could not lose him…not now when she'd only just fully realized how very much she needed him.

She would do whatever it took to keep him safe and away from the evil that had destroyed her life once.

Leberman, the soulless devil, would not win this time.

Though she had never been able to prove it, she knew Errol Leberman was responsible for her husband's death. She couldn't be positive he was the one who had taken her son, but in her heart she knew it was a strong possibility. He had done all within his power for twenty long years to destroy her. Just a few short months ago he'd almost succeeded.

The ruthless bastard had lured first Lucas, then her, to St. Gabriel Island. Lucas had been badly hurt…and she'd known that she could not let Leberman win.

He had to be stopped.

Permanently.

Chapter 3

Lucas always enjoyed his time with Victoria, but today he'd been distracted. She had noticed, and to some degree there had been nothing he could do about that. She read him too well.

"You're sure that's all that's bothering you?" she asked again as she closed the door of her office behind them. He hadn't felt she was secure until he'd gotten her back into this building, this office. His concern at the cemetery as well as at the quiet, out-of-the-way restaurant where they'd dined had apparently been obvious.

Her own suspicions had been raised and she didn't intend to let it go. No one could accuse Victoria Colby of being anything less than persistent. As she awaited his response she shouldered out of her jacket and hung it on the coat tree in the corner, unknowingly providing him with an opportunity to simply look at her in a rare, unguarded state.

He suddenly wished he could see her dark hair loose. He knew it would be long, though she always kept it in a serviceable, upswept arrangement. The silver highlights enhanced the depth of the woman. As she turned to face him once more, he stole yet another moment to admire her effortless beauty. Great personal loss had etched her porcelain skin with fine lines, yet failed to detract from the gentle, sophisticated elegance.

He had been in love with Victoria from the moment he first laid eyes on her thirty years ago. But she had been the fiancé of his best friend and colleague, later to become his wife. As much as Lucas loved her...wanted her...he would, even now, undo the past, resurrect her husband and son in a heartbeat to make her happy, if only he possessed the power. But he could not, of course. He could, however, love her and protect her until the day he took his dying breath.

That he *would* do.

He produced the expected smile and stuck to his original story that would tie in to his immediate plans. "It's nothing, really. Casey has gotten it into his head that I need a vacation and, well—" he shrugged, using all the tactics he had learned over the years in the spy business to hide what he didn't want her to see "—you know how I am about work. I can't see myself taking off that kind of time. But Casey is the boss and he keeps insisting." He heaved a sigh. "I have a feeling he isn't going to take no for an answer. This little trip away from D.C. won't be enough to appease him."

Victoria looked thoughtful for a moment. "I've been getting the same hassle around here," she said, her brow furrowing. "Everyone but me thinks I need a vacation. I suppose even I realize it's past time I took some time off." It was her turn to shrug. The gesture drew his eyes to her slender but proud shoulders and the white silk blouse she wore. The contrast of the delicate, feminine fabric to the strong, tough-as-nails woman beneath only served to widen his smile into the genuine article. "Maybe I should," she went on as she looked directly at him, a new kind of sparkle in those brown eyes. "Maybe *we* should." Her expression turned inquisitive, the barest hint of a smile curled the corners of her lips. "What're you grinning about?"

He held her gaze for a couple of beats, weighing her words and the emotion that looked very much like desire he'd noticed there. "Is that an invitation, Victoria?" he ventured, ignoring her question for the moment. His heartbeat accelerated, sending a surge of heat through his body. He wanted this. Wanted it very much. But it had to be her choice...her decision.

She unconsciously rubbed her left hand, missing the ring she'd worn for more than half of her life. "Yes," she said succinctly. "It is."

Scarcely breathing for fear he would somehow break this spell, Lucas took her hands in his and considered how she'd tucked that precious gold wedding band into the ground next to her husband's headstone. That act had taken a great deal of courage, and he respected what it surely meant. She was ready to move on. But he would not push the issue. He had waited a lifetime for this woman, a few weeks longer wouldn't hurt. But her safety was another issue altogether.

He was getting closer.

Lucas had sensed his presence today at the cemetery. During lunch he'd excused himself briefly to meet with his security team leader in the restaurant's bar. His suspicions had been confirmed.

The man, who they assumed at this point to be a hired assassin, had taken up a position about fifty meters from Victoria. He'd been armed with a special police-style rifle, complete with tactical scope and bipod. At one point, one of the two specialists assigned to Victoria's secret security detail had almost engaged the target. Lucas had warned his men that the assassin was to be kept alive if at all possible. But he'd gotten damned close today. The only thing that had kept Lucas's man from taking out the assassin was the fact that he'd visually verified the weapon's positive three-position thumb safety was still locked. The shooter had had no intention of killing Victoria today.

He'd simply been watching.

Lucas could only assume that he was standing by for final authorization to complete the mission. He'd had at least three opportunities so far and hadn't acted. But there would come a time when he would, that was a certainty. Lucas had to take countermeasures before that happened. Somehow, while keeping Victoria safe and allowing the assassin to stay on their trail temporarily, he had to get someone close to this guy. It was the only way he could hope to catch the real threat: Leberman.

Victoria would never be safe as long as Leberman was alive. If he had hired this assassin as Lucas suspected, there might be a chance of tracking this hired killer right back to the bastard's hiding place. Which was the only reason they hadn't taken out the shooter already. They needed him to get to Leberman.

"Then we have plans to make," Lucas offered as he dispensed with the other troubling thoughts and focused on her invitation. "Where would you like to go?"

She searched his face, looking for some hint of what was on his mind. Suspicion still nagged at her, he knew. "Shall I have Mildred bring us coffee while we discuss the possibilities?"

The prospect of planning their joint vacation pleased

her, and he hated like hell to disappoint her. They were so close. He groaned and glanced at his watch. "I have another meeting in thirty minutes. I could try and re-schedule or—" he pretended to mull the idea over "—why don't you think about the destination possibilities and then we'll discuss the options over dinner tonight?"

"That would be lovely."

He squeezed her hands once more before letting go. "I'll see you at eight, then."

She nodded, her hopeful expression wilting just a little. He would make this up to her.

Victoria watched Lucas leave her office, the ever-present limp only adding to his distinguished demeanor. He looked so handsome today. The gray shirt emphasized his eyes. The elegant charcoal suit fit his lean frame perfectly. Their time at lunch had been more relaxed than any they'd shared since before the incident on St. Gabriel Island. It had felt good to simply be, with no talk of Leberman or the past.

She wanted it that way from now on.

He wanted it, too. She knew he did.

The only thing she couldn't figure out was why he insisted on lying to her.

Chapter 4

Lucas leaned against the examination table in the small treatment room and waited for the others to arrive.

The door opened, and a nurse with a cheery expression peeked in at him. "Mr. Camp, would you like some water or coffee?"

"No, thanks."

She shot him a cheeky smile and disappeared, allowing the door to close with a slow whoosh behind her.

He couldn't risk detection of this meeting. Complete secrecy was crucial. If Leberman or any of his people—and he could only assume that the assassin might be one of several—saw Lucas with Victoria's most-trusted investigators, they would know he was on to them. He didn't want that to happen any sooner than necessary. Nor could he risk that any part of the Colby Agency offices were bugged. It was a long shot since the offices were swept for foreign electronics on a regular basis, but one he wasn't willing to chance. As long as Leberman thought they were one step behind, he wouldn't get nervous and perhaps do something rash, like giving the final execution order.

The door opened again and Ian Michaels entered the room followed closely by Simon Ruhl. They were the kind of spit-and-polish guys who epitomized the term *spy*. But Lucas knew the gritty, less glamorous side of the business. He couldn't be deputy director of Mission Recovery without having been exposed to the worst that man was capable of. The highly trained Specialists in Mission Recovery were only called in when all else failed.

Ian acknowledged Lucas with a mere nod while Simon commented, "Nice place for a meeting."

This wouldn't be the first time Lucas had used a physician's office for a clandestine meeting, but it had been a long time. Not since his surgery after bringing down the traitor who'd almost destroyed Mission Recovery before Casey came on the scene as director. Had it been four years already? At any rate, this physician was an old friend from his military days. His Chicago clinic, situated mere blocks from the Colby Agency's location just off the Magnificent Mile, was a perfect front for conducting covert ops.

"You have any trouble with the transportation?" His lips twitched when he noted the slightest flinch in Ian's carefully controlled exterior.

"Not if you discount the siren," Ian commented dryly.

Though Lucas had walked into the office like any paying patient, Ian and Simon had arrived by ambulance and were hustled in through the rear emergency entrance. Anyone watching Lucas enter the clinic would never know that two Colby agents had arrived via the back door.

"So, what's going on, Lucas?" Simon was the first to call the meeting to order. Ian remained occupied with sizing up Lucas and his intentions. The man was good at that. Could tell more by watching his prey for mere minutes than from listening to hours of interrogation. Victoria had bragged to Lucas long ago about Ian. He was good at the business of peeling away the outer layers and getting to the bottom of things.

"I told you two weeks ago that I suspected Victoria was being watched." He spread his hands in a speculative gesture. "I couldn't be sure of the source of the problem—still can't be absolutely certain. But we now have reason to believe that this man may be connected to Leberman. He may be on the verge of making a move."

Silence reigned briefly while the two men absorbed the ramifications of that bit of information. Anyone who had been with the Colby Agency for any length of time knew about Leberman. The bastard had made it his life's mission to destroy Victoria Colby and all that she stood for. Lucas was certain he'd killed James Colby as well as the boy, Victoria's only child. But even that wasn't enough for the devil. He just kept coming back for more. Playing his sick games and then going back into hiding. He hybernated for years…until it was safe to surface again. Then he'd strike.

But this time was going to be different. This time Leberman was going to die.

"We don't have any real evidence to support our assessment, of course," Lucas went on pushing the disturbing memories away, "but I'm certain enough to take the appropriate action. I've put a security detail in place."

"We've reviewed every case that might carry enough significance to warrant this sort of vengeance," Simon informed him, bringing him up to speed on their end and lending even more credence to Lucas's conclusion. "There simply isn't anyone out there related to a Colby Agency case who we have reason to suspect at this time."

Lucas stroked his chin as he considered how to broach the next step. Neither of these gentlemen was going to like his strategy, and their cooperation was essential.

"What is it you're not telling us?" Ian cut to the chase.

Lucas almost smiled. Two minutes and the guy had nailed him to the floor. Judging by the fierce glare he had trained on Lucas at that moment there was no way around giving him a straight answer.

"The man watching Victoria may be a professional assassin hired by Leberman. I believe his mission is to complete what Leberman started on that island."

The air thickened with a new level of tension. All three were well aware of the events that had unfolded on St. Gabriel Island in a matter of hours. Events that had been years in the planning. The tiny island off the coast of Georgia had proven the perfect stage for his devious plans.

"Then she is no longer safe in any public setting," Ian suggested.

"I would have to agree with you." Evading the issue would be pointless. "To be frank, he's had ample opportunity already, but has chosen not to take the shot. My conclusion would be that he's keeping surveillance and waiting for final authorization from Leberman."

"But you can't be certain that Leberman is the one behind this," Simon countered. "You don't have any actual proof. No factual intelligence."

"No." Lucas looked from one to the other, reading the skepticism they wanted to cling to. No one wanted to believe Leberman was back, least of all Lucas. "Everything I have is speculation. But we all know he's the most logical candidate."

"Why haven't you taken out the assassin already?" Ian pressed as his own sense of anticipation obviously moved to the next level. To his way of thinking that would have been the most strategic move. Hell, it made perfect sense, but Lucas had his reasons.

This would be the tricky part. "We all know that Victoria will not hide from this once she's briefed on the situation. Nothing any of us could say would change her mind. And we also know that she will never be safe as long as Leberman is alive—"

"We've had this conversation already," Simon noted matter-of-factly. His agitation was somewhat more evident than Ian's. Tension radiated in every aspect of his posture.

"We have," Lucas agreed. "My stand on the matter has not changed. We need to get Leberman. If this assassin can lead us to him, we have to take the risk."

"The risk you speak of," Ian interjected calmly, his subdued tone more lethal than if he'd shouted the words, "involves Victoria's life, correct?"

Their gazes locked for two beats. "Correct."

"And you are willing to take this risk?" Ian pushed for finite clarification.

"It's our only option."

The two Colby agents exchanged a look.

Simon spoke up first. "Lucas, I'm confident that Victoria's best interests are your primary concern. I know you'll do whatever is necessary to protect her, but you must know that we can't simply pretend this isn't happening. We have to take some sort of action."

"The only action that will make a difference requires Victoria's cooperation, which will compromise our efforts." He divided his attention between the two somber-faced men. "I have an alternate approach in mind. First I have to persuade her to take a vacation with me. I've plotted a destination. She'll be completely cocooned by my team of Specialists until we can reel this guy in. I won't allow anything to happen to her, you can rest assured of that."

"You'll keep us informed of every step," Simon persisted.

"I'll keep the two of you informed." Lucas gestured from one to the other. "I don't want anyone else to know the plan. *No one,* is that understood?"

"Are you implying there might be a traitor inside the Colby Agency?" Ian inquired, one brow raised slightly higher than the other his only outward indication of surprise.

"I'm not implying anything," Lucas asserted. "I'm simply not taking any risks. No one but the four members assigned to her security will know exactly where she is. And even those four won't know where they're going and for what reason until they get there. If there is a breach in security it won't be on my end."

"If you spirit her away to safety," Simon countered, "how is that going to affect the situation with the assassin and his leading you to Leberman?"

Another dicey maneuver. "I'm going to send someone undercover to get close to him."

"Since complete anonymity is essential, who will you utilize for that assignment?" Ian wanted to know, his tone reflective of his uncommitted stance on the matter.

"I'm going to use someone who isn't affiliated with my people at Mission Recovery or the Colby Agency. Someone completely out of the game."

"You think that's wise considering who we're up against?" Simon prodded, his arms folded over his chest. He clearly didn't like this any more than Ian did. For that matter neither did Lucas.

"This agent is a recruit fresh from the CIA's training

facility. Our Forward Research group has been tracking her progress since before she entered the program. She's good. Damn good. She has a degree in psychology, which could prove useful. And she has no stake in the matter either way."

"What makes you think she'll go for this assignment?" Simon looked even more suspicious of the whole strategy. It did sound like a suicide mission, even Lucas had to admit it.

"If she's got half the fire burning in her belly to impress the brass as it appears, she'll go for it."

"But is she good enough to do the job?" Ian voiced the remaining variable.

Lucas smiled as he thought of the hotshot he'd observed steamrolling her peers, female *and* male alike. He'd been waiting for the right kind of opportunity to bring her onboard. "Oh, yeah. She's good enough."

"She'll try to get close to this guy in hopes that he'll lead her to Leberman, is that it?" Simon relaxed, but only marginally.

"She'll get close to him, and then when Victoria vanishes he won't have any choice but to contact Leberman for additional instructions." Lucas hoped like hell it would be that easy.

Five seconds lapsed into thirty as the two men closest to Victoria at the Colby Agency considered his proposal.

"I can see how this might work." Simon was the first to edge toward commitment.

"And what about you, Ian? Do I have your support?" Lucas couldn't move forward without both these men on board. Timing and synchronized reactions were everything. There couldn't be a single glitch.

"I have no reason to doubt your loyalty to Victoria," he said in response, without actually answering at all. "I

do, however, have reservations as to the plan you've outlined, but I can't conceive of a better strategy." His gaze
locked fully with Lucas's. "As you say, Leberman must
be stopped. It's past time we got this done."

"All right, then. I'll set things in motion on my end.
The only thing I need on yours is full cooperation and
complete secrecy."

"You have that unconditionally," Ian said with that
quiet intensity that would unnerve most men.

Lucas nodded. "I'll keep you posted."

With the preliminary plans out of the way there was
nothing further to discuss. "We'll ensure status quo at the
office until we hear from you," Simon offered in parting.

"I don't want Victoria to suspect anything," Lucas reiterated as they moved toward the door. "She's already
picked up on my uneasiness."

"We understand." This from Ian. He paused before following Simon into the corridor. "Just one more thing." He
looked directly at Lucas. "I have no doubt that you will do
all in your power to protect Victoria from this assassin."

"I will," Lucas assured him.

"If," Ian qualified in that low, deadly tone, "you take
this risk and fail, it will be the last thing you do."

Their gazes held for a beat of screaming silence.

"If," Lucas allowed grimly, "I fail, you can use my
gun to do the job."

Chapter 5

Tasha North tossed her bag into her car and yanked off the confining double-breasted suit coat that had felt like a straitjacket all day. This stuffy attire was just one more thing she hated about her new job. She flung the inside-out garment into the back seat and dropped behind the wheel of her Volkswagen Beetle. She breathed a sigh of pure, unadulterated relief. Whenever she settled into the white leather seat of her little yellow Bug she felt normal...almost.

Jerking the pins loose from her hair, she shook the blond shoulder-length mass free and pushed her sunglasses into place. She cranked and revved the engine. Thank God it was Friday. She couldn't wait to get out of here.

Tires squealing she rocketed out of her designated parking slot and zoomed toward the exit of the mammoth parking garage. At the security checkpoint she slowed for the guard to ID her, gave him a big, friendly smile, which he returned sheepishly, and then proceeded forward.

Once off Langley property she floored the accelerator and headed home.

Frustration pounded in her brain. She hadn't joined the elite CIA to sit behind a desk. All day long she did the same thing: reviewed intelligence reports, looking for tidbits others had missed. Oh, she'd found an item here and there, especially the past couple of days. But that wasn't how she'd seen herself fitting into the agency she'd been in awe of all these years. At any rate, when she'd graduated from training, her superiors had insisted that her battery of assessment tests had determined that this was the best assignment for optimum use of her skills.

In her opinion that was a load of crap.

So what if she had a near-photographic memory and felt like cyberspace was her second home or that she could hack into the Pentagon's computer system as easily as checking her e-mail? Would they never forget that little incident?

She rolled her eyes as she merged onto the expressway. She'd only done it once. Good grief, she'd been seventeen. Kids did stupid stuff like that. She was more sensible now, played by the rules, thought before she acted... Well, most of the time, anyway.

But at seventeen she'd been impetuous. Still, once the hoopla had settled down, especially the part about no charges being filed, and her parents had stopped having cardiac episodes, she'd actually gotten a little excited about having stepped knee-deep in national security shit. A CIA recruiter had come to see her at high school. It had all been very secretive. Her first covert briefing. He'd told her how impressed he was with her skill and how he'd personally kept her out of trouble. Had said that he'd be watching as she moved through her college career. Then, with a mysterious "I'll be in touch," he'd disappeared just like the spy she dreamed of being. And just as he'd promised, on graduation day he'd shown up at the university to recruit her.

And what had they done?

They'd stuck her behind a metal desk reading boring reports all day every day.

Oh, the training program had been great. She'd loved it, kicked ass and taken names, coming out top in her class.

Those intensive weeks had been exhilarating...had felt like the CIA she'd dreamed of joining.

This—she glared at the skirt and low-heeled pumps she wore—was not. She looked just like her mother for heaven's sake.

Tasha took a breath. Okay, okay. She knew the deal. Paying her dues wasn't the end of the world. Impatience had always been her most glaring flaw. She was almost twenty-three. It was past time she'd learned how to take the waiting in stride.

"Grow up, Tasha," she grumbled. "You have to earn your way in the real world." How many times had her father told her that theatrics didn't pay off? "Patience is a virtue," he'd say at least once a day while she was growing up. Be that as it may, in high school she'd gotten noticed by proving she could do what no one else could—like cracking the Pentagon's cyber security.

Another sigh heaved from her chest. This wasn't high school. Being slick and cagey and, as bad as she hated to admit it, irreverently arrogant wasn't going to put her at the top of the food chain when her superiors, those rating her ability, were all replicas of her dear old dad. She had to be patient. Had to prove her worth behind a desk before she graduated to field operations. Hadn't she learned a good deal about the human psyche in college?

A degree in psychology taught her one thing if nothing else—meet the expectations of the humans in charge and life was much easier.

She could do it. Five days a week, eight hours a day, for a while longer. Her time would come…eventually. All she had to do was play it cool and bide her time. She reached to turn up the volume on the CD player just as the sound of her cell phone ringing drew her hand in another direction. Groping around in her bag she fished out the phone and flipped it open.

"North."

"Tasha, this is Martin."

Her respiration came to a screeching halt before accelerating into double duty. Her recruiter. A major player amid the powers-that-be at the Agency. Could this be the call she'd hoped for? "Martin, how's it going?" she asked when she had reclaimed her voice, then moistened her lips in nervous anticipation. Why would he be calling now? She hadn't heard from him for nearly three months… not since surviving training…and being shackled to that damned desk. She'd all but given up.

"We have to talk. Can you meet me right now?"

A frown worried her brow as she considered the urgency in his tone. What was up with that? "Sure. Where?"

"Take the next exit. There's a gas station on the right once you've cleared the overpass. I'll be waiting."

Her frown deepening, she closed her phone and tossed it in the general vicinity of her bag.

What the hell was going on?

She slowed for the upcoming exit ramp and took it as instructed.

But…she glanced at the discarded phone, then back at the expressway she'd veered from…how did he know where she was?

Tracking device. She'd heard rumors that all new agents were injected with the latest technology. A device so small that it could be installed with nothing more than a subcutaneous pin prick. With all the immunizations required in training, she could have been injected with anything and not known the difference.

She shrugged it off. Just part of the business. If they wanted to keep tabs on her comings and goings she didn't mind. Anything for the job.

She stopped at the end of the exit ramp, then made a sharp left.

The highway that cut beneath the overpass was one of those takes-you-nowhere kind that sprawled off into the woods in either direction. To her surprise there was a gas station up ahead. It looked deserted. As she eased into the parking lot her assumption was confirmed. Not simply closed but out of business.

On the far side of the lot Martin waited, leaning against his shiny black Jaguar. Smiling in spite of the buzz of warning going off in her head, Tasha pulled up next to him and climbed out. This was Martin. The man who'd held the door to the CIA open for her. He'd assured her that he had his eye on her and would see that her future turned out the right way.

Maybe he had news along those lines for her now. A jolt of irritation shot through her. He'd better have good news. She was sick of all talk and no action.

"I'm glad you came," he said as he removed his dark glasses. "We need to talk."

She nodded, slipped off her eyewear and tossed the designer sunglasses onto the dash of her car. He was right. They did need to talk. If he didn't have an offer for her now, he'd better get things in motion. She'd had about all the nine-to-five grind she could tolerate. Moving closer, she propped a hip on the rear quarter panel of his sleek automobile. "I hope you've got good news for me."

He studied her for a moment, then asked the last question she'd expected to hear, "You have the codes, don't you?"

The hair on the back of her neck stood on end. "Codes?" Her posture stiffened before she could stop it. He noticed. Dammit. "I don't know what you mean."

"They're watching you." He surveyed the wooded area around them. "They know."

"Who knows?" She straightened, adopted a fight-or-flight stance and did a little surveying of her own.

He reached into an interior pocket of his high-priced suit jacket and pulled out a 9 mm handgun. "Take this. You may need it."

She stared at the nickel-plated weapon before accepting it. "How do you know?" She'd reported the breach the moment she stumbled upon it while reviewing endless boring text. Someone, inside the agency, had hidden the codes in the documents. She had no idea how or why, she'd simply done her job. But, as Martin said, she had, in fact, uncovered some sort of code. Her supervisor had appeared agitated that she'd made such a discovery. And it wasn't like she could forget what she'd seen. Once she viewed data—any data, written, visual, whatever—it was in her brain for all time.

"I always know what's going on with my special students."

He'd been an excellent mentor. She'd counted on him. Trusted him…but somehow this felt off. The psych evaluators who'd assessed her prior to advancing into the CIA's training program had called the little sixth sense she possessed elevated precognitive reception. Well, whatever the hell it was, her little precog receptors were humming like mad.

"Is there something else I should know?" Was he only here to warn her to be careful? She resisted the urge to shake her head. It just didn't make sense.

"You'll need—" The rest of his words were cut off by screaming tires and a roaring engine.

Tasha dove for the ground, hitting the asphalt hard and rolling behind his car just as a hail of gunfire erupted.

Martin followed suit, their movements like a well-choreographed dance.

She shifted into a crouch and prepared to return fire when the world suddenly went dark.

Her head ached.

Tasha slowly opened her eyes and surveyed the room around her. Plain white walls. No furniture other than the chair in which she sat.

Where the hell was she? She blinked and even that small movement cost her. The ache in her head sliced through her skull like a machete.

Her hands were secured behind her back. She twisted her wrists, the flesh there burning from the tightness of the ropes.

Martin.

Her heart skipped a beat.

Had he been shot?

The code.

Surely this wasn't about that code...she didn't even know what it related to.

The door across the ten-by-ten room suddenly opened, and a man dressed in black combat gear walked in. He closed the door behind him and leaned against it.

"Hello, Agent North."

She looked up at him from beneath her lashes and told him her position in no uncertain terms. "I don't know what you want. You're wasting your time."

He tugged at first one leather glove and then the other, pulling them firmly into place. "You think so?"

She laughed softly, anticipation already rushing to steady her spinning head. Let him take his best shot. "I know so."

"We'll just see about that."

He started toward her, and Tasha did as she had been trained.

She shut down all nonessential functions.

Closed him out.

Closed *everything* out.

Chapter 6

They'd covered her head and tied her hands behind her back again. Tasha stayed very still, absorbing the details around her as best she could in her current state of near numbness. The vehicle—a cargo van maybe—she'd been shoved into glided smoothly toward its destination. City streets, well maintained. No back road. Not yet. Wherever they were taking her she had a pretty good idea they planned to execute her and dump the body.

She hadn't given either of the men who'd interrogated her what they wanted. She was of no further use to them. Those words echoed through her throbbing skull as she allowed her senses to awaken more fully, inch by slow inch. The bruised ribs and split lip were the least of her worries. Unless she finagled an escape she was dead.

Just in case she managed a getaway, she had studied each face she'd encountered very carefully. Had even gotten a DNA sample under her nails when she scratched one of them. She almost smiled when she thought of the head butt she'd pulled off, taking one guy down. She hoped his nose was broken.

Well, at least she'd put up a good fight and she hadn't given them the code.

That was something.

Though an alien emotion, what felt like fear, moved through her. She had to admit that the thought of dying so young lacked any appeal whatsoever.

The vehicle rocked slightly as it slowed, then stopped briefly. She listened intently. No traffic sounds. A left turn. Then a right. They were likely nearing their final destination now. Her heart rate quickened.

The vehicle bumped over a rise and then stopped. Parking lot, she surmised. The sound of metal sliding over metal and a rush of cool air told her the cargo door had been opened.

It was now or never. She had to make a move.

When she would have pushed herself up, brutal hands shoved her forcefully from behind, sending her hurtling out of the vehicle.

She landed hard. Her skin, wherever exposed, identified asphalt beneath her. Struggling frantically, she maneuvered into an upright position, her legs folded painfully under her. If she could only get up…

Those hands pushed her back down.

She braced for the impact of a bullet.

Silence.

Footsteps retreating.

Tires squealed as the vehicle spun away.

Stunned as much by the shock of being left alive as by the pain now making itself known in a big way, for one long moment Tasha could only sit there, bewildered.

The sound of clapping jerked her out of her state of dazed confusion.

She stumbled to her feet, battling with the bindings on her wrists. Within seconds she was free, the knots oddly easy to escape. Not like before.

"Bravo, Agent North."

She jerked the cloth sack from her head and glared in the direction of the voice. *Martin.* Her mentor. Her recruiter. The man she trusted above all others.

"What the..."

Her words drifted off as realization seeped into her muddled gray matter. She'd been set up. He hadn't needed a tracking device...he'd planned this.

"You son of a bitch," she snarled as she charged toward him.

He held up both hands to halt her attack. The streetlamp on the outer perimeter of the abandoned parking lot provided sufficient light for her to see his features. "Now, don't go taking it out on the messenger."

"What the hell was this?" She swiped at the blood leaking from her split lip, wincing at the burn.

"Just a small—" he held his forefinger and thumb close together "—*final* test," he assured her with a knowing nod.

"Test?" she roared. "You people played enough mind games on us during training. I've been out of training for three months! What else do I have to do to prove my loyalty?"

He sighed and braced one elbow on the other arm so that he could rest his chin in his hand as he'd often done when pacing before the class. "You see, Tasha," he offered quietly, his easygoing tone making her want to slug him, "there are a chosen few who get special notice. For those, like you, we have exclusive plans. But, there's always one final test. And that test can only be administered *after* you have access to negotiable information, otherwise it's pointless. You, of course, passed with flying colors."

Some of the fire went out of her fury. But she was still as mad as hell. "What does this mean?"

He smiled. "It means, my dear Tasha, that you are on your way. Very soon you'll be brought into that exclusive club."

She narrowed her gaze, her suspicion mounting. "How soon?" She wanted more than an empty promise. She'd had that.

"Soon." He surveyed her haggard appearance. "Now go home, take a long hot bath and enjoy your weekend."

Before she could demand any other information, he got into his Jag and drove away.

"Bastard," she muttered as she staggered to her own waiting, considerably more modest, vehicle.

She'd lost one of her shoes, so she kicked the other one away before climbing behind the wheel of her Bug. Her panty hose were shredded, and one knee was skinned. She dragged off the ragged nylon and tossed it out the window. Only one button held her blouse together. But at least she still had all her teeth, she mused, sliding her tongue over her undamaged pearly whites.

A quick glance in the mirror and she grimaced. She looked like hell. Well, as long as it got her where she wanted to be. No pain, no gain, right?

She started the engine and pointed the car toward home. Damn she was beat.

Literally.

Half an hour later she braked to a stop at the curb outside her small Crystal City duplex. Swearing profusely she eased out of the car. Every muscle in her body screamed in protest of each move. Fat lot of good three nights per week of martial arts had done her. With her hands tied behind her back she'd scarcely landed a single blow.

Appeasing herself with the memory that Martin had said *soon,* she padded barefoot up the steps and to the front door. Soon she would join an exclusive club. She knew what that meant—field operations. Smiling, she reached to insert the key into the lock. She stilled. A chill raced over her skin. Her pulse tripped into the rush zone.

Something wasn't right.

It was past midnight and damned dark. Most of her yuppy neighbors were in bed already. Like her they all worked too many hours to bother with pets, so the whole neighborhood was dead silent. They were all good little robots, spinning their wheels in their white-collar world by day and playing nice, tidy little home owners by night.

Boring…boring. Not the life she'd planned for herself. Hopefully that was almost over for her.

At the moment *over* might very well have an altogether different meaning.

Cautiously, not making a sound, she moved around the side of her house. Her unit was the last one on the block, which gave her quick access to the rear of the property without passing a neighbor's window. Keeping close to the brick wall, she edged around to the back.

She flattened against the wall next to her back door and listened intently. No sound came from inside, but the goose bumps raised across her skin warned her that things were not as they should be.

During training she'd met a few other recruits who had this elevated sense of alert. Advanced precognitive warning system, whatever the shrinks wanted to call it. She'd always had it…had banked on it more times than she cared to recall. Whenever her gut clenched and her flesh pebbled she paid attention.

She eased a little farther across the rear of the house until she reached her bedroom window. A smile slid across her lips when she found it open an inch or two and with one broken pane. The bastard. He'd climbed through her window. Just who the hell did he think he was? He'd likely been damned disappointed that she didn't even own a DVD player much less a Blu-ray. She preferred making her own entertainment.

Another thought struck her on the heels of that one. This was too easy. Not right. She considered her options and decided that going in was the best route. She'd be prepared for whatever waited inside. And she knew someone was there…she could feel it.

In less than ten seconds she was in the room with scarcely any effort and without having made the slightest noise to warn her prey.

The bedroom was dark but Tasha didn't need any light. She knew her way around her own home.

She reached into the tissue box on the bedside table and snagged her weapon. A .38 that she'd purchased the day she graduated from college. A girl had to have her protection. Besides, she'd thought she was going into the spy business. Didn't every spy carry a weapon? Fleetingly she thought of the 9 mm Martin had lent her for about five seconds. It probably had been loaded with blanks, just like the ones that had sent her diving for cover when the van came barreling into the gas station's parking lot. She gritted her teeth against a new surge of fury. This sure as hell better not be another one of his games.

She frowned. The .38 felt wrong. She weighed it in her hand…too light. She crouched down and felt under the edge of the bedside table for her backup piece. A sinking feeling kicked in. This business of game playing had gone too far. A burglar would have taken the gun, not just the bullets.

She eased across the bedroom and through the open door. She had memorized each spot where her floor creaked and avoided those areas as she made her way down the short hall that connected the five rooms of her home like spokes on a square wheel. The bathroom was clear...the kitchen was, too, except for three nights' worth of dirty dishes. She didn't have to see them to know they were there, her memory provided a vivid image. Nothing in the guest room.

With each breath expertly controlled to avoid audible detection, she locked her right elbow and leveled her .38. She kept her left hand slightly behind her, the .32 grasped firmly there. She didn't want to give away her backup piece just yet. Giving herself a mental three count she entered the living room, her gaze sweeping left to right until she visually engaged the dark outline of the target framed in the meager light from the streetlamp outside the window.

On the sofa. Looked tall. Male probably.

The barrel of her .38 zeroed in on his torso. "Don't move or you're dead."

"Do you mind if I turn on a light? I prefer to look a person in the eye when conversing."

A new kind of wariness slid over her, and she squinted to make out the details of his face, which was impossible. "Who the hell are you?"

"I'm reaching for the light," he informed her as one arm moved toward the table next to him.

The lamp switched on and she blinked to adjust to the brightness. The warm glow from the sixty-watt bulb spilled over the intruder who looked to be about fifty or so. Graying hair...eyes the color of a winter's frost. Business suit, designer quality. His hands were propped on a cane in front of him. Briefcase sat at his feet.

Resisting the urge to frown, she cocked her weapon. "You'd better start talking, old man, before I decide to shoot first and ask questions later."

He opened his left hand and showed her his palm and the brass rounds gleaming there. "You might find that difficult without these."

She leveled the .32 in her left hand on him then. "I don't think it'll be difficult at all." She tossed the useless .38 aside.

He smiled, approval gleaming in his eyes. "You are good."

"I don't know who the hell you are," she growled, "but I can tell you that I've had a really bad day. So bad in fact that I could shoot you right now and blame it on post-traumatic stress and probably get away with it."

"Sit," he ordered. "And we'll talk."

That sounded a little too damned familiar. Talking had done nothing but get her in trouble today. Still watching him warily, she moved to the closest chair, which put her directly across the antique-trunk-turned-coffee-table from him. She eyed his cane skeptically and let him see her dubiousness. "How the hell did you manage to climb through my window?" she asked bluntly. Beating around the proverbial bush had never been her style.

He smirked. "Who said I climbed through the window?"

Her gaze narrowed then cut to the front door. Sure enough the lever was turned to the unlock position. She'd known the whole window thing was too easy…staged.

"I only opened the window to make you think I'd climbed through," he explained unnecessarily. But then he did that on purpose, wanted to rub it in.

"Okay, so you have my attention now. What's this about? I've endured about all the head games I intend to play today. And you don't look like the type who has to force the ladies to do his bidding. So what do you want?" Despite being over the hill and using a cane, the guy was attractive, in a smart-ass sort of way, definitely distinguished looking.

That last jab won her a genuine smile. Her heart fluttered. When he smiled, wow! Those gray eyes sparkled with mischief and something deeper…something curiously fascinating. She scolded herself. That was just the kind of thinking that usually got her into trouble. This stranger had broken into her home and had unloaded her weapon. He could be armed. She surveyed him again. Probably was. Besides, she wasn't supposed to notice how cute he was. He wasn't a frigging stray dog looking for a home. In fact, she'd bet he was about as far from domesticated as one could get. Another concept crept into her thoughts. Had Martin's schemes moved to a new level?

"My name is Lucas Camp. I'm here because I need you for a mission."

Whatever he'd said after his name was lost on her. "Lucas Camp?" She lowered her weapon. "You're a legend."

Another of those charming smiles. "Some would disagree with you on that."

What the hell was a superspook like Lucas doing in her living room? "Former Military Intelligence turned CIA," she said aloud, recalling all the rumors she'd heard about the legendary Lucas Camp. "Then the story gets a little murky. Everyone knows you're out there, but no one knows any more than that. You're the best of the best. No one can touch you." She'd never say it out loud but he represented all that she wanted to be. Made Martin look like a pussy. Well, okay, maybe not a pussy, but she was a little pissed at him right now.

"Unless I choose to allow them access," Lucas said with a pointed look at her.

Her breath caught in her chest. He was allowing *her* access. This was Lucas Camp—in her home—talking to her. Her eyes rounded and she passed the back of her hand over her burning lip. "Would you like something to drink? Water? Beer?" Dammit, he probably preferred coffee and she didn't even own a coffeemaker. She winced again at her stinging lip.

"No, thanks, Ms. North. As I said, I'm here to discuss a mission with you."

She felt her eyes go even wider. A mission? Had he said that before? "With me?"

He nodded. The amused expression he wore told her she was making a complete idiot of herself. Time to pull it together and act like a professional. She'd survived CIA training after all. And today's *final* test. She was no lightweight. She squared her shoulders and looked him directly in the eyes. "What kind of mission?" She sounded strong, professional. Just when she would have given herself a mental pat on the back she remembered how she looked—like hell for sure.

While she tugged at her blouse to keep it closed he reached into his briefcase, withdrew a phone, entered a code and offered the device to her. "The profile is pretty sketchy, but this is what we have."

She reviewed the meager contents, scrolling forward one screen at a time. John Doe, estimated age thirty, approximate height and weight six-two, a hundred and ninety pounds. Living somewhere in Chicago, specific address unknown. She surveyed the shot someone had taken from a considerable distance, probably zeroing in with a mega zoom lens. Blondish hair, similar to her own. Blue eyes. Chiseled good looks.

She looked up at Lucas and asked, "You don't know who this guy is?" Which was a dumb question since he was listed as John Doe. Duh.

Lucas shook his head. "Not a clue. We believe he's an assassin."

Now that got her full attention. "Who's his target? The president?" Another rush of adrenaline seared through her veins. This might just be her lucky day.

"Nothing politically related or that high profiled," he told her without going into specifics, which was par for the course. Intel was doled out on a need-to-know basis only.

"What part do you need me to play in this mission?" She emphasized the word *need*. No matter how he downplayed the scenario, this had to be big or Lucas wouldn't be involved. Maybe not White House big, but big in any case.

"We need to know who this guy is and, more important, we need to reach out and touch the man who hired him." Lucas pointed to the phone. "The next face you see is the one we're looking for."

Tasha studied the final image on the screen with new curiosity. This one was older. Gray hair, gray-blue eyes. Five-ten, a hundred and sixty pounds. This one looked almost harmless. She flipped back a screen or two. Now this one—she studied the younger man's grim features— looked deadly. "So, you want me to get to know the assassin. In hopes he'll lead me to the man who hired him." Her gaze connected with Lucas's. "Is that it?"

Lucas nodded, then quirked one brow a fraction higher than the other. "That is, if you think you're up to it. The personal requirements might be steep. To get as close as you need to…" He allowed the unfinished statement to linger in the air a moment before he continued. "We'll be watching from a distance, but not close enough to keep you safe. You'll be on your own."

Another charge of excitement went through her. "I'm up to anything you can throw my way." She knew what he was worried about, and she could handle it. Her training had included intensive profiles to see if she could tolerate mental as well as physical abuse of all kinds. All results indicated she would hold up under pressure exceedingly well. She licked her busted lip for emphasis. She would die before she'd break. Fooling a polygraph as well as tactics to fight the effects of certain drugs were all a part of her vast repertoire. "Sounds almost too easy," she admitted.

"We don't know anything about this assassin," Lucas said grimly. "We have to assume he's extremely dangerous. There's no way to guess how many people he's killed in his career or what his MO is. If the man who hired him is who we believe he is, then you can rest assured that our assassin is highly trained and well experienced."

She could read between the lines. This was a mission that contained a definite "suicide" element. Getting close to the target and staying alive would entail a great deal of skill and more than a little luck.

"What's in this for me?" she wanted to know, undeterred. They might as well get to the heart of the matter. "If I'm going to risk life and limb for you, what will *you* do for me?"

Lucas looked pleased that she'd asked. "You succeed in this mission and you'll come to work for me with the best of the best."

Struggling with the desire to do a victory whoop, she clamped down hard on her outward reactions. *Stay cool, don't let him see that you know this is an opportunity of a lifetime*. A route through all the BS and straight to the kind of work she longed to do. It was rumored that the elusive Lucas Camp headed some sort of elite top secret organization. A club far more exclusive than anything under the CIA umbrella.

"And if I fail?"

"Then it won't matter," he said flatly. "Because you'll be dead."

That was the answer she'd expected. If she got close to this guy and he suspected for one nanosecond that she was a spy, she'd be history. Tasha shrugged. "So, I won't fail." She looked straight into the knowing eyes of one of the most powerful men on the planet and watched for the slightest flicker of deceit. "Just one more question, Mr. Camp, why me?"

"Because you're good." No hesitation, not even a glimmer of deception. "Too good to be stuck behind some desk." A smile curled one corner of his mouth. "Too good to be working for the CIA period."

She inclined her head and pushed for a little more. "What's so bad about the CIA? The whole world is convinced that the CIA has ultimate power and prestige." That much was true. But those with the real power were few and far between, that was the part they never showed in the movies.

Lucas chuckled. "Agent North, my organization is what the CIA wishes it were."

His statement validated the rumors she'd heard. "When do I go to work?"

"Tomorrow. A cab will pick you up early and take you to the airport. Someone will be waiting at O'Hare to take you to your temporary quarters. This assignment may last a few days or a few weeks. I can't be sure at this point. Don't take anything from home. We'll furnish everything you need."

She knew a moment's uneasiness, but only a moment. "What about my work at Langley?" If this didn't pan out and she miraculously survived...

"Time off has been cleared with your immediate superior. He doesn't know why and doesn't need to. Once this mission is over, you can decide if you want to take me up on my offer or go back to your job with the Agency."

Sounded fair enough. "All right." This was the opportunity she'd waited for, a chance to prove what she was made of. "Once I'm in Chicago where do I start?"

"Our boy hangs out most weekends in a club downtown called the Metro Link."

She'd read that in the sketchy personal info on the phone.

"You'll need to commit to memory the meager intel we have on this guy."

"Already did." She passed the phone back to him. "How come there's nothing on the guy who hired him except a visual image?" That part struck her as odd. Lucas certainly sounded as if he knew more about the guy than what he looked like.

"Intel will be provided as necessary." He dropped the phone into his briefcase as he stood. "I think you understand what to do from here."

Nothing she hadn't expected. "How do I let you know once I've made contact with the target?" she asked as she followed him to the door.

"I'll be in touch with you when the time comes."

Translation: Lucas Camp would be watching.

"By the way." He hesitated before going out the door. "Just in case you were wondering, Agent Bauer's nose *isn't* broken."

Before she could ask how the hell he knew about Martin's little test and her performance he'd disappeared into the night.

Just like a ghost.

Chapter 7

Victoria stared at her reflection in the mirror for a long time that night, the brush clasped in her hand as she stroked her long, dark hair. The silver streaks gleamed in the light, reminding her of just how old she really was. So much time had passed...and nothing in her personal life had changed. Beethoven's "Moonlight" Sonata played softly in the background. The music usually relaxed her, but it wasn't working so well tonight.

She sighed and laid the brush on the vanity table next to her bottles of perfumes and cosmetics, all lined in a neat row awaiting her attention. There was moisturizer for her skin, anti-aging cream for the fine lines that marred her eyes and mouth. And, of course, the skin firmer for less delicate parts of the anatomy. Everything that one could need to remain youthful looking.

Maybe she should have started using the products long ago. Then perhaps she would not look quite so old. But nothing she applied to her skin would change the way she felt inside.

Ancient would be the best description.

Age had never really bothered her until now. She looked down at the bare ring finger of her left hand, and for a moment her chest tightened with anxiety. She'd made a new commitment today. One that in no way lessened the old one, but rather, forged a new path for her to move forward. Looking back was definitely not good for her peace of mind. James was gone. It was well past time to move on. Lucas was alive and ready to move into the future with her.

She peered at the weary face in the mirror. But was she really ready for that journey? Her right hand moved to her chest, settling over her heart. On a conscious, cognitive level she felt ready. It was her heart that hesitated, that worried about starting over.

Victoria stood and moved away from the vanity table. She paused in front of the full-length mirror mounted on the wall near her walk-in closet. She was almost fifty. What did Lucas see when he looked at her?

Tugging the silk belt free she shrugged out of the robe, allowing it to puddle around her feet. She studied her nude body then. Her skin was still slightly flushed from her long, hot soak in the tub. Her dark hair, even with the silver streaks, contrasted sharply against her pale flesh. She'd never really noticed that before. Would the contrast please Lucas? Or did it only make her look pale and haggard?

Pushing that worrisome detail aside, she moved on to other features. Her breasts were still reasonably firm and high, not that they'd ever been that large, but they were presentable, she supposed. Her husband had never complained, but then, that had been a very long time ago.

Her waist narrowed nicely and her hips flared just enough, though she couldn't quite claim a flat tummy.

Time and gravity had taken its toll there as well as behind, she noted as she turned slightly. Her legs were fairly
toned, mostly from the treadmill she used every morning.

She wondered what kind of women Lucas had been
involved with in the past. Though he'd never been mar-
ried she felt certain there had been numerous lovers; after
all, he was a very handsome man with endless charm. A
smile relaxed across her lips and affection twinkled in
her brown eyes. Did her eyes glitter that way when she
smiled at Lucas? She sighed, anxiety gnawing at her insides. Just something else to wonder about. She would
know soon enough.

Locating panties and a nightgown, she dressed for bed,
then turned off the lights except the one on her bedside
table and crawled beneath the covers. She didn't have to
bother with turning off the music, it was on a timer. An
hour from now it would end on a graceful note and, if she
were lucky, she would be fast asleep. The day had been
long and tiring. Going to the cemetery always affected
her that way. She thought of the way she'd buried her wedding band and took a moment to search her heart now for
regret or guilt but found none. She stared up at the ceiling and wondered at the lack of the emotions she'd fully
expected to experience. Fifteen years was certainly long
enough to grieve. She needed to move on. Living in the
past had taken a heavy toll on her in the past few months.

It wasn't really moving into a relationship with Lucas
that weighed so heavily upon her, she felt reasonably sure.
James would want her to be happy, there was no question
there. It was her son.

He'd been gone for eighteen years. His twenty-fifth
birthday would have been last month.

Her heart felt like a load of bricks in her chest as she
sat upright and struggled for breath. Tears burned her eyes

even now, after all those years. If only she could have had closure. The not knowing was the worst. She could only imagine the horrors her child had suffered before his death. Oh, she'd tried to pretend that some kind family had found and raised him. A couple who had been desperate because they couldn't have a child of their own. But that wasn't likely. She didn't need an FBI profiler to tell her the score. She was all too well aware of what happened to most children who vanished into thin air.

She closed her eyes and forced away the thought of Leberman. Both she and James had been certain he had had something to do with Jimmy's disappearance, but they'd never been able to find any proof. And as the years had dragged on that possibility had diminished. Leberman wanted to hurt them. If he'd been the one to take their child, wouldn't he have used him to wield the ultimate pain? Another part of her was utterly convinced that Leberman was indeed the culprit. But she would never be certain.

They'd searched the lake for weeks. James had hired special diving teams even after the authorities had given up. He and Lucas had worked personally with those men. If he'd somehow ended up in the water, surely they would have found something...anything. But there was always the possibility that he was out there...beneath the glassy surface of that lake near the house she'd once called home. She shuddered at the thought.

She hadn't been able to stay in that house after James had died. It was a splendid home. They'd planned its design together, had enjoyed every moment of the work involved in bringing it to life. The place was beautiful still...but she couldn't go back there. Too many memories. Yet she hadn't been able to part with the property, either. Too much of James was there, and then one of the

FBI agents working her son's case had told her that sometimes when stolen children grew older, assuming they survived, they found their way back home…to the last home they'd known with their families. So she'd kept the house. The agency used it as a safe house or for the occasional VIP since it wasn't that far outside the city. But she never went there…never.

She didn't like thinking about it. The memories were too painful.

Victoria threw the covers back and climbed from the bed that had felt like heaven on earth a few minutes ago but now closed in on her like a prison. She padded to the kitchen and peered into the refrigerator to see what looked good. She wasn't really hungry, but she'd do anything to take her mind off the past. Lucas crossed her mind briefly, but she dismissed the idea. Too late for coffee and conversation…too soon for anything else. Food would have to suffice. Carrots, salad fixings. She made a face. Not in the mood. Yogurt. Not tonight.

Ice cream. Now that was more like it.

She pulled the freezer door open and reached inside, spotting her favorite flavor right off the bat. Her hand stalled halfway to its destination. A box of chocolate ice cream sat next to her vanilla. The bright yellow smiley faces drawing and holding her attention.

Why would there be chocolate?

She never ate chocolate. It gave her hives.

She frowned, but then remembered that her housekeeper sometimes brought along snacks on cleaning day… but she was on a diet. The carrots and celery in the vegetable bin were hers.

Victoria picked up the full quart of forbidden indulgence and studied it. The cold from the open freezer door, from the package, leeched through her skin, settling deep inside her. She shivered…tried to think why this carton's presence should disturb her. She hadn't seen those smiley faces for years.…

Jimmy had loved chocolate anything…ice cream…milk. Especially the kind that came in this carton.

Just as Beethoven's sonata reached a crescendo the box slipped from her limp fingers.

She backed away from the refrigerator.

Her head moving from side to side, she told herself it couldn't have anything to do with him.

She should call Freda and see if she had brought it…if she'd gone off her diet—

The security alarm wailed, jerking Victoria from the unsettling thoughts.

Confusion pulled her in different directions before she gathered her wits. She should turn the music off. Pick up the box of ice cream that lay on the floor. Needed her robe…

Shaking off the confusion, she rushed to the keypad near the front door. She'd set the alarm before her bath. It was habit…she scarcely remembered the act. The display flashed a warning that a failure had occurred in area fifteen.

The den. Grabbing the closest object for protection, which turned out to be a long-handled umbrella from its stand, she moved quietly toward the den, the siren wailing in the background, drowning out Beethoven. She wasn't really afraid. The community security guard would arrive almost immediately. As if to punctuate that thought the telephone rang. She ignored it. If she didn't answer, the authorities would arrive post haste, as well. Any burglar worth his salt would know that and run like hell. She huffed under her breath, any burglar worth his salt wouldn't have tripped the alarm in the first place.

The den stood in complete darkness. It was past midnight and any moonlight there might be was blocked by the trees shading this side of the house. She stood very still, listening, watching, but sensed no movement...no presence. Holding her breath, she reached for the wall switch by the door and flipped on the lights.

The problem wasn't immediately evident. All looked as it should be. The sheer panel hanging between her drapes suddenly shifted. A new kind of tension climbed up Victoria's spine. Moving cautiously, listening for any sound besides the insistent alarm and the rushing piano notes, she edged toward the window. Another slight shift of the sheer fabric. Every muscle tensed for battle, she jerked the panel back. The window was open only four or five inches. Just enough to allow a breeze to drift into the room. Just enough to break the connection of the security contact.

She exhaled the breath she'd been holding and peered down at the open sash. How had that happened? It had to have been closed when she set the alarm, otherwise she'd have gotten a default message. When she would have reached to push the sash down she saw a small black, mangled object, not much larger than a quarter on the sill. She leaned closer and visually inspected the object. Knowing better than to touch it and contaminate any evidence it might offer, she stood back and considered the possibilities.

She always kept the windows locked. Always. Unlocking it from the outside without breaking the glass would be impossible. Plus, this was a gated community, it wasn't as if vandalism or burglaries were commonplace. Had someone intended to open her window earlier, before she came home, and somehow failed? That didn't make sense. How would they have gotten in with the alarm set?

Pounding on the front door startled her from her thoughts. Surprised that security had arrived even more quickly than she'd anticipated, Victoria disarmed the security system as she passed the keypad on the way to her front door. Perhaps the police had arrived, as well.

"Mrs. Colby!"

She hurried to the door and peered through the peephole. Better to be safe than sorry. She drew back at what she saw. "Identify yourself, sir," she demanded. This was no policeman. At least, not one in uniform. Nor was it the grounds security who donned clearly marked blue uniforms.

"Mrs. Colby, my name is John Logan. I work for Lucas. I need to know that you're all right."

He worked for Lucas? She remembered the name John Logan from that nightmare on St. Gabriel. She looked again. Her breath caught as she recognized the young man this time. What was he doing here?

She unlocked the door and jerked it open. "Is Lucas here? Has something happened?"

John Logan looked worried...or maybe upset. "No, ma'am, he's not here, but he's on his way."

A frown furrowed across her brow. "Why are *you* here?"

"Ma'am, if you'll let me come inside so I can ensure that the house is secure, Lucas will explain everything when he arrives."

Irritation wiggled its way up her backbone as a scenario formed in her mind. Oh, he would explain all right. She'd known he'd been keeping something from her. She just hadn't expected it to include John Logan.

"Come in, Mr. Logan," she said with a welcoming, utterly fake smile pushed firmly into place. "Look around all you'd like. There's an open window in my den. That's what triggered the alarm."

"Yes, ma'am." He nodded and walked right past her in the direction of her den.

Her mouth dropped open as she realized that he knew the layout of her home. But then, why was she surprised? Lucas always was thorough.

The golf cart security used to buzz around the small exclusive community came to a bone-jarring halt in her drive. Beyond that blue lights flickered, drawing her attention farther down the street. She knew without taking a second look that the SUV on the police cruiser's tail was Lucas's.

She left the door open and went in search of her robe. Dignity was required when exerting power over one's own domain. Lucas was about to find out just how much *indignation* she could rally.

"Just how long were you going to wait before you told me?"

Lucas thought about that for a moment but one glance at Victoria told him he'd be better off just to tell her the truth rather than some concocted story. "Until we were safely away on our vacation."

She blinked, fiddled with her robe a bit more, then looked up at him again. "So this man, this assassin, has been following me for two weeks."

Lucas nodded. "At least. We're trying to identify who he's working for."

She looked heavenward and made a disgusted sound. "Please, Lucas, spare me the supposition. You don't need evidence. You know it's *him*."

He sighed. It was after 3:00 a.m. They were both tired. Pursuing this discussion was pointless, but she wasn't finished punishing him just yet. "Yes, Victoria, I believe it's him. But I have to be certain."

"How are you planning to pinpoint his involvement?" Her expression boasted her considerable doubt. "You know how he is. He can stay underground for months—years even. He could be anywhere, posing as anyone, providing this assassin with his instructions over the Internet."

That was all true. She knew it and so did he. "I'm moving someone into position to get close to this assassin as we speak," he explained. "Once you and I have disappeared, he'll have no choice but to report to Leberman, leading our source straight to him." Lucas couldn't help glancing around the room even though he knew his own man had swept the entire house for surveillance bugs. Still, it was habit.

Victoria stood, abruptly announcing she'd heard enough. She was furious and he couldn't blame her.

Lucas supported his weight on his cane as he got to his feet. Damn, he was exhausted. "Logan has removed the device from your windowsill and locked the window. The house has been swept for bugs and any other sort of foreign gadget or substance. Are you sure you'll feel comfortable here the rest of the night?"

He would like nothing better than to take her back to his hotel with him. But she would refuse. He knew her answer before he asked. He didn't really like her being here after what happened tonight, but his men would be watching.

The intruder had obviously gotten in while Victoria was at the office today. He'd disarmed her security, since she said she always set it before leaving for work, and then planted the device that contained a small explosive charge—just enough to push the unlocked window up at a later time, breaking the security mechanism's contact. Then he'd reset her alarm and left. Lucas assumed that the small explosive had been coated with a substance that deteriorated when subjected to air. The slow deterioration, likely calculated to the very minute, had allowed for the timing of the explosion and thus the security breach. Ingenious. Lucas knew before he looked there would be no prints. This intruder was a professional.

It was *him*.

The assassin who feared no one—not even Lucas and his men. Lucas wasn't stupid. He felt certain the guy was well aware his men had noticed his presence. And still he stalked Victoria. Fearlessly.

The idea that he could have left more explosives in the house tied Lucas's gut in knots. There was no end to the damage he could have done—poison and any number of other booby traps. He should have had someone watching the house at all times…but he hadn't even considered that avenue. His only concern had been keeping Victoria safe in real time. He'd failed to properly evaluate the threat. He was too close to this…not thinking clearly. It wouldn't happen again.

"No, thank you, Lucas," she said finally, the annoyance she'd felt at his deception visibly draining away. "I'll be fine here. Besides—" she gestured to the door "—your capable men are right outside."

That reminded him. Ian and Simon were still waiting outside with John Logan and Vincent Ferrelli. Lucas imagined the two of them would be dressed down next. Victoria had already told them in no uncertain terms that she would speak to them *later*.

Lucas nodded his understanding of her decision to stay home. As he had known, Victoria Colby would not run from any sort of threat. "We'll talk again later this morning. We still haven't reached a decision on where we'll take our vacation."

One brow winged higher than the other. "Do you really expect me to believe that you haven't made that decision already?"

He tugged at his collar. Even without a tie binding his neck she could make him squirm. "We can discuss it over lunch." He wanted her a lot calmer and more cooperative than she was right now before they made any decisions.

Damn, this was too close.

He hoped like hell Tasha could move in on their guy in a hurry. She'd be settled into her apartment by noon today. Maverick and Ramon, two more of his specialists, would serve as her backup, and bring her up to speed. She had to get next to this guy. Lucas needed something…anything to go on. He was counting on her to move quickly. He just hoped it didn't get her killed.

He swallowed hard. If it did, it would be entirely his doing. She was young and reckless. Far too reckless to fully comprehend the level of danger involved. But he'd needed her, and Lucas had never failed to take whatever risk required to accomplish his mission. For the first time in his career, he wondered if he had done the right thing.

Victoria squeezed his arm. "I'm okay, Lucas. Really."

He snapped back to the present. She'd mistaken his preoccupation for concern. And he was concerned. About a number of things. "That's all that matters," he said as much for his own benefit as hers. Keeping her safe was all that really mattered. He leaned down and brushed a kiss to her cheek. "Good night, Victoria."

He didn't want to leave her. She looked so vulnerable in that white silk robe with her dark hair falling down around her shoulders. He'd never seen her like that and it was all he could do not to stare in awe.

Allowing her one last smile, he turned away and started for the door.

"Oh, dear God," she gasped.

He turned back to her, performed a quick visual inspection. Had she only now realized she was injured in some way? "What?"

"In all the excitement I completely forgot," she murmured. Her frightened gaze collided with his and she gestured vaguely toward the kitchen. "I don't eat chocolate ice cream."

Chapter 8

The insistent throb of the music from the Metro Link nightclub kept a rhythmic pace with her confident stride as Tasha made her way to the entrance. Black thigh-high leather boots and skintight, cheek-baring silk shorts gave the illusion of legs that went on forever. Legs toned from all those five-mile runs, making every guy she passed stop and stare.

The strappy halter top showcased her flat belly and the contour of her spine, covering nothing except her breasts, and even then the gossamer-thin, lacy fabric scarcely left much to the imagination. A small leather bag, hardly large enough to hold some cash, a couple of loose cigarettes and her car keys, hung from a long, delicate gold chain that draped over her shoulder. The bag bounced against her hip with every step she took. An ankle-length jacket that was as sheer as air and designed from black netting so thin and fragile that it felt like a midnight fog against her skin completed the daring ensemble.

She possessed all the bait and weapons required for a manhunt.

At the main entrance she paused for the bouncer to wave his security wand around her body. She opened her purse to show her keys when the wand passed over it and hummed a warning.

She smiled wickedly at him. "Baby, you don't have to worry about me," she crooned. "The only thing I'm packing is a raging desire to find just the right guy."

His slick bald head stilled, his eyes level with her waist when the wand hummed another warning at the top of her right boot. He looked up at her, one eyebrow cocked in question.

"It's just my cell phone," she insisted. She reached into her boot and tugged out the slim communicator that had triggered the metal detector. "See." She waved it in front of his face before slipping it back into her boot. "Anything else you need to see?"

He straightened, glanced at the crowd lining up behind her and then back at her. He wanted to see more. No doubt. The gleam in his eyes gave away his every thought.

"Come on, man, we don't got all night," his co-worker groused. He waited impatiently, the official Metro Link stamp in his hand. A veteran on the job, she surmised. One who wouldn't be impressed by a half-naked woman and a sexy come-on line.

The guy with the wand waved her through. "Have a nice night," he offered, his tone chock-full of innuendo.

She leaned close to him and whispered, "Believe me, baby, I will."

"Let's go," the other guy grumped.

Tasha squared her shoulders and gave him a look that said, Buddy, you need to get laid, and held out her hand. He glared at her then smacked the stamp in place.

An eerie ML glowed on her skin between her wrist and knuckles. She flashed him a "bite me" smile and moved on.

Heavy-metal music blasted from the surround-sound system as she strode into the crowded club. The maximum occupancy posted was five hundred, and she'd bet Martin's Jag that they'd long passed that limit. Patrons were jam-packed into every available square foot. A long, sleek bar of black-and-mirrored glass flowed along one wall. Up front the crush of the crowd made it difficult to distinguish one couple from another on the dance floor. It more accurately resembled a sea of body parts, all connected somehow like a scene from a gruesome horror novel as they gyrated to the beat.

A laser light show splashed across a screen high above the band jamming on the stage. Booze and beer abounded like manna from heaven, and she quickly spotted a number of other less-than-legal stimulants. Leather, lace and tattoos. Smoke, heat and sex. Women with men and all variations in between. It was all out there. Just like Sodom and Gomorrah.

So this was his favorite haunt, she mused, scanning for her target. Tall, blond and deadly liked it trashy. Well, she could play any way necessary. Backup knew where she was at all times. The handy dandy tracking-monitoring device looked just like a skin patch, the kind people used for kicking the nicotine habit or for birth control. Skin colored and shaped like a small round bandage. Rafe "Maverick" Scott, one of the two men Lucas had assigned as her backup, had instructed her to place it under her left breast. The device would send out a constant signal providing her location as well as her cardio stats. If her heart rate escalated to panic level Maverick would come to her rescue.

But she wasn't going to need that kind of backup tonight.

She did a double take, her gaze landing on Mr. John Doe himself.

"Mmm-hmm," she muttered under her breath. "You are one amazing Y chromosome." For a killer, she added.

John Doe sat on a stool about center of the long bar, those ice-blue eyes scanning the dance floor like a hungry panther ready to pounce on his dinner.

Looking for a little action, big boy? Taking her time as she crossed the room, she took stock of his numerous physical assets. Whoever had estimated his height and weight had done a stellar job. Those broad shoulders tested the seams of his black shirt. Powerful thighs filled out a well-worn pair of jeans. Black ankle boots, the kind made for walking and climbing, soft leather uppers, ribbed soles. For stealth and traction. Smart.

He wore a watch, but no other jewelry that she could readily see. The slight bulge at his left side about midway of his torso would indicate a shoulder holster. She wondered how he'd managed to get in here with a weapon. Official ID, perhaps? Just something else she'd need to check out.

The couple sitting next to him got up and headed for the dance floor, presenting the perfect opportunity for her. "The gods are watching over me tonight," she murmured.

She slid onto the stool next to J.D., John Doe just sounded too cliché. "Great band," she said when he glanced in her direction.

He didn't respond.

Okay. She crossed one leg over the other, offering up a length of thigh for his perusal. He never even looked her way. She leaned toward him. "What time it is?" she asked, ensuring she spoke loud enough for him to hear her.

He held up his wrist so that she could see the face of his watch. She splayed her fingers over his muscled forearm and drew it closer to her face. He tensed and pulled free even before she was ready to let go.

Not the reaction she'd hoped for, but a reaction nonetheless.

She leaned close again, ensuring that her shoulder rubbed against his. "Thanks. What's your name?"

Again nothing.

Five minutes passed with her sitting there gazing out over the mass of swaying, twitching bodies and him doing the same. Not one word was spoken.

Time for drastic measures.

She hopped off her stool, standing as close to him as possible. "Hey!" she shouted at the bartender. "How about a beer?"

A long-necked bottle slid down the counter toward her. She snagged it and took a long draw. "Hmm," she purred as she wiped her chin. She sighed and plunked her bottle back onto the counter. She resisted the urge to wince. Although her lipstick did a great job of camouflaging her split lip, the alcohol still burned on contact.

She leaned against the bar and adjusted her position slightly so she could look her target directly in the eye… well, she could if he turned his head a mere five degrees and allowed her to. Jerk. Maybe he just wasn't in the mood?

Only one way to find out.

She pulled a cigarette out of her purse, a girl never knew when she'd need a conversation starter, and provocatively leaned in his direction. "Do you have a light?" she asked, peering up at him as if the world just might come to an end if he gave the wrong answer.

He looked at her, that piercing gaze cold enough to

give her frostbite, then glared at her breasts for a fraction of a second. "No," he growled before looking away, clearly unimpressed.

Dammit.

Well, at least he'd spoken to her.

She tossed the cigarette onto the bar and propped fully against the counter, pressing her shoulder into his, as she drank her beer and contemplated her next move.

The beer was cold and refreshing once it got past her lip, but he was making her sweat. Usually she didn't have this much trouble getting a guy's attention. Surely three months sitting behind a desk at Langley in a two-piece suit hadn't thrown her off the game this badly. Giving herself grace, she hadn't actually ever attempted to bait a killer. It must be tricky, she mused. Rising to the challenge, she studied him out of the corner of her eye. His profile was strong, his jaw chiseled. A scar running from the corner of his mouth to the middle of his cheek served as a kind of permanent dimple. Otherwise, movie-star-quality features, but more rugged. She squinted for a better view. There was something in his hairline.

Another scar...

No.

Tattoo.

A number: 6...6...*shit*...

She stiffened.

He turned his head and pointed those laser-blue eyes directly at hers.

She opened her mouth but it took about three seconds for the words to come out. "Is that...?"

She couldn't say the rest. He knew what she meant. She saw it in his eyes. Damn. Was this guy for real? Focus, Tasha. Stay calm. She forced her heart rate to slow before that cowboy Maverick could come bursting through the door.

He was still staring at her.

"What do you want from me?"

An involuntary shiver raced over her skin at the sound of his voice. Or maybe she was just freaked out by the bizarre tattoo. But the deep, gravelly sound scraped over her flesh, leaving every single nerve ending raw and tingling.

"I…" She moistened her lips and grappled for the cocky attitude she'd waltzed in here with. "My name's Tasha. I just thought you were cute and that maybe we could—"

He looked her up and down. Not a fast and furious sweep, but a slow, methodical perusal…as if he were devouring every square inch of her with his eyes. She shivered again. Jesus, what was wrong with her?

When that unyielding blue gaze collided with hers once more, he said, "Go away."

Had this encounter tanked or what?

She mustered up a properly pissed-off look and the body language to go with it. "Maybe I don't want to. Maybe I like it right here." She guzzled the rest of her beer. "You know," she said, her gaze focused on the mirror behind the bar, but her voice just loud enough for him to hear, "I knew moving here would be a mistake. My first night on the town and I get the brush-off from the best-looking guy in the club." She turned toward him then, pressed even more intimately against him. "Why is that, do you think?"

He shifted just enough so that his face was about two inches from hers. "Maybe it has something to do with that big mouth."

She laughed softly and then sighed, allowing her breath to feather across his lips. "Well, now I know, don't I?"

He turned away as if he hadn't even noticed her seduction attempts. How the hell was she supposed to crack this guy?

Lucas's offer echoed in her ears…*succeed in this mission and you'll come to work for me with the best of the best.* Failure was not an option. The cell phone tucked into her boot vibrated. Maverick, no doubt.

She braced a hand against J.D. as she fished out her phone. He flinched. Great, he didn't even want her to touch him. "Yeah." She turned away from the exasperating man, straining to hear over the music.

"I take it we have contact."

Maverick's call would show up as a cell phone listed to her fake roommate, Patti. Under normal circumstances he would call if he didn't like what he saw on the monitor, if in distress she would say the right phrase or her inability to answer would equate to the same, and the cowboy would create a diversion, allowing her to escape whatever trouble she was in. But tonight's call was just to ensure contact had been made and to tie her to his monitoring link. Once he'd put a call through to her cell phone, as long as that phone was turned on he could trace her. Backup to the other apparatus, he'd told her. He liked playing it safe. She glanced at the brooding man at her side. "Definitely. I thought you were coming back to pick me up, Patti."

"Our friend is nearby," he said knowingly. "Very good."

"Yeah. Forget it, I'll figure out something." She hung up, closed her phone and tucked it back into her boot. She heaved a disgusted sigh. She couldn't be certain how this would go from here, but at least she'd made contact. That's all Lucas had wanted for tonight. But she wanted more. She wanted to prove how fast she could work… how deep she could go right from the start.

Her target suddenly stood.

Damn.

He tossed a couple of bills onto the counter, clearly preparing to split.

"You leaving already?" She shifted as close to him as possible. "We didn't even get to dance."

She looked up at him with all the sensual invitation she could muster. For two beats he stared right back at her without a word…without a reaction at all.

Abruptly he snagged her by the arm and moved away from the bar. Startled on one level but grateful on another, she allowed herself to be dragged around the fringes of the dance floor, zigzagging to avoid gyrating bodies. His fingers were like iron vises around her wrist. He didn't slow down until they had cleared an emergency exit and were standing in the alley behind the club. Fear trickled through her but she quelled it instantly. Somewhere in the back of her mind she wondered vaguely why no alarm went off when they pushed through the exit. The fire marshal needed to start doing his job. She suddenly hoped like hell Maverick was doing his.

"Decide you want to take me home with you?" she encouraged, blocking the internal alarm going off inside her head. She was playing with fire here. Pushing the limit… but at least she had his attention now. When she would have reached toward him he shoved her to her knees.

"You know what to do," he said savagely.

Oh, damn.

She took a breath, looked at his crotch and the sizeable bulge there, then peered up at him, careful not to let her uneasiness show. "You know, you're really cute and all, but I don't go down on a guy on a first date. Especially when I don't even know his name."

When she would have pushed to her feet he snagged her chin in a punishing grip forcing her back down. "I guess you don't know how to use that big mouth after all."

She glared right back into that icy gaze and countered, "Considering your attitude, I guess you'll never know."

His gaze held hers a second longer before he released her and started to walk away.

Tasha lunged to her feet and went after him. Dammit, she couldn't let him get away. "Wait a minute. I—"

"Shut up." He kept moving…didn't look back.

She hurried to keep up with his long strides. "Look, my roommate left me here. I really need a ride. Could you at least give me a ride?"

This could go either way…all she wanted at this point was to find out where he called home while in the Windy City. That was more than Lucas had asked for, but then, that was the point. Considering this guy's attitude, however, that might be all she could hope for period.

Glancing down his shoulder at her, his stride never slowing, he growled, "Call a taxi."

"Wait!" She stayed right on his heels. "Don't be a jerk. I just need a ride. Is that such a big deal?"

He stopped. A straining ray of light from a distant streetlamp filtered through the darkness where they stood, softly illuminating those Arctic eyes and highlighting the hard planes of his face.

She held her breath…all she needed was half a chance….

"A ride, nothing else."

"Nothing else," she promised.

He turned and started walking again. She followed.

Two blocks later he clicked the remote on his keychain and the headlights of an SUV came on.

She climbed into the passenger seat while he slid behind the wheel. When she snapped her seat belt into place he asked, "What's the address?"

She gave him the address for her apartment and relaxed back against the seat as he pulled out onto the street. "Oh, no!" she groaned and smacked her forehead with the heel of her hand. "My roommate called me…" She looked over at him. "In the club, you know. She needs the apartment to herself tonight. I have to hang out somewhere else."

"A hotel, then." This he said, as usual, with no emotion and without even sparing her a glance.

She moistened her lips and reached way down deep for her whiniest voice. "But I don't have any money for a hotel. It took most everything I had to pay my share of the rent when I got here. Couldn't I just crash at your place for the night? I swear I won't be any trouble. I'll even sleep on the couch. I don't usually go home with strangers but I don't know anyone else in town and—"

He slammed on the brakes. The seat belt was all that kept her from an up-close encounter with the dash.

"Get out."

She glanced around the dark neighborhood. They'd already left the cluster of night spots behind. Rush Street and Division were safe enough, she knew from Maverick's briefing, but it was after midnight…who knew? Of course, she had backup, but this guy didn't know that. Mr. Coldhearted Snake apparently didn't give a rat's ass.

"Fine." She muttered a couple of fitting expletives as she jerked the seat belt loose and scrambled out, then slammed the door as hard as she could.

When she walked away she gave it everything she had, swaying her hips like a hooker on a desperate mission.

She might not have his home address, but she had his license plate number. That was something.

When he didn't immediately drive away, an uneasy feeling quivered up her spine. She resisted the urge to turn around and assess his intent. If he gunned the engine she'd hear him in time to dive to safety.

She forced herself to put one foot in front of the other and to pretend he wasn't even there, watching, waiting, for God knows what. The memory of that bizarre tattoo made her shiver again. There was something really wrong with this guy. Her sixth sense hadn't stopped vying for her attention since she walked up to that bar.

As if she didn't have enough trouble already, a drunk staggered from an alley a few yards ahead. A friend joined him five seconds later. Both watched her steady progress without making a move. She braced herself for a scuffle.

Was everything determined to turn out badly tonight?

The SUV rolled slowly forward.

She sensed the movement more than heard it.

Just before she reached the plot of sidewalk where the two winos waited, the SUV stopped next to her, and the passenger-side window powered down.

"Get in."

She folded her arms over her chest and turned a belligerent glare in his direction. "Are you sure? You know they have medication now for bipolar disorders."

"Get in."

Those cold eyes cut through the darkness with a warning. He wouldn't be pushed any further.

"All right." She opened the door and climbed back into the luxurious leather seat. "So," she ventured when he'd eased into forward motion once more. "You'll put me up tonight?" She resisted the urge to smile in victory. Why had she ever doubted herself?

He braked for a traffic light and swung that piercing gaze toward her. "If you're certain that's what you want."

She blinked…knew a foolish moment of panic. "Of course I'm sure. Is there some reason I shouldn't be?"

That relentless stare bored into her for several seconds more. "That depends."

The light changed and he shifted his attention to the task of driving.

She swallowed, wet her lips and considered whether or not she had made a serious mistake. "Depends on what?" she inquired nonchalantly, uncertain as to whether he would even bother to answer.

He didn't look at her…just kept driving. But his voice when he spoke was every bit as icy as she knew his eyes would be. "On why you picked me out in that club tonight." He relaxed into his seat, still not so much as glancing her way. "You see, I don't believe in coincidences. Everything happens for a reason. And—" he did look at her then…the fleeting stare chilled her to the bone "—I will know your reason."

Chapter 9

"We lost her."

Maverick stared at the handheld monitor, hoping like hell he'd pick up her signal again.

Nothing.

"Dammit."

"He could have a jamming device in his vehicle," Ramon offered from behind the wheel.

"Just keep driving," Maverick barked. Ramon had been in this business almost as long as he had, but that didn't give either one of them an edge at a time like this. If they couldn't pick up a signal on the tracking device or the cell, the bastard had to have a jammer on board. It was that simple. "We gotta find that son of a bitch."

He studied the electronic map of the vicinity where they'd last picked up the signal...where they'd last known Tasha North to be. She'd climbed into the SUV with the guy, and they'd lost her signal but had visual contact, so Maverick hadn't worried. Then, when she'd gotten out a couple minutes later, the signal had come through loud and clear once more. He shook his head and hissed another curse from between gritted teeth. The bastard had a jammer in his vehicle, all right. He knew all the ropes and wasn't taking any chances.

Able to maintain visual contact for a while, they'd followed him for several blocks. But, erring on the side of caution, they'd had to lag too far behind to keep up. He'd moved out of visual range...the signal hadn't returned.

Now she was gone.

Maverick called up on the screen a ten-mile radius relative to the last visual sighting. "We'll take this area one block at a time and hope we spot his SUV."

"And if we don't?" Ramon asked, his expression as disgusted and worried as Maverick's surely was.

"Then we report in."

He didn't have to say the rest. If they couldn't find her soon they'd have to let Lucas know...and start looking for her body.

Chapter 10

"What did you learn?"

Lucas settled on Victoria's sofa in the very den where approximately twenty-four hours earlier the assassin had been setting his little booby trap. He leveled his attention on the woman waiting expectantly for his response. She looked as regal as ever; the coat dress, the color of ripe peaches, flattering to both her complexion and her figure. One would never know that she'd been through pure hell. She sat in the elegantly brocaded chair directly across from him as if a briefing related to her home's intrusion were an everyday affair.

"How are you holding up, Victoria?"

Though she looked prepared for anything, her shoulders square, her chin lifted high. He knew better. This couldn't be easy.

"Lucas, I need to know what you've learned. Please don't attempt to spare my feelings. It's far too late for that."

He set his cane aside and looked her straight in the eye.

"He's been in your home, as you know. Planting the device that opened your window would have been impossible by any other means. He left no prints that we can find. Nor did he leave any other surprises."

She shifted slightly then. He resisted the urge to shake his head. No matter what she said she wasn't as ready for this as she wanted him to believe.

"So you'll keep my home under twenty-four-hour surveillance now."

It wasn't a question. She already knew the answer. Lucas had hoped to conceal the depth of his awareness regarding the assassin's movements, but that was impossible now. He would note the increased surveillance on the home. That couldn't be helped. But keeping his suspicions from the assassin that Leberman was behind this was imperative.

"Yes."

"He'll realize that we know, then," Victoria noted, reading Lucas's mind.

He nodded. He tried without success to keep the other worry from interfering with his concentration. They'd lost contact with Tasha at one this morning. If the bastard had killed her...

Lucas forced the idea away. Tasha was too good to go down this easy. He refused to believe she was dead... just yet.

Something changed in Victoria's eyes. Her expression went from firm and solemn to fragile and frightened. "What about the ice cream."

This was the part he'd dreaded the most. "Freda didn't bring the ice cream." He managed a smile. "She swears she's still on a diet."

Victoria nodded stiffly. "I thought as much."

Lucas leaned forward, braced his forearms on his

knees. "Is there a possibility that you picked it up by accident. Didn't notice that one of the flavors was chocolate."

The weariness that settled over her expression then tied his insides into knots. "You know, I've considered that possibility over and over." She clasped her hands together in her lap. "I'm nearly certain I didn't…but then I can't be sure." She looked at Lucas. "I've even wondered if I'm losing my mind entirely. Having memory lapses maybe." She looked away and shook her head. "I just don't know."

"Yours are the only prints we found on the carton."

Her gaze met his once more, and the anxiety there almost undid him completely.

"But that doesn't really mean anything," he hastened to add. "Since he didn't leave his prints anywhere else, either."

He didn't want her to go through another moment of this. Couldn't bear it. "Victoria, I think it's time for us to make those plans. I'd like to get you away from the danger. I don't like how close he's gotten."

She appeared to consider his suggestion for a few moments, but before she could respond, Logan came to the door of the room. Lucas pushed to his feet and strode across the room to see what news Logan had brought. When he moved into the entry hall, farther away from Victoria, Lucas's tension ratcheted up a notch.

"I just received additional information on the brand of the ice cream."

His people were analyzing the chocolate ice cream from every standpoint, from taste to the manufacturer.

"I assume it's a local manufacturer."

The look in Logan's eyes set him even closer to the edge.

"It used to be. But that brand hasn't been manufactured at all for more than ten years."

Chocolate. Little Jimmy Colby's favorite. Even the brand was the one Victoria remembered buying for her only child. But it had been off the market for ten years.

"So he's been keeping it all this time," Lucas suggested.

Logan nodded. "The age of the product would be consistent with that theory."

The memory of those hours on St. Gabriel Island when he'd been face-to-face with Leberman for the first time in nearly two decades came pouring into his mind. The bastard hadn't said much...had apparently gotten his jollies from merely watching Lucas squirm when faced with the realization that Victoria was somewhere on that island and he couldn't protect her. Lucas hadn't cared if the bastard killed him but he couldn't bear the idea of him hurting Victoria any more than he already had.

Something had been different.

For all those years Leberman had lain in wait. Then, out of the blue, he struck. He could have killed Lucas... possibly even Victoria. But he'd disappeared instead. He'd played them. Lured them into his trap, dangled the possibility of death, then disappeared, leaving someone else to finish the task. But that had been a ploy. Leberman had known the effort would fail. Everything that happened on that island had been a precursor. Some sort of test or preliminary tactic for the real thing. An appetizer to the main course, so to speak.

He'd killed James Colby fifteen years ago. Lucas was certain of that. Though Leberman had not claimed responsibility he'd left his calling card. James had been tortured relentlessly then shot twice, once in the back of the head execution-style, then once in the heart. The first shot had killed him...the second hadn't even been necessary. It had made a statement from the killer.

From Leberman.

Just as the ice cream did now.

He was here.

He'd devastated Victoria all those years ago. Could have devised a way to kill her a dozen times over since… he was far too cunning for anyone to believe otherwise. But he'd chosen not to strike. The little drama he'd set in motion on the island had been to prove something. Otherwise why would he have simply walked away, leaving both of them still alive? Lucas's gaze narrowed as he thought about that. The answer was suddenly so simple.

He'd played out that whole ridiculous scenario to make sure Victoria was ready for the next step. He'd waited all these years to make sure he could hurt her as deeply as he desired. She'd needed time to get over losing both her child and her husband…to finally get on with her life. He'd waited for her to fall in love again.

With Lucas.

It all made sense now.

Killing her years ago when she'd already lost so much that she'd wished for death anyway would have lacked the zenith he yearned for…the fulfillment he needed.

So he'd waited. Waited for her to feel again.

Waited for the ultimate moment.

When Lucas was prepared to make her his once and for all.

The weight of the epiphany crushed down against him.

The game this time would be for keeps. Lucas could feel it in every fiber of his being.

If the bastard had his way, both Victoria and Lucas would die.

Soon.

But first he would play, draw out his pleasure.

Lucas gritted his teeth against the fury that whipped through him...and that one obsession would be his doom.

Lucas would see to it.

Errol Leberman was dead already...he just didn't know it yet.

Chapter 11

Tasha jerked awake.

She sat up straight and took stock of her environment. The room was dark.

She couldn't be sure how much time had passed but she was certain it should be daylight by now.

The perpetual darkness, along with the dank, musty smell confirmed her suspicions that she was in a cellar or basement. Someplace underground.

She lifted her right foot, crossed it over her knee, the metal on metal clanging a noisy reminder that she was shackled to the cot. Rubbing at her ankle where the metal chafed her skin, she stretched her neck first one way and then another. She had a hell of a crick in her neck and shoulder from sitting in such an awkward position while she dozed. Her side still hurt from the beating she'd taken during Martin's little exercise. But she'd slept, anyway.

She hadn't meant to sleep at all, but exhaustion had finally claimed her after hours of trying to get loose. He'd taken her boots and her tiny purse, leaving her with nothing to pick the lock or attempt to pry it open.

After feeling around on the cold concrete floor and stretching the chain as far as she could and finding nothing, she'd admitted defeat and plopped back down on the cot to wait. She'd decided to conserve her energy for kicking ass.

She set her jaw firmly when she considered the heartless bastard who'd locked her down here. When he showed up again she intended to let him have it, shackled or not. To punctuate her heated thought she jerked on the confining chain with all her might.

"Don't waste your time."

The deep voice cut through the darkness like a knife, piercing her defenses. She gasped in spite of herself. Dammit. She hated even the implication of weakness. Hated even worse that he could rattle her so easily. How had he sneaked up on her like that? She'd always been a very light sleeper.

Since Maverick hadn't shown up, she could assume that being underground had silenced the tiny electronic pulse her tracking device emitted. *He* had taken her cell phone and likely turned it off.

Just her luck he had a brain to go with the awesome bod.

Renewed fury raged through her.

She rocketed to her feet and moved as far in the direction the sound of his voice had come from as the chain would allow. "Why the hell are you keeping me here like this?"

The silence thickened as she waited for an answer. Her heart banged painfully against her rib cage.

"To watch you."

She laughed, a dry, totally pissed-off sound. "Yeah, right. You can't even see me."

"Sure I can."

She drew back slightly. He was right in front of her. Her expression hardened with the anger sizzling inside her as she pushed all thought of playing it safe aside and leaned toward him. "Then read my lips." She mouthed a detailed description of what she thought of him.

He snagged her chin in one iron grasp. "So you don't think I'm cute after all?"

She stilled. He couldn't see her...reading her lips was impossible. Her eyes narrowed. Unless he was wearing night vision goggles. She reached for his head. He manacled her wrists but not before she touched his face and found no goggles. The idea that he actually could see that well in the dark startled her all over again.

"Why didn't you leave when I told you to get lost?"

She tried to analyze his tone but it proved impossible. He spoke firmly, harshly almost, but there was no underlying emotion. No anger...no concern...nothing.

"Well, we both know it wasn't because of your sparkling personality."

He jerked her closer still. So close that she could feel his breath on her face when he spoke once more. "What do you want?"

Tasha took a moment to shut down her emotions. So far she'd been pretty much going with the flow, but things were different now. He was dead serious. She couldn't screw up. Her reactions had to be calculated.

She peered up at him, though she couldn't see a damned thing in the dark, and relaxed in his hold. "I thought you were cute. I...I was attracted to you." Then she lifted her chin and glared belligerently since he, apparently, could see. "But that was before I found out what a jerk you are." She tried to wrestle her arms free from his hold. "What are you? Some kind of serial killer or something?"

"And what if I am?"

She stilled, allowing him to think that the idea startled her. Well, it did, sort of, but not enough for the drama queen performance she was laying on at the moment. "You're…you're not going to kill me, are you?"

He made a sound…a laugh, only too soft and with no humor whatsoever. "I don't know. Maybe."

Time to pump up the theatrics. She tried to pull free again. "Let me go!"

He released her, and she stumbled back a couple of steps. "Look, just let me go and I won't say a word. I don't even know your name."

"That's what they all say," he countered, his tone purposely sinister.

He wanted her afraid…he didn't like it that she wasn't scared of him. Tasha pondered that assessment briefly. He wanted to be in complete control. Testing the waters of her theory, she summoned the proper emotion and pleaded, "I swear I won't say anything!"

Another of those soft, humorless laughs, scarcely more than a breath. "With that mouth do you really expect me to believe you can keep a secret?"

She balled her fingers into fists and suppressed the urge to slug him. Jerk. "Just tell me what you want," she urged, going for a placating tone and forcing her muscles to relax from their battle-ready stance. She had to remember he could see. "I'll do anything you ask."

He moved closer…a step, maybe two, the movement soundless. But she didn't have to hear him, she felt him, as if they were somehow connected on some weird level.

"But, if I'm a serial killer as you suggested, anything you do won't make a difference. You'll die anyway."

He liked the power…wanted her helpless. She was sure of it. Reacting as he would expect to the encroaching sound of his voice, she backed away, the chain rattled as she bumped into the cot. "Just my luck to hit on a psycho," she muttered, forcing a tremor into her voice. "But my luck has always sucked anyway." She had a hunch. It was a long shot, but what the hell. "My own mother ran out on me as a kid, but I managed to get by." She glared in his direction, lifting her chin with a hint of defiance. "Looks like fate had it in for me all along."

He moved again…close enough that she could have reached out and touched him.

She collapsed onto the cot in a show of defeat. "Just get it over with." She hugged herself and exhaled a shaky breath. "I don't want to play any sick games. I got enough of that crap from my old man before he cut out on me, too."

"You just don't know when to shut up, do you?" Before she could make an evasive maneuver he grabbed her by the shoulders and pulled her to her feet.

Surprisingly, she sensed anger in his tone, felt it in his punishing grip. She thought about that for the three seconds she dared permit the distraction. He didn't want to hear about her fictional childhood distress. Was there something like that in his past? Maybe she'd play up the whole "beaten down" strategy and see where it took her.

"Look," she said wearily, "if you're going to kill me you'd better let me pee first otherwise I'm going to make a hell of a mess on your floor."

He grabbed her right hand and pried it open. Before she could fathom his intent he placed a key in her palm. Startled all over again by his actions, she crouched down and unlocked the steel bracelet around her ankle. She rubbed the raw skin there and then straightened and offered him the key back. Could this guy be human after all?

"Does this mean you're not going to kill me?"

He didn't answer, just manacled her arm and dragged her across the room. The stairs were a little tricky in the dark, but he didn't seem to have any trouble.

She wondered how he could possibly have such excellent night vision. There were people like that she knew, but generally there was some physiological reason. He'd have one, as well.

When he opened the door at the top of the stairs, she blinked rapidly to allow her eyes to adjust to the light.

She studied the layout of the house as he led her through the kitchen and down a hallway. Back door in kitchen near sink. Three more doorways in the hall. One leading to what looked like a living room, the one they'd exited from the kitchen and the third one led to a bathroom. The stairs climbing to the second level started where the hall ended opposite the front door. No pictures on the walls. No other decorating touches.

At the bathroom door he stood aside. "Make it fast."

She sidled past him but hesitated before closing the door. "You mean you're not going to watch."

He folded his arms over his chest and leaned against the wall without responding.

Tasha closed the door and sagged with relief.

She exhaled some of the tension tightening her chest, but instead of relaxing, she quickly surveyed the small room for a means of escape. Not that she'd decided she needed to make a run for it yet…but just in case. She was pretty sure that if he'd intended to kill her he would have, whether she needed to relieve herself or not. Besides, she was trapped.

The only window was one of those small rectangular ones above the tub/shower combination. As slim as she was there was no way she was getting out that route.

Knowing he was waiting right outside, she pushed off the door and took care of nature's call.

As she flushed the toilet she couldn't help smiling. She'd done it. Gotten him to bring her to his lair. *Lucas Camp,* she mused, *wherever you are, I'm in.*

Chapter 12

They'd driven around most of the night.

And found nothing. Her signal had restarted briefly at one point, but not long enough for a lock on her location.

Maverick scrubbed a hand over his face and cursed himself for letting her get away.

He was her backup.

If she was dead…

Ramon was part of her backup, as well, but Maverick was the one in charge. In nearly two decades of this kind of work he'd never lost a team member. Not once. He didn't want to start with one so damned young.

An almost inaudible beep sounded in the silence of the truck.

He jerked to attention, his gaze going instantly to the monitor he still clutched in his hand.

The two previously flat lines he'd stared at for hours on end blinked into activity.

"We've got her back," he said in a rush, the words scarcely more than a relieved whisper.

Ramon sat up a little straighter behind the wheel. "Give me some directions, amigo."

He rattled off the necessary information, not once taking his eyes off the tiny pulsing lights that represented Tasha North's heart rate and location.

They were back in business.

He had to get word to Lucas.

Chapter 13

Tasha moistened a cloth and washed her face. She couldn't be sure how long he would give her in here alone, but she needed some time to get a better grip on her strained emotions. She might be tough but she was still only human. Playing this guy's game had been hard work.

There was something not quite right here, but she couldn't put her finger on it. If he'd been the stone-cold killer he appeared to be she'd be dead now. It didn't take a master's degree in psych to see it...and she had one.

She'd be lying to herself if she didn't admit that a small part of her wanted to get the hell out of here ASAP. But the professional in her needed to see this through. She was close—right where Lucas wanted her. If she could just stay alive she could bring this guy down.

Whether he was as bad as he wanted the world to believe had nothing to do with her mission. Lucas wanted her close to him so he could be stopped. She got the distinct impression that as soon as he had led them to the man who'd hired him, he would be terminated.

That thought gave her an uncharacteristic pause. The hesitation confused her...but it was there. She'd have to deal with it.

She shook off the thought. That was the number one rule in the spy business—never, ever let the enemy close enough to make it matter.

The door opened, and the enemy in question barged in.

"Did you forget how to knock?" she asked the face glaring at her in the mirror.

"You never answered my question."

Back to that again, huh?

She spun around on her bare heel, bracing herself against the sink and staring up at him. "I already told you that I hit on you because you were the cutest guy in the club. Deal with it." The images Lucas had captured of this guy didn't do him justice, especially his eyes. Nor had the dim lighting in that club last night. His eyes were...amazing.

Suppressing a shiver she started to give him her back. He stopped her with a hand on her shoulder. "What's this?" He tipped her chin up and looked first at her healing lip then at the fading bruise on her cheek.

Concealer and makeup had covered the evidence of the roughing up she'd taken night before last. The low lighting in the club had helped, as well. But with the makeup long gone and in the bright light of day, there was no hiding her battle scars.

"My roommate and I had a disagreement." She drew away from his touch. "It happens." She turned back to the mirror and grimaced at her reflection. She looked like hell. Nothing she could do about that since she had no cosmetics, not even a brush. She combed her fingers through her tousled hair. The net jacket that had looked so sexy last night reminded her of snagged pantyhose this morning. She peeled it off and stuffed it in the trash can next to the toilet, purposely bending from the waist to startle her *host*.

"And this?" He gestured to her right shoulderblade when she straightened once more. "Did your roommate take a knife to you as well?"

Dammit, she'd forgotten about that old battle scar. Her first scuffle with a would-be mugger once she'd moved out on her own in college. He might have drawn first blood, but he'd also been the only one lying on the ground when the police finally arrived.

"I guess I forgot to mention that between my successful attempts at running away from the system, I survived a couple of foster homes. Nobody really wanted to deal with a rebellious teenager, but they didn't want to lose the government check with my name on it." She shrugged as if it didn't matter. And it didn't, because she was only making this stuff up. But, like a good movie, it was based on true stories she'd heard while interning in a social services office. "People don't bother with troubled teens unless it's for one of two reasons." She looked him straight in the eye via the mirror, sensing that she would see a reaction. "For the money or the sex."

He flinched. She resisted the urge to pump her fist in the air and scream yes. She'd gotten to him…maybe just barely beneath the surface, but someplace under the skin all the same. She'd sensed a resistance in him before when she brought up the past. He definitely did not like going there. The first piece of the puzzle. She might not have the opportunity to dig more deeply, but she'd learn what she could until it was over.

She turned around, stared up into those cold, hard eyes once more. "What about you?" She touched his jaw, tracing the outline of an old scar that gave him a permanent dimple before he could evade her touch. Her gaze moved lower, to another scar where his shirt opened into a vee at his throat. She hadn't been able to see that one last night in the low lighting. A jagged little line a shade or two lighter than the rest of his skin.

Some unknown force driving her, she reached toward him with her other hand. Oddly he didn't move away. She released the next button of his shirt. And then another and another until it lay open to his waist where he'd tucked it into his jeans. Too caught up in the moment to note his reaction other than the fact that he allowed her to continue, she pulled the shirt free of his jeans, pushing the sides farther apart so that she could see more of his well-defined torso.

For one long moment she couldn't breathe. There were too many scars to count…some small, thin lines…others much more lethal looking. She wanted to ask him about them, but when she opened her mouth no words would come. Instead she touched one particularly brutal-looking scar so damn close to his heart she couldn't imagine how he'd survived the wound. She felt him tense beneath her fingertips, but, again, he didn't move away.

That extra instinct she possessed was screaming at her now, warning that she was about to dive headlong into dangerous territory…delve past some unseen boundary of no return, and still, she couldn't stop herself. She looked into those ice-blue eyes, letting him see every confusing emotion she felt at that moment.

"Still think I'm cute?"

Right now—this moment—was the turning point. Her response to him now would determine whether or not he allowed her full access. He refused to trust her, but some part of him wanted to believe that she was telling him the truth.

Her future depended upon this one defining second.

She went up on tiptoe, and even then, reaching that grim mouth was a task. He stood several inches taller than her. She brushed her lips lightly to his. Something electric zipped through her...startled her.

He pulled away...eyed her suspiciously.

Just when she felt certain he wouldn't respond, he grabbed her, whirled her around and pinned her against the wall with his big body. His mouth came down hard on hers. The kiss was punishing, savage. A mixture of desire and fear surged through her veins. She couldn't deny the attraction, but his touch was brutal.

She shoved at his chest. Every muscle her body encountered was like granite. Her lip burned, the wound reopening beneath his onslaught. The tang of blood had her pushing harder against him.

"Wait," she murmured breathlessly when he broke the seal of their lips just long enough to take a breath. She touched her lip, swiped at the trickle of blood. He watched her intently, his own breath ragged, but a good deal more controlled than hers.

Just then she remembered the monitor and made a conscious effort to slow her respiration...her heartbeat. If Maverick was still monitoring her activity, she didn't want him barging in.

"Not like that," she whispered. "Like this." She told herself it was a mistake, but that didn't stop her. She kissed him tenderly...slowly. He didn't move a muscle... held perfectly still. She kissed those firm lips until her own unexpected reaction forced her to break the contact. Not taking the time to evaluate her motives, she pressed her lips to the tiny scar on his cheek and then moved lower. Scar after scar she acknowledged with her lips... tracing each with her tongue. Her fingers fisted in the worn soft cotton of his shirt, and she fought the crazy need swirling inside her. This was work, she repeated mentally over and over. She dropped down to her knees, careful not to break the contact of her lips against his skin.

She was winning this battle. He braced his hands against the wall, his eyes closed and for the first time since she'd met him, the hard lines of his face softened just a fraction. But that was the only thing soft about him. Flirting with danger, she drew her tongue along the warm flesh just above his waistband. If she didn't stop now... she might have to finish this but every instinct told her that seduction was her only chance of reaching this guy.

Without warning, he grabbed her by the shoulders and pulled her to her feet. When her gaze collided with his, he looked totally unaffected. Anything he'd felt was long gone.

"I'll take you home now."

He released her and walked out of the room. Tasha let go a shaky breath and sagged against the wall to pull herself together. She was hot...damn hot and wet. She'd enjoyed that more than she should have—definitely more than he had, it seemed.

Damned fool, she railed at herself silently.

She knew better than to let that happen.

Staring at her reflection in the mirror, she just shook her head. The chance of a lifetime and she was going to screw it up playing amateur psychologist.

Whatever this guy's problem, it wasn't her job to save him. Her mission was to deliver him up to Lucas Camp for one thing and one thing only.

To die.

Chapter 14

When he pulled the SUV next to the curb outside her apartment building, Tasha couldn't help thinking she'd had her chance and now it was over.

This wasn't the kind of guy to allow any sort of strings. She most likely would not see him again. But at least she knew where he lived, for the moment. She had his license plate number and a damned up-close description. But that's it. She knew absolutely nothing else about him.

"You didn't tell me your name," she said in the silence that ensued after he'd shifted into Park.

He turned toward her, his gaze cutting right through her like cold, hard steel. "Does it matter?"

She nodded, feeling startled by and wholly unprepared for the emotions he wrought in her.

"Seth."

"Seth," she echoed, thinking that it somehow fit. Some Egyptian slayer or something. "I like that."

He stared at her for a second that turned into ten before she started to squirm. There was something about his eyes…

She couldn't just get out now…she had to leave him with some reason to contact her again. She grabbed a pen from the console that separated them, then reached for his hand. He resisted at first, but eventually allowed her to draw it to her lap. She jotted her number on his palm.

He stared at his open hand for a moment then at her, but he didn't say he would or he wouldn't use the number.

"Bye, Seth."

She opened the door and climbed out, but his voice stopped her before she walked away.

"Just one thing."

She looked at him expectantly, her hand on the door ready to push it closed.

"Tell your roommate if she touches you again she's dead."

Tasha entered the building without allowing herself to think. She needed a long, hot bath. She needed to think… but first she had to get that final look she'd seen in his eyes out of her head.

He'd looked directly at her and issued that warning as if she belonged to him, and anyone else who touched her would be risking life and limb.

It didn't make sense.

On the elevator she stabbed the button for floor fourteen and leaned back against the wall. God, she was exhausted, mentally and physically.

The lift stopped on thirteen and she opened her eyes to see who would be boarding an upbound elevator with only one floor to go.

The doors slid open and Maverick waited in the corridor. "This way, North," he instructed.

Coming to immediate attention, she exited the elevator and followed the big cowboy down the quiet corridor. Though he didn't wear a hat, he had the boots and the attitude. She'd never been so glad to see anyone in her life. He was tall, broad-shouldered and had just a sprinkle of gray in his dark hair. Just enough to tell a girl he'd been around the block a time or two. She was glad to have him on her team.

At the fourth door on the right, he opened it and stepped back for her to enter the apartment before him.

"This whole floor is ours," he said in answer to her questioning look. "The escape route I showed you in your apartment upstairs will bring you here."

The escape route he spoke of was an oversize laundry chute accessed from her walk-in closet.

Inside the thirteenth-floor apartment, Maverick's partner, Ramon Vega, waited. He was much smaller in stature but quite confident and capable looking as well. His Latin heritage showed in his good looks, but he'd long since banished any accent from his dialect. He pressed a couple of buttons on a remote control and a wide-screen monitor came to life. Lucas Camp behind a desk blinked into vivid focus, his gaze zeroed in on her as if they were face-to-face in the same room.

"You look like hell, North," Lucas said by way of greeting.

She noticed the Webcam then and knew that, for all intents and purposes, they were face-to-face. She plopped down on a chair directly across from the screen and accompanying camera. "Feel like it, too."

"Tell me what you've got."

Before Tasha launched into a detailed report of the events since making contact with her target, she needed to get one thing out of the way.

"Something isn't right with this guy," she said, confusion lining her brow. She could feel it but couldn't quite label it.

"You mean something besides his being a sociopath?" Maverick ventured.

She nodded. "Yeah. Something besides that."

"Give us a profile on how he lives," Lucas said, setting the direction of the briefing. "Maverick has already told me where he lives and a brief summary of the neighborhood, but what did you see inside?"

"Not much at first. The lights were out when he took me in and he locked me in the basement until this morning."

Lucas frowned. "Locked you in the basement?"

"Shackled me to a cot down there. The cot was bolted to the concrete floor. There was no way to escape. I had my doubts as to whether or not I'd see the light of day ever again." She sighed wearily. "I can't be the first person he's held prisoner down there. His preparations were too well thought out."

"That's why we couldn't get your signal back," Maverick concluded. "I'm certain he had a jammer in his vehicle, but after that I couldn't be sure what happened. He stashed you underground, that explains it. You had me worried for a while."

She nodded. She'd been a little worried herself. "This morning he brought me back upstairs. I didn't get a good look around, but the place looked fully furnished with the usual household goods. I imagine his private space was on the second floor. I didn't get that far."

"Do you think you made enough of an impression to see him again?" Lucas wanted to know. He was watching her closely, assessing her state after her first encounter with the target.

She moved her hands over her face and through her hair. "I think so. Maybe. It's difficult to tell. He's so guarded." She looked directly at Lucas then, or at least at his image. "There's something wrong with this guy, Lucas. Something really wrong."

"Anything you picked up on could be helpful. I've got a profiler standing by."

She nodded. "It's more than just the fact that he kills for a living, obviously." She tried to think how to label it…but nothing that came to mind felt accurate. "He's deeply troubled. I got the distinct impression that he's not afraid of anything, death included." She shrugged. "It's weird. It was nearly impossible to get any kind of reaction out of him. It's like he blocks all emotion. Doesn't feel a thing. And the scars." She shook her head as she thought of the marks on his body. "I've never seen so many. He's had it rough at some point. But the lack of emotion was the biggest thing I noticed. I could scarcely get a reaction out of him at all."

Ramon lifted a skeptical brow and eyed her skimpy attire. "Are you sure he isn't dead?"

A pained laugh burst from her. "Oh, no. He's very much alive…just buried somehow."

"What about prints?" Maverick tossed into the conversation. "We could ID this guy if he's in the system."

Lucas nodded. "Possibly, but we've run his picture through the system and didn't find anything. Still, there's always the possibility that he's had his appearance altered. Did he give you a name?"

"Seth." Tasha tugged off first one boot, then the other. She reached into her right boot for her cell phone, handling it carefully. "He handled the boots and the phone."

Maverick and Ramon took custody of the items.

"I don't think that's his real name, though. Not that I

expected to get the real thing," Tasha said to Lucas. "But I studied Egyptian mythology as an elective in college. Seth was a sort of dark god, a slayer. The irony of it is too coincidental I think."

Lucas nodded his agreement. "We'll see what we can find on the name Seth. It may be an alias he's used before."

"What now?" she asked Lucas, then glanced at the two men who served as her backup.

"Now we wait," Lucas announced.

That felt like such a waste of time. Tasha spread her hands in a gesture of uncertainty. "Maybe I should have tried to plant some sort of tracking device on him. He could be meeting with the guy who hired him right now and you can't allow a tail to get close enough to find out." She didn't want Lucas disappointed in her performance and he certainly hadn't given her any real reason to think he was pleased at this point.

Maverick spoke up first. "No way, little lady. This guy's a pro. He'd have found it, known you were the one who planted it, and that would have been the end of that, if you get my drift."

She nodded. The end of her, no doubt. "You're right. It just feels like I should have done more. He has my number, but who knows if he'll call."

"You got a lot farther than we expected for a first encounter," Lucas said pointedly. "And you're alive to tell about it. He'll call."

She supposed that was close enough to a pat on the back. And she sure as hell hoped he was right.

There was only one thing she could do now.

Wait.

Chapter 15

Tasha moaned softly as the steam rose around her. It felt so good to just soak for a while. She'd taken a shower after her debrief this morning, then a power nap that lasted for three hours. But this...this was pure luxury. She needed this. Her muscles loosened...relaxed as the heat chased away the stress and soreness. It might just take hours to soothe all the kinks and stiffness.

She apparently had the time. *He hadn't called.*

Her eyes opened and she lay there, her gaze searching for anything in the foggy room to focus on. She didn't want to think about him...not yet. Draping her arms along the sides of the tub, she forced his image away.

But not quickly enough. An entirely different kind of heat coiled inside her. She cursed herself for allowing it. He was a killer...the enemy. And yet, somehow he'd gotten to her on a level over which she had no control. It was totally unbelievable. She tried hard to pinpoint the precise root of the feeling. It wasn't sympathy. There was a definite physical attraction, despite his lack of personality.

But that wasn't such a big deal. As Ramon would say, she wasn't dead. Any woman breathing would be attracted to Seth on a physical level. But she could handle that. He was an assassin…a very dangerous man…a bad guy…the enemy. Taking him down wouldn't be a problem.

That last thought echoed hollowly. "Shit," she muttered. This couldn't happen. She'd just met the guy. Taking him down was her mission…but something felt wrong.

How could she even think about screwing up this badly? She shook her head slowly from side to side. This was the opportunity of a lifetime. Lucas Camp had come to her! She couldn't let anything get in the way. Why the hell had she chosen psychology for her major, anyway? If she hadn't, maybe then she wouldn't have bothered looking beneath the surface.

She scrubbed a hand over her face and cursed herself again. This wasn't about what made the guy tick. This was about stopping a killer—a hired assassin—before he accomplished his mission. Her primary goal, outside seeing that he didn't accomplish his, was making the connection between him and the man who hired him. Nothing else mattered. All those scars… The overwhelming feeling that he was as much a victim as those he hunted was of no consequence.

He would be stopped, one way or another. And so would the man who'd hired him. Lucas's intentions were crystal clear. He wanted this guy dead. Tasha felt it all the way to her bones. It was personal somehow.

A knock at the front door jerked her from her troubling thoughts. Water sloshed as she pushed upright. Her heart kicked into a faster rhythm.

She shifted to her feet, the steam rising off her skin, and stepped out of the tub onto the fluffy bath mat. Shouldering into the robe without bothering to towel dry, she reached for her weapon next.

As she padded down the short hall, her bare feet leaving a trail of water, she chambered a round in the weapon Maverick had given her. Another knock rattled the hinges as she crossed the living room. She peered through the peephole, her heart pounding, and saw Maverick.

Heaving a relieved sigh, she shook off the tension and opened the door. "What's up?"

Maverick stepped inside, and she closed the door behind him. "Just wanted you to know that we lifted his prints from your cell phone but they were useless." He passed the phone back to her.

A frown nagged at her forehead. "He wasn't in the system?" The guy was clearly a high-end professional, getting caught wouldn't be in keeping with his skill level. And unless he'd been caught and charged with some crime, he wouldn't be in any system.

He shook his head and handed her the boots she'd worn last night. "Can't tell. There's too much alteration, not enough legible lines to go for a match."

"He doesn't intend to be ID'd." This just kept getting better and better. Seth was really on top of his game. He'd had his fingerprints altered.

"It's professional work, too, not a homemade job."

That's why she hadn't felt any particular roughness when he'd touched her. This wasn't a hack job to alter any prints he'd leave behind, this was one of those cutting-edge "escape clinic" laser jobs. Very expensive, very cleverly done. Either Seth or the man he worked for knew how to remain anonymous.

"If he calls," she offered, "I can try and get a look around his place. See what I can find."

Maverick nodded. "Just be careful." He looked at her

a moment before he continued. "Lucas would like you to try and get a DNA sample. We don't know how much good it'll do, but it's another avenue of identification."

The various ways a sample could be obtained flashed quickly through her mind. "All right."

Maverick looked away briefly before adding, "You know a shed hair won't get us what we need. If you could lift his toothbrush or razor, assuming it's not the electric type, that would be better."

She nodded. "Got it."

"Just be careful, North." Maverick shook his head, his expression cluttered with more concern than she would have expected from a man of his background. "You're right when you said there's something off about this guy. He worries me more than most I've run across in my time. Lucas said the same thing."

At least she wasn't the only one picking up those vibes. "Don't worry, I've got it under control."

That was a flat-out lie, but he didn't need to know it. In the event that he was fishing for Lucas, she wasn't about to give him any information that could discredit her in any way.

"I'll be right downstairs." He glanced at her robe. "Don't forget to put another patch in place."

"Will do."

When he'd gone, she retraced her damp path to the bathroom, drained the tub and cleaned up the mess she'd made. She set her weapon aside, reached into the medicine cabinet and got the box that contained the patches. To anyone else they looked like a simple birth control prescription. Lucas's people covered every base. If her target decided to check her out, he'd find nothing that would suggest she wasn't who she said she was. They'd even furnished the second bedroom of the apartment, complete with young, female wardrobe, to give the illusion of a roommate.

Tasha pressed the patch into place and checked out her reflection. The bruise on her cheek was pretty much gone now, and her lip was way better. A dab of makeup and she'd be good to go. Her side was still a little tender, but not so bad.

The firm knock on her front door made her jump. Damn, she was edgy. Forgetting her appearance for the moment she strode back into the living room. What did Maverick want now?

She opened the door without bothering to check the peephole.

Her target filled the doorway, those piercing blue eyes covered by dark shades.

For one second she was sure she had to be imagining things, but she blinked and he was still there.

He removed the concealing eyewear and focused that fierce gaze on her. "Ask me in."

A shiver raced across her skin as much from the sound of his deep voice as from those eyes. She summoned a semblance of control and stepped back, opening the door wide. "Come on in."

He reached down and picked up a bag she hadn't noticed since she was too busy staring at those unsettling eyes. Idiot, she railed silently. Details. She wasn't supposed to miss any.

Once he'd stepped inside, he closed and locked the door behind him. That move should have set her on edge but didn't. Maverick and Ramon would be watching. Her apartment was rigged for surveillance. Seth looked at her, surveyed her lack of proper attire and then settled his gaze on hers. "I have a job for you."

For just a second it kind of annoyed her that she found

not a glimmer of approval in his eyes. She was standing there naked but for the robe, and he didn't even notice. God knew that she'd absorbed every damned detail about him. Black T-shirt beneath a pale blue cotton button-up shirt. The telltale bulge of the weapon he wore, well-fitting jeans and those made-for-traction ankle boots. If she hadn't enjoyed the perusal so much she could have chalked it up to merely being part of her job. But the heat funneling beneath her belly button made a liar out of her. She pushed the disturbing sensation away.

"What kind of job?"

"You need money, right?" He said this as he surveyed what he could see of her apartment. It was a nice enough place and wasn't the reason he asked the question. She remembered telling him that she didn't have a job yet and was pretty much broke from coughing up her share of the rent.

"Yeah, I need money," she said bluntly. "But not badly enough to do anything illegal." She looked him up and down, pausing briefly at his crotch. She looked away just as quickly. Either the guy stayed aroused all the time or he was extremely well endowed. Why she would notice and why it would have such an effect was beyond her. What the hell was wrong with her?

"There's nothing to worry about." He offered her the shopping bag he carried. "Put this on."

Still trying to read his expression, which was impossible, she accepted the bag that turned out to be a good deal heavier than it looked. Inside was a brown uniform. "What's this?" Her senses moved to a higher state of alert. Even folded up as it was she recognized the delivery-service getup.

"I'd like you to make a delivery for me. It's very simple."

"What kind of delivery?"

When he looked at her this time, there was no way to miss his impatience. That he allowed her to see the emotion surprised her and served as a warning at the same time.

"Don't ask so many questions."

She shrugged and headed to the bedroom with the bag in hand. For a second or two she allowed the elation of his return to bolster the nagging worry over where this might be headed. For the moment he was back, and that was all that mattered.

Moving quickly, she dragged on a pair of panties and a bra. Surprisingly the uniform was a good fit. Maybe he'd noticed more than he'd let on. The weight in the bag was the shoes. He'd thought of everything.

She brushed her hair and pulled it up with a claw clip, grabbed her purse and sunglasses and readied for whatever the hell he had in mind.

He waited right where she'd left him. Maverick and Ramon would know whether he'd looked around. She would find out later.

Seth scrutinized her from head to toe. "Perfect."

"Why not just have the package delivered in the usual manner?" she asked as they exited her apartment.

"I have my reasons."

She locked her door and followed him to the stairs. Fourteen floors, either the guy had a phobia where elevators were concerned or he didn't want to get trapped in one in case he had to make a run for it.

He didn't speak again even after they were in his SUV and headed into city traffic, which was no big surprise. He only spoke when he had something to say or she forced a response out of him. She occupied herself with attempting to determine their destination.

A few minutes later he parked in the lot of a large office building right off the Magnificent Mile, Chicago's main street of shops, restaurants and ritzy office buildings.

He reached into the back seat and picked up a package. Eight-by-ten, she estimated. Wrapped in a plain brown paper. Addressed to... She leaned toward him slightly to read the name and address.

The name slammed into her with all the force of a runaway train.

Victoria Colby.

She was his mark.

"You know..." Calm, stay calm. She forced her heart rate back to a normal pace and focused on slowing her respiration. She couldn't let him see that she recognized the name. "Maybe this isn't such a good idea."

He nodded toward the building. "Fourth floor. The elevator opens right into the Colby Agency lobby," he went on as if she'd said nothing. "Ask for Victoria Colby. Don't let anyone else sign for the package except her. Do you understand?"

She moistened her suddenly dry lips. Somewhere in the back of her mind, she realized that he'd just said more to her at one time than any other time since they'd met. "What's in the package? You're sure—"

"Go." He pushed the package and an electronic clipboard toward her and pressed her with a gaze that warned her not to argue. "Now."

She took the package and the clipboard and climbed out of the SUV. She walked slowly across the parking lot, praying that Maverick had her location. She forced her mind to consider what could be in the package. It felt a little light for any kind of elaborate explosive. A detonator would be required. But then again there were all kinds of lightweight devices. She considered the possibility of some sort of poison. Something absorbed through the skin or inhaled like anthrax.

Resisting the impulse to scan the lot for Maverick's vehicle, she opened the main door and stepped inside. She strode straight up to the lobby desk.

"I have a package for Victoria Colby," she said in as professional a tone as she could manage. He could be listening, watching even. Who knew what sort of gadgets he could have added to the innocuous-looking uniform. There'd been no time to check it out thoroughly.

"Fourth floor," the watchman said without even asking for ID.

It was the uniform. It was too much a part of everyday life for anyone to give it a second thought.

Tasha went to the bank of elevators and pressed the call button. She let her respiration and heart rate increase faster and faster as a signal to Maverick that something was wrong. By the time she reached the fourth floor, her skin felt flushed and she'd all but hyperventilated. Even if Seth had some way of monitoring her now, he would expect her to be nervous going in.

The receptionist greeted her with a smile and a pleasant, "May I help you?"

"I have a delivery for Victoria Colby."

The receptionist reached for the package. "I'll take it for you."

Tasha knew a moment's panic. "I'm sorry," she said, grabbing back control. "Ms. Colby has to personally sign for the package."

"Oh." The woman's expression turned to one of confusion, or maybe irritation. She pointed to the corridor on Tasha's right. "Her secretary's office is the first one on the left."

Tasha forced a smile. "Thank you."

She passed a couple of people in the corridor, both male and wearing suits. Colby Agency investigators, Tasha presumed. Each one surveyed her thoroughly before moving on. She wanted to scream, "Doesn't anyone suspect anything is wrong here?" But she only smiled stiffly.

"Good afternoon. You have a delivery?" This from a pleasant-looking middle-aged lady whose name plate read, Mildred Parker.

"Yes, for Victoria Colby."

"Well, generally the receptionist would sign for any packages," she offered kindly.

Tasha glanced at the clipboard. "The sender requested that Ms. Colby sign for the package personally."

"Very well."

The secretary stood and moved toward the door on the other side of the room. Tasha followed. The older woman knocked once and pushed it open.

"Victoria, there's a special delivery for you. This young lady needs you to sign for it."

Mildred opened the door wider and stepped to one side for Tasha to enter.

Her pulse racing, Tasha met the dark gaze focused on her from the other side of the massive mahogany desk. So this was Victoria Colby. She looked every bit as dignified and sophisticated as Tasha had expected.

What she hadn't expected was the incredible complacency where security was concerned. Wasn't Lucas supposed to have men watching her? Forcing her feet into action, Tasha moved across the room.

Victoria Colby reached for the clipboard Tasha offered. "Good afternoon," she said with a smile.

Tasha forced an answering smile and nodded.

Victoria signed the clipboard and passed it back to her, her open hand waiting for the package.

As she slowly extended the package toward the woman, Tasha tried to warn her with her eyes...tried to make her see that something was wrong.

If Victoria noticed, she didn't show it.

"Thank you," she said as she settled the package on her desk.

Tasha managed a stiff "Have a nice day" and left. She punched the down button at the elevator and fought the need to tell someone that this was all wrong. A part of her braced for the sound of an explosion or for a scream of agony.

When the elevator doors finally slid open, what felt like a lifetime later, Tasha drew up short when a tall, dark-haired man moved to exit the arriving car. He paused and looked directly into her eyes for two beats. She prayed he would see the warning there. When he at last moved past her he allowed his hand to brush hers.

The rush of relief was so profound that she scarcely stepped forward quickly enough to catch the elevator before the doors closed.

Whoever the guy was he had to be one of Lucas's men. The look he'd given her was one of assurance, the physical contact a sign that he understood something was wrong. Maverick had gotten word to Lucas.

She stabbed the button for the lobby and sagged against the closest wall. Taking long, deep breaths she calmed her racing heart and slowed her frantic respiration.

When she reached the SUV, Seth didn't ask any questions, just drove away once she'd climbed inside.

The silence that hung in the air ignited a fury in her belly. By the time he pulled up to the curb in front of her apartment building her temper had raged out of control.

"I want to know what was in that package." She turned on him, glared at him with all the anger she felt inside.

He didn't even bother taking off his sunglasses or looking her way, he simply offered her a wad of cash.

She almost told him where he could shove the money, but that would be out of character for the role she played. Instead, she snatched it from him, startled to note that it was five one-hundred-dollar bills.

"You can dispose of the uniform."

She grabbed her purse, shoved the money into it before slinging it over her shoulder. She started to get out, but hesitated, then shook her head. No way was he getting off this easy.

"I don't like being used," she told him. "If that package was dangerous and that lady—"

"There was nothing in the package that could physically harm anyone. It was merely a message…a reminder."

She closed her eyes for one second as another blast of relief hit her.

"Get out."

Renewed fury obliterated all other emotion. "You're unbelievable. You come to me for a favor, then you treat me like a piece of trash you can toss away."

He remained silent, motionless, seemingly oblivious of her heated emotions.

In a lightning-flash move, she snatched off his sunglasses and glared at him. "You really are—"

Before she could finish the statement, he'd jerked her across the console and trapped her between his chest and the steering wheel. The look in his eyes was murderous, his expression hard, his breathing shallow and harsh.

"Don't ever do that again."

Ignoring the fury seething in every part of him, she

lifted her chin defiantly and demanded, "And just what will you do about it if I do."

He kissed her.

Savagely.

Then he drew back and looked into her eyes. "Get out."

She didn't hesitate this time. She scrambled out of the vehicle and strode to her building without looking back. Not until she was inside her own apartment, with the door closed and locked behind her, did she allow herself to breathe easy.

She thought of all she'd learned about him from their brief encounters. The way he'd locked her in that basement. The bizarre tattoo…the way he tried to hurt her even when he kissed her.

Whatever else she felt or imagined she felt, one thing was a certainty…this guy was dangerous.

Extremely dangerous.

To her.

Chapter 16

"Where's Lucas?"

"He's on his way, ma'am," Logan told Victoria. "I've checked the package thoroughly. It appears to be safe, but I'd rather you wait for Lucas's arrival before we open it."

Victoria looked to Ian and then to Simon. Both men looked as uncertain about this as she felt.

She hadn't needed John Logan to rush in and snatch the package from her hands to know something was wrong. The young woman who'd delivered it had given her the undeniable impression that she should be afraid.

Victoria closed her eyes and tried to steady the spinning in her head. She wasn't sure she possessed the fortitude to get through this. It was bad enough that an assassin was stalking her, but the ice cream...now this.

Leberman, the son of a bitch, why didn't he just confront her face-to-face? Why all the subterfuge? All the games?

Because the sick bastard gets off on the pain he inflicts. She knew the answer. Understood perfectly why he was doing this to her. Still, she couldn't fully come to terms with it.

Victoria opened her eyes and stared at the package. Her only regret was that she couldn't kill the bastard here and now.

From his hotel only minutes away, where he'd set up a mini command post, Lucas arrived just then, his gaze going first to her, then settling on the package lying in the middle of her desk.

"That's it?" He looked to Logan and then to Ian.

Both men nodded. Logan told him, "I can't find any indication of explosives or poisonous substances. Scans indicate a nonmetal object."

"Clear the room," Lucas commanded. "I don't want anyone in here when I open it."

"Absolutely not," Victoria argued. "The package is addressed to me, I'll open it."

"I'll open it." Simon stepped toward her desk.

Simon had a new wife. Ian had a wife and two children. And Logan had a wife, as well. Victoria looked to each of the trusted men and ordered, "Leave my office. I want to do this alone."

Ian shook his head. "Not going to happen, Victoria. Either allow one of us to open the package, or we'll stand here and debate the point all evening."

She surveyed the determined male faces around the room. All were prepared to die to protect her. Every damned one of them was as stubborn as she was.

"All right." She stepped back. "Open it."

Simon quickly stepped in front of Ian. Simon had done time with the FBI and was fearless when it came to doing his duty. He was just one of many fine investigators Victoria employed. She prayed the evil that had followed her life for nearly two decades would not touch him now.

Using the gloves and utility cutter Logan had brought into the office, Simon carefully slit the packaging. He pulled back the outer wrapping and cut the tape sealing the lid on the small box. He dragged the package a little closer and cautiously lifted the lid.

He studied the contents for a moment before allowing his gaze to meet Victoria's. She saw the uncertainty there a split second before he turned the box around where she could see what it held.

A small blue sneaker was the only item in the box.

She didn't have to touch it or inspect it in any way. She recognized it immediately. She knew everyone in the room was waiting for her to say something…but she couldn't speak. She could only stand there, as the tears spilled down her cheeks, and stare at the small shoe her son had been wearing the day he disappeared.

Chapter 17

He drove back to the house in Oak Park well after dark. He'd waited until Victoria Colby had left her office, her protector, Lucas Camp, and his two men close by, and then he'd followed her home.

It hadn't been necessary for him to see her face as she opened the package. He saw all he needed to in her pained, stoic profile while she pretended to go about her daily routine as she left the office. He was satisfied.

They knew he was watching, but they did nothing. He'd wondered at that in the beginning but he understood now. They had what they considered an ace in the hole. And Victoria Colby would want to see how this game played out. She wanted the truth. She wanted Leberman.

As, he imagined, did Lucas Camp.

He laughed softly as he considered what lay before them. Victoria Colby couldn't possibly imagine the horrors in store for her before the blessed relief of death would come. He almost hated to allow it to end that way.

He backed into the driveway that flanked the house

he used for the time being. He hated coming back here, but it was a necessary part of the strategy. Though he enjoyed the buildup, the crescendo of death would be lessened immensely, in his opinion, by this grandstanding.

But it was not his decision to make.

As he did each time he returned, he searched the grounds, considered the windows and doors for any subtle change in the way he'd left them.

He knew immediately that he had a visitor.

A careful one.

Like smoke, soundless and camouflaged by the darkness, he stole into the house. His visitor waited in the darkness of the inner hall, like a cancer lying dormant before it struck its unsuspecting victim. Being in this house again with him gnawed at Seth's gut like the sharp hunger pains he'd once known in that dark place he'd called home.

"What do you want?" he demanded.

He didn't want him here. Had no desire to speak with him or to see him.

Leberman flipped on the overhead light switch, leveling the playing field since he could not see so well in the dark. He blinked to adjust his vision.

"You made the delivery?" he demanded without preamble.

"Yes." Seth squashed the sensation of fear that, even now...after all these years, tried to surface. He reminded himself that he was not afraid of anything—most especially this son of a bitch.

Leberman nodded. "Good. And the rest is on schedule?"

"I don't want you here." He clenched his jaw hard to hold back the emotion he refused to allow. Control was essential.

Leberman met his gaze, those beady eyes showing no fear. The tables had turned in recent years. He was a fool not to fear him. "I know you don't want me here. You despise me now." He circled him slowly, inspecting him as he had hundreds of times before. Seth resisted the instinct to stiffen. "I know exactly how you feel about me," Leberman continued. He moved back in front of him. "But that changes nothing. You owe me this. You will see it through."

Seth didn't respond. Leberman knew he would not fail. As he said, he owed this to him. And then they would be even…finished.

Leberman leaned closer and sniffed. "You've been with a woman. I smell her perfume."

He didn't bother to respond to that comment, either, though a tendril of uneasiness slid through him. He banished it with the same indifference he displayed for his unwanted guest now. Theirs was not a relationship based on friendship or fondness of any sort. They had only one thing in common. Sheer hatred for the Colby name.

"Did you fuck her?" Leberman inclined his head thoughtfully. "I think not. Perhaps that's the reason for your foul mood." He smiled grotesquely. "She must have seen you for what you are. Pure evil…a beast. Did you let her live in spite of her rebuff?" He sniffed again. "You're not getting soft are you?"

Seth locked down all emotion and moved a step closer to the bastard, his fingers fisting tightly to resist the urge to wrap around that scrawny throat. Only with him did he still struggle with the human weakness of baser emotions. "Unless you came here to provide additional instructions, we have nothing to discuss."

Leberman peered up at him, studied his face, seemingly oblivious to the hatred radiating in his direction. "I trained you so well. You don't show the first hint of emotion. Anger now and again, perhaps, but nothing more."

This was a waste of time. "Say what you came to say and *go.*"

"Pain, death, none of it touches you, does it?" Leberman persisted. He smiled. "You are magnificent." He shook his head slowly from side to side. "You have no idea how proud I am. Every moment I've waited will have been well worth it." He sighed mightily. "You're prepared for tomorrow?"

The question was unnecessary. "Of course."

"Good. I'm looking forward to this step more than you can know."

Seth said nothing.

A beat of silence passed. When Leberman would have gone, Seth reluctantly issued a warning of a different sort, "They're watching me closely now. I don't think I was followed, but it's a possibility." Though he didn't really care if Leberman was caught or not, it would ruin his own plans at this stage.

Leberman cocked his head. "Really? I'm surprised you let them that close." His eyes narrowed. "That's not like you. It's *her,* isn't it?"

"I'll create a diversion so you can go undetected," he offered and walked away, leaving the bastard to think what he would and not bothering to answer his question. He didn't give a damn what surprised him.

If Lucas's men were out there, as he suspected, all he had to do was set a course for Victoria Colby's private residence, and they would follow.

He glanced back at Leberman once more and warned, "Don't come back."

"Just so you know, I will be watching tomorrow," Leberman told him, an underlying threat in his tone. "I'll be very careful to stay out of sight, but I will be watching."

Seth just wanted him out of his sight. If he chose to watch tomorrow it was of no consequence to him as long as he stayed out of the way and away from him. The death of Lucas Camp only served one purpose as far as Seth was concerned.

To torture Victoria Colby.

Chapter 18

Tasha lay in bed at midnight with no sign of sleep in sight. She couldn't stop thinking about what Lucas had told her. The package had contained a small boy's shoe. One of the shoes Victoria Colby's child had been wearing eighteen years ago when he'd gone missing.

Victoria had been devastated then and today.

Tasha thought of the woman she'd met briefly when she delivered the package. Strong, steady, still very attractive at fifty or so. But that woman had been brought to her knees by a horrible reminder of the past.

Why would Seth do that? Tasha felt certain that he was following Leberman's orders. Lucas had told her that they suspected this man named Leberman of having taken the child. Once he'd disposed of the body he'd obviously kept souvenirs for later.

Leberman wanted to make Victoria suffer before he ended her life. Lucas was sure he had more dirty tricks up his sleeve. Tasha also fully understood Lucas's personal ties now. Victoria Colby.

Tasha's thoughts turned to Seth then. Was it about the money? She'd turned the uniform and the bills he'd given her over to Maverick for fingerprinting in hopes of finding Leberman's or anyone else's who might be connected. She wondered how much a man like Leberman would pay to hire a man as skilled and ruthless as Seth to carry out this well-planned drama that was supposed to end in death.

She wondered at the brutalities Seth must have suffered to make him the kind of man he was. She flopped over onto her other side. Why the hell did she care? He was a killer. It didn't matter what made him that way. Her only job was to stop him once they'd located Leberman.

Tasha pushed up from the bed and shuffled into the kitchen for a drink. Sleep wasn't coming. She might as well give up and do something useful. Maybe some yoga. She could definitely handle some relaxation exercises.

The telephone rang, startling her.

She blew out a breath. Damn, she was going to have to get a grip here. She strode over to the table next to the sofa and picked up the receiver. It wouldn't be Maverick, he'd knock on her door.

"Hello," she said softly as if she'd been awakened, though she really didn't expect to hear from Seth again this soon.

"There's a cab waiting outside."

Seth.

Anticipation seared through her. "A cab? Where am I going?" She glanced at the clock, 12:35 a.m.

"I think you know."

An audible click told her he'd hung up.

She lowered the receiver and dropped it back into its cradle.

For a while Tasha simply stood there trying to decide if she could take this step or not.

She knew what he wanted.

Had felt the primal urgency in his kiss that afternoon. Had also felt his resistance. He didn't want to want her.

She closed her eyes and ordered her heart rate to slow. Sleeping with him was supposed to be a last resort. But nothing was as it should be with him. She needed that closer connection with him. She needed him to need her. Seduction was her only option.

Rather than stand there rationalizing further, she did what she had to do.

She dressed for the occasion.

Short black skirt, matching thong, even shorter gold top, no bra, no hose. She slid her feet into strappy black sandals and looked herself over. The hesitation she saw in her own eyes was unlike her…she shouldn't hesitate. This wasn't personal. It was business—essential to the mission. She'd known going in that it might come to this. She shook her head and looked away from the lie in her eyes. Somehow, stupidly, she had waited for this moment. She hoped like hell her motivation was grounded in the mission. But she had a very bad feeling that it wasn't.

Tossing her toothbrush and other essentials into a bag, she glanced at the gun she'd left lying on the toilet tank. But she couldn't risk him finding it. She had mace. That would have to be sufficient. He was a lot bigger than her, but she could fight as well as any man. On second thought she removed the patch and tossed it into the trash. Maverick knew his location. She wasn't going to risk having to explain the patch to Seth. Or worse, have him detect its signal if he chose to do a body sweep.

As he'd said, a cab waited at the curb. She climbed in, and the driver pulled out onto the street without asking for directions. Maverick would be furious, but it wasn't like they didn't know where Seth lived now. Her apartment was monitored, they would know she'd left.

She relaxed into the seat and cleared her mind. She wasn't going to argue with herself anymore. Whatever happened happened. End of subject.

She knew what she had to do.

A few minutes later she leaned forward and surveyed the street signs.

"Why aren't we headed for Oak Park?"

"That's not the address I was given," the cabbie offered with a shrug. He smiled then. "Maybe it's a surprise."

Uneasiness slid through Tasha. An all-too-familiar sensation these days. There were surprises and there were *surprises*. This was definitely one she hadn't anticipated. Failure to anticipate her target's moves was a dangerous weakness. He looked more and more as if *he* was a serious weakness.

Thirty minutes later, after traveling through several exclusive neighborhoods, the cab braked to a stop in front of a massive ornamental gate. She squinted to make out the house that lay beyond but couldn't.

After a moment the gate opened and the cab rolled through and toward the house at the end of the drive. As they neared the structure she could make out the soaring, contemporary lines and angles. A high wall enclosed the property for as far as she could see, and if her sense of direction was on track they were near the lake. That would explain the elegant homes they'd passed.

"Here you are." The cabbie glanced back at her and smiled with masculine approval. "The fare has already been taken care of."

"Thanks." Tasha stepped out of the cab and looked

around for a bit before moving toward the house. The cab left through the gate, and she heard it close behind him. The house looked dark except for foundation lights that up lit from the well-landscaped shrubbery. But Seth liked the dark.

She moved toward the front entry, wondering where his SUV was parked. A side entry garage perhaps.

As she moved up the steps, the front door opened and he stood there waiting for her. He didn't speak, just waited. Her pulse reacted and she chastised herself for the lack of control.

If Maverick had tried to follow her, he was nowhere to be seen. But then, that was her fault for removing the one link between her and her backup.

It was just *him* and her.

She was on her own.

When she'd stepped inside, he closed the door behind her and turned on the lights, the setting far dimmer than she would have preferred.

"Looks like you've moved up in the world," she said to him when he remained silent. Even in the low light she could see that the house was elegantly decorated and expensively furnished.

"This way."

She followed him up the grand staircase. Surely this wasn't his home. Maybe Leberman's? That didn't make sense, either. Lucas and Victoria would certainly know if he were this close. This place didn't exactly have a lived-in feel, but it didn't have that closed-up smell or feel about it, either.

When he stopped again and turned on a light, they were in a generously sized bedroom with French doors that likely led out onto a balcony. She imagined there was a view of the lake. The furnishings were just as exquisite as the ones downstairs, including the massive king-size bed.

He took her purse, then leveled that piercing gaze on her. "Take off your clothes."

She walked over to him and reached for the buttons of his shirt. "How about we take off yours first?"

Strong fingers encircled her wrists and pulled her hands away from his shirt. "Take them off."

She backed up a step and considered her limited options. She could refuse and blow this now—maybe have to fight her way out of here—or...

He unzipped her purse then removed a thick fold of bills from his pocket and dropped them inside. When he'd tossed the bag aside he issued his order again. "Now, take off your clothes."

Unbridled fury scorched through her. "You think I'm some kind of hooker?" She glanced at her bag for emphasis.

When he didn't answer she huffed in disbelief. "Oh, man." She stormed out, didn't even bother with her purse. She wanted to make the right connection with the guy. Earn his trust. This kind of connection would get her nowhere fast.

By the time she reached the landing he was right behind her. She ignored him and kept moving. She was down the stairs and halfway across the entry hall when he stopped her. He whirled her around to face him, his hold on her arms brutal.

"No one walks away from me."

"Let me go," she warned.

Something changed in his expression. "I thought you needed a job," he countered, his eyes narrowing suspiciously.

She tried without success to jerk free of his savage hold. "I need a job not a john. Now let me go!"

He released her as suddenly as he'd grabbed her. He took a step back physically and emotionally. "Get your bag. I'll take you back."

Tasha couldn't move for a moment, unable to look away from that fierce gaze just yet. When she could break free of the spell, she turned and hurried up the stairs. She cursed herself every step of the way for being the fool she was. She should be glad that he hadn't out-and-out raped her. Instead, he'd turned off the desire she knew he had felt as easily as he turned off a light switch.

And, unbelievably, she was disappointed.

Chapter 19

He performed his usual check of the perimeter of the Oak Park property before entering. Thankfully no one waited for him this time. A quick sweep for alien electronics and he relaxed.

If Leberman showed his face once more he might just kill him now and put them both out of their misery. Dread, or something on that order, hardened in his gut. He tamped it down. Hated those old sensations Leberman so easily engendered in him. When Victoria Colby was dead they would be even, anyway. What difference would a few days make? Once his score with Leberman was settled he intended to kill the bastard if he ever came near him again. Just looking at him made Seth remember the past, and he didn't want to remember.

He climbed the stairs to his room without bothering with light. He was as much at home in the dark as he was in the light, maybe more. The dark had always been his friend. No one could see him in the dark.

Before he could stop the mutinous memory, Leberman's words echoed in his head. He knew what he was all right. He was pure evil…a monster. Hadn't he been marked long ago? That was just one more reason he couldn't trust Tasha. She pretended to see what wasn't there…pretended not to care what he was.

But he knew differently.

He knew a great deal more than she suspected. He knew exactly what she was doing. Leberman had his sources. He untied his shoes and toed them off, then shouldered out of his shirt and dropped it to the floor. The weapon and holster he shrugged off and lay on the bed. A gun had been his only sleeping partner for more than a decade. He was never without it. Never intended to be, as long as he was still breathing.

As he peeled his T-shirt up and off, he caught a glimpse of himself in the mirror. He moved closer to inspect the numerous scars that marred his otherwise well-maintained body. Ugly, brutal marks that told the story of his past. A past he wanted to forget. He studied his face and the slash on his jaw that had been the last one inflicted by the bastard who'd trained him.

He banked the fury that ignited instantly whenever he allowed himself to dwell on the past. His lips flattened into a grim line. The bouts of anger he'd been dealing with lately were nothing but an indicator of his one weakness—the past. When he had paid his final debt he would never think of the past again.

The image of Tasha flashed through his mind, sending a new kind of fire straight to his groin. She was proving a weakness, as well. He'd allowed his curiosity to get the better of him…. That had been a mistake.

It wouldn't happen again.

He had no reason at this point to kill her, but he would if she got in his way.

The curiosity she'd sparked in him was the only reason she wasn't dead already.

But she was toying with him…there could be no other explanation.

He knew what he was, and no woman would want that.

Unless she was paid to want it.

He shook his head in self-disgust when even the mere thought of her got him hard. Not once since becoming a man had he allowed any woman to hold that kind of power over him.

Sex, he decided, was only about his body's need for physical release, nothing more. He stepped back into his shoes and tied them. Then reached for his shirt and weapon. Well, physical release would be easy enough to obtain.

There were plenty of women out there who knew how to use their mouths for something more than talk.

He didn't need Tasha.

Any woman would do.

They were all alike—manipulative, clingy, untrustworthy. Though admittedly they had their uses, he had never met one he needed.

He didn't need anyone or anything.

Chapter 20

Tasha sat in the darkness of the compact car Lucas had provided. She peered at the house where Seth had held her prisoner just forty-eight hours ago. Though the place was dark, she knew he was in there, his SUV was in the drive.

Tonight—this morning, actually, since it was well past midnight—when he'd dropped her back at her apartment, she'd been too furious to think before she reacted. He hadn't uttered one word to her the entire trip. He'd simply driven her back as he said he would and stopped only long enough for her to get out.

Even now renewed fury burned away all reason. She'd entered her apartment building, given him thirty seconds and then exited again. She'd jumped in her car and driven straight back to the lake house with no rational thought as to the consequences. She'd sat there for a few minutes watching the eerily dark house, but that extra instinct of hers had nagged her into going back to the Oak Park residence. She'd sensed that he wasn't at the lake house. Somehow, incredibly, they'd connected on a level that

she couldn't begin to understand. The only thing she did
know with a certainty was that she'd lost a good deal of
her objectivity way too fast. She felt angry at him for
drawing her close, only to turn her away when she refused to do things his way. The idea that he could so easily turn off any need or desire made her want to scream
with frustration.

Bottom line, she'd wanted him to want her. Which
meant one thing, she'd crossed the line. Hell, she hadn't
simply crossed the line, she'd pole-vaulted over it.

This wasn't supposed to be personal, even if sex were
involved. It was business—the mission. Somehow she'd
allowed the amateur psychoanalyst side of her to get
sucked into his world. She was so busy trying to figure
him out that she was losing all perspective on reality.

He was a killer.

An assassin.

He tortured and murdered people for money.

Her career would be over if the Agency or Lucas Camp
discovered that she'd crossed that line. Worst of all, she
feared her lack of objectivity was even more deeply personal than her overwhelming need to know what made
him tick.

Maybe her career should be over if she couldn't maintain proper perspective any better than this.

The headlights of his SUV suddenly glared through
the darkness.

She tensed…forgot all else and moved to a higher state
of alert. Where the hell would he be going now? To Victoria Colby's house? That didn't feel right. He was surely
aware that she would be tucked in for the night with maximum security. He was on to Lucas now, probably had
been from the start.

The SUV he'd backed into the driveway rolled forward onto the street, in the direction of Chicago proper and away from her position.

Slowing her respiration and pulling her focus on track, Tasha eased into a nearby driveway, turned around and followed him. Maintaining a visual would likely be impossible since she couldn't risk getting too close. At this hour the very idea of tailing a target was ludicrous. There were no other vehicles on the quiet residential streets with which to blend.

But she'd give it her best shot.

Even if he didn't spot her, she was in deep trouble. Maverick would have her hide whenever she showed up back at her apartment. She was supposed to wear the monitoring device at all times. When Seth had called about the taxi she'd foolishly assumed the destination. Now she had nothing to blame but plain old stupidity. She'd been so angry she followed him without taking the proper precautions. She'd acted on the moment…on instinct. What the hell good was backup if she left them in the dark? She imagined Maverick would report her carelessness to Lucas.

Somehow she had to make tonight worth the risks she'd taken. Going back empty-handed wasn't an option. She needed something.

Something only *he* could give her.

And that was the bottom line. As much as his actions had rubbed her the wrong way, pushed some button he shouldn't even have access to, she'd walked away with nothing and no guarantee that she would see him again. Unacceptable. She was better than this. She would get to him…she would give Lucas Camp what he wanted: Leberman.

As they neared downtown, traffic appeared, which facilitated her ability to duplicate Seth's turns without the risk of detection. Since she'd never visited Chicago before this assignment, she didn't know the name of the area he selected for his middle-of-the-night cruise. But it didn't take her long to recognize he was headed toward the seedier side of town.

Block after block of adult-entertainment joints, hole-in-the-wall newsstands, pawnshops, dive bars and the occasional sleazy-looking motel. The heavy flow of pedestrian traffic made it look like a Saturday night on Bourbon Street in New Orleans rather than a plain old weeknight in the low-rent section of Chicago.

He pulled over to the curb, and Tasha did the same. From her vantage point a block behind him and parked between two other vehicles, she watched a hooker approach the passenger side of his SUV. Since he'd passed at least a dozen in the past three blocks, she could only assume that he'd decided this one suited his taste.

Try as she might to watch the scene evolving before her with cold, clinical objectivity, a mixture of rage and something she wasn't prepared to label seethed inside her. He wanted someone he could control, someone who would play the game his way.

Seth eased away from the curb, drove to the end of the block and turned into a small parking area. Seconds later he approached the woman waiting outside an adult entertainment club. He followed her inside.

Tasha, wishing like hell she had her weapon, fished for her cell phone. She had to let Maverick know where she was. She might not be thinking as clearly as she should, but she wasn't completely stupid. According to the display, she'd missed three calls. Oh, yeah, Maverick would be pissed. With the phone set on vibrate there had been no ring. "Dammit." Even worse, she had no signal now.

No signal. How could she be in a city this large and not get a signal?

"Hell with it." She tossed the phone to the passenger seat and emerged from her car. Her senses on full alert she started in the direction of the club. She ignored the comments tossed her way by the men, as well as the women, she passed along the way. At least she was dressed to fit in.

The club Seth had entered was a narrow two-story building sandwiched between a pawnshop and a sleazy restaurant that was closed for the night. No bouncers waited at the entrance to check for weapons or to stamp her hand. Management apparently had a lax door policy. No surprise there.

Inside, music blared and multicolored lights flashed and throbbed in sync with the rhythm. Tasha surveyed the crowded room, careful to stay in the shadow of the tight clutch of weirdos hanging near the entrance. Seth and his hooker were nowhere in the throng. Tasha peered beyond the masses enjoying lap dances and watching porn videos on the array of wall-mounted screens, her gaze locked onto a dimly lit corridor and set of stairs on the opposite side of the club. She moved in that direction.

"You got an appointment?"

The male voice halted her in her tracks, and she glanced over to the man standing at the end of the battle-scarred bar. The numerous body piercings and tattoos did little to enhance his thin, haggard frame.

She smiled flirtatiously and leaned on the counter to look up at him. "Do I need one?"

He jerked his head in the direction of the corridor marked Employees Only. "You do if you're going in there." He looked her up and down when she stood back and adopted a put-upon expression.

She reached into her purse and withdrew the wad of cash Seth had dropped in there earlier. "I only want to watch."

The bottom feeder behind the counter grinned grotesquely. "Baby, this'll buy you just about anything we have to offer." He flexed his bare, tattooed arms as he braced against the counter and leaned forward. "Including me."

How could she resist? she thought loathingly. "As tempting as that sounds," she lied, "there's something else I need to do first. A big guy, blond hair, dark glasses came in here a couple minutes ago with a redhead."

He nodded to the corridor again. "Last door on the left upstairs."

She gave him a million-dollar smile that suggested a promise she definitely didn't intend to keep. "Thanks."

Tasha pushed through the crowd and made her way up to the second floor. Nine doors lined the dark corridor, most were partially open, offering glimpses of sexual depravity involving whips and chains and parties of three. The music still thumped loudly, adding a sick score to the nefarious acts taking place.

She slowed as she came nearer to the final door. Like the others it stood slightly ajar. A warning blaring in her skull, she eased into the entryway, allowing the door to shield her to an extent. She peeked into the room, telling herself that she just needed to know what he was up to. But that was a lie. This had nothing to do with her mission...this was personal. She knew it, but the realization didn't stop her. She had to know. Had to see.

Swaying provocatively the woman undressed in front of him. Tasha watched his unchanging profile as the hooker gave it all she had without eliciting the first visible reaction from the man. Completely naked, her body pressing close to his, she reached for him, but he pushed her hands away. Yet something passed between them. He hadn't spoken, Tasha was sure of that. The hooker must have seen some indication in his eyes of what he wanted.

She knelt in front of him, her red hair swishing around her shoulders as she moved her upper body brazenly, showing off her large breasts. Taking her time, to draw out the tension, she unfastened his jeans. First the single button at his waist, then slowly, ever so slowly, she lowered the zipper of his fly.

Tasha watched in morbid fascination, unable to move or think…she could only watch as some heretofore unknown genetic defect allowed her body to respond as if it were her touching him. Her breath stalled in her lungs. Heat slid through her, and she was helpless to stop it.

With his fly gaping wide, even from across the room, Tasha could see that he was naked beneath the worn-soft denim. Her mouth parched unbearably as the hooker took him. The breath hissed out through Tasha's parted lips as his fingers plunged into the woman's hair. His reaction startled Tasha…damaged her somehow. He hadn't reacted to her touch…hadn't allowed her to reach him.

Stunned by her own fierce reaction, she forced her gaze upward to look at his face…to measure his response…

But he was looking at her.

She jerked with the impact.

He held her in a firm grasp with nothing but an Arctic glare. The sheer force of it cut all the way across the room. She stumbled back a step.

"See something you like?" another male voice uttered harshly in her ear.

She froze. The fine hairs on the back of her neck stood on end.

"He's beautiful, isn't he?"

Behind her, to the left. Hidden from Seth's view as well as hers.

She cautiously reached for the mace in her purse.

"Don't move," he threatened as he pressed a cold, steel muzzle to the back of her head. "Keep your hands where I can see them, and I'll let you watch. Make the slightest move and you'll die on the floor of this den of iniquity."

Tasha tried frantically to place the voice. Refined, no accent whatsoever...evil.

The music rose and fell, punctuating the wanton cries and demands echoing from the other rooms.

Seth never took his eyes off her. He still couldn't see the other man, the one with the gun to her head. Tasha wanted to tell him somehow but between the cold barrel poking into her flesh and the woman drawing her mouth back and forth along his hardened length, she could only stare helplessly, wishing that she could taste him, that it was her hair that his fingers were plunged into. She licked her lips...need sharp and demanding unexpectedly paramount to all else. It was crazy...but she couldn't stop it.

Seth abruptly shoved the hooker away.

Tasha blinked. The strange spell suddenly broken.

He fastened his jeans and was across the room before his intent fully assimilated in her brain. He drew his weapon and plowed through the doorway, knocking her out of the way in the process.

By the time she regained her balance he and the man who'd jabbed her with his weapon were facing off in the corridor. The hooker cowered in the room, belatedly holding her blouse to her chest.

"I warned you not to let anyone too close," the other man said.

Tasha scanned the details of his face, recognition slammed into her instantly.

Leberman.

"I told you," Seth growled, his tone chilling, deadly, "to stay away from me."

"She followed you here. *This* is a mistake."

Tasha's fingers itched to grab the mace and do what she could to take control of the situation but that would only get her killed. If Leberman didn't get a round off, Seth would. He wouldn't hesitate to kill her. She knew it. It made her obsession with him all the more insane.

"I'm out of here," she announced, determined to take some sort of action. If she could only get to a phone while they continued their standoff...if she'd only worn that damned tracking monitor.

Seth manacled her arm and jerked her back when she would have walked away.

"Don't move."

Tasha held perfectly still and used the time to study Leberman. He wasn't very tall, five-ten or -eleven maybe. Hundred fifty pounds, she guessed. Gray hair...but those eyes were dark and menacing. He glowered at Seth with a mixture of awe and irritation. The situation was too weird to explain, but one thing was crystal clear. Seth hated Leberman. He might be working for him but he damned sure didn't like him.

"Come near me again and I will kill you," Seth warned him. There was more than anger in his voice this time... fear or desperation maybe.

Leberman stiffened ever so slightly, but Tasha picked up on it. He didn't like being ordered around by his hired help. Seth's reaction was a little harder to assess. What power did this man hold over him? How could this weasel instill any sort of fear in a man like Seth?

"Your mission is too important to let anything—" he glanced at Tasha "—get in your way."

Seth tightened his grip on his weapon. Leberman flinched. "Nothing—" every muscle in Seth's body looked taut, ready to snap "—will get in my way, including you."

Leberman lowered his weapon. "This is not the time to allow mistakes."

Seth kept his weapon aimed directly at the other man's frontal lobe. "I never make mistakes."

"See that you don't." Leberman turned his back on them both and walked way.

Startled, Tasha looked from one man to the other. Not until Leberman had descended the stairs did Seth lower his weapon. He turned on Tasha then.

When that icy gaze collided with hers there was something new there...something she couldn't quite define. Whatever it was, she shivered at the intensity of it.

"If I see you again, you're dead."

He walked back into the room where the hooker still cowered like a frightened animal and slammed the door behind him.

For five trauma-filled seconds Tasha didn't move, just stared at the closed door. Then she blasted into action, running for the stairs.

Leberman couldn't have gotten far. Weapon or no weapon she had to do something. She had to find him. Had to get word to Lucas.

Leberman was here...in Chicago.

Chapter 21

The minutes ticked past like hours.

Victoria roamed her den like a prisoner anticipating his final walk down death row. She'd slept less than an hour…hadn't been able to turn off the images inside her head long enough for more than that.

She remembered so well dressing him for school that morning. The jeans…Cubs T-shirt…and those blue sneakers. His favorite pair.

After school she'd picked him up and they'd gone home, just as always. She never stayed at the office when she could be with Jimmy. The sun had been shining… spring had arrived after a long, arduous winter. She'd loved the spring.

He'd gone out into the yard to play.

She'd been distracted for only one moment.

And then he was gone.

Her life had plunged into an abyss of pure hell. James had done everything he could to find their son. Lucas had helped, as well. But none of it had mattered…he was gone.

She stopped in the middle of the room and closed her eyes in an attempt to regain her equilibrium.

Why had he waited all this time?

She had assumed that since he hadn't tortured them with the idea that he had possession of their son, that he wasn't the one. Leberman wanted to hurt them...used every means at his disposal. But this—this just didn't make sense.

It had been eighteen years.

Did this particular time of year hold some significance for him? It had been October when James had interviewed Leberman's wife, nearly twenty years ago. Nineteen to be exact. James had long since left his work with military intelligence, choosing instead to start the Colby Agency where he would never have to worry about being separated from his family. But an old friend had needed him to help with an investigation involving one of James's former men, Leberman. Errol Leberman had served under James's command. Had been an excellent intelligence officer.

But Leberman had committed treason, had sold military secrets to the enemy, and James had uncovered the evidence, had driven the final nail in Leberman's coffin.

When Leberman went into hiding to escape prosecution, James questioned his family as to his whereabouts. But his wife had claimed no knowledge of her husband's whereabouts or his troubles. She had feigned shock at the news that he was wanted for treason. James had pushed... that much was true. If only he had known how unstable the woman was...maybe he could have prevented what happened next.

Mrs. Leberman had taken her life that same night, but only after taking the lives of her two children first. She'd left a note stating that they simply could not live with the weight of her husband's shame.

That had been the beginning of the end.

Leberman had successfully evaded capture and made it his life's work to get even with James Colby for, in his twisted way of thinking, killing his wife and children.

Victoria exhaled a heavy breath. Dear God how he had gotten even.

He'd killed their son. She closed her eyes and fought the tears that welled. All this time she had hoped…for a miracle. Had hoped that her son was alive and well somewhere with people who loved him. But he wasn't. He was dead. Leberman wouldn't have allowed him to live. It hurt too much to even imagine what the bastard had put her child through before taking his life. Then, when she and her husband had suffered through endless nights of praying and hoping and endless days of searching—three long years' worth—Leberman had killed James. Though there was no rock-solid proof it had been his evil work, she had known.

Just as she knew he was behind this assassin…this heartless reminder of the child she had lost. Her fingers tightened into fists of rage. He'd let her hope all these years only to dash that hope. Just when she'd been ready to resume a real life. It was as if he knew. As if he'd waited for this moment to start sending back the pieces. He had done the unthinkable. She knew it.

Lucas knew, as well.

Leberman wanted to destroy them both. He wouldn't stop until he did. If Victoria went into hiding as Lucas urged her to do, it would change nothing. He would just keep coming back until he destroyed everything connected to the Colby name. She felt certain he was the one responsible for various troubles the agency had run into over the years. She had to face this monster once and for all. Or she would never be free...and neither would Lucas, for he was guilty by association.

Victoria had lost enough.

This time Leberman was going to be the one to die.

Her doorbell rang, and she glanced at the mantel clock above her hearth—7:00 a.m. It would be Lucas. He'd decided not to go back to his work in Washington until the Leberman situation was resolved or until he could talk her into disappearing, whichever came first. He wasn't going to like her decision.

As much as she hated to admit the weakness, his concern warmed her. She needed him right now. But she also needed him to understand her position.

She checked the peephole in the front door for safety's sake, disarmed the security system and opened the door for him.

"Good morning," he said as he stepped inside, his gaze scrutinizing her immediately.

He would see that she'd had no sleep and would guess that she'd lacked any appetite as well. He would fuss. She sighed wistfully. And she would be thankful for him...for his constancy in her life. She inhaled deeply, enjoying the subtle, clean scent that was the same one he'd worn for as long as she'd known him. An enticing combination of sandalwood and plain clean skin. She resisted a shiver. Only Lucas could make her feel so alive under present circumstances. And she was so very tired of reliving the haunting past. She couldn't bear it any longer.

"Good morning, Lucas." She decided to do something she rarely did, go to the office late. "Would you like to have coffee with me this morning?"

That charming smile he had perfected to a science—the one that warmed her insides—spread across his handsome face. "I can always handle a second cup of coffee." He locked the door behind him and followed her to the kitchen.

It had been a long time since she'd prepared morning coffee for someone besides herself, but it felt good. Once she'd slid the carafe into place and pressed the start button, she turned to Lucas.

She might as well get this part out of the way while they were in her territory. "I've decided to stick by my schedule for the next few days. Mildred reminded me last night when I'd pulled myself together a bit that I have that Woman of the Year luncheon this evening." She held up a hand to hush his protests and continued, "You know I don't care about the honor. It isn't about that at all. It's about not allowing that bastard to put my life on hold again. He's not taking anything else from me."

"Victoria." Lucas propped his cane against the closest cabinet and took her hands in his. "You wouldn't let me comfort you last night." He searched her eyes for answers. She knew what he wanted to hear…but could she give him what he longed for after all that had happened?

It would feel too much like running.

They'd both waited so long. But she was so very tired of living with the threat of Leberman hanging over her head. He represented all of her past pain…she wanted to banish him forever. Wanted to make him pay for what he'd done to her son.

The worry in Lucas's eyes very nearly undid her. "You refuse to go away with me. You have to give me something to work with here. Please." He squeezed her hands. "Please, let me keep you safe."

She had known Lucas Camp for more than half her life, and this was the first time in all those years that she had sensed his emotions so near to the surface. Certainly it was the first time she'd heard him skate so close to out-right begging.

She looked into those loving gray eyes and she tried with all her might to ensure that the depth of her feelings for him shone in her own. "Lucas, I know you want to keep me safe, but I can't run from this. If I do, it will never end. We have to stop this bastard. Face this enemy. Now."

"I have a strategy in place," he countered. "One that doesn't require you to take these kinds of risks. Whatever precautions we take at this evening's affair, there is still a strong possibility that he'll get close enough to hurt you. Let me bring him down my way. You have my word that I'm working on that as we speak. I *will* make it happen."

He wasn't making this easy. She looked away, gathered her scattering courage before allowing her eyes to meet his once more. "Lucas, I'm certain that you're doing all you can. But it might not be enough." Pain tightened her chest as she saw the new lines of worry forming on his beloved face. "Yesterday when I looked into that box and saw that shoe I almost slipped over a precipice that I'm not completely sure I could have returned from. It's been that way for a while now. It's like I'm performing a balancing act on an emotional high wire."

She shrugged, hoped her words were making sense. "I can't do this anymore. *He* won't let me put the past behind me and move on as I'd hoped to do. You and I will never be free to live our lives as long as that bastard is breathing."

Lucas nodded, his eyes suspiciously bright. "You're right. I know that, but knowing the facts won't prevent me from going crazy with worry for you."

Tears brimmed behind her lashes and she took a breath, moistened her lips and tried her damnedest to hold them back. "And that's just one of the many things I love about you."

He searched her eyes again, his own clearly startled by her admission. Though they had each recognized for some time how the other felt, they'd refrained from verbalizing that emotional commitment. Not out of fear or uncertainty, out of respect for the man they'd both loved in different ways. But James Colby wasn't coming back.

"Victoria, you must know," Lucas began, his voice filled with the same emotion she saw in his eyes, "that I am deeply, profoundly in love with you."

She smiled. God, how she did love this man. "Of course you are. I've known it all along."

For several boundless moments they simply stood there, holding hands and staring into each other's eyes while the scent of fresh-brewed coffee filled the air around them. She moved first, leaned forward just far enough to lift her mouth to meet his.

And then he kissed her.

His lips were as firm as she'd known they would be, his taste pleasant, sugared coffee flavored with just a hint of French vanilla—the kind they sold at the coffeehouse near his hotel. When he reached up to gently cup her face in those strong hands she moaned softly. How long had she waited for that simple touch? Desire sung vibrantly through her veins, sending a long-forgotten heat to the very core of her being...to the part of her that made her woman.

And then she forgot to think at all.

Chapter 22

At seven-fifteen on Tuesday morning Tasha walked into her apartment building on North Dearborn. The strappy sandals she'd donned the night before hung precariously from her right hand.

The long walk had cleared her mind of the confusing emotions she'd experienced in that club. She'd gone from outraged and obsessed to furious with herself to numb. Total exhaustion had left her defenseless and completely disillusioned about who she'd thought she was.

Some jerk had stolen her car while she acted like a jealous lover. Her useless cell phone had been in there for all the good it would have done her. And, on that sleazy side of town, there hadn't been a cab to be seen in the wee hours of the morning.

She walked. Oh, she'd turned down a couple of offers for rides, but she had known, judging by the sleazebags tossing out the invitations, that she would have ended up walking, anyway—after she'd had to beat the crap out of one of them.

But worst of all, she'd looked Leberman straight in the eyes and hadn't been able to do anything about it.

That screw-up alone was enough to get her tossed back to Langley. She jabbed the call button for the elevator, too damned tired to even consider the stairs.

Not that she could blame Lucas for sending her back. She'd failed. Gotten personally involved practically overnight. She shook her head in self-disgust. All this time she'd thought she was all set to become a hotshot undercover operative. She could do anything. Kick ass all day long and never miss a beat. Boy, had she been wrong.

She slunk onto the elevator when the doors opened and selected floor thirteen. No doubt it would stop there, anyway. Might as well save Maverick and Ramon the trouble.

The elevator surged into motion making her stomach turn over with renewed dread. She hadn't wanted it to end like this…she hadn't meant to…

The gentle bounce that signaled she'd reached her destination dragged her attention from her self-pity session. This was it. The doors slid open and Ramon waited in the corridor, one elbow braced on the arm folded over his middle so he could tap his chin like an impatient teacher.

He did a quick but thorough appraisal. "You look like hell, honey."

"Where's Maverick?" Why beat around the bush? She was done. *Finito.*

Ramon hitched his head in the direction of the apartment directly beneath hers. "He was too pissed off to greet you in the corridor." His expression turned sympathetic. "You might want to brace yourself."

She nodded, appreciative of his concern, but wholly undeserving.

Ramon led the way. She followed, not bothering to brace herself. Whatever she got, she deserved. She could be ready to head back to the east coast in less than an hour. Martin might not even want her back after this fiasco. She gritted her teeth and blocked the image of Seth that tried to haunt her. If she never saw him again it would be too soon.

Yeah, right.

He was the whole reason she'd screwed up so badly… he'd messed with her head. Another image, this one involving him and the hooker, flashed before she could stop it. Seriously messed with her head.

"Just one thing," Ramon said, hesitating outside the door, "the car thing was his idea. Not mine."

Bewildered but too depressed to care, Tasha followed him into the apartment to face the wrath of Maverick.

He stood in the middle of the living room, his arms crossed over his wide chest. Every feature of his formidable frame vibrating with tension. "Sit," he ordered with a distinct nod toward the chair directly in front of him.

She dropped her sandals onto the floor, flinched at the loud *thwack,* and took the seat he'd indicated.

"Do you know how stupid what you did this morning was?"

She looked straight into those furious eyes. "Yes."

"Did you also know that I have never lost an operative? Never. And you're hell-bent on smudging that perfect record."

"I just—"

"Don't speak," he warned, his tone lethal. "It was a rhetorical question."

His high-handedness kind of ticked her off, but she knew he was right so she squashed the retort that had risen immediately at his scathing remark.

"You went into that club—*without backup*—after a

known assassin. He could have killed you and there would have been nothing we could do about it."

"But I—" His words echoed inside her head, derailing the thought before she could voice the rest of it. Club? How the hell had he known about the club?

She looked up at him. Her confusion no doubt obvious. "How did you—" And then it hit her. These guys were specialists—the best of the best. They would have all bases covered well in advance.

"I'm an old hand at this business, North. You're nothing but a green recruit." Before she could argue the point, he went on, "Did you really think I'd give you enough rope to hang yourself?" He shook his head. "No way. I knew you'd screw up."

Before the mental order to stay seated issued by the more reasonable side of her brain could synapse she was on her feet. "Okay, you're right, but I got through it. And…and I came face-to-face with Leberman. You should—"

"We know." His expression went from furious to grim in less than a heartbeat.

She blinked. "You know?"

"We had a tracking device in your car. A new one we're trying out. It's supposed to be undetectable, but we're not prepared to take unnecessary risks with it yet. Still, we figured bugging your vehicle would be safe enough since you usually rode with our target anyway."

"Why didn't you do something?" she demanded before she could catch herself. "I mean," she said in a more controlled tone, "what did you do?"

"When one of our men spotted Leberman he tailed him in hopes of getting a clean shot. Halloween's this weekend, some prick in the local adult entertainment industry decided that every night this week they'd party like the world was coming to an end over in that crime-ridden zone where we located you. The cops probably won't even bother trying to stop them as long as no one gets murdered. But the whole scene made for crowds, and my man lost Leberman before he could take a clean shot. But we have confirmation that he's here."

She nodded. "Yeah, he's definitely here." The stand-off between Seth and Leberman tugged at her thoughts for a few seconds before Ramon's insistence that the car wasn't his idea jarred her gray matter from its distraction. "You took my car," she accused as her gaze connected with Maverick's once more, then narrowed with suspicion as the concept solidified.

"Damn straight I did. Once I knew you'd live through your stupidity, I figured you needed a lesson in humility."

So Maverick was the jerk who'd stolen her car.

She shook her head in defeat. Might as well admit now that she wasn't good enough for this mission. It wasn't as if she hadn't given them a clear picture of her inadequacies. Lucas was looking for sharp people like Maverick…not impulsive hotheads like her. "So, I guess it's over then. I failed. I'm out, right?"

Maverick laughed, which really pissed her off. "Lucas said you'd feel that way."

Her humiliation was complete now. "You've talked to Lucas already?" She felt every bit as hollow as her voice sounded.

"Honey, I talked to Lucas the moment you sashayed outta here in that taxi right after midnight."

This was it. She'd get her walking orders now.

"Look, North, you screwed up," Maverick offered, his tone gentled now. "You survived it. But that doesn't mean you're not cut out for this gig."

How could he know exactly what she was feeling?

"This is the real thing, not training. You're inexperienced in the field. No way can you expect to perform in that setting the way you did in training. Not in the beginning. It's a whole different world. We understand that and so should you. Lucas picked you for this mission because he knew you were good." He gave her a knowing look. "He also knew that you possessed a key element that would get you closer to our assassin than anyone else on our team. You're a virgin."

"Like hell," she blurted, then cringed. There were some things she was experienced in, but she hadn't meant to say it out loud.

Maverick chuckled. "Not that kind of virgin."

Tasha just wanted the floor to crack open and swallow her up. Could this get any worse? Her face flamed so hot, she cringed.

"Our guy obviously picked up on your innocence in a professional sense or you'd be dead now."

Admittedly, a part of her had known that. He hadn't been threatened by her. Annoyed maybe, but definitely not threatened or intimidated in any way. She'd almost convinced herself that he trusted her just a little. But that wasn't the case. He just didn't see her as a threat.

"You not only got close to him," Maverick continued, his tone openly approving now, "you got to him on some level or he would have killed you last night."

Damn, the man was a mind reader. "Leberman told him not to let me too close…said I'd get in his way. But he let me walk despite that warning."

"You got to him," Maverick reiterated. "He doesn't want to hurt you."

Her brow furrowed into a frown as she recalled Seth's final words to her. "Well, he did say that if he saw me again he'd kill me."

"That's bullshit, baby," Ramon piped up.

Tasha turned toward him.

Ramon smiled at her, his apparent approval shoring up her resolve. "You did good, girl. If our boy had wanted you dead, he wouldn't have wasted time talking, and you wouldn't have been walking."

The guy missed his calling, she mused. He should have been a poet. "I guess that's true." A big part of her sure hoped like hell it was.

"We know Leberman is close," Maverick said, drawing her attention back to him. "That means whatever is going down will be happening soon. We have to be ready. We could still use an ID on that assassin. Anything we can learn would be helpful."

Tasha shrugged and dropped back into the chair. Damn she was tired. "I can try going to his place. Making contact again."

Maverick shook his head. "You have to play by his rules. He has to make the next move. You don't want to push his generosity. He doesn't want to see you again, but if you got to him the way we think you did, he'll be back."

If only she could be that lucky. "So we wait." She looked from Maverick to Ramon and back. "Again."

"We wait," Maverick confirmed, then gave her a quick once-over. "You look like you could use some rest, anyway."

She nodded and pushed to her feet. The memory of that house by the lake zoomed to the forefront of her thoughts. "He took me to a house by the lake. Could it belong to Leberman?" That seemed the most likely scenario. If they'd been tracking her movements, they would know which house she meant.

Maverick and Ramon exchanged a look. "No," Maverick told her. "That house belongs to Victoria Colby."

Chapter 23

Lucas surveyed the palatial lobby of Chicago's Cultural Center as Victoria chatted with well-wishers. Soaring arches created a kind of echo chamber and allowed the classical music to gently resonate throughout and then upward. It was 6:45 p.m. and they had just started to move toward the grand staircase. He didn't like the crowd pressing in around them. Liked even less the endless possibilities the Greek and Romanesque architecture offered in the way of hiding places.

His men had scoured the five-story building and had set up the tightest security net possible, considering that hundreds of guests were expected for tonight's gala. Every single person who entered the lobby had been screened, as was the current protocol for all major public events. Not one of the tuxedoed or sequined attendees looked villainous. Every security guard and police officer on site had been briefed as to the descriptions of Leberman and the assassin. All imaginable precautions had been taken. And yet, he somehow knew that it would never be enough.

His team had not been able to pick up either Leberman's or the assassin's trail since four o'clock this morning when things went to hell in that sex club.

But there was nothing else Lucas could do. Victoria insisted on going through with this. His gaze moved to her and his heart surged into his throat. She looked incredible. More beautiful than he had ever seen her. The exquisitely simple white gown didn't need any glittering embellishments. The woman wearing it was jewel enough. His mouth parched as he remembered the kiss they had shared. He'd waited so long for that moment. The kiss had held many promises, and even now made his body harden with desire.

He couldn't help wondering if tonight would be the night. That, too, would be Victoria's decision. He would not rush the issue. As much as he wanted to make love to her, he would wait until she made the first move. Just as he had with the kiss. He took a deep breath, every fiber of his being anticipating more of those wonderful kisses.

Moving farther up the staircase, he studied the walls of white marble. Shimmering mosaics winked in the light of the bronze sconces and the chandeliers draped from the three-story, vaulted ceiling. This was the kind of place where Victoria belonged, amid luxury and beauty, the grandest of which could not rival her own. She deserved all that life had to offer, and he would go to his death trying to give her whatever her heart desired, including this moment.

Every instinct warned him that this was a dangerous risk, but his heart would not allow him to deny her.

When they reached the landing, the staircase spilled into Preston Bradley Hall and more of the palatial savoir faire. Spectacular stained-glass domes, lush ornamentation and intricate coffered ceilings. Lavishly decorated tables filled the enormous hall. A stage and podium had been erected beyond a towering archway adorned with mosaic scrolls and rosettes. Opulence abounded. The perfect setting for this prestigious honor. His gaze settled on Victoria once more. And it was all for her.

Lucas smiled in spite of the tension vibrating inside him. No one knew better than he what an amazing woman Victoria Colby really was.

Standing before the full-length mirror, Seth adjusted the lapels of the tuxedo, then checked the bow tie. Perfect.

He picked up the elegantly embossed invitation from the dresser and walked out of the master suite belonging to the man whose name was inscribed beneath the words *requests the presence of*... He would be among the last to arrive at the gala event, but no one would notice since he had taken meticulous steps to alter his appearance.

The eyeglasses, brown-tinted contacts and the temporary rinse he'd used to darken his hair provided a slight resemblance to the man who had been conveniently called away on business. Leberman had seen to every necessary detail. But the most important aspect of Seth's camouflage tonight was the layers of skin-colored latex that added fullness to his face and neck and simultaneously covered his one readily visible distinguishing mark, the scar on his jaw. The carefully applied makeup that allowed for the other man's lighter coloring, face, throat and hands, and finally, the padding that piled on the extra forty pounds that completed the image.

All in all he felt confident that no one, not even Lucas himself, would recognize him.

Twenty minutes later, after allowing the valet to take

his borrowed Mercedes, Seth put his skills at disguise to the test. As he expected, he was waved through by local security without a second glance.

Now all he had to do was move into position.

Five days ago he had come to the Cultural Center in response to their frantic call for maintenance on the heating and cooling system. With an electronic monitor on the land line he had easily intercepted the telephone call. The problem was simple, especially since he was the one who'd rigged the fault. He'd taken his time, explored the ventilation and return ductwork until he found what he wanted. Access to Preston Bradley Hall. The necessary returns placed about the enormous room provided several different angles in the event the stage was not positioned as he expected.

Escaping once he'd accomplished his goal would not be such an easy task, since he would still need to get out of the building and would have already shed his disguise. So he had arranged a couple of diversions. With a crowd this size it wasn't a difficult task. A fire alarm and then, ten seconds later, a small explosion near the first-level rear entrance. The hysteria that followed would provide all the distraction he needed.

Once he'd reached the access area, he shucked the tux and peeled off the disguise, contacts included, and shoved them out of sight. He donned the coveralls and assembled the weapon he would use for the job, all of which he'd stashed five days ago.

After attaching the silencer, he eased into the long galvanized-steel tunnel that wound around and eventually took him to Preston Bradley Hall.

He slipped into position and peered through the louvers he'd pried apart just enough to facilitate the tip of his weapon. He'd disposed of the filter, which left nothing but the thin louvered metal door between him and the crowd settling at their respective tables.

Now he would wait.

Because of the large crowd anticipated, the thermostat had been set to a lower temperature to ensure comfort during the exclusive event. Despite that step, sweat had already beaded on his forehead.

Leberman was here already. It wasn't necessary to spot him in the crowd or to recognize the disguise he used. Seth sensed his presence just as one sensed a coming storm in the air. The very atmosphere changed. Every nerve ending cracked as an anxiety he'd thought behind him inched up his spine. He gritted his teeth and forced away the memories that threatened. He would not be distracted.

Forty-one long minutes passed with one politician after the other raving about their beloved city of Chicago and the glorious Victoria Colby and all her worthwhile accomplishments as an entrepreneur and businesswoman.

His gut clenching with anger as every accolade echoed in the enormous hall, he tuned out the meaningless words. Politicians were fools, anyway. He wondered how lofty Victoria Colby would feel a few moments from now. A smile stretched across his face. Now, there was something to look forward to.

Finally the mayor stepped up to the podium to make the presentation they had all waited for.

A standing ovation accompanied her as Victoria Colby rose like a regal queen and advanced to the podium. When she began to speak, the crowd stopped clapping and resumed their seats. She made what she must have considered a moving speech that garnered her yet another round of enthusiastic applause.

As she concluded, Lucas Camp made his way to the

stage, dressed in his black tux, his silver-handled black cane making him look all the more distinguished. He extended his hand to Victoria as she descended the first of three steps leading down from the stage. The delicate crystal Woman of the Year award clutched against her chest with one hand, she reached out to her beloved protector with the other.

Seth squinted into the scope, snugged his finger around the trigger as he steadied his aim, then took the shot.

Lucas Camp fell forward.

The Woman of the Year award shattered on the marble floor.

Victoria caught Lucas in her arms, his weight pulling her downward, the blood from his head wound turning her lovely white gown a sinister crimson.

Chapter 24

He stood in the darkness, his eyes closed as he absorbed the sounds. Allowed the tension to drain from him. His respiration slowed as he gradually became one with the night. Years of surviving in the darkness had given him power over the night.

He was not afraid…not afraid of anything or anyone. Not anymore.

The stillness crept closer…the night sounds like a familiar lullaby. He'd learned to embrace the darkness and to let go of all else. That had been his only means of existence.

It was true that he was alone, but that had never mattered. He needed no one…nothing.

Her image slipped into his meditation, etching a frown across his brow. She'd followed him last night, not that he was really surprised. He had wondered at her seeming innocence. She was not like any of the other women he had known. Certainly not what he had expected considering her chosen occupation. He almost laughed at that.

There had never been a time when he'd bothered to know anyone. He wouldn't miss or need what he didn't know.

He didn't need her.

Perhaps it wasn't about need.

He simply wanted her.

His eyes opened and he stared beyond the dark, beyond the cloak of trees that sheltered his position, to the lake that glistened like glass beneath the moon's pale glow. She was out there. Not so far away. He could have her. He was certain of it. Her eyes had given her away...the way she'd licked her lips as she'd watched another woman take him. Even now his body reacted to the yearning that had clearly surprised her. Though, like him, she'd sensed the connection from the beginning.

She'd wanted to touch him that way. To feel the weight of him in her hands, the thrust of him inside her hot, lush mouth. He'd wanted the same thing. It was the thought of her that had sent his fingers plunging into the other woman's hair. Not once had he touched a woman that way— with tenderness or intimacy on any level other than the requisite physical contact necessary for release.

But he longed to touch Tasha that way. He couldn't shake the fiercely primal craving. Couldn't completely block thoughts of her.

His frown deepened. Mere curiosity kept his thoughts going back to her. It couldn't be anything else. Desire alone would not be enough. He'd conquered that emotion long ago.

The intensity of her own desire had shaken her, and still she hadn't been able to look away from the carnal act taking place before her.

But *he* had interfered.

Seth clenched his teeth at the thought of Leberman. He should have killed the son of a bitch then and there. But he'd sworn to repay this one final debt. He might let the bastard live to see that debt fulfilled and then he would finish him if their paths crossed again. Never again would the bastard control him…punish him. *Never.*

His lips tipped into a smile when he thought of how outraged Leberman would be that the day had not ended as he had decreed. He'd laid out the plan he wanted carried out step by step. Every move calculated so carefully.

Too bad. Seth had developed his own plan. The end result would be much the same, but it would be carried out his way whether *he* liked it or not.

He cut his eyes to the right, his senses moving instantly to an elevated status of alert. He inclined his head, listening for any sound that would confirm his instinct. A leaf crunched under the weight of a silent footstep. Ten meters away.

He was certain no one had followed him here tonight or any other night. No one had any idea he came to this place. Tasha had been to the house once…but he'd warned her to stay away. There was only one who knew of his draw to this particular spot. That singular, deep-rooted urgency to occupy this place and know control over his own destiny.

The brush of foliage against fabric…closer.

Seth stepped back, shielding himself behind a towering oak tree. His skin prickled with a familiar warning.

"I knew you'd be here."

Seth moved toward him with the stealth he'd learned long ago to avoid punishment.

The tip of his 9 mm pressed against the man's skull before he suspected Seth had approached him. "Are you ready to die?" he asked from between clenched teeth. He'd warned him twice already.

Leberman turned, faced him and the weapon with its

chambered round as if the risk of death were of no consequence to him.

"You disobeyed my orders."

The statement was spoken far too casually. Seth tensed. Tightened his grip on his weapon. This was not like his hated mentor. He resisted the apprehension nagging at his gut.

"This day was very important," Leberman rambled on, as if discussing the latest political uprising in some third-world country. "It was the perfect occasion. I had waited for this moment so very, very long. Yet you blatantly disregarded my wishes."

"The result was the same," Seth ground out, quickly growing sick of the bastard's presence despite his uneasiness. "You saw the look on her face the same as I did. The horror...the surrender. She would gladly have traded her life for his in that split second."

"That's all quite true but not the issue at hand." He eased closer, allowing the business end of the weapon to bore into his chest, then slapped Seth hard. Seth refused to flinch...clenched his jaw. His grip on his weapon tightened so that his arm trembled, but he would not back off. Wouldn't give the bastard the satisfaction.

When Leberman spoke again, his tone was accusing... threatening. "You expressly disobeyed my order. I will know the reason for such insubordination."

For one instant panic trickled through Seth, but he brutally squashed it. He would not feel that fear again. "The job will be finished on schedule," he said between gritted teeth. "But I have decided that the manner and timing of events will be at my discretion." He lowered his weapon. "End of subject."

"Your discretion?" Leberman echoed haughtily.

Seth turned his back on the man he despised almost as

much as he did the final target of this mission and walked away. The past was over. Only the future could bring him the peace he sought.

"This is how you thank me for saving your life."

Seth stilled. The words rang out like a death knell from the church tower in a medieval village, dragging him back in time regardless of his determination not to go, twisting his gut with remembered agony. The pain... the confusion and endless punishments. He didn't want to go back there. Wouldn't go back there.

Taking his time, he faced his ruthless, self-proclaimed savior. "Yes," he said harshly, his breath growing more shallow and rapid with each passing second. "You saved me from certain death, and I will repay that debt."

Leberman released a melodramatic sigh and waved his arms in orchestration as if the words he intended to utter were a garish symphony regaling his selflessness. "I taught you everything you know...made you all that you are. Without me you wouldn't have survived. I am your maker...the man who created you. You owe me *everything*."

Claimed by renewed fury and hatred, Seth took two long strides toward Leberman before realizing he'd moved. He beat back the emotions that would undermine his control, but it proved more difficult than usual. "You made me all that I am, rightly enough. I have the scars to prove it." Before he could stop himself he was toe-to-toe with Leberman once more. "I suffered your endless beatings... days on end without food...and the training." He laughed, the sound as evil as that of the very savior who had schooled him so well. "Do you have any idea what they did to me?"

Long-exiled memories came flooding back...threatened his already strained hold on control.

"They did only what I instructed," Leberman said bluntly. "Everything happens for a reason. The torture made you untouchable...made you stronger."

"Go to hell, you bastard," Seth snarled. "I'll do what I came here to do because I want it." He pounded on his disfigured chest. "I want to watch Victoria Colby die just as much as you do, maybe more." He took a moment to slow his ragged breathing, to steady his shaking hands. "Final warning. Don't come near me again. Or the teacher will become the student, and I don't think you'll like your first lesson."

He walked away without looking back.

For the last time.

Chapter 25

AT 4:00 a.m. Victoria took a deep breath and made the journey to the private waiting room where Ian and Simon, as well as two of Lucas's men, waited. She produced a faint smile for the police officers, Chicago's finest dressed in their stiffly starched dark blues, gathered in the corridor outside the doors marked No Visitors Beyond This Point that she had just exited.

Chicago PD had gone above and beyond the call of duty. The shooting as well as the fire alarm and minor explosion had sent the crowd into a panic-stricken mass exodus. Only with the quick and levelheaded thinking of the boys in blue had the evacuation occurred without additional injuries or worse. That was the only level of involvement by the local authorities that Lucas had allowed thus far.

At the waiting-room door she drew together the lapels of Ian's jacket. He'd cloaked her shoulders with it hours ago, more to cover the gruesome bloodstains on her dress, she imagined, than to shield her from the brisk

October night. One last deep breath and she prepared to deliver the news.

She entered the room and all talk ceased.

Vincent Ferrelli and Ramon Vega, two of Lucas's Specialists, Ian and Simon all turned their attention to her and waited expectantly. Each still wore his tailored tux—except Ian's jacket was missing—and all looked very much like the remainder of the old regime still standing after a conquering military invasion.

"You'll all be able to see him soon," she announced, knowing the words would banish a good deal of the tension thickening the air in the room.

A collective sigh of relief sounded.

"But first," Victoria said, pushing all emotion away, "I'd like to clarify my position on this latest turn of events."

Dead silence settled over the room once more.

Victoria looked from Ian to Simon, her most trusted men, and then to those Lucas trusted just as much. "Leberman was there last night, just as the assassin was. You can be assured that he's close now, waiting to hear if the assassination attempt was successful. Lucas wants him to believe that it was." She allowed the one emotion that would get her through this. Absolute fury flamed as hot as Hades inside her. "I don't give a damn what he believes. I want him dead. Do you understand what I'm saying?" She surveyed the grim faces. "I want him dead...*today.*"

Ian moved toward her. "Victoria—"

She stopped him with one upraised hand. "No one is going to change my mind. I want both of those bastards dead. I don't care what it takes."

Ferrelli shrugged nonchalantly. "Sounds like a plan to me."

Ramon shot him a quelling look. "Mrs. Colby," he

offered, "we should wait to see what Lucas has to say about this."

"Listen to him," Simon put in, "he's right. Besides, Leberman isn't coming out anytime soon. You know that. He'll stay in hiding, savoring his coup for at least a couple of days or until he finds out the attempt failed."

Victoria shot Simon a scathing look. "I think I know Errol Leberman better than anyone in this room and I know what he wants." She turned to Ian then. "You put the word out on the street that I want a face-to-face meeting with him. Anyplace, anytime as long as it's soon."

Ian gave his head a slow, deliberate shake. "I won't let you do that. That's what he wants."

Victoria lifted her chin in challenge. "That's what I want as well. I don't care if I have to put out a personal plea on the local radio stations. Whatever it takes. I want a face-to-face with Leberman *today.*"

"Over my dead body."

The sound of Lucas's voice propelled her into an about-face. "What're you doing up?" she demanded.

John Logan and a tall young man in a surgical scrub suit trailed behind him. Victoria recognized the young man as the surgeon who'd taken care of Lucas. "He won't listen to a word I say," the doctor lamented.

Victoria doubted anyone in the room was surprised.

A bandage covered Lucas's forehead. He looked pale, weary, and her heart lurched as the whole scene played out in her mind's eye once more. He'd fallen into her arms, blood pouring from his head wound. For three endless beats she'd been certain he was dead. And then he'd taken her down to the floor with him, telling her to stay down as blood covered his face completely.

"He wouldn't even let me put him under to do the repairs," the doctor who'd patched him up told her. "Had to do it with local anesthetic."

Lucas flitted a glance at him. "I didn't live this long without enduring a little pain. I'll be fine."

The doctor's eyebrows shot up. "I removed a sizable section of skin from your back to repair the damage on your forehead. You might be tough, Mr. Camp, but don't be foolish. Infection is still a serious risk."

Victoria felt the bottom drop from her stomach and she had to work to keep her legs from wobbling. The bullet had more or less grazed his forehead, tearing away a portion of tissue. Though the wound wasn't deep, like all head wounds, it had bled profusely. All the blood. She shuddered. That had been the most frightening part. Not knowing exactly how badly he was hurt had almost sent her over the edge.

"Thanks, Doc. I'll be in good hands." Lucas looked from the doctor to the men in the room. "We have work to do."

With a defeated sigh the doctor added, "I'll write up your release order." He turned to go without further argument. He, apparently, knew a brick wall when he hit one.

Victoria also knew, without doubt, that it wouldn't have mattered what the doctor said, as long as Lucas was breathing and able to stand, he would go on with his work. He was that much like her. Or maybe she was like him. She couldn't help smiling at the thought.

"We're going to go with the assumption that Leberman thinks I'm dead," Lucas said when the door had closed behind the doctor. He rubbed his jaw a moment then. "I do find it difficult to believe that our assassin missed. I had him pegged as a lot more worthy than that." He snorted a laugh. "God knows I'm glad his game was a little off. Still, it doesn't feel right. For now we'll—"

"Excuse me." A nurse eased into the room, her hesitation evident in her expression and in the way she loitered in the doorway. She held a large floral arrangement in her hands. "Mr. Camp?" She looked to Lucas since he was the one wearing the bandage.

"Yes?" He looked annoyed but tempered it with a stab at a smile.

"These were delivered down at the E.R. a little while ago." She blinked a couple of times as if befuddled. "We usually don't get deliveries at this hour. But, anyway, they're for you."

Lucas's less-than-stellar smile drooped. "Thank you."

When he would have reached for the flowers, Logan stepped in. "I'll take those."

The nurse nodded jerkily and rushed away.

Victoria couldn't help wondering if they looked that intimidating. She surveyed the classically dressed, well-trained agents in the room, and then hers as well as Lucas's bloodied attire and shivered. Oh, yes. They definitely looked lethal.

Logan settled the vase onto a nearby table and fished out the accompanying card.

The smell of freshly cut white carnations drifted across the room and only then did Victoria really look at the arrangement. A frown furrowed her brow. Something about the flowers disturbed her somehow.

Logan passed the card to Lucas. "It's him."

Those two simple words tightened like a steel band around Victoria's chest, drawing her attention away from the flowers.

"Next time," Lucas read aloud, "will be for real." He looked up, his gaze settling on hers. "He signed it 'Fate.'"

"You were right," Simon commented dryly, "he wasn't off his game. The miss was intentional."

Lucas nodded. "It would seem so."

Victoria started to shake. Couldn't control it. She hugged her arms around her middle. "We have to do something. We can't let him get away again." The scent of the flowers drew her gaze back there once more. Carnations made her think of death...funerals...graves.

Lucas came to her, pulled her close. "I won't let him get away this time," he murmured for her ears only. Then he turned to the men awaiting instructions. "Ferrelli, you and Simon go to the house in Oak Park our assassin calls home. Tear it apart." His jaw clenched, he added, "If there's anything there I want it found."

"Won't we need a warrant for that?" Simon suggested, ever the rule player.

Lucas smiled, but the grim expression held no humor. "Not for this." He leveled his most intimidating stare on Simon. "You only need paper if you fear repercussions, which I don't, or when you plan to prosecute. This man isn't going to live to go to trial."

Just then a memory struck Victoria. Carnations. She'd ordered carnations for James...for the funeral. She'd placed a single carnation in his hand...before they closed the lid. That one had been for the son they'd lost.

The little boy they hadn't even been able to bury.

The lights dimmed.

She could hear Lucas calling her name.

Arms grabbing for her.

Then the darkness took her.

Chapter 26

Lucas sat on Victoria's bedside and held her hand. His head throbbed viciously, and the spot on his back they'd robbed of skin burned like hell, but he couldn't worry about that right now and any sort of pain reliever that might actually help was out of the question.

He had to stay sharp. Couldn't let down his guard.

"I should be at the office," Victoria said, her voice thin with exhaustion and the devastation of the night's events.

"You won't be going to the office today," he insisted as gently as he could while remaining firm. "Ian has everything under control. He said he'd call you this afternoon for a general briefing."

She nodded resignedly and lapsed into silence.

There was so much Lucas wanted to say. He wanted to reaffirm his love for her with more than just words. But now wasn't the time. She was far too fragile. He could practically see her breaking apart right before his eyes.

And he was helpless to stop the momentum.

"I want you to rest now. I'll be right here."

She nodded again, not bothering to look him in the eye.

But she didn't have to say anything for him to know what she was thinking. She wanted this over...she wanted Leberman dead. She was more than ready to face death herself to end this nightmare. Lucas would not allow that to happen.

He left her resting and moved quietly to her den. He scrounged up the remote for the television set and the DVD player and switched them on. After locating the surveillance footage in his briefcase he slid it into the machine and fast-forwarded to the part that kept nagging at him.

On the video, Tasha North opened the door and allowed *him* inside her apartment. Lucas studied the way he moved, the sound of his voice. There was something vaguely familiar about the bastard who had taken a chunk out of his profile, but he couldn't place it.

He was smart. Damned smart and well versed in all the right tactical maneuvers. As soon as the Cultural Center had been cleared, Logan and Ferrelli had determined exactly how the shooter had pulled off his hit. He'd posed as a repairman the week prior, plotted his access to the hall where the Woman of the Year banquet would be held, then stored his necessary equipment. Since the equipment was stored within the cooling system's metal frame, their scans for weapons hadn't picked it up. He'd used C-4 for his explosive, not enough to do any real damage, just a little fear factor tossed into the mix to create mayhem. The smoke bomb had been a stroke of genius, as well. It had set off the fire alarms and assured mass hysteria.

He'd thought through the whole scenario very thoroughly. Hadn't missed a trick. He'd known that escaping would be impossible without a diversion, so he'd planned ahead.

Lucas would bet his life that Leberman had been there, too. Ramon was reviewing the Cultural Center's surveillance tapes right now, but Lucas doubted he would be able to ID the scumbag. His disguise would, like the assassin's, be elaborate. The man the assassin had impersonated had called the police this morning to report that his home had been burglarized while he was away. It was yet to be determined how Leberman had managed an invitation and under what name. But Lucas would find all the answers in time.

He restarted the footage a third time and watched it once more, concentrating hard in an attempt to capture that fleeting sense of recognition. What was it about this guy?

"What's that?"

Lucas looked up to find Victoria standing behind him. He switched off the TV. She didn't need any more stress today. When Simon and Ferrelli reported in with their finds from the Oak Park house, he would have to see that Victoria was distracted. He intended to suggest that the timing of Ian's briefing would coincide.

"Just some surveillance I wanted to take a second look at," he said, as he pushed to his feet. "Join me and I'll call out for some lunch." Neither of them had eaten today. Nourishment of some sort would be good right now.

Victoria didn't bother to sit down. "I've been thinking for the past few minutes."

Lucas tensed. He didn't want her coming up with any plans that included her personal involvement in baiting Leberman.

She moved toward him, her eyes glittering with unshed tears. He blinked, kicked himself for not noticing her emotional state sooner. "Don't let him get to you any more than he already has," he urged. "He wants to hurt you. Don't give him the pleasure."

He reached for her and she came to him without hesitation. She walked into his arms, pressed against his body and it felt right. So right. Lucas closed his eyes and reveled in the feel of her...the warmth...the softness.

"It's not me I'm worried about," she murmured, then drew back to look at him. "I can't bear to lose anyone else. Especially not you." She shook her head as one tear, then another slipped past her lashes. "I've been selfish. Only thinking of my own need for revenge." She peered deeply into Lucas's eyes. "He almost killed you last night. Every time I play it over in my mind I lose my breath. I can't allow that to happen again."

"Victoria, I swear to you that I will stop him."

She moved her head side to side. "No more. I want us to leave. To go far away. Someplace where he'll never find us. I want this over even if it means I have to walk away from everything."

Dear God, could she know how much he wanted to believe that? He would love to take her away and keep her safe forever, but she would never be happy. He knew that for a certainty. The Colby Agency meant too much to her. Running wasn't her style.

He pulled her to him again. Inhaled the delicate scent of rose oil. So sweet and elegant, just like the woman. "We will go away." He drew his head back far enough to meet those worried eyes. "But we're not running. We're only taking precautions. I'm going to get him before this is over. That's a promise."

"Kiss me, Lucas," she urged. "Kiss me and make me forget for just a little while."

He'd waited a lifetime for this moment. She wanted him to take her to bed. She didn't have to say the precise words. He understood what she wanted…needed. He wanted and needed the same. As much as he feared her request might be based on the stress of the past few hours, he couldn't resist or deny her anything.

He pressed his lips to hers. For one long moment he simply savored the taste of her…the gentle heat that made him crazy with desire. How he loved this woman, wanted to make her happy above all else. She melted into his arms, the tender contours of her feminine body making his harden in an instant.

Her kiss was greedy, desperate, and her arms tightened around him as if she feared she might lose him. He held her tighter to reassure her. She was his, and no one was going to harm her. Heat flooded his body, and he surrendered to the kiss…putting all else aside.

This was their time.

A knock on the front door jerked him from the heady embrace of desire. He stilled, praying it was a mistake and whoever was at the door would go away. But the banging came again, more insistent this time.

He drew his mouth from hers, his whole body crying out at the loss of contact. "I should get that."

She smiled, all signs of tears gone now. "You should. We'll continue this as soon as you've gotten rid of whoever it is."

A grin tugged at the corners of his mouth. "You'd be surprised how fast an old man like me can work."

She stepped aside and he reached for the cane he'd abandoned on the sofa. "Don't move," he told her. "I'll be right back."

"I'll be waiting," she tempted as he made his way toward the entry hall.

It felt good to hear her tease him. Going away now was not only necessary but it would be beneficial to both of them. They needed time to themselves, where work and the past couldn't touch them.

When they had consummated and solidified their fledgling relationship, then they could return to face the past.

Logan waited on the other side of the door, Lucas noted with a quick glance through the peephole. A part of him wanted to threaten that this interruption had better be important, but Lucas knew it would be. His men were too well trained for him to expect anything less.

"The postman just delivered this package for Mrs. Colby."

Lucas glanced at the package, then back at Logan. The grim expression on his face told Lucas he'd already checked it out and it wasn't good.

"It's from him?"

Logan nodded.

Lucas reached for the package, but Logan stopped him with a warning, "You'd better close the door. I don't think you're going to want Mrs. Colby to see this."

Lucas moved forward a step and pulled the door closed behind him. He propped his cane against his hip and reached for the package once more.

When he raised the lid, tissue paper concealed whatever was inside. A note read: A memento from the past.

Lucas shoved the note aside and drew back the layers of delicate white tissue paper.

His breath evacuated his lungs. Ice slid through his veins as his heart pumped one last time before shuddering to a near stop.

A small T-shirt bearing the Cubs logo, the best he could make out, lay neatly folded in the box.

The entire shirtfront was soaked in dried blood, an ugly brown with age.

Lucas didn't need Victoria to identify the shirt for him. He knew whose it was.

This was the shirt her child had been wearing the last time she saw him.

Chapter 27

Tasha paced the length of her living room once more. She knew Maverick could see her. He had to know she was going crazy down here, and still she heard nothing.

Seth had taken a shot at Lucas. Thankfully he was okay, but it had been a close one. According to the last word she'd gotten he hadn't intended to kill him.

This time.

Failure stung sharply.

Dammit. Why hadn't she been able to get close enough to the guy? She was better than this.

She kept playing that scene in the sex club over and over in her mind until she was going crazy with it.

He'd watched her watching him. Had known how bewildered and, at the same time, fascinated she'd been by the intimate act playing out before her.

How sick was that?

She'd gotten turned on watching another woman go down on him! She'd been so damned caught up in the twisted moment that she hadn't even sensed Leberman coming up behind her.

She *always* sensed danger.

Her advanced precog receptors had never failed her.

But this time had been different.

This time she'd let herself get infatuated with the target. Obsessed with the mystery of him. What made him kill? How had he gotten all those scars?

She'd been so focused on playing the voyeur that she hadn't even felt the enemy coming.

Maverick told her not to beat herself up, but he hadn't been there, and she wasn't about to tell him exactly what had distracted her.

She'd lost it. Hell, maybe she'd never even had it.

She spun on her heel and stormed across the room again.

The waiting was driving her mad. It was worse than sitting behind that damned desk at Langley, reading those monotonous reports.

She had to get out of here.

It had been almost a week since she'd run or worked out at all. Her physical as well as sexual frustration capacity had maxed out.

She couldn't stand it any longer.

Turning thought into action, she strode determinedly toward the door, flipped the lock and yanked it open. At least a walk out in the open air would be better than this. Maybe she'd run into some safe-looking guy on the street, screw his brains out and get this crazy obsession out of her mind.

Maverick towered in her doorway.

"Lucas wants to talk to you."

She blew out a breath and waved the big guy in. "It's about time." Her body literally vibrated with tension.

The suspicious way Maverick looked at her as he entered the room had her hoping he couldn't read minds. While the big cowboy turned on the monitor and Webcam for the briefing, Tasha made herself comfortable on the sofa. She rolled her shoulders, took a couple of deep breaths and banished the thoughts that had haunted her for the past forty-eight or so hours.

When Lucas's image filled the screen, she produced a smile. "Good morning." She made a conscious effort not to scrutinize the bandage on his forehead. Seth had gotten too damned close. And where the hell was the hatred she should be feeling for the bastard right now?

"Morning."

Lucas's tone told her immediately that whatever he had to report wasn't good.

"Yesterday afternoon Victoria received another package."

The memory of the package she had delivered on Monday and its contents sent dread pooling in Tasha's stomach. "What was it this time?" Her voice sounded stilted, but it was the best she could do. She couldn't even begin to imagine what a mother who'd lost a child went through—even eighteen years later.

Lucas hesitated and in that moment she saw the anguish in his eyes. But it vanished in a flash as he composed himself once more. "It contained the T-shirt Victoria's son was wearing the day he disappeared. We're waiting for DNA analysis."

DNA analysis. She swallowed hard. That most likely meant blood. The shirt had probably been bloody. She closed her eyes for a fraction of a second and sucked in a steadying breath. Leberman was ruthless.

"There's still no sign of Leberman or the assassin."

She'd noticed that Lucas refused to call him Seth.

They still didn't have a last name. She wondered if using first names made it too personal. Lucas always called her North. With a shudder she imagined that it would be easier to kill a man you'd never called by his first name.

"Did you find anything at the house?" Ramon had told her that they were going through the Oak Park house where Seth had held her hostage, but she hadn't heard any results.

Lucas nodded, his expression going even more somber if that were possible. "We have reason to believe that Leberman and/or our assassin have used that house on and off for some time. We found a few usable prints. Some old magazines on guns, mercenaries and porn. But not much else. There's indication that the basement where he held you has been used for that sort of thing before but that's about all we know for now. We've got a couple of forensics techs going over the place from top to bottom to see if they can find anything else."

Tasha nodded. The gruesomeness of it weighed heavily on her chest. How could she have feelings for such a monster? She thought about the number...666. Who had marked him that way? Branded him a beast? "Tell me what I can do, Lucas." She looked straight into the Webcam and turned up the intensity in her eyes. She had to do something. She couldn't just keep sitting here, waiting. It was Thursday, she hadn't heard from Seth since just before dawn on Tuesday when he warned her to stay away.

"I know it's difficult, but I really need you to sit tight for a little longer. Considering this latest turn of events Victoria has agreed to disappear. That means Leberman will get desperate."

She lunged to her feet and braced her hands on her hips. "How the hell is that going to help me get close to

Seth again?" She had to do something. Get out there and find him. Take her chances.

"Sit down, North," Lucas ordered.

With a disgusted sigh, she dropped back onto the sofa. "Dammit, Lucas, I just need to do something." Her eyes widened the moment the words were out of her mouth. What was wrong with her? She'd just addressed him as if he were her buddy not her superior.

"I didn't want it to come to this," he said quietly.

Oh, God, here it was. She'd screwed up one time too many. He'd ship her back to Langley—if they'd have her.

Lucas heaved a breath. "But we're out of options."

Okay, so maybe he wasn't sending her back. She dispensed with the self-pity session and listened up. "Just tell me what you need me to do. Whatever it is, I'm ready for it."

Lucas looked at her from wherever the hell he was, but those gray eyes peered into hers as if he were right there in the room. "When Victoria and I disappear, we need our man to lead us to Leberman."

Tasha nodded. "Right. That's been the plan all along."

"Yes, we discussed that strategy in the beginning. But our guy hasn't responded to you the way we'd hoped. He's chosen to keep you out of the game."

It was her fault. She'd failed. She hadn't possessed the skills to reach a man as far gone emotionally as him. "If you'll let me get back in the game I can find him. I'm sure of it."

"We're going to have to take extreme measures," Lucas suggested, either in conjunction to her offer or oblivious to it.

"I agree," she said quickly, maybe a little too quickly. Uneasiness slid through her and goose bumps rose on her skin. "What's our first move?" She resisted the urge to flinch at the intensity emanating from that screen.

"I'm going to give you up, Tasha. It's the only way. He'll try to get to us through you. Are you prepared for that?"

It was the first time he'd called her by anything other than North. That alone gave her pause. She moistened her lips and held the fear screaming in the back of her mind at bay. "You're going to put the word out that I'm part of your team."

It really wasn't a question.

She knew the answer.

And it made perfect sense.

Lucas nodded. "Only if you're prepared to take that risk. I'll tell you now that if I were in your shoes, I might choose to stand down. I won't hold it against you if you do," he hastened to add. "My original offer still stands. You've got a job with me for as long as you want it. Your decision now won't change anything."

Well, she appreciated his leniency. But then, if she got the job that way she wouldn't really be earning it. And Victoria Colby would never be free. She wouldn't even allow Seth to enter the equation. If she was successful—major *if* considering her recent job performance—she might just have to kill him herself. Protecting Victoria Colby was top priority. His attempts to complete his mission had to be stopped at all costs.

The real question here wasn't whether or not she was prepared to take the risk, because she was.

What escaped her completely was whether or not she could kill Seth if it became necessary.

Chapter 28

"You plant this somewhere in his SUV." Maverick handed her the tiny electronic bug. "It'll be useless, since he has a jammer, but he doesn't know that we know that. He'll find this thing in a hurry, so don't hang around after you've put it in place."

She nodded. "Then I wait some more." That was the part she hated the most.

"Not for long. As soon as he's found the bug he'll know you're working with us, or at least that will cross his mind. Then when he realizes Victoria and Lucas have skipped out on him, he'll come looking for you."

She understood that part perfectly.

"Now, this," Ramon said, drawing her attention to him, "is an entirely different matter." He showed her a small object about four inches long, similar in design to an ink pen. "Don't try writing any checks with this baby."

She picked it up and looked it over. "What is it?"

"It's a high-pressure puncture device, kind of like the ones diabetics use to deliver a blast of insulin, only this one delivers a drug that debilitates the human body within seconds." He took the pen-shaped device from her to demonstrate. "Just stick him with it, ensuring that you push with your thumb against the button as if you were clicking the pen into place to write."

"It takes a tough enough punch that you're not likely to do it accidentally just by rummaging around in your purse," Maverick added.

That was a good thing. She looked to Ramon for confirmation. "This will render him unconscious?"

He nodded. "For about an hour. It's powerful stuff. You could put down a bull elephant with that stuff. And since you'd never get in the club with a gun in your purse, this is the only protection you'll have."

Tasha gingerly dropped the pen into her purse, then tucked the tracking device into the bag's small, zippered compartment.

She glanced at the clock. Half past nine. Things would be jamming at the club by now. "I should get going."

Maverick and Ramon exchanged a glance. "Just be careful," Maverick warned. "Don't take any unnecessary chances. And remember, press against the implant if you need us. We won't be far away as long as we don't lose the signal."

The latest technology in tracking-warning devices had been inserted subcutaneously on the underside of her right forearm. It was a passive transmitter which emitted its signal only once per hour. If Seth swept her for tracking devices he'd find nothing. However, all she had to do if faced with trouble she couldn't handle was press hard against the device and an altered signal would be generated immediately, indicating distress. This one had a longer range and a better warning system than the patch. It also fluctuated the pitch of its signal to help override jam frequency. But it was brand-new and could present unforeseen glitches. Still, they had decided that it offered the technology they most needed at this point.

"I'm ready." She took a breath. "I'll see you guys when I see you."

They all three stood there for a moment, just looking at each other, not saying anything. There was really nothing to say. Seth had warned her to stay away, but she was going after him. If she survived the encounter, the likelihood of surviving his fury when he discovered who she really was amounted to something less than zero.

That was the deal.

Tasha drove past the lake house. The one she now knew belonged to Victoria Colby. There was no sign of Seth. Maverick had given her the entry code for the gate and front door, but going in that way would give her away too quickly if he did happen to be in there.

Instead she hung around outside for a while, watching and waiting. When she felt reasonably sure enough time had passed for him to have approached her if he were there, she headed back to town. It was only Thursday night but there was always the possibility that he would be at the Metro Link. En route she had driven down the street past the Oak Park house. Though she felt fairly confident he wouldn't go back there after Lucas's order to take the place apart.

Before she headed over to the Metro Link, she decided to cruise down *porn* avenue and see if she saw him there. Maybe he liked the redhead enough to go back for a repeat performance.

The street was almost too crowded to maneuver. The Halloween festivities were in full swing tonight, masks and elaborate disguises included. Though Halloween wasn't actually until Saturday, that didn't appear to bother any of this party-hearty group. No sign of his SUV. Of course, he could be driving something else now. She couldn't be sure. Shooting a guy like Lucas definitely upped the stakes. Seth might feel it necessary to change a lot of things, including the places he usually frequented.

The possibility that she might not find him at all nagged at her but she refused to think that way. She had to find him. Lucas had said that the club where she'd first met him was his favorite hangout. Maybe she'd find him there.

She had to find him…she needed this second shot at proving she was as good as Lucas Camp had thought her to be when he'd brought her on board for this mission.

Maybe he didn't consider her performance so far a failure, but she did.

And that was unacceptable.

The music thumped loudly, its rhythm inviting, as she strolled up the walk to the Metro Link's main entrance. The place was almost as crowded as it had been on Saturday night. Thankfully she didn't find any Halloween masks here. The same bouncer was waving his metal detecting wand. He smiled when he caught sight of her, then gave her a slow perusal.

She'd opted for a skirt. Very short, very tight. Very red. A red spaghetti-strap top that showed off her flat midriff and four-inch leather stilettos that accentuated her legs. She might not be supermodel material but she knew how to use what she had. Returning the flirtatious bouncer's smile, she opened her matching red bag for him to survey the contents. She'd made sure a package containing a neon-purple condom would be right on top.

He lifted it between two fingers and waved it in front of her. "Got big plans tonight?"

"You bet, sugar." She leaned a little closer. "I've always got *big* plans."

He dropped the condom back inside and glanced briefly at the cell phone and pen, lip gloss and few bills, then waved her through. His no-personality partner stamped her hand a little more gently this time.

"Great shoes," he commented, eyeing her legs lasciviously.

She moistened her lips and gave him a sexy smile. "Why, thank you."

The only thing she could think as she entered the crowded club was that the guy must have gotten laid this week. His mood had certainly improved.

She cruised the place for a while, weaving through the crowd, watching, smiling, keeping a constant eye out for Seth. Just when her hopes started to plummet she saw him near the bouncers at the entrance. Her gaze narrowed as she watched him slip something to the guy with the wand who then waved him through without hesitation.

So that's how he got inside with a weapon. He'd either given the guy money or drugs. Making her move before he spotted her, Tasha latched on to the closest available guy.

"You wanna dance?" the guy asked, his words slurred.

"Absolutely." Her arms went up around his neck, and he pulled her close.

"I haven't seen you before," he muttered close to her ear. The music made hearing almost impossible this close to the band.

She kept the shouted conversation going as she slowly but surely lured him farther from the band and closer to the bar...to Seth. He'd claimed an empty stool and was surveying the crowd the way he had before.

She sensed the instant he saw her, felt his eyes on her.

Snuggling up to her dance partner, she widened her smile from time to time as if he had her undivided attention. He seemed to be thrilled with her attention, though she wasn't sure how he stayed vertical considering the degree of his inebriation.

"I need a drink," she finally told him.

He walked her to the bar, keeping one arm around her shoulders. Plopping unsteadily against the counter, he ordered himself a beer and then looked down at her.

"The same for me," she said sweetly, keeping her adoring gaze focused on him, though she could feel Seth's cutting right through her.

When the bartender set the beers in front of them, she leaned closer to the guy. "What was your name again?" she asked, though they hadn't exchanged names, but she doubted he would remember.

"Kevin," he said after downing a gulp of his beer.

"I'll be right back, Kevin," she assured him. "Gotta find the ladies' room." She gave him a quick peck on the cheek. "Save my spot."

Kevin smiled down at her, his eyes blurry. "Count on it."

Tasha looked for the signs marked Rest Rooms and headed in that direction. She passed right by Seth without sparing him a glance. She rounded the end of the bar and followed the narrow, dimly lit corridor to the bathrooms. There was an emergency exit at the end of the hall. This one exited to the opposite side of the building from the main parking area, probably into another alley. She shivered instantly as she thought of the one Seth had dragged her to the first time they met.

As she reached for the ladies' room door, her skin instantly pebbled with goose bumps.

Strong fingers manacled her arm. "What're you doing

here?" that deep masculine voice growled, sending shivers up her spine.

She whipped around and faced him. Before she could utter the scathing comeback she'd planned her gaze moved over his body, taking in every last detail. Well-fitted jeans, faded chambray, button-up shirt. And those eyes. She could never get her fill of looking into those eerily clear blue eyes…so ice-cold and yet so intense.

"I'm having a good time," she told him with an indignant little sway of her shoulders. "Now, if you'll excuse me—" she tried to tug free of his hold "—Kevin is waiting."

Fury blazed in those eyes, turning them a glistening aquamarine blue. Her pulse reacted. "I know what you're doing. I warned you to stay away from me."

She laughed ruefully. "Don't flatter yourself. I have better things to do. Besides—" she moved in close and peered up at him, allowing her breath to feather across his lips and simultaneously hoping he wouldn't see the way his proximity affected her "—I don't think I'm your type."

For three seconds he didn't move…she held her breath.

"Guess there's only one way to find out." He yanked her toward the emergency exit and once again no alarm sounded as they barreled through the door, allowing it to slam hard behind them.

"What the hell do you think you're doing?" she demanded, tugging uselessly against his barbaric grip. A thread of panic needled its way through her.

He didn't stop until he'd reached his SUV and jerked the passenger-side door open. "Get in."

She drew back as far as his brutal hold would allow. "No way. I'm not going anywhere with you." It was a lie, of course. But she couldn't make this too easy.

He trapped her between the SUV and his muscular body. "I don't like games."

Her breath caught at the renewed intensity in his eyes. "I'm not playing games with you."

"Don't lie to me. I know what you're doing and I know what you want. Now you're gonna get it."

She swallowed, moistened her lips and reached for the calm that had promptly deserted her. "Maybe I changed my mind about what I want."

"Get in."

Exhaling shakily, she looked away from that intimidating gaze and climbed into the passenger seat. He shut the door and moved around the front of the vehicle, his gaze never deviating from her.

Focus, she ordered her whirling mind. This was good.

This was the first step.

She had to get close to him and find his vulnerable spot…had to do this right.

He got behind the wheel and drove straight to a hotel a mere five blocks away. She recognized the chain and felt some amount of gratitude that it wasn't a complete dump.

"Don't move." He cut her a look that would form icicles in the desert.

Steeling her nerves, she watched as he entered the lobby and paid for a room, a mixture of anxiety and anticipation welling up inside her. There would be no talking her way out this time.

The point of no return, Tasha, she told herself.

Prepare to go through with it or get out and run like hell.

The decision had to be made *now*.

She watched the clerk accept the cash he offered.

Tasha reached for the door handle.

If she ran, this one last chance would be over and there wouldn't be another.

Seth took the key card.

But if she stayed…

She reached into her purse and retrieved the small tracking device. She tucked it into a niche in the console then dropped her hand back into her lap as he exited the lobby.

This was the only way.

He slid behind the wheel and drove to the far side of the parking lot.

A test, she told herself. A simple test to see if she had the right stuff to do this job.

As determined as she was resigned, she followed him to the room, first floor, facing the parking lot. Quick access to his vehicle if he needed to make a run for it.

The room was small but neat. She purposely looked away from the bed as he locked the door behind them and tossed the keys to his vehicle onto a table.

She dropped her bag on a chair and went into the bathroom and closed the door. On second thought she locked it. She braced her hands on the sink and stared at her reflection in the mirror. She could do this. Operatives often sacrificed a great deal more.

Summoning her resolve, she pushed off the sink and turned back to the door. If she gave herself too much time to think about this, she'd lose her nerve. That couldn't happen.

She opened the door and took a deep breath. She was attracted to him…she could do this.

The room was dark, the dim glow from the bathroom providing the only illumination. But then, he was most at home in the dark. She blinked rapidly to adjust her vision, and located him sitting in the chair near the door where she'd left her purse. He'd tossed the red handbag onto the table next to his keys, the contents scattered across the laminate top. He'd gone through her bag.

"Take off your clothes," he ordered, a raw edge to his tone.

She knew what he thought. He thought she would run away again. Well, this time she intended to see it through. He would be the one wishing he'd run. If she had this guy pegged even half to rights, he wasn't accustomed to a woman like her. Tasha had never believed in doing things halfway.

Seth the slayer was about to learn a very important lesson.

Slowly, taking her time, she released one button after the other, until her tight little top fell open, revealing her unrestrained breasts. He watched. The pale, frosty blue of his eyes cut right through the semidarkness, like those of some unearthly nocturnal being.

She shouldered out of the blouse, allowing it to fall to the floor. Without hesitation she reached behind her and lowered the zipper to her skirt. She slid it over her hips and down her thighs until it, too, puddled on the floor like a circle of blood.

Stepping out of the ring of shed garments, she stood before him naked but for her thong and stilettos. "Now your turn," she said tautly, the anticipation of seeing his nude body already making her want to squirm. She reached for his hand and pulled him to his feet, which would have been impossible had he not wanted to do her bidding.

"Turn out the rest of the lights," he ordered in that ominous growl she'd come to associate with the man.

She shook her head. "I want to see you." Her nipples pebbled at the thought.

He stood perfectly still as she reached for him. When she released the first button of his shirt, she expected him to bolt, but he didn't. She released button after button until she'd reached the waist of his jeans, then she tugged his shirt free of that confinement. His only reaction was a slight increase in the rate of his respiration, but he remained very much in control. She had to fix that.

She pushed the shirt off his shoulders, ensuring that her hands molded to his bare skin and that her breasts grazed his chest as she leaned close. Heat sizzled deep inside her. When she reached for the shoulder holster he captured her hand and shook his head firmly side to side.

She moved on to the closure to his jeans but all those scars captured her attention once more, startled her all over again. They were so brutal…and there was so very many. Trying her level best to keep the shock from her expression, she touched each one, committed it to memory. Had he been some sort of prisoner?

Slowly, not wanting to set off any internal alarms, she moved around behind him. Her breath caught in her throat, the resulting tremor quaked all the way to her hands. He tensed beneath her trembling touch. If she'd thought the scars—the hideous indications of torture—on his chest were unsettling, the ones on his back were indescribable.

Grappling for composure, she did the only thing she could, she slowly kissed first one and then the next. Soothing each injury with a gentle touch. She could feel the tension rising in him with every graze of her lips. His fingers tightened into fists. Before she could finish he turned to face her, his expression hard, angry.

"I don't need your pity," he snarled. "I am what I am."

She looked deeply into the fiery depths of those eyes

and said what she knew in her heart with complete certainty, "I know."

Before he could demand to know what she meant by that remark, she dropped to her knees and released his jeans, her heart pumping fiercely, foolishly as she considered that she had longed to do this since watching him with the other woman. She didn't slow down to think how insane it was. She only wanted to touch him…to taste him. She lowered the worn soft denim over his hips, freeing his engorged sex. Her pulse leaped as she inhaled the earthy smell of him. She pressed a kiss to his hip, allowing his long, hard cock to nuzzle against her neck. He was so hot.

His move came lightning fast and with all the brutality she knew him to be capable of. He jerked her up and pinned her against the door, his body pressing hard against hers.

She started to ask why he'd stopped her, but before she could his mouth came down savagely on hers. He ripped her panties from her body and crushed his pelvis against hers, the full size of his rigid sex grinding into her bare mound.

She braced her hands against his chest, knowing she should stop him…at least slow him down. The condom… it was right behind him on the table. But she couldn't slow the momentum, every part of her begged for his touch… yearned for his possession. She couldn't have stopped him…he was just as far over the edge as she was. Her thoughts fragmented, forced all reason from her mind as her hands learned him, molded to the muscular contours of rock-hard flesh.

Her fingers went into his short, thick hair and her mouth opened wider, inviting his invasion. She couldn't stop herself. She wanted this…wanted him. He thrust his tongue inside, then retreated, over and over again as if he couldn't get enough of tasting her, delving inside her. He lifted her legs up and she obediently wrapped them around his waist.

Long, blunt-tipped fingers parted her expertly. She writhed anxiously, needing to feel him inside her. The insistent nudge of his cock sent a spasm racking through her entire body a split second before he rammed into her, stretching her opening and dragging along her feminine walls until she cried out at the sweet unbearableness of it.

He hesitated only for a second, his lips mere centimeters from hers, his breath ragged, then he drew back and thrust hard again, jamming that generous length deep inside her, his mouth plundering hers once more. His hands latched on to her breasts, squeezing savagely, his fingers still damp from delving between her slick folds.

He pumped long and mercilessly, every stroke pushing her closer to the edge, slamming her against the solid wooden door at her back. Her flesh was on fire, her insides quivered with the urge to ignite…to erupt with the tension mounting. He hitched her legs higher, increased the depth of his penetration. She cried out with the pleasure-pain of it, the sound a primal signal that set him off. He pounded harder, flexed those powerful hips back and forth, allowing the full length of him to slide in and out… over and over again—base to tip.

The release that had felt faraway, deep, deep inside her abruptly crashed down around her, as if he'd dredged it from the farthest recesses of her soul. She screamed with the force of it…. Her body bucked in his powerful arms.

And then he came. Hard. Long. The heat and fury of it setting her on fire all over again.

He thrust one last time, a guttural sound escaping from between his clenched teeth. The agonized sound caused her eyes to flutter open. Her brow creased in confusion as she watched the dance of unreadable emotions across his face. He pushed her legs off his hips and withdrew, his cock gleaming with their commingled fluids, leaving her sagging against the door, her limbs quivering.

While she stood there trembling, her entire body limp and tingling, her mind swathed in bewilderment, he hoisted up his jeans and fastened them. He reached for his shirt and then looked straight at her, "Get dressed."

She took an unsteady breath and pushed away from the door, her legs so weak she very nearly staggered in the high heels. As quickly as she could she went into the bathroom and cleaned herself up, then put on her clothes, sans her destroyed silk thong.

When she came back into the room he still stood there silently waiting, the keys to his SUV in his hand.

Unable to bear the silence any longer, she looked directly at him, not bothering to shield her utter confusion, and asked, "What's with you?"

"You were right. You're not my type."

Chapter 29

It wasn't even midnight when he pulled up alongside her sedan in the parking lot of the Metro Link. The club was still packed, the music still blasting. How could she have failed yet again in less than two hours' time?

He was her target...and she'd fallen for him.

Fallen hard. Let things get personal.

Her mission was to stop him...terminate him if necessary. After all, he was a cold-blooded killer, a man who tortured innocent people for money. And yet, more than anything else, she wanted to save him.

She was seriously messed up.

"I could stay the night at your place," she offered, her voice sounding too fragile. God, this was totally pathetic. But she had to try. It was her job—the whole mission depended on her being able to get to Leberman. She had to do this. Had to find a way to stay close to him.

He didn't respond, just sat there waiting for her to get out. Even in the dim glow cast by the dash's display, his profile looked stony, every line and angle rigid with some conclusion only he understood. Dammit, she was certain he'd felt something.

She'd watched the unreadable emotions play across his face…had felt his body's response to hers. It went beyond the physical, she couldn't shake the connections. But he didn't want it that way…he didn't want any strings. For some reason her response to him disturbed him. It damn sure disturbed her.

Was it the scars? Had someone made him feel ugly? Deformed? Or did he simply choose to be this way to facilitate his profession? From the beginning she'd felt something wasn't right here…something intrinsic to his very being.

But it went too deep to be recent or merely about sex. This was way bigger than that.

Then again, maybe she was reading too much between the lines in an effort to let herself off the hook for indisputable failure.

He looked directly at her, giving her a start with the abrupt move. "Do yourself a favor and walk away."

She shifted in the seat to face him more fully. Anger, mostly at herself, frustration and hope, dammit, *hope,* funneled inside her, making her desperate to reach him… to salvage this operation.

"I don't want to walk away. I want to know you." She blinked, only then realizing that moisture had gathered in her eyes. What was wrong with her? This shouldn't be happening. And then she knew…if she couldn't get to Leberman—if she were factored out of the scenario for good—Lucas and his men would have no choice. Seth would die. Because he wouldn't stop…they would stop him. She'd totally screwed up this mission. Broken the first rule of ops: never get personally involved.

That penetrating gaze focused fully on her, the feroc-

ity of it making her tremble in spite of her determination
not to react outwardly. "There's nothing to know." Two
endless beats passed before he shifted his focus forward.
"Now, get out."

Tasha didn't argue this time. She couldn't risk letting
him see more of the emotions that hovered far too close
to the surface. The moment she'd scrambled out of his
SUV and closed the door he drove away.

Just like that.

Her heart rammed against her chest as she tried with
all her might to focus on getting the keys into the ignition of her car. She had to get out of here before she lost it
completely. She needed a bath. A long, hot soak to wash
away his scent…the very feel of him lingering on her skin.

She sucked in a jagged breath and put the car in gear.
No way could she consider the consequences of her futile act right now. They hadn't used a condom, and the
sacrifice she'd made had been for nothing. She'd still
failed to keep his attention. She didn't have it in her to
go there…to analyze it. The next time she saw Seth—if
she saw him at all—it would be on a whole other playing field. He would be seeking her and it wouldn't have
anything to do with sex.

She leaned against the wall in the elevator as it moved
upward, eventually stopping on the thirteenth floor.
Vaguely she wondered if they'd chosen that floor in defiance of the significance of the unlucky number. Or maybe
it was the only one with every room vacant. After all, who
wanted to live on the thirteenth floor?

Her mind was rambling…her emotions a wreck.

She couldn't think…couldn't reason.

It was over.

What was there to think about? Other than keeping

herself alive when he turned those killing instincts on her. Well, if her performance continued on its present course she was dead already.

Fury ignited inside her. She was a complete idiot. She'd let this guy get to her. Let him draw her into some kind of spell, and she'd lost all illusion of being in control.

Not once in all the scenarios they'd thrust her into during training had she failed so miserably.

It was the human element, she knew. They'd warned her that when it was for real she might not feel so damned cocky. But she'd convinced herself that she was better than that. Didn't need any warning. She could handle anything. Well, she'd handled it all right. She'd handled herself out of the game.

The elevator doors slid open, and Maverick waited in the corridor for her. She didn't know and didn't ask how they'd gotten back to the building before her, but the flicker of concern in his eyes was impossible to miss.

They'd been tracking her every move…they knew just how far south this op had gone.

"Did you plant the bug?" he asked as they strode side by side to the apartment that served as a sort of command center.

She nodded. "He'll find it next time he sweeps the SUV."

"Good." Maverick opened the door leading to the apartment and waited for her to go in first.

Ramon turned toward her when she stepped inside. "You okay?" he asked, surveying her disheveled appearance.

She shrugged. "I'm okay."

"Our boy opted not to take you back to wherever the hell he's staying now," Maverick stated the obvious. "We'd hoped he would keep you close long enough to pinpoint that location."

Tasha moved to the couch and sat down. "Thanks for reminding me." Like she needed the cowboy to rub it in. She'd failed. "He told me to get lost, as usual."

"Did you have to approach him or did he approach you in the club?" Maverick wanted to know, the analytical wheels turning in his head.

"He approached me," she said wearily, though for the life of her she couldn't see what difference it made at this point. She was out. Another wave of anger washed over her, and she racked her brain for possibilities of what she could have done differently. There had to be a way to reach this guy on a level he couldn't resist.

"That means he's hooked," Ramon suggested, jerking her from her troubling thoughts. "He'll be back in touch."

She looked up at the two men, regret pricking her. She hated to burst their collective bubble of hope, but that wasn't going to happen. "He's not the kind who can be hooked," she said, setting Ramon straight. "He doesn't want any connections. If he comes back it'll only be because of the bug and his assumption that I'm connected to Lucas."

"There's nothing we can do but wait and see," Maverick said pointedly, either to get her to lighten up on herself or in an effort to thwart her self-pity session. She'd seemed to be doing a hell of a lot of that lately.

"There is the other..." he began, looking directly at her.

"I got it," she said before he could ask. That was the one thing she'd done right in all this. Her means might lack originality, but success was the bottom line. She looked directly into his expectant gaze and said, "I got the DNA sample Lucas wanted."

"That'll be helpful." Maverick's expression didn't show

his relief but she heard it in his voice. "I'll notify Lucas right away. He'll want analysis started immediately."

She moistened her lips and said the rest, the reality that they hadn't used a condom reverberating in her head again. "There's just one thing. We're going to need a rape kit to retrieve it."

Chapter 30

At dawn Seth took up a position with Victoria Colby's private residence within his sights. Lucas Camp had taken her there from the hospital two days ago and she hadn't left since. But Seth knew she couldn't stay holed up in there forever. Eventually she would come out. Quite possibly this very day if his calculations were correct.

Lucas's men had the gated community staked out quite thoroughly, but that didn't present a problem for Seth. He didn't need to be that close. All that he required was a position within striking distance. He was a top marksman, had learned the skill from the best snipers in the mercenary business. He'd risen above even the masters. A weapon felt as much a natural extension of his body as his right arm.

His focus shifted back to the small but grand house Victoria Colby called home now. He wished he had been there to see her open the package containing the T-shirt. He couldn't fault Leberman's uncanny foresight. All those years he'd kept the evidence of his crime. Anyone else would have wasted no time in destroying any and all evidence. But not Leberman. The bastard had known the power it held. The soul-deep anguish it would awaken. He had planned this final game for nearly twenty years. Now the end was near. There would be one last moment of shocking discovery and then death would swoop down upon Victoria Colby and her protector before they could hope to escape.

Seth was the instrument of that certain death. He existed for that sole purpose. It would fulfill his obligation. Would sever the connection between him and Leberman. Once and for all. A twinge of something that felt too damned much like regret twisted inside him. He almost laughed out loud at the sensation. Was he supposed to grieve the loss of his *creator?* The only caretaker he'd ever known? He thought of the endless persecution and decided the answer was no. He hated Leberman. Despised him.

It was that very hatred that made him good at his work—he had no fear and no hope for anything beyond the moment. Death was no threat to him. Nothing could stop him.

She slipped into his mind…made his body tighten with remembered visions of them together. He clenched his jaw and pushed thoughts of her away. He'd given her what she wanted…what she needed to accomplish her part in the grand finale. He wouldn't see her again. Like he'd told her, she wasn't his type.

Another laugh rumbled in his throat. He didn't have a type. And he knew without reservation that there was a reason for her physical reaction to him as there was for everything. Leberman had taught him that unforgettable lesson well. However innocent on certain levels Tasha appeared, he was not fooled. Nor was he a fool.

He knew that no woman would want him...would look at him with anything other than disgust in her eyes. Even the hookers he hired to relieve his sexual tension didn't want to look at him except for the money. And if at any time he started to forget just what he was, Leberman always reminded him. He was nothing, could depend on no one...trust no one. But he could deliver death without fail...without flinching. And when his own death came, that ability would define who he had been. Nothing...no one—a ruthless killer.

They thought they had him figured out, thought they knew what he was about. But they had no idea.

The bug she'd left in his SUV hadn't been necessary. He had known she was the enemy from the moment they met. The only reason he hadn't killed her that first night was because she had tripped some internal trigger he hadn't known existed...made him curious. Made him feel a strange kinship with her. He usually didn't allow distractions of any sort, but he hadn't been able to deny himself this one indulgence. It could prove a mistake, but he wasn't concerned at this point. She knew what he wanted her to know, nothing more. She had not hindered his task. To the contrary, she had facilitated his effort, unknowingly of course.

Tasha North would be the messenger who carried the final blow to the mighty Victoria Colby.

Leberman didn't like that part. He'd wanted her out of the way from the start, but Seth had refused. Considered his inspiration to make her a participant as ingenious as any of Leberman's schemes. The more he'd thought about it the better he liked it.

She would provide the pivotal key without even realizing it until it was too late.

She wasn't part of the Colby Agency or any member of

Lucas Camp's organization. Lucas had selected her from someplace else. She had some training, he knew, but she lacked real experience. Just another unknown factor that nagged at his curiosity.

Though he knew it was her job to get close to him, to learn what she could for Lucas Camp, her sincerity gave him pause. He'd felt her body's reaction to him. That kind of response couldn't be faked. Irrationally, his own body reacted instantly at even the thought of thrusting deep inside her. Admittedly, he had been shaken somewhat by the overwhelming physical connection. Had experienced unfamiliar sensations deep in his gut. But there had been much more on her part. She was either very, very good at pretending, which he doubted, or she'd let herself get emotionally involved.

The last didn't make sense, since Lucas Camp would never select someone so lacking. Yet, Seth was anything but convinced of her ability to pull off such a genuine performance. His instincts had screamed a warning at the depth of her vulnerability when he'd pushed her away afterward. That was the part that didn't make sense to him.

He needed to know more.

He lowered his binoculars and considered more closely his motivation for such a step. What did it matter who she really was or where she had come from? Or even what made her react as she had? She was simply a useful tool, one he would, without hesitation, dispose of if she got in the way.

His teacher had ensured that he possessed no emotions, other than rage. Determination, if one considered that an emotion. His ability to block such distractions was necessary to his existence…to his mission. Nothing else mattered.

Still, he needed to know about her. Some aspect of her background might prove useful at a critical moment.

Not that it would change the outcome.

Nothing could change the events to come.

Chicago's CIA field office, like all offices even remotely related to national security, worked more man-hours now than in the past two decades. The Domestic Resources Division and its once-secret collection-and-analysis work within the boundaries of the United States were no longer a closely guarded secret. Constant analysis and briefings were expected from every available source. The pressure was on.

But one CIA officer, Walter McCone, now understood just how scary things could get in his otherwise sedate job.

Three seconds after Seth pressed the muzzle of his 9 mm to the man's temple, he had provided the necessary retinal and thumb print scan to allow access to the Central Intelligence Agency's vast database. The moment he'd entered his personal identification code and the screen confirmed its acceptance, Seth had landed a swift blow to just the right spot, rendering him unconscious. Killing him hadn't been necessary. Seth wanted him to report the security breach. It was time Lucas Camp realized just how much Seth knew.

He shoved the man's limp body aside and settled into the chair behind his desk. He typed in the name Tasha North and waited for the search results.

Half an hour later, despite the dead ends he'd encountered, his persistence paid off.

Everything he wanted to know about Tasha North spilled across the screen in front of him.

The more he knew, he reminded himself, the more power he possessed.

Chapter 31

"You know," Victoria said thoughtfully, "Max has that cabin near Crystal Lake. We could go there." It certainly wouldn't be the first time the Colby Agency had used one of their own people's hideaways for a safe house.

She tried to read Lucas's face or his eyes as she waited for his response to the suggestion, but he'd guarded his emotions very closely for the past two days. The assassin must be closing in, she concluded, it was the only reason he would work so hard to keep her in the dark. He feared for her safety…worried that he wouldn't be able to do enough to spare her from harm. Lucas was not so young anymore, the worry was taking its toll on him.

Her jaw clenched tightly. She hated Leberman and his assassin for that. They still knew nothing about this killer—where he'd come from, his reputation. She wondered, fury and hatred seething inside her, if this man, this assassin, felt even a moment's remorse for what he'd been hired to do. She knew the answer. No. He felt nothing.

What kind of man could kill without thought or hesitation? Could induce the kind of pain she had endured having to look at her child's bloodied T-shirt? Tears welled instantly at the thought. She would not think about that. Leberman, the bastard, had kidnapped and killed her child. She didn't need the DNA analysis Lucas had put a rush on to confirm it. The shirt was his...the blood was his, as well. She could feel that truth in her very soul.

Though she had known that her son was most likely dead, had accepted that fact on some level. The knowledge did little to lessen the devastation when she'd peered into that box and seen that small, bloodied garment. Agony squeezed her chest whenever she considered what her baby must have endured at that bastard's hand. She would kill him. Whether Lucas wanted her involved or not. She wanted to fire the weapon that ended his pathetic life. That was precisely why she had no intention of going too far from here.

As much as she feared for Lucas's life, and she did, dear God, she did, she had to end this. They would never be free of this horrible past until Leberman was dead. The delivery of the T-shirt had driven that point home. She wanted him dead soon.

And she hoped he burned in hell for all eternity.

"I had a more remote location in mind," Lucas said after lengthy consideration of her suggestion. He braced on his cane a little more heavily than usual and walked over to join her at the hearth. Just another indication of how hard the past week had been on him.

Though it wasn't that cool outside, she couldn't seem to get warm. She'd had Lucas light the gas-powered fireplace. The heat from the flame scarcely made a dent in the cold cloak of dread that had swathed her. The chill came from deep inside and she had a feeling that she wouldn't feel warm again until this was over.

She looked directly into Lucas's caring gray eyes and told him the truth. Being evasive wouldn't help matters. "I know you want to keep me safe, Lucas. There's nothing in this world I want more than to see that you're safe, as well." Tears burned in her eyes as the images from that night—when he'd fallen into her arms…blood streaming down his face—rushed one after the other through her weary mind. "We can't risk allowing Leberman or his assassin to get too close. But, by the same token, we can't run from this. We have to get him this time. There's no other option."

Lucas nodded. "I agree. I have a place in mind that isn't so far away. We'll be safe but close enough to react in a timely manner if the need arises. I just don't want to risk utilizing any known locations."

There it was. Ian and Simon had warned her that Lucas considered even her trusted employees at the agency a possible threat. She could scarcely believe it then or now. Of course, her two most trusted men hadn't told her about their covert meetings with Lucas until after there was no way to hide the truth any longer. But that only proved their dedication to her welfare.

Still, it annoyed her that Lucas would even consider one of her people less than trustworthy.

"I know what you're getting at," she said flatly. "You won't find a traitor at my agency. Can you say the same for your own?" That was unfair. She didn't have to see the surprise in his eyes to know that she'd tossed out that scathing remark without grounds. Lucas's Specialists were above reproach just as her Colby agents were. "I'm sorry. That was uncalled for."

Lucas splayed his hands in uncertainty. "Perhaps it

isn't. I can't be positive." He leveled that knowing gaze on hers. "Just as you can't. There are too many variables in this world to be that certain."

"True," she admitted, though with great reluctance. "That's why you chose someone outside yours or my sphere of professional affiliation to make contact."

"Exactly. The woman we have undercover is someone I selected personally for this mission. Someone outside this circle."

Victoria had wondered about that. She remembered her from the day she'd delivered the package. This young woman was risking a great deal. She hoped that the personal wager was not more than she realized. "Does she know the full risk involved?"

Lucas nodded. "I believe so, though I'm certain her youth colors her perspective a bit."

Victoria's instincts went on point. She read the regret in Lucas's eyes in a heartbeat. "You're that worried about her?"

He exhaled mightily. "I am." He turned away then, looking at something beyond her…or maybe nothing at all. "I chose her because she was untried in the field, lacked the hard edge of experience. I wanted her vulnerability to show. I didn't want him seeing through her cover. But I may have overestimated her emotional limitations to some degree."

Victoria definitely knew how that felt. She'd done the same once. But only once. She'd chosen a young woman right out of the Colby Agency's research department—unaware that the woman had a congenital heart condition—for those very reasons and sent her out to bring in the kind of man, though a good guy, not unlike this ruthless assassin. Fortunately that mission had succeeded… this one might have an altogether different outcome.

"Are you going to pull her out?"

Lucas regarded her for a moment before he answered. Something more bothered him but he wouldn't tell her until he was ready. "Yes, I am."

Victoria's heart skipped a beat. As hard ass as Lucas Camp would have the world believe him to be, he would not risk a life unnecessarily. His honor wouldn't let him. Just more proof of the many reasons that she cherished him so dearly.

She put her arm through his and drew closer. "Tell me about this place you plan to take me." Warmth spread through her and she allowed it, let it wash away the cold worry and fear. She loved this man, wanted to spend the rest of her life with him if it amounted to nothing more than a few hours. She wanted those precious moments to be with him.

He laid his hand over hers. "It's definitely off the beaten path."

Victoria smiled. "That sounds perfect." She very much needed a place just like that right now. A place where she could forget the past and concentrate on whatever time she and Lucas would have in the present.

If destroying Leberman took her life, she wanted to spend the time they had left wisely. She'd wasted far too much already.

Lucas readied for his conference with Tasha.

He considered again the intel he'd only just received, and his decision solidified. He had to pull her out now. Whatever happened from this point forward, he could no longer in good conscience ignore the risk to her life.

When her image appeared on the monitor, he produced a smile for her benefit. "Good work, North," he told her. Maverick had already informed him that she'd taken the assassin's rebuff far too personally. "The DNA evidence you provided is being analyzed as we speak. If this guy is anywhere in the system, we'll find him."

She nodded firmly, but her eyes gave her away. She knew she'd failed to accomplish the ultimate goal, and the guilt weighed heavily upon her. "Thank you, sir."

"I received intel a few minutes ago," Lucas told her, paving the way for the blow to come, "that indicates our assassin has accessed CIA's database. He now knows who you are. I had hoped that change in our strategy might facilitate our efforts to locate Leberman, but now I'm not so sure. Considering the risk involved, I've decided to sequester you in a safe house until we eliminate the threat."

Something changed in her eyes. All signs of uncertainty vanished. "No."

Lucas leaned forward a bit, wanted her to see the irritation in his expression. "That wasn't a suggestion, North, that was a direct order. You've done all you can. Certain additional developments have greatly reduced your value as an asset in this mission. Now, you *will* go into protective custody until we neutralize this situation."

"With all due respect, sir," she said with just as much annoyance as he'd shown, "I'm not finished yet."

Lucas tightened his hold on his cane. A part of him wanted to give her a lesson in following orders, but another part of him wanted to cheer her undying determination. "I'll be taking Victoria to a safe house as planned. When we've disappeared he will come after you in hopes of discovering our location—"

"That's what you wanted, right?" she countered. The determined tilt of her chin as well as the rigid set of her shoulders warned him that she wouldn't give in easily.

"That's what I wanted before," he allowed, "I have reason to believe your objectivity has been compromised."

Personal involvement on that level spelled disaster. He knew it, and so did she. That was the first rule of deep cover. Though he didn't relish the necessity to dash it in her face.

"That's why you picked me in the first place, isn't it?" she accused, hitting the proverbial nail right on the head. "I lacked any field experience which would prove to my advantage in fooling our target. The fact that I lost perspective only lends more credibility to my act."

Well, she certainly had him there.

"The bottom line is I won't let this go any further," he said pointedly.

"Pulling me out will blow your best chance at getting Leberman," she retorted, knowing he couldn't deny her words. "I think you're smarter than that, sir. I'm a more valuable asset than ever at this point. I'm willing to take the risk. You'd be a fool not to take advantage of the opportunity."

A flare of fury ignited inside him. She might be right about many things, but she was wrong about him. He wasn't going to knowingly get her killed. She'd gotten too close to the guy. Every instinct warned him that she wasn't thinking like an agent...she was thinking like a woman.

"I may be a fool, but you have your orders. We'll bring down Leberman another way." He'd already considered his options. She wasn't the only bait he could offer. Once he and Victoria disappeared, he had a feeling that this guy would gladly follow any available avenue. He was too focused to let anything get in his way.

"In that case, I guess I'll head back to Langley," she said as she stood. "I have no desire to work for a fool."

She was angry. If there hadn't been some credibility in the words she'd flung at him he might have been angry himself. But she was more right than she knew. For that reason he let her insubordination go.

She walked out of the camera's visual range. He let go a heavy breath as he heard a brief, heated exchange between her and Maverick and then the slamming of a door.

"You want me to take her into custody?" Maverick asked as he moved in front of the camera.

Lucas nodded. A new kind of fury flamed inside him. Leberman always had a way of turning everything to shit. Even his own life. Leberman blamed James Colby, had tried to destroy all that was his because *he* had screwed up. "Don't let her get away or she'll be out there looking for him."

"Will do."

Maverick signed off to catch up with Tasha. She had a stubborn streak about her, Lucas had to give her that. But that determination he'd so admired was going to get her killed under the circumstances. He should have seen this coming. But he hadn't.

Maybe *he* was too personally involved to make reliable decisions. He shook his head and closed the laptop that had provided the face-to-face encounter without his leaving Victoria's home.

"Lucas."

He looked up to find Logan waiting in the doorway of Victoria's small home office.

"Yes." He stood and moved toward the door. "Did we get the results of the analysis?"

Logan nodded. "It's a match. The blood on the T-shirt definitely belonged to Victoria's son. And the age of the sample tested is consistent with the time frame of his disappearance."

There it was.

Leberman wasn't merely playing with Victoria's emo-

tions, this was the real thing. Her son's actual shirt...
his blood. The bastard had killed the child—violently
probably.

Fury twisted inside Lucas. He would see that he died
in a similar manner...screaming for mercy.

Chapter 32

Tasha didn't bother slamming the door to her apartment since she knew Ramon was right on her heels. The door closed behind him but she didn't look back, just kept moving until she was in her bedroom, then she slammed the door as hard as she could. She wanted him to know how pissed-off she was, for all the good it would do. It was his job, she imagined, to keep an eye on her until Maverick finished up with Lucas, and then she'd be under house arrest so to speak.

Lucas wanted her out. Not that she could blame him. She'd crossed the line. It was true. But that didn't mean she was out. She could finish this if he'd only let her. She was very nearly positive that she'd gotten to Seth on some level. She'd felt it.

It wouldn't matter now because he was a dead man. Lucas's men would take him down. Every instinct told her that Leberman would get away. He was too smart to get caught by the usual means. Lucas knew that. That was another thing she was certain of. Yet, he refused to allow her to do what needed to be done.

He was protecting her.

Because she'd failed.

And, ultimately, it was his responsibility to know when an agent was no longer reliable.

A blast of fury obliterated the mixed emotions playing havoc with her ability to think.

Yes, she'd crossed the line. But she was still an asset.

And that left only one thing to do.

She went into the bathroom and lifted her arm, surveying the tiny healing cut where they'd inserted the tracking device two days ago. Tasha moistened her lips and braced herself for the discomfort.

Using a pair of tweezers she tore the tiny incision open and dug around under the skin. Her stomach roiled and a thin line of sweat broke out on her upper lip before she made contact. She grasped the tip and pulled out the matchstick-size device. Letting go a ragged breath, she wiped away the blood, careful not to leave any signs of her little surgical procedure, and shoved a small strip bandage into place. Another deep breath or two and the nausea had passed. She swaddled the device in a tissue and set it aside.

After pulling on her denim jacket, she tucked her handgun into the waistband of her jeans and groped around in her purse for that nifty little ink pen Ramon had given her. She tucked the pen into the right pocket of her jacket and shoved what cash she had and the tissue containing the tracking device into the other. Her sneakers would allow for stealth. She was good to go.

When she heard Maverick's voice in the living room of her apartment, she made her move. The hidden door inside her walk-in closet that concealed a laundry-chute-like egress route into the apartment directly below opened with ease. Five seconds later Tasha stood in the kitchen of the command center Ramon and Maverick called home.

She hurried to the front door, unlocked and opened it, praying that one of them wasn't one step ahead of her already.

The corridor was empty.

Releasing a tense breath she ran for the stairwell. She listened intently for someone else to enter the stairwell as she double-timed it down one flight after the other. Just as she reached the final dozen steps, she heard the echo of footsteps above her. She had to get out of there before she was caught. Whichever of the two wasn't bounding down the stairs would be coming down in the elevator. Time was not on her side.

She burst through the stairwell door into the first floor lobby and, without pausing, exited the building. Five-o'clock rush hour had turned frantic with drivers and pedestrians alike determined to get home to begin their weekends. She didn't hesitate. She pushed through the crowd on the sidewalk and shot into the street, dodging and weaving to avoid the cars. A horn blew and tires squealed, but she made it to the other side without ending up a hood ornament. When she would have darted into the alley between two upcoming buildings a taxi, sans fare, slowed to a stop practically right beside her.

It had to be fate.

She jerked his rear door open and rattled off an address. "How fast can you get me there?" she demanded, leaning forward, needing him to feel her urgency.

He shrugged. "In this traffic, I can't say."

"Just get me there as fast as you can. I'll make it worth your trouble."

No sooner than the words were out of her mouth than

there was a break in traffic and the taxi eased left, then zoomed forward. At that precise moment she caught a glimpse of Maverick and Ramon on the sidewalk panning the street. She slumped down in the seat and didn't breathe easy again until the taxi had moved ahead several blocks.

When he reached the address she'd given him, she paid the fare plus a generous tip. "Do me a favor," she said, peeling off another hundred bucks, "drive around for a while. Maybe on the other side of town."

He took the money and smiled. "Sure, I got some errands I could take care of before I call it a day."

"Thanks." Tasha climbed out of the car, leaving the tracking device tucked safely in the back seat. She'd watched for a tail and hadn't noticed one. Maverick and Ramon were likely caught in the traffic. The chase the taxi would lead them on would buy her some time. But she couldn't afford to waste a second. Lucas would be notified and more of his men would pick up her trail. Unless he decided she wasn't worth the time and manpower.

When the taxi was gone and there was still no sign of Maverick or Ramon, she surveyed the Oak Park house. This was as good a place as any to start looking for Seth. Though she felt fairly confident he wouldn't come back here, there might be something inside that would give her an indication of where to start looking. Something the others had missed.

The fine hairs on the back of her neck suddenly stood on end.

The sound of a vehicle braking to a stop sounded right behind her. She swore, certain it would be Maverick.

"Get in."

She whipped around as recognition of the voice exploded in her brain cells. Seth's SUV sat at the curb, the passenger-side window down, his 9 mm aimed directly at her. Was this her lucky day or what?

"Now," he commanded.

He hadn't needed the gun. She would have gone with him anyway. But he didn't know that. She climbed into the vehicle as ordered.

"Give me your weapon."

"What makes you think I'm armed?" she tossed back as he eased away from the curb.

Those piecing blue eyes cut in her direction. "The weapon," he reiterated, "give it to me."

She reached behind her and removed the gun from her waistband and placed it on the console between them. "This isn't necessary," she told him quietly. "I know you found the bug. But there are things you don't know."

He just drove, not even bothering to glance her way.

"We need to talk," she said bluntly, hoping like hell he would at least listen to what she had to say before he killed her.

He picked up her weapon and tucked it into his waistband. "Don't talk."

She should have expected that. He didn't mince words. She was the enemy. He would kill her.

Tasha faced forward and relaxed into the seat. She ignored the ache in her arm where she'd removed the tracking device. The idea that she'd probably made a mistake doing that flitted through her mind. No, she decided, that had been necessary. She had to do this on her own. Staring out the window, she couldn't be sure where he would take her to do the job, but between here and there, she needed to come up with a plan that would keep her alive and accomplish the mission at the same time. She resisted the urge to laugh. Piece of cake, right?

Yeah, right.

One glance at her captor's stony profile and she decided that staying alive might just be impossible. But impossible had never stopped her before.

The sun was setting, casting an orange glow over the treetops, by the time he reached his destination. She didn't recognize the house or the thinly populated neighborhood as he parked his SUV in the deserted drive. Woods bordered the back of the property. The house was dark, empty looking. A For Sale sign tucked into a front window told her the reason why.

"Get out."

His voice startled her after the long minutes of silence. She moved to obey, knowing that a play for her weapon would be futile, not to mention suicide.

As they crossed the yard, her heart rate accelerated. He nudged her from time to time to keep her moving toward the wooded area.

"Where are we going?" Her voice sounded as shaky as she felt and she hated the weakness. He was taking her into the woods, to kill her no doubt. Panic trickled through her, but she pushed it aside. She wasn't dead yet. The pen in her pocket gave her some comfort. She hoped like hell it worked as fast and efficiently as Ramon had said, since it was the only thing standing between her and certain death.

"Just keep walking," he said in answer to the question she'd almost forgotten she asked.

After about fifteen minutes he finally said, "Stop here."

The broad canopy overhead blocked most of the sun's waning light, leaving them shrouded in gloom. She glanced around the area. There were trees on all sides but the smell was different here. She inhaled deeply, noting the deep woodsy smell and something else...something damp and earthy.

Water.

The lake.

She suddenly knew where they were.

Victoria Colby's lake house.

"Why are we here?" she asked, her skin prickling with a familiar warning. This place held some significance... that's why he kept coming back.

He leveled that chilling gaze on hers. Despite the near darkness, those eyes of his seemed to draw whatever light there was and reflect it as if he possessed some sort of supernatural power. She suppressed a shiver. Reminded herself that he was likely about to kill her. How had her instincts failed her so miserably where he was concerned?

"I told you to stay away from me," he growled.

She looked straight into those haunting eyes and told him the truth. "I couldn't do that."

That assessing gaze narrowed. "You want to die, is that it? Is your job worth dying for?"

She took a step closer to him, ignored the alarm bells going off inside her head. He was way bigger than her. And strong. The memory of those arms holding her firmly while he pumped in and out of her made her shiver in spite of her best intentions not to.

"I came back," she told him as she stared up into that unyielding face, "because I thought you were worth saving." Unfortunately for her, it was the truth. That's why she'd failed...because she felt something deeper...stronger. He was more than just a killer. Every instinct urged her in that direction.

He laughed, the sound a harsh bark bursting from his chest. "And just who do you think you have to save *me* from?"

"Lucas will eliminate you," she said flatly, a fierce combination of emotions warring inside her. Her loyalty to Lucas battled relentlessly with her yearning to save this man...this killer. "You could walk away now. All he wants is Leberman. Tell me where Leberman is and you can disappear."

Rage claimed his rock-hard expression. "You think you know what this is about? You don't know anything."

She held her ground beneath that intimidating glower. He hated talking about the past. She'd learned that very quickly. And this had everything to do with the past. "Then why don't you explain it to me."

"I have an obligation to fulfill, and nothing will stop me." His voice sounded calm and collected but she could sense the building tension, the hot fury beneath it. "Not Lucas Camp. Not you."

She shook her head. "This is about more than money. Whatever Leberman is paying you to do his dirty work, that's not what drives you." His guard went up instantly. Checkmate. She gave herself a quick mental pat on the back. "There's a lot more involved. It's something in your past."

He tensed visibly. "Shut up." His fingers tightened on the weapon in his hand. "You don't know what you're talking about."

"Someone did this to you. Made you what you are. Your father, maybe?" she ventured, her pulse racing in anticipation of his answer. "A caretaker for certain. You don't trust anyone...you don't need anyone. You're a classic case of abused child turned raging adult. You don't even know why you do this...you just do it because it's the one thing you have control over. It's *all* you have."

"I said shut up!" He shoved the weapon against her

temple. Every feature of that chiseled face turned to granite.

She ignored his threat and went on, "I knew when I saw those scars that someone had done terrible things to you. Someone you trusted to take care of you…someone you cared about."

"I've never cared about anyone," he said through clenched teeth.

"What did your father do to you, Seth?" She didn't let up. Laid her hand against his chest, knowing he hated to be touched. He flinched. "Tell me what he did to you." She threw down the gauntlet, knowing he wouldn't be able to resist the challenge. "Or are you too afraid to talk about it? I thought you weren't afraid of anything."

He laughed softly, the sound almost sinister. "You want to know what he did to me? You think all those stories you read in your psychology books have prepared you?" He tangled the fingers of his free hand in her hair, dragging her closer. "He punished me each time I didn't live up to his expectations. Kept me shackled in the dark in a basement like an animal…fed me when he decided it was convenient."

Her heart was pounding. She was getting closer. "What about school or training?" She winced as his fingers tightened a fraction more in her hair.

"I've only had one kind of training. The kind—" he leaned closer, until she could feel his breath on her face "—you can only get from men who are no longer men… they're animals who crave violence, who live for nothing else. The kind that teaches a fourteen-year-old how to be a ruthless killer."

"But you were just a kid," she protested, her heart aching at how horrible it must have been.

"That's right. And do you have any idea what they did

to me? They beat me within an inch of my life for every misstep I made. They withheld food and water for days at a time if I failed in some way. Far more frequently and far worse than anything Leberman had ever done." A muscle jerked in his tense jaw. "When they couldn't break me that way, they made me their personal whore."

The brunt of his words made her shudder, brought the sting of tears to her eyes. Dear God...how...

Before her thought could mesh fully in her mind, he continued, "But I kept growing bigger and stronger until I wasn't a kid anymore." He made a guttural sound, a laugh maybe. "Then I had my revenge. I'd killed half the bastards who'd ever touched me before the others could stop me. They kept me locked up, afraid to come near me, until Leberman arrived to take me away." He tapped his head, right where that bizarre tattoo was. "That's when I got this. Leberman laughed and said that I wasn't human... that I was a beast."

Her whole body sagged beneath the weight of the words he's spoken. How could anyone hope to overcome that kind of violence. "How..." She cleared her throat and moistened her trembling lips. "How did you survive?"

He shook his head. "You don't get it, do you? *I didn't.*"

She saw the change in his eyes...knew what his next move would be. Her fingers wrapped around the pen in her jacket pocket. "I just want to help you," she urged.

"I don't need your help."

She jerked her arm upward and brought it down hard against his neck.

His body tensed.

For two beats she was certain she was dead.

The weapon bored more deeply into her flesh.

And then he dropped like a rock.

Chapter 33

Logan entered Victoria's home office, and Lucas looked up from his final preparations. "Any word on Agent North?"

Logan shook his head. "No luck with the CIA. Since she hasn't been upgraded to field work yet she didn't receive a tracking implant."

Lucas hissed a curse. He'd hoped they could locate her that way since she'd removed the one Maverick had implanted. He leveled his gaze on Logan's. "You keep me posted. Ramon and Maverick are on this?"

"I called in Blue and Noah to help them out. They're combing the city along with Maverick. Ramon's hanging out at the Metro Link in case our guy shows up there."

Blue Callahan and her husband Noah Drake were two of Mission Recovery's finest assets. Lucas should have thought to call them in. He sighed in self-disgust. "I appreciate the way you've stayed on top of things, Logan. I haven't…" His words trailed off as a wave of weariness washed over him. He'd tried to keep the exhaustion clawing at him at bay, but his efforts were quickly losing ground. "I haven't been at the top of my game this go-around."

"That's understandable, sir. Are we ready to go?"

They had waited for the cover of darkness. A switch-off would take place in the event that the still-unidentified assassin was watching. Ian Michael's wife, Nicole, disguised to look like Victoria, would leave with Lucas and two of his men in the SUV waiting outside. Nicole had arrived dressed as a man so anyone watching wouldn't suspect just such a setup. Thirty minutes after their departure, Victoria, disguised in the male clothing and wig Nicole had worn, and her two most trusted men, Ian and Simon, would leave in an SUV parked in a neighbor's driveway. Another of Lucas's men, along with two more of Victoria's, would be watching the small gated community for any sign of the assassin as Victoria departed. Vince Ferrelli would follow as backup. They'd covered every possible base.

Lucas didn't like the idea of being separated from Victoria, but it was the only way to ensure her safety at this point.

"Almost ready," he said in answer to Logan's question. "Victoria is briefing her people before leaving. Since we can't be sure how long she'll be away, she wants to ensure that both Ian and Simon feel comfortable in their positions as codirectors of the agency until her return."

"I'll be waiting outside," Logan said before he turned away.

"One more thing," Lucas said, waylaying him. "I've decided to change my orders on the assassin."

Logan looked surprised. Lucas rarely made last minute changes without overwhelming motivation. "In what way?" Logan inquired.

"Until now I've wanted him alive so he could lead us to Leberman. I think that might be a mistake. It's now clear to me that Leberman has grown impatient and will want this over just as swiftly as we do. I think he'll make a move with or without his hired help." Lucas looked directly at Logan then to ensure there was no misunderstanding. "If you get our assassin in your scope, take him down."

Logan nodded slowly. "Do you want him alive for any reason?"

"No." Lucas didn't hesitate. "I want him eliminated."

"Understood."

Lucas watched Logan go, then took a moment to ensure he'd taken care of everything in his makeshift command center. He considered the possibility of any loose ends and could think of none. Director Casey would continue to handle ongoing operations at Mission Recovery until Lucas's return. Assuming he returned.

Lucas closed his briefcase and exhaled another heavy sigh. His top priority right now was getting Victoria to safety. He touched his still-tender forehead and the fresh, much smaller bandage that had been secured there today. His back was still tender as well. There was no doubt in his mind that he would be dead right now had the assassin wanted him that way. More of Leberman's games, Lucas had decided. Well, he'd had enough games. It was his and Victoria's turn now. Whatever it took, Leberman was going to die.

He thought again of the video he'd watched when the assassin dropped by North's apartment. He couldn't shake the feeling of familiarity in the way the man moved. But he'd studied that video over and over and nothing had come to him. Familiar or not, he was a dead man, the same as the man who'd hired him.

* * *

"Are there any other questions?" Victoria looked from Ian to Simon and back. The two men sat on the sofa, both watching her closely as she stood before them. She couldn't sit for more than ten seconds without squirming.

"None," Ian said.

Simon chimed in as well. "No questions."

Victoria nodded. "Very good." She propped her hip on the arm of a chair and pretended to relax, knowing she wouldn't be able to tolerate it for long. "If for any reason I don't return," she stated succinctly, "Zach has the proper instructions for continuing to conduct business." Victoria suddenly wished Zach were here. She missed his steady support. As the Colby Agency's top legal eagle, they worked closely together. But Zach was on leave back home in Indiana where his lovely wife was giving birth to their second child.

Victoria couldn't help a pang of jealousy. They had their whole lives ahead of them, just as Ian and Nicole, Simon and his Jolie did. Time was running out for her and Lucas, and here they were wasting it on a horrendous part of the past that wouldn't go away.

God, how she wanted Leberman dead. She wanted this over so she could move on. Eighteen years was long enough to grieve and keep fighting the same old battle. She couldn't change the past...couldn't bring her husband and son back. It was time to move forward.

She closed her eyes and thought of the way Lucas made her feel when he kissed her. So warm and contented. Happy in a way she had not known in a very long time. His kisses had been chaste the past couple of days, because of the mounting tension and all the horrible reminders of the past, she knew. But she was ready to move beyond that. She was sick to death of having her painful history dashed back in her face. Life was so fleeting. Why couldn't she have this time with Lucas?

"Victoria, are you all right?"

Nicole's voice dragged her back to the present, and Victoria's eyes fluttered open. She managed a smile for the young woman. She nodded then. "Yes. I guess I'm just tired." A frown worried her brow. "Nicole, are you absolutely certain you want to do this?"

Nicole Reed-Michaels smiled. "I'm positive. I can handle it. Don't worry about me." Nicole was former FBI. She knew how to take care of herself.

But that didn't keep Victoria from being concerned. A dark wig covered her blond hair, and she wore one of Victoria's suits. If the assassin or Leberman were watching, she was a target. Leberman was an evil bastard. His assassin had proven every bit as devious. Those kinds of men were capable of anything. Killing a lovely woman, wife and mother of two, would be nothing to them.

Victoria stood abruptly. "Excuse me a moment."

She rushed to the guest room to take care of a task she'd forgotten. A quick flip of the wall switch and light filled the space. Her gaze went immediately to the bed. A box, its contents scattered across the pale green comforter, drew her deeper into the room. Settling on the edge of the bed, she reached for a photograph of her young son. Tears gathered in her eyes as a bittersweet smile tugged at the corners of her mouth. If only she could have protected him.

She'd failed.

Laying the picture aside with trembling fingers, she surveyed the mementos of his short life. This was all she would ever have of him…it wasn't enough. She'd dragged out the box of painful memories earlier that afternoon, she had to look one last time.

He was gone.

She had to face the finality of that glaring fact.

With a heavy heart she pushed up from the bed and moved to the door without looking back. Freda would put things away...she didn't need to bother—to put herself through the pain. It was time to forget.

As hard as it was to do, Victoria turned out the light on that part of her past.

"It's time," Lucas said as she entered the den once more.

She nodded her understanding. "All right." She looked back at her trusted Colby agents and reminded herself to be strong.

Determined not to allow this moment to become an emotional farewell, she produced an appreciative smile for Ian and Nicole. "Thank you for everything." To Ian and Simon, she added, "I'll be in touch."

When the decoy party had moved to the entry hall, Lucas glanced back to Victoria. He wanted to take her in his arms, she could see the need shining in those caring gray eyes. But he wouldn't, not now.

"We'll rendezvous in one hour," he told her.

Somehow she managed to keep her smile tacked in place. "One hour," she repeated. "Be safe."

"Let's step back into the den, Mrs. Colby," Vince Ferrelli, one of Lucas's specialists, said.

Victoria's heart pounded so hard she feared she might be incapable of a response just then so she nodded and followed him from the entry hall. She wanted to say so much more to Lucas before he left. Wanted to tell him again how very much she loved him. She'd only told him that once.

Please, God, she prayed, don't let that be the last time.

"We'll wait here, Mrs. Colby," Ferrelli said. He gestured to the sofa. "Everything will be fine."

It had to be, she thought as she settled onto the sofa's edge. Fate couldn't be so cruel as to take Lucas from her. She'd already lost too much.

Lucas's cellular phone vibrated in his jacket pocket. He frowned at the intrusion. He didn't need any distractions right now. But if it was one of his people it had to be important, otherwise they wouldn't risk talking over the air waves and interception by anyone who might be listening.

He hoped like hell it wasn't bad news involving North…or Victoria. He'd only left her minutes ago.

He fished the damned phone from his pocket and flipped it open. He didn't recognize the number of the caller. "Yeah," he said instead of identifying himself.

"Lucas?"

His frown deepened. "Ebb?" Dr. Ebb Deason was the genetics expert Lucas called upon whenever he needed the very best in DNA analysis. Not to mention he could count on his old friend dropping everything and working his team until he had results.

"I apologize for calling you like this," Ebb hastened to explain. "Maverick insisted it would be all right, considering the subject matter."

Maverick had given the doctor this number? It had to be important. "It's fine. Go ahead, Ebb."

"I finished that latest analysis you sent me."

The seminal fluid specimen North had provided. The memory pinged Lucas's conscience. "That's good to hear. What have you got for me?" Unless the doc had found a match in some database, a mere analysis wouldn't be much help.

"Well, I was a little bewildered at first. I knew immediately that I'd seen this DNA strand before."

Anticipation seared through Lucas. "You found a match in CODIS?" The FBI's Combined DNA Index System proved a useful tool for all government agencies. It contained DNA specs for violent criminal offenders. That would be the most likely source of a match considering the specimen donor's occupation.

"No...the match was with another specimen you provided."

Lucas stilled. Every sensory perception stood at attention.

"This specimen was a perfect match to the one from the Cubs T-shirt."

Lucas blinked, breaking the paralyzing spell the news had cast. "You're certain of that." Of course he was certain. He wouldn't have called otherwise.

"Yes. Quite certain," the doctor confirmed.

"Thanks, Ebb."

Lucas didn't remember terminating the call, but somehow his cell phone made it back into his pocket.

"Dear God," he muttered.

This was...impossible...

The assassin determined to kill Victoria was...*her son.*

Chapter 34

Tasha collapsed on the floor in the massive entry hall. Her breath heaved from her chest as if she'd run a marathon.

It had taken her at least thirty minutes to drag Seth's unconscious body to the house. The woods, she discovered, bordered the side of Victoria Colby's lake house opposite the water. She'd used the code Maverick had given her to open the gate and then the front door. For once, since taking finals in college, she was thankful for her fantastic memory. She'd only seen the code once but it was forever imprinted across some brain cell that floated around in her gray matter just waiting for her to access it.

After getting Seth into the house, she'd tied him to one of the massive columns in the entry hall. She'd used the electric cords for the coffeemaker and the toaster to secure him. She glanced at the clock on the wall. She couldn't be sure what time she'd injected him, but she imagined he would be coming around anytime now.

She had both weapons and his cell phone.

Leaning back against the wall, she watched him and considered all that she'd bullied him into telling her. She would bet her life, which ultimately she'd just already done, that he'd never told anyone that horrifying story before.

She closed her eyes and fought the sting of tears when she thought about the child he'd been and how that bastard Leberman had brutalized him. Shackling him in the basement like an animal, restricting his food and water. No wonder he had such excellent night vision, he'd spent his formative years in the dark.

Then, worst of all, sending him to stay with those scumbags who'd done far worse things to him. At fourteen he must have believed that nothing could be worse than what he'd faced so far in his young life, and then he'd been left to discover that his nightmare had only just begun.

They'd tortured him…starved him…dear God, and they had raped him. Anguish roared through her. Leberman had made him a monster. He'd disfigured his body and then he'd killed his soul.

How…how did you survive? Even now tears burned in her eyes as that moment replayed in her mind. *You don't get it. I didn't…*

Seth was right. He hadn't survived. Whoever he had been back then had died. The man that he was now had been born of violence and despicable evil. A beast. Like Leberman said. Her fingers tightened around the weapon. She wanted to kill that bastard with her bare hands and now she had the bait.

She flipped open the cell phone and went through its menu. There were no numbers entered into the speed dial function. She checked the incoming call log and dialed the number from which he'd last received a call. Three rings passed before a very pissed off, male voice answered.

"Where the hell are you? They're on the move."

It was him. A shudder of dread quaked through her. It was *Leberman*.

"Seth's a little tied up right now," she said flatly, almost smiling at her own wit. "Why don't you come and help him out. I think you know where we are." She ended the call and tossed the phone aside. "Bastard," she hissed beneath her breath. She would kill him all right and never feel a moment's remorse.

"That was a mistake."

Seth's voice jerked her attention to him. His eyes burned like a high-octane blue flame. Fury didn't begin to describe what she saw there. She swallowed back the fear that threatened to clog her throat. "Maybe," she allowed, then cocked the weapon in her hand. "I'm of the opinion that he's got this coming to him."

Seth made that noise in his throat that was probably as close to a laugh as he got. "You think you have what it takes to stop him? Others have tried and they've all failed. Just ask your boss, Lucas Camp. He'll tell you."

That he'd tossed Lucas's name into the equation with such glibness made her want to shake the hell out of him. She eased out of her sitting position and moved toward him, settling again near his bound feet so she could read him better. She wanted to see even his subtlest reaction to what she was about to say.

"After all he's done to you, why would you care if I kill Leberman or not?"

He looked straight at her from beneath lids still heavy with the lingering effects of the drug. "Who says I do?"

She shrugged, deciding to go with her gut and not pretty this up in the least. "I don't know. Maybe it's because you haven't killed him yourself in all this time. After all, he did all those cruel things to you and still you let him live." She said the last with as much repugnance as she could muster, then pressed him with a fierce gaze of her own. "Maybe you liked it."

The change evolved instantaneously. The fury she'd noted before morphed into pure, unadulterated rage. But even that savage ferocity didn't hold a candle to the lethal intensity of his voice when he spoke. "Cut me loose now and I'll let you live. Drag this out and you'll end up dead."

She inclined her head and stared at him in amazement. With complete certainty she knew that what had happened between them in that hotel had affected him, maybe not to the extent it had her, but he'd felt something. And yet, he still appeared prepared to kill her. Or maybe the suggestion was his offhanded way of trying to save her.

"Still think I'm worth saving?" he taunted.

She looked him straight in the eye and said what she felt in her heart…in her gut. "Yes. I do. Despite the kind of man your father is—despite everything he did to you—I know there's something good inside you. It's just buried under so much pain and cynicism that I can barely see it."

He made another of those humorless sounds. "You don't know anything about my *father*. He was responsible for the death of an innocent family and caused all of this."

She'd tried hard to keep her emotions in check—to keep an objective prospective—that went out the window. "I know he did everything in his power to turn you into some sort of unfeeling monster. But it didn't work, did it?" She pushed to her feet, circled him slowly. He held very still, not even breathing. When she faced him again, she crouched down and peered into that feral gaze. "You felt something when we were together. I know you did. I felt it, too. So don't try and play dead with me, Seth. I know better."

He pushed forward as far as his bindings would allow

and with heart-gripping sensuality and intimacy whispered, "Just because I fucked you and liked it doesn't mean I won't kill you and like it just as much."

The words were a direct hit to her more fragile emotions. Hurt hurdled through her, and she drew back slightly before she could stop the outward reaction. He smiled, the expression sinister.

"See, Tasha, that's the difference between us. We both have our causes, but I'm prepared to see mine through no matter what it takes. Can you say the same?"

For one long moment she stared into those eyes, knowing with complete certainty that he spoke the truth. He would kill her here and now if given the chance. Whatever it was about him that her instincts urged her to believe in, she damn sure couldn't see it at the moment. No matter the atrocities he'd faced as a child, as a man, he was still a killer.

And it was her job to see that he didn't fulfill his mission.

Long minutes passed in silence. There was more she wanted to say, but it wouldn't matter. The only thing she could do was wait.

He looked away abruptly…appeared to listen intently. The fine hairs on the back of her neck stood on end. Every fiber of her being went on alert as his gaze returned to hers.

"He's here. Cut me loose and I'll protect you."

She gave her head a little shake and rolled her eyes. "I think I'll take my chances on my own."

"Then you'll die."

Ignoring his comment, she stood, tucked his weapon in her jeans at the small of her back, and, at the same time, heard what he'd likely picked up on five seconds earlier. Leberman had come in through the back. The slightest shuffle of a single step touched her auditory senses. Moving away from the dim light of the entry hall and into the darkness of the dining room, she listened intently for more movement.

The kitchen.

A faint scuffling sound.

Moving in the direction, she frowned. What the hell was he doing? Trying to give himself away?

"Turn on the light, Agent North."

She flinched. The haughty sound of his voice grated across her nerve endings.

"Put your weapon down, Leberman," she ordered. Squinting, she could barely make out his silhouette in the darkness. Something was wrong...

"Turn on the light or she dies *now*," he snapped. "You see," he went on in a much calmer voice, "after your call I picked up a little insurance."

She. Tasha's senses charged to a higher state of alert, she eased toward the wall nearest the door leading into the entry hall, where the light switch was most likely located. The fingers of her free hand located and activated the switch. She blinked quickly to adjust to the brightness and then her heart surged into her throat.

Leberman shielded his body with a young girl. Sixteen or seventeen, tops. Her eyes were wide with fear. Judging by the way she was dressed she was probably a prostitute. New at the profession, Tasha immediately determined. Her hair was too shiny, too full of body and life, her skin still looked clear and smooth. Dammit. Where the hell were her parents?

Leberman held a knife, probably from this very kitchen, close to her throat. She cried out as he pressed the sharp stainless steel even harder against her soft flesh.

The swift bloom of bright red tears beneath the shiny blade jerked Tasha from the stunned spell.

"All right," she relented. "Let her go and I'll put down my weapon."

Leberman laughed with the same haughtiness that he'd spoken. "You put down your weapon and I'll let her go. That's the way it works. You see, Agent North, I'm in charge of this game. Not you. And certainly not Lucas Camp."

She now had the distinct feeling that both Leberman and Seth had known from the beginning who she was…it couldn't simply have been since she'd planted the tracking device in his car to give herself away. Leberman exuded the kind of confidence that went with knowledge held over time…not recent, surprising news. He wasn't the least bit surprised. He'd known. She was sure of it. She just didn't know how.

She didn't want to give up her weapon…but those bloody tears slid down the girl's long, slender neck.

"Put it down now!" Leberman commanded.

Slowly Tasha laid her weapon on the closest counter. The thought of dying left a bad taste in her mouth, but at least she'd managed to distract both Leberman and Seth while Victoria and Lucas escaped to safety. That was something.

Then again, she wasn't dead yet. She looked straight at Leberman. "Your turn. Let her go," she said pointedly.

He shook his head. "Not quite yet." He nodded to the counter. "Lay the weapon on the floor and kick it over here."

She had one split second to make the decision.

Tasha reached for her weapon. It was cocked already.

She bent at the knees as if she planned to do as he'd asked.

Instead she fired.

He jerked when the shot hit his right shoulder.

The knife clanged to the floor.

Shrieking, the girl scrambled away from him.

When Tasha would have taken a second shot, one aimed right between his beady eyes, the muzzle of his weapon stared right back at her.

He'd been holding a gun in his left hand. The girl's blouse where he'd held her anchored to him by her waist had covered his hand and the weapon.

Shit.

Tasha straightened to her full height, kept the weapon leveled carefully between his eyes. "I guess we have the proverbial Mexican standoff."

Leberman smiled sardonically. "Well, I do have a bit of leverage, Agent North."

"Really?" She lifted a brow in question. "And what would that be, scumbag?"

"The man standing behind you."

She held perfectly still, allowing the rush of goose bumps over her skin to tell her that Seth was, in fact, right behind her. She'd tied him securely, but somehow he'd managed to free himself. He tugged his weapon from her waistband and she cursed herself.

Curled in the fetal position, the young girl sobbed quietly in the corner. That was the worst atrocity of all, Tasha told herself in the next moment. She was a trained agent. She'd known going into this thing that death was a possibility. But the girl—she was innocent on that score. Tasha's call had dragged her into this. For that she suddenly felt a truckload of remorse.

"You know," Tasha said, deciding she might as well get her dig in while she could, "I just can't figure out why Seth would do your bidding after all you've done to him."

Leberman laughed again, that ugly, evil noise that erupted straight from hell. "Didn't he tell you? I rescued him…saved his life. He owes me everything. Without me…he wouldn't exist at all."

None of what he said made sense. "Saved him from what?" she demanded, unconvinced and allowing him to clearly see her doubt and disgust.

"Why from his negligent parents, of course. They didn't care what happened to him…left him all alone and lost. But payback is always a bitch, isn't it, Seth?" Leberman said the words to Seth but never took his eyes off Tasha. "You see, Agent North, we've both waited for this for a very long time. Final vengeance is close at hand, and you're not going to stop it. Neither is Lucas."

What was he saying? If he wasn't Seth's father, then who was? "I'm afraid you've lost me," she tossed back at him. "Call me dense, but I just don't get it."

Fury streaked across the slight man's face. A ferret, she decided. If not for the gray hair, he'd look just like a weasel-faced ferret. She shook off the thought no doubt spawned by hysteria and focused. She had his attention. He would want her to fully understand before she died. One didn't have to be a psych major to know his type. She had his number already. He only enjoyed the kill if the proper emotional impact was achieved.

"I told his father all those years ago before I killed him what I planned to do." Leberman laughed, his gaze suddenly distant. "You see, I knew watching *her* suffer from the loss of her husband would never be enough. So I waited all these years for her to finally put the past behind her and fall in love again before I staged the grand finale. But I told her beloved husband every detail fifteen years ago. He died with those horrible images in his head. God, it felt so good. It was almost enough…but not quite."

James Colby. He had to be talking about James Colby. Lucas had said that they suspected Leberman had killed Colby fifteen years ago. But what did that have to do with Seth?

"My God," she murmured as the realization rammed into her brain like a bull charging toward a taunting matador. Seth was…James Colby Jr. He was Victoria's son. Her gaze focused back on Leberman and a new kind of rage went through her. "You son of a bitch, you stole him away from his parents and then you did…" All those despicable things to him.

"I didn't have to steal him," Leberman lashed out, his control slipping marginally. "They left him all alone in those woods. He would have died from exposure or drowned in the lake if I hadn't rescued him. *I saved him.*"

That's why he'd taken her to the woods…that's why he kept coming back to this place. It had once been his home. A dozen sensations whirled inside Tasha all at once. She so wanted to face Seth and make him believe the truth that she knew. But she couldn't risk turning her back on Leberman.

"You're a liar, Leberman," she said flatly. "Maybe you've got Seth fooled, but I know the truth. You stole him from the people who loved him. Victoria still grieves for the son she lost…the one you *stole.*"

"No! She left him, just like his father did. And now, the son she threw away will have his vengeance, as well as mine. He owes me that. I kept him alive…made him what he is. He will finish this. Kill her now!" he shouted at the man behind her.

She might be headed to hell but she was taking Leberman with her. Her finger tightened around the trigger.

The gun blast echoed in the room.

Chapter 35

Lucas stared out over the dark water as it rushed toward the shore. The moon and blanket of stars overhead cast down an ethereal glow which only made the water look more menacing. The isolation suddenly pressed down on him…made him feel small and completely inadequate in the scheme of things.

He had chosen this location precisely because of its isolation. Well north of Chicago, the small waterfront property was owned by the doctor who'd allowed Lucas to use his clinic for his covert meetings with Victoria's people. But not even the good doctor knew that Victoria and Lucas were here now. He'd long ago given Lucas a standing invitation as well as a key to the property.

Complete secrecy was essential.

He hated like hell to think that there was a leak of some sort or, worse yet, a mole in either his or Victoria's agency. But there were far too many factors weighing in at the moment to deny that possibility.

Leberman was all too aware of Victoria's every move, as well as Lucas's.

As soon as the bastard was taken care of, looking for that inadvertent leak or, God forbid, mole would be Lucas's next order of business.

No, that wasn't right.

His next order of business had to be the assassin.

He had already briefed their security detail. Logan, Ferrelli, Callahan and Drake already knew that the assassin was Victoria's son. No one had questioned the announcement, they'd merely nodded gravely. Ian and Simon knew, as well, both were keeping watch on things at the Colby Agency.

Maverick and Ramon were still searching for North.

Lucas hoped like hell that little girl kept herself alive. For the first time in his career, he wasn't quite sure he could live with the weight of her death on his shoulders.

And then there was Victoria. How was he supposed to tell her the truth? She had finally accepted the past for what it was—the past. She was ready to move on, to love him. Now that very past threatened not only that love, but also their very lives. How could fate be so cruel? How was he supposed to tell her that her own son wanted her dead?

That he was a brutal, relentless assassin who cared nothing for human life.

Lucas remembered the small boy…had kicked himself over and over for not recognizing him as a man. He'd felt there was something familiar about him, but hadn't been able to nail down just what it was.

Now he knew.

And he had to figure out some way to tell Victoria.

More important, however, he had to keep her safe. Her son wanted her dead, would likely stop at nothing to see his mission to fruition.

Lucas had recanted his previous order and had issued a new one, that his and Victoria's people were to maintain visual contact but not to engage the assassin unless absolutely necessary if they located him. As much as he wanted to stop him, he wanted him alive. He couldn't imagine having to tell Victoria that one of his people had killed her son.

He shuddered at the thought…told himself it was the cool breeze wafting in off the water, but he knew better. The quake he'd felt was one of uncertainty…of fear. Fear for the woman he loved. Fear of losing her.

There was no way to even guess how this would end.

As much as he loved Victoria and wanted to ensure her safety, he knew with complete certainty that she would not survive losing her son a second time.

For one fleeting moment the possibility that he could conceal that truth from her flashed through his mind. If keeping her safe meant killing her son, was there any real reason to tell her the truth? What would it accomplish, other than to bring her more pain?

"Lucas."

The sound of her voice tugged him from his troubling thoughts, and one look into those dark, caring eyes gave him the answer he sought. He would tell her because he couldn't lie to Victoria. There had never been a lie between them; he wouldn't start now.

"Are you coming inside?" she ventured hesitantly.

She looked so lovely with the gentle breeze lifting those loose tendrils of hair around her throat. He longed to see it down again. Longed to touch her…to kiss her. This was the first time he'd seen her dressed so casually. Petal-soft, pale yellow slacks and matching sweater and low-heeled slip-on shoes made her look like a fragile flower.

This was the Victoria he had yearned to know for so

very long. The vulnerable, soft side that lacked the tough professional veneer she wore at the office.

Yet he loved both personas more than life itself.

"The bread is warm and the wine has had plenty of time to breathe. Everything's ready."

She'd insisted on cooking, swore it would take her mind off things. He'd offered to help, but she'd wanted to do it alone. She'd been right. She looked more relaxed than he'd seen her in months. Since before those horrifying hours on that island when Leberman had been close on that last occasion. The total change, considering all that had happened the past few days, abruptly unsettled him. Had she resigned herself to some fate she'd decided inescapable? Had the presumption that her son had suffered a violent death pushed her over some unseen precipice? Should he tell her right now that her son was alive?

If only he knew the right words to say....

"I won't let you down, Victoria," he felt compelled to say as he reached for her, unable to restrain any longer the need to touch her. "I swear to you that I won't let him harm you in any way."

The smile that spread across her lips warmed his heart despite his seemingly overwhelming concerns. "I'm not afraid, Lucas," she said quietly, patiently. "I'm not resigned, either, if that's what you're thinking. I have complete faith in your people as well as my own. Leberman won't win." She took his hands in hers. "What I am at this moment, more than anything else, is determined." She let that sink in for a moment, then continued, "Determined to get on with my life. To put the past firmly behind me. I can't live with it anymore." She looked deeply into his eyes, the hurt there evolving into need. "Now, come inside, Lucas. We're going to eat and then we're going to make love."

"But—" he began, his body already racing full steam ahead on the very course she'd drawn in his active imagination.

She shook her head, cutting him off. "No buts. Tonight nothing else in this world matters except us."

Victoria brimmed with nervous anticipation, so much so she'd scarcely eaten the meal she'd gone to so much trouble to prepare. When Lucas had offered to make coffee, she hadn't been sure she would be able to contain herself. Finally she'd simply had to spell it out for him.

"We'll have coffee later," she'd said simply, then she'd taken him by the hand and led him to the cabin's spacious bedroom.

Now he stood waiting for her to make the first move as she'd known he would. Lucas had spent half a lifetime being patient…waiting for her to come to terms with the tragedies fate had dropped like bombs into her life.

But that was all behind her. She would not look back. Lucas had highly skilled people who would take care of Leberman and his hired killer. Her own people would see to the agency. This—here and now—was going to be their time. She didn't want anything else to get in the way of this precious moment. Here they were safe.

She stepped out of her shoes and scooted them aside. Next she removed her sweater. She loved the feel of it, so soft and warm. She'd known when she packed it that she wanted to be wearing it at this moment. The pastel-yellow color looked good against her skin, and the fit was flattering.

For just one moment as the exquisite fabric drifted to the floor, she suffered a pang of panic. What if her body failed to please Lucas? She was not so young anymore. Almost fifty.

She forced the thought away. She'd been down that road, had considered what he might think, and she knew there was only one way to find out. Youthful beauty only went skin-deep. What she and Lucas shared went far deeper than that.

Far, far deeper.

She reached behind her and unzipped her slacks, then slid them down and off in one, smooth motion. She stepped forward, out of the confines of the garment puddled around her ankles.

His cane propped against the night table, Lucas watched her intently, his breathing visibly more ragged. Was he half as worried about pleasing her as she was about pleasing him? She smiled, realizing that he likely was. Even men suffered that plight…to some degree.

As she tugged at the pins restraining her hair, he shouldered out of his jacket. Anticipation soared through her. He wasn't going to keep her waiting.

She watched his capable movements as he tossed the jacket into the nearby chair. While he removed his tie she freed the length of her hair, allowing it to fall down and sway around her shoulders, the feel of it against her bare skin making her shiver. She blinked, nearly certain she'd seen him shiver, as well. Could he have waited for this…allowed himself no other as she had? The mere idea made her tremble again.

Moving closer to him, she watched as he slowly released one button after the other along the front of his shirt. She moved more quickly now, wanting—needing—to be close enough to touch him. The final button was scarcely freed before she boldly pushed the starched cotton from his broad shoulders. Her heart pounded hard at the sight of his well-defined chest. A twinge of trepidation plagued her at the thought that her body was not nearly so nicely toned.

"You're beautiful," he whispered, as if reading her mind.

She took a deep breath and met that hungry gray gaze. Though she'd carefully selected delicate, feminine undergarments, she still felt like an old woman dressed in pastel-yellow designer lace and satin.

"So are you," she whispered back, unable to resist touching him a moment longer. Her palms smoothed over the masculine contours, tingled at the raspy feel of his chest hair. She traced every line and ridge, reveled in the powerful muscles that felt so hard and smooth. He had such an amazing torso. She wanted to see more.

She reached for his belt and he stayed her hands. "There are some things that you might not find so appealing," he reminded gently.

Her heart thumped hard. The prosthesis. All those years ago as a prisoner of war, he'd saved her husband's life, but he'd lost his right leg from the knee down while doing so. She'd forgotten all about that. Lucas Camp was the kind of man who exuded power and strength, obliterating any doubt in his physical prowess. She'd completely forgotten the matter of his prosthesis.

She looked up into his eyes and said the words she knew he needed to hear. "I love you, Lucas. I can't imagine a man more appealing in every way."

He removed his shoes, then unfastened his belt and his trousers. He sat down on the side of the bed and removed the trousers as well as the prosthesis. He sat there a few moments, wearing nothing but his boxers, before meeting her eyes.

"You sure about that?" he asked, looking more vulnerable than she could ever have anticipated. Lucas Camp

was not a man one associated with any sort of vulnerability.

She sat down beside him and took his hand, his unguarded fragility leveling the playing ground more than
he could possibly know. "Positive."

He touched her hair, his expression reverent. "I've
wanted to touch you this way for so very long."

Her pulse leaped at his words. "I know. I'm sorry I've
kept you waiting."

His fingers trailed down her back and she turned to
give him better access to the closure of her bra. He released the hooks and she shed the bra without hesitation,
allowing him to see her slightly less-than-firm breasts.

His deep, satisfied sigh made her head spin just a little.
"If you were any more beautiful I'm not sure my heart
could take it." Moving slowly, giving her ample time to
stop him, he reached up and cupped one breast.

A surge of longing made her gasp. The feel of his palm
against her nipple, his strong fingers around her made her
inner muscles quake with renewed anticipation. No one
had touched her like this in more than fifteen years. How
she had missed knowing a man this way.

She reached for him, taking her time, exploring his
body more fully, careful of the bandages, while he acquainted himself with hers. He leaned closer and kissed
her, his mouth hungry, his desperation undeniable. She
drew away from him, scooted back onto the bed and lay
down in invitation.

He slid off his boxers, revealing well-formed buttocks
and muscled thighs. He eased down next to her and gently tugged her panties down her legs and off. He tossed
the lacy scrap of fabric across the bed.

When he'd stretched out beside her once more she felt
complete just feeling his warm body along the length of

hers. "It feels so good just lying next to you," she admitted.

He played with her hair, allowing it to slip through his fingers and feather down against her skin. "You truly are beautiful, Victoria," he told her. He caressed her cheek. "Right now, before we take the next step, I want you to know that I love you and I will never allow anything to hurt you again. No matter what it takes."

His eyes were far too solemn…that worried her. "Lucas, is something wrong?" Was he having second thoughts? Had he learned news that he hesitated to share with her?

He shook his head. "Everything is perfect." With that he kissed her. Kissed her softly at first. His firm lips moving skillfully over hers, the taste of wine making her want to drink him in. His hand moved down her abdomen, and her entire body quivered with need. He tangled his fingers in the curls between her thighs and her breath caught harshly.

"It's been a long time," he whispered between kisses. "We need to take this slowly."

His touch was as skilled as his kisses. His fingers magical. He knew just how to touch her…how to draw out the desire. And then his mouth moved downward until those masterful lips had latched on to her breast.

Her fingers plunged into his silky hair, urging him on as her body built toward an almost forgotten crescendo. Every draw of his mouth, every dip of his fingers and she edged closer and closer to release. The heel of his hand rubbed firmly against her clitoris, making her writhe with longing. How much longer could she stand this building tension? It coiled harder, deeper until…her senses erupted. Her feminine muscles throbbed with climax… her whole body shuddered with it.

He parted her thighs and nestled himself there. The feel of his hardened length made her whimper his name. Her arms went around his waist as he slowly, carefully nudged inside. They both cried out as he sank deeply inside her. And for one long beat neither of them moved. They could only lie there, gasping for breath, caught in the sweet, sensual trap of pure desire.

He started to rock, gently at first, allowing her body to adjust. Eventually the pace and depth increased and then all else was forgotten.

He took her back to that place of sensual bliss before he plunged over the edge himself.

But Lucas Camp had never been a selfish man. He pleasured her well before taking his own and that only made her love him more.

When they lay side by side, still panting, and utterly sated, she hugged him tight to her side. "Lucas," she whispered.

"Hmmm," he murmured, his voice still rough with desire.

"I've made a decision."

"That we should have an encore?" he teased, then kissed her forehead.

"Well, that, too," she agreed. "But no, I was just thinking. I believe it's time you made an honest woman out of me."

Chapter 36

The gun dangled from his fingers as Leberman stared down at the hole in his chest. Blood spread quickly across the front of his shirt, like the center of an ever-expanding bull's-eye.

He lifted that beady gaze and stared at the man who'd shot him. "Why?" The single word came out more a hiss of disbelief than pain.

Seth took aim again. "I told you if you came near me again I'd kill you."

"You swore you would fulfill this promise to me. You owe it to me," Leberman snarled with more strength than a man already dead should possess.

Seth made that sound that wasn't quite a laugh. "You're right. I do owe it to you and I won't fail to deliver."

"I was supposed...to see it...for myself," Leberman shouted the words between frantic gasps for breath.

"Use your imagination." The next shot split Leberman's skull right between the eyes. Blood and brain matter sprayed across the wall behind him like a bad

Impressionist painting. He crumpled to the floor, and the girl he'd kidnapped screamed hysterically.

Tasha looked from Leberman's body to Seth. He stood in the doorway, his weapon still leveled, ready to fire, his face a blank canvas, devoid of any emotion whatsoever.

He had shoved her to the floor and fired a fatal shot in Leberman's direction before she could depress her own trigger. As she stared at the aftermath, she felt frozen by emotion. Not quite fear...not quite relief and confusion. Something in between.

Before she could gather her wits, Seth had snatched her weapon from her hand and stalked over to the girl cowering in the corner. She shook uncontrollably as he jerked her to her feet and pulled her arms away from her face. He surveyed her wound, which, to the best Tasha could tell, was superficial.

He pushed the girl toward the back door. "Get out."

The girl didn't hesitate, nor did she look back.

Tasha dove for the gun Leberman had dropped a split second before Seth's attention swung back to her.

She grabbed the weapon and lunged to her feet, shoving the barrel into Seth's face when he took a step in her direction. "Stop right there," she ordered.

He tucked the weapon he'd taken from her into the waistband of his jeans. As he did so she noticed the blood streaking his hands. She blinked, uncertain where it had come from. Then she knew. He'd ripped open his flesh while freeing himself.

Maybe she tied a better knot that she'd realized.

"Give me the weapons," she demanded. She tried to calm her racing heart and her whirling thoughts, but she kept seeing Leberman's head explode and wondering what had made Seth decide to kill him. And the girl...? He'd looked to see that she wasn't hurt that badly before he sent her scurrying away. Where had this sudden burst of compassion come from? It was like that first day when he'd taken her home and told her to warn her roommate that she'd better not hurt her again. How could this killer care what happened to anyone?

But somehow he did. On some level, anyway.

"Hand over the weapons," she repeated, her aim steady.

He looked at her with that impassive face and those ice-cold eyes. "You decide I wasn't worth saving after all."

If he'd uttered the words with any emotion whatsoever she might have felt a pang of regret. "I just don't want to end up dead like your friend over there." She jerked her head in Leberman's direction. "Why did you do that?" She had to know. The analytical part of her screamed for answers.

"Why I didn't let him kill you or why I killed him?" he asked, seemingly oblivious to the inhumanity of his own words.

"Why you...both," she demanded, annoyed at her inability to keep perspective here.

He glanced at the weapon in her hand then settled that arctic gaze on hers. "I warned him. He just kept coming back."

She swallowed, moistened her lips. "And what about me? Why am I still breathing?" As if to emphasize her words, a little soblike mewl escaped her lungs. She steeled herself, tightened her grip on her weapon. She might have to kill him yet. He didn't need to know how his actions had affected her.

But God, he was Victoria Colby's son.

Did Lucas know by now? Had the DNA test told him that?

And could she...could she actually do *it* if necessary?

He didn't answer her question, just turned his back on her. The move startled her from her worrisome quandary.

"Where are you going?" she demanded, altering the aim of her weapon to keep a bead on him.

He hesitated at the door just long enough to glance back at her. "I have a job to finish."

She followed him onto the rear deck of the house. "Wait," she shouted. "He's dead. What does it matter now? Don't you understand what this all means? Victoria Colby is your mother."

Even in the moonlight she could plainly see his savage glare when he spun around to face her. "She's nothing to me," he ground out. "I hate her more than I hated Leberman."

She had to stop him—distract him—and she wasn't sure, knowing what she knew, that shooting him was actually an option. "Because you think she abandoned you," she called out after him, "left you to be rescued by the likes of Leberman. She loved you, Seth. He stole you away from her. This isn't her fault. They both loved you."

He turned around again but this time instead of just glowering at her he strode straight toward her. The murderous look on his face had her backing toward the house. He pinned her to the wall with his free hand. The light from inside the house cut across his face highlighting the fury contorting his features.

"If she loved me so damned much then why didn't she stop him?"

And there it was…the tiniest, almost imperceptible crack in his impervious armor. The little boy who'd been praying for a savior all these years peeked out.

"Because she couldn't find you," Tasha said softly. "She tried…but Leberman kept you hidden from her."

"I was right here," Seth snarled. "Right here in Chicago all that time. She didn't want me. Neither of them did. He told me that every day of my life. Every time he punished me, he reminded me that I would be nothing without him. So you tell me, Tasha, why the hell didn't she stop him?"

Pain flickered in his eyes for just one second before he banished it, but he couldn't erase the memory of what she'd seen. The emotion had been so achingly profound that her lips trembled with the empathy welling in her chest.

"You can't believe anything Leberman told you," she urged. "He did this to you to get back at the Colbys. He—"

"Just shut up!" Seth roared. "I know what I lived through. What *she* let me live through. And now she's going to pay for that. I've waited a long time to have her look me in the eye and know." A muscle jumped in his tightly clenched jaw as he struggled to restrain the emotions she sensed were raging inside him. "I want her to know what he did to me and then I want to watch her die."

Tasha blinked back the tears that brimmed behind her lashes and glared right back at him. A part of her wanted desperately to hold him and make him see that it would be all right now, but part of her just wanted to kick the shit out of him and tell him what a jerk he was. "Then I guess you'd better go ahead and kill me now because I'm not going to let you do this." She was betting that he wouldn't kill her. That he couldn't. She hoped like hell her instincts were on the money this time.

He pressed the muzzle of his weapon beneath her chin. She tensed. "Do you really want to die? Is Lucas paying you enough to die for him?"

"This isn't about Lucas," she said, her voice shaking

despite her best efforts to keep it steady. "This is about you and your mother."

The weapon bored painfully into the soft flesh. She winced. "I don't have a mother," he said softly, lethally. "I have a target."

The sound of sirens in the distance snagged his attention. He swore. The girl had probably made it to the closest neighbor, which was quite a distance, and called the cops. A smidgen of Tasha's tension eddied away.

He snatched Leberman's weapon from her hand and tossed it into the grass. "I guess you got yourself another reprieve. Just remember that you might not be so lucky next time." He released her and bounded across the deck and down the steps.

"You're not leaving me here to straighten out your mess," she yelled at his back as he headed toward the woods. She followed. If she planned to keep him in sight, she didn't have time to search for the weapon he'd tossed.

As hard as it was she managed to stay within a few meters of him. Thank God she'd kept in shape. At one point he tried to lose her, but she didn't take the bait. She just kept dogging his steps. When they reached the clearing where he'd originally brought her, to kill her she imagined, he stopped abruptly and turned around.

"Why are you following me?"

She took a moment to catch her breath. "Because I have to stop you."

He charged up to her, didn't even bother to draw his weapon from his shoulder holster. But then, he was a lot bigger than her. She held her ground, refused to let him see her uneasiness.

"That's not going to happen. Don't try to pretend you're not afraid of me," he murmured. "I know you are."

"I've had sufficient training to give you a run for your

money if you want to go hand-to-hand," she shot right back, hoping like hell she wouldn't have to back that up.

He laughed softly. "I can see your pulse fluttering. You're definitely scared."

She touched her throat, had forgotten how well he could see in the dark. She parked her hands on her hips. "How do you know it's fear?" She couldn't be sure of the exact timing of Lucas's and Victoria's departure. Keeping him away from Victoria's private residence for as long as possible was essential. Not to mention it would keep him alive. The last word she'd heard, Lucas's men had been ordered to take him out.

A beat of silence passed. Her tension escalated to an unbearable level in that one moment.

"Your cover is blown, Agent North," he taunted. "No need to keep up the pretense. You don't have to pretend to be attracted to me any longer."

"Who says I was pretending?" Her heart was racing all over again, only this time it had nothing to do with having to run like hell to keep up with him. It was hard to believe that she'd just watched him kill a man—low-life bastard though he was—and still he could make her respond to him this way.

She couldn't see his face clearly, but she knew she'd given him pause. She could sense his hesitation…his need to pursue the issue. But he never catered to his own needs.

"Stay away from me," he growled. "If you know what's good for you, stay away from me."

She didn't hesitate. When he walked away this time, she followed him again. How else was she supposed to get out of here, anyway?

When they reached his SUV, he glared at her once more before climbing inside. Not about to back off now, she glared right back and climbed in herself.

She stared at the vacant house while he shoved the keys into the ignition.

"Last chance," he said quietly. "Get out while you still can."

She looked at the digital clock on his dash— 11:00 p.m. Surely Lucas and Victoria were gone by now. She could very well get out...she'd done the only thing necessary to fulfill her mission. She'd kept him out of the way while they escaped. Though she hadn't been able to lead Lucas to...

Leberman was dead.

The realization penetrated the confusing layers of emotion that had wrapped around her good sense. He was dead. She had to get word to Lucas. That bastard was dead...would never bother them again.

But then there was Seth. He was hell-bent on killing Victoria for her part in what happened to him. A part of Tasha understood what he felt...but she knew the truth. How could she make him see that truth? What could she do to ensure a safe conclusion to this assignment?

Victoria's son was alive.

She should have the opportunity to know him...to make everything right.

But if he had his way that would never happen.

His mother would die.

Somehow she had to keep that from happening.

Since she made no move to get out, he started the vehicle and backed out into the street.

He drove in silence until he pulled into the parking lot of a gas station not unlike the one Martin had lured her to. That felt like a lifetime ago. Would he want her back, knowing she'd screwed up so badly here? Then again, Lucas had told her she had a job. She pushed away the thoughts. All she could think about right now was the moment.

The gas station was closed, ruling out the possibility of a fueling stop, since the pumps were the old-fashioned kind that didn't accept credit cards.

"Why are we stopping here?"

He didn't answer. He simply got out and walked around to her door. He opened it and barked an order. "Get out."

With a roll of her eyes and a huff of disgust, she obeyed. Somebody needed to teach this guy some manners. He opened the door to the men's room and ushered her inside.

Even in the dark she imagined the worst about the place. The smell wasn't as bad as she'd expected, but bleach would camouflage most anything and the bleach smell was damn strong. He flipped on the light and she was relieved to see that the bathroom was actually halfway clean, which was so not what she needed to worry about right now.

When he unzipped his jeans she cursed under her breath and gave him her back. He couldn't have taken a leak in the woods where it was dark? She huffed in frustration. Maybe not...the police had been headed their way.

He ignored her sounds of protest, simply did his business. She tried to block the sound of him taking a piss, but it just didn't work.

She knew this wasn't right. Why hadn't he just disposed of her? Gotten her out of his way? He knew her intentions and yet he allowed her to live. No matter how he denied it, there was some kind of weird connection between them, and it wasn't just the sex. She wished she could understand it. The toilet flushed and the water in the basin came on. She turned around and watched as he washed the blood from his wrists and hands. The cuts her bindings had made were nasty, but he didn't even flinch. She wondered if he'd learned to ignore the pain when Leberman punished him. Had he ignored all the other atrocities he'd suffered in much the same way?

She blocked the vivid mental images the words echoing inside her head evoked. Just the thought of all that he'd suffered made her insides quake with emotion. Victoria would be devastated when she learned the truth. No matter how this ended, both of them would suffer. But there could be light at the end of the tunnel...if he'd only listen to her, open up fully to her. Trust her.

He tossed the paper towel he'd used to dry his hands into the trash, then gestured to the toilet. "It might be a while before we see another one."

"No, thanks."

She studied his eyes, his face. How could she get through to him? Could anything touch him at this point?

He reached for the door but she snagged his hand, her pulse leaping at the contact. "Does it hurt?" She turned his hand over, inspecting the damage he'd done freeing himself. "Must have hurt like hell," she murmured. If he hadn't gotten free, Leberman might have killed her before she could kill him.

He pulled his hand away. "Don't start anything you're not prepared to finish."

Did her touch have that effect on him? She definitely felt something when he touched her.... What difference did it make? She would never be able to get through to him. She definitely wasn't qualified to analyze this guy. She had to stop thinking that way.

She turned her back on him and reached for the door herself. There was nothing she could say to that remark. She wasn't prepared to go there again...didn't trust herself to hold on to any semblance of perspective and go there.

"I guess reality dampened your case of the hots for me," he accused. She didn't miss the edge in his voice. She'd hurt him somehow by turning away.

She did an immediate about-face. "Do you want to know the truth? Do you think you can handle the truth?" she challenged.

Anger slashed across his face, but he tamped it down. "Don't play with me, Tasha."

She couldn't stop the shiver that trembled through her at the sound of her name on his lips. "The truth is that hearing about your past made me sad for the little boy you used to be. Made me wish I could do something to change it. But I can't. Nothing I could say or do is going to change how twisted you are. But none of that has anything to do with how I feel about the man standing in front of me."

She watched that wall go up as he went on guard.

"I hate what you do," she told him bluntly. "You're a cold-blooded killer. But there's still something decent inside you, and that part cries out to me. I can feel it." She peered into those ice-cold eyes. "I can almost touch it. Don't bother denying it, I know it's there…just waiting to break free."

He forked the fingers of his left hand into her hair and pulled her close. "The only thing crying out for you is right here." He pressed her hand against his crotch. "Can you handle that truth?"

She lifted her chin in defiance of his challenge. He needed the contact. Had just killed his long-term care-taker. He needed her even if he would never admit it. "I can handle it, but we do it my way this time." As much as she knew she shouldn't let this happen, it would delay his discovery that Victoria was now out of his reach. It would… help him forget.

He shrugged. "As long as your way is right now." His mouth claimed hers. He kissed her so hard it hurt.

She pushed him away and shook her head. "Not like that." She tiptoed and kissed him softly. "Like this." She kissed him again and again, feather-soft kisses. He resisted at first, hating the very idea of doing things her way. But then he relented, gave himself up to the temptation she offered.

Forcing all else from her mind, she put everything she had into kissing him. She wanted him to know how it felt to really be kissed, sweetly, passionately...tenderly.

He responded in kind, gentling the pressure of his lips, moving more slowly, mimicking her moves. His hands moved under her blouse...found her breasts and squeezed hard. She drew back and murmured, "Not so rough."

He tensed briefly, then lightened his touch. She let him hear how much his touching her that way pleased her. He released the buttons of her blouse quickly, fumbling once or twice, and then he laved her bare breasts with his mouth. She closed her eyes and groaned with the pleasure of it. He sucked urgently, but not to the point of pain as he had before. He dropped to his knees and unfastened her jeans and dragged them downward, along with her panties. She toed off her shoes and kicked free of the garments he'd peeled down to her ankles.

He tongued her navel, then lapped her skin. Slowly, surely driving her out of her mind and making a path to her sex, spreading her legs until his mouth was centered where he could thrust his tongue inside. Every thrust grew stronger, more impatient as her legs quivered beneath her. She plunged her fingers into his hair and urged on his ministrations.

Her whole body verged on climax. She couldn't stop

panting…couldn't catch her breath… Then he stopped. Sat back on his heels and just looked at her.

She made a desperate sound. "You can't stop now," she pleaded. She closed her eyes. Damn, she was so close. Her heart pounded even harder in protest.

He dragged her hand to where she was burning up with slick heat for him. "Finish it. I want to watch you come."

She laughed, a breathless sound. "I…need you to—"

"Finish it," he ordered, his eyes aglow with blue heat.

She flattened her spine against the cool metal of the door and groaned. She was so close…and he was watching her so intently. A ghost of a smile tipped one corner of his mouth, and victory claimed his expression. "Can't do it, huh?"

He thought he'd won…had turned the tide.

No way.

She touched herself and gasped at the sensitivity. He had her so close that any contact would likely set her off. Oh, yes, she could do this. She squeezed her eyes shut and slid her fingers into the heated flesh…lost herself to the rhythm. Her free hand fisted in the cotton of her blouse as she strained to reach that elusive pinnacle he'd brought her to the very crest of. And then she flew over the edge. Her body stiffened then quivered as wave after wave of sensation washed over her.

When the last of the release had shuddered through her, her eyes opened to find him still watching.

She sighed and shook her head. "You bastard, now you're going to pay."

He pushed upward to his full height, going for intimidation, but she was way past being intimidated.

She unbuttoned his shirt, revealed his scarred chest and relished the feel of his warm flesh beneath her palms.

"Sit down," she ordered. She pushed him back toward the toilet.

He sat without much persuasion, his curiosity piqued.

She straddled his lap and pressed herself intimately to him. The bulge in his jeans told her he was doing a little suffering of his own.

Carefully tracing every line and mark on his flesh, she kissed him repeatedly. His mouth, his eyes, his chiseled jaw. Too many places to remember, all the while she rocked against his hardened sex. Finally, when he'd had all he could take, he drew her back to look him in the eyes.

"This isn't enough," he said breathlessly.

"It'll have to be enough," she threatened. "Or maybe you want to finish it yourself."

Those blue eyes closed as she pressed against him yet again. "No," he growled, the sound strangled. He reached beneath her and unfastened his jeans, pulled his throbbing penis from its confines. "I need…" He lost his voice… groaned as she lightly rubbed herself against his tip.

"You need what?"

"You," he confessed in desperation.

She smiled. "That's all I wanted to hear."

That hot, hard flesh touched her, and a ripple of pleasure went through her. She lifted her hips slightly, while he positioned himself. She let her weight down just a fraction, bringing him inside an inch or two. She moaned with the exquisite feel of him, but she held on to control, resisting the urge to sink down fully onto that incredibly hot length.

He arched upward but she reacted too quickly, not allowing him additional penetration. A ragged breath hissed from between his clenched teeth.

She kept up the game a while longer, easing down an inch, then lifting until she couldn't stand it any longer…

until he visibly shook with need. Then she plunged downward, sheathing him fully inside her. His startled gasp
almost sent her over the edge again.

She kissed him…softly, as she set a slow, steady pace
of rising and falling…of squeezing and tugging. When
he came, his whole body jerked with the force of it and he
cried out her name. She followed him over that edge, her
climax so powerful her chest ached with the gravity of it.

He held her for a long while after that, the feel of his
heart beating bringing a new rush of tears to her eyes.

Somehow she knew that this moment was a first for
him. The way he held her…awkwardly almost. He didn't
know how to do this…how to relate on this level.

It would be morning soon, and then he'd know that
Victoria and Lucas were gone.

That moment was one she had no idea how to control.

She just hoped they all survived it.

Chapter 37

Tasha watched the sun rise from the darkness of the SUV. Seth had parked in a position where he could watch Victoria Colby's private residence from the neighboring residential area. A few more minutes, an hour tops, and he would realize that something was wrong. How fitting that it was Halloween. A holiday celebrating the dead. A group they would both likely join before the day was up.

She glanced at his profile now. A fresh wave of emotion flooded her. Each time she thought of what he'd experienced as a child she wanted to weep.

Lucas had shown her that grainy photograph in the beginning, had estimated his age at thirty, but that was wrong. Seth, James Colby Jr., was a mere twenty-five years old. But he looked several years older. The cruelty Leberman had dealt him was engrained in his very flesh. The scars, the memories he carried of each one, the damage to his state of mind were unfathomable. There were ways, she knew, to deal with that kind of damage, but it would be a long, drawn-out process. Leberman had likely used a form of intensive brainwashing. He'd instilled a certainty in Seth that his parents didn't love or want him. That they were evil. The little boy had forgotten any memories he'd made with his family; those memories had been replaced with sheer hatred and terror. He'd been punished every day of his life for his parents' perceived sins.

Was it possible to overcome such abuse? Years and years of physical and mental torture that accumulated like the dust on an air filter, eventually, if unchecked, clogging the system, shutting it down. She now understood why he had killed Leberman. Though the man had held immense power over him as a child and even to some extent as he became a man, Seth reached a point where Leberman no longer controlled him. The two men had simply shared a common goal—the destruction of the Colbys. That common goal had dragged out the relationship when it would have otherwise ended.

If the house at Oak Park was, as she suspected, the one Leberman had used to hold him hostage as a child, the memories it evoked in Seth might have pushed him closer to the edge. Might have given him the necessary determination to end Leberman's control once and for all.

The part she couldn't begin to comprehend was how to awaken those old memories of his seven years with his family before Leberman. If she could just reach that place somehow. Make him see how much they'd loved him, maybe—just maybe—some emotion would surface and strike a chord of recognition…alter his course.

Every bit of it was nothing but speculation. She was not a psychiatrist just a psychology major. She understood to a degree the workings of the human psyche, but there was a lot more involved than her minimal understanding could encompass. What she did know with complete certainty was that she had to find a way to let Lucas know that Leberman was dead. To make sure he knew who Seth really was.

The police. She suddenly remembered the sirens at the lake house. They would have found Leberman's body. Lucas would know by now, she felt certain.

She could only imagine how this turn of events would affect Victoria Colby. When she learned how Leberman had treated her child and how very close he had been—literally hidden in plain sight—it would devastate her. But she had to know.

The past was here…right in front of her.

"Something's wrong."

The sound of his deep voice startled her back to attention. Tasha folded her arms over her chest to hide her trembling fingers.

"What do you mean? It's still early." Only 5:00 a.m. But he'd likely watched Victoria long enough to know her routine. He would spot an inconsistency in a heartbeat.

"She's usually up by now." He started the engine. "I'm going to take a closer look."

The guards at the gate didn't arrive until 6:00…that could only mean that he had the access code to the small supposedly secure community.

"How will we get in?" she ventured.

"The same way you got into the lake house," he answered, tossing a look that said "don't yank my chain" at her.

She nodded. "Right." She might as well chill out and follow his lead.

Seth's instincts were humming. Tasha knew something. He could feel it.

He drove to the gate, braking long enough to enter the

access code. The gate opened and he drove into the small *secure* community Victoria Colby called home.

He stole another covert glance at Tasha. She'd been strangely quiet all morning. Nothing at all like the sassy girl he'd met that first night, but then, that had been an act. Just as, he felt certain, was her physical responses to him. Though some of her reactions couldn't be faked, the tenderness she displayed…the compassion, that was likely part of her job. She wanted him to believe she'd fallen for him. But he knew better.

No one would want him. He was nothing.

Less than nothing.

And that didn't matter…all that mattered was accomplishing his goal.

His jaw hardened instantly at the memory of Leberman aiming that gun at her. Had the bastard really believed that he would allow him to continue to interfere with his plans? Seth would follow through with the commitment he'd made, but doing so was no longer for Leberman. It was for him. He *wanted* to watch Victoria die. Had waited for years to experience that climatic moment.

Leberman had told him over and over how his parents hadn't wanted him. He'd only been in the way. They had only cared about the Colby Agency and he had been left to fend for himself. The memories twisted in his gut, burned in his brain. He'd been alone and helpless… vulnerable. But no one had given a damn. All that he had suffered had been because she had allowed it. She didn't deserve to live.

Leberman hadn't deserved to live either. He had punished him one time too many. He would never touch him again. Would never gloat about how he'd created him… saved him. Seth owed him nothing. He only owed himself. He felt no guilt, no regret, no nothing for what he'd done.

Leberman had trained him too well.

Seth blocked the thoughts from his mind. Focus and absolute control were essential to the success of his mission. Lucas would want him dead…would be guarding Victoria closely. But that wouldn't change the outcome.

Victoria Colby would die.

And so would anyone else who got in the way.

His gut clenched when his gaze shifted to Tasha for one fleeting second. She was not important, he reminded that part of him that hesitated. The fact that she had brought him to his knees, in a manner of speaking, last night in that rest room, made no difference this morning. It was true that sex had never affected him that way and that no woman had ever reached so deep inside him. But, ultimately, it meant nothing. He'd learned the hard way never to trust a single emotion…only his instincts.

He parked across the street from the Colby house and waited. Watched. The sun climbed above the treetops and poured its warming rays down on the small cul-de-sac and still nothing changed. No lights came on inside. No movement anywhere on the grounds.

There was no one here.

He opened the vehicle door and climbed out.

"What're you doing? You shouldn't—"

He shut the door, cutting her off.

Moving slowly, scanning continuously for any movement, he walked across the street, up the sidewalk and to her front door without encountering resistance.

Fury started to simmer deep in his gut.

Tasha moved up behind him. "We should get out of here before Lucas's men spot us," she urged.

He turned on her, then, his patience at an end. "There's no one here." He reached into his pocket and retrieved the key and unlocked the door and then disarmed the security system. They'd changed the code but he already had the new one. Leberman had never failed to provide the essential details.

"You have a key?" She stared at him, slack-jawed with surprise and still standing on the outside of the threshold.

"Close the door," he ordered. The last thing he needed was a neighbor calling the police to report an unknown intruder. He needed time to assess the situation. When she obeyed, he locked the door and reset the alarm.

Seth moved through the house, checking room after room. Nothing. He went back to her bedroom and checked the walk-in closet. He had memorized exactly how it looked before. Several items were missing. She'd packed light, but she was gone. Her scent still lingered in the air making his jaw clench and his gut tie in knots.

He spun around and pointed the rage building inside him directly at his only connection to Lucas. "Where is she?"

Tasha shook her head. "I don't know."

He grabbed her by the shoulders and shook her, control slipping away. Leberman always provided the details…gave him the orders. Confusion slowed his ability to think but he quickly regained control. He was in charge now. He didn't need Leberman. "Tell me where she is."

"I swear I don't know."

She was telling the truth. He could see it in her eyes. He could also see the fear. She didn't want to be afraid of him but she was.

He gritted his teeth.

She should be. He could not fail.

The telephone on the table next to Victoria's bed rang. Seth released her and glanced at it.

"Answer it," he ordered, turning back to her. "It'll be for you." They were watching. He didn't need to recognize the number on the caller ID or make visual contact with the enemy to confirm it. He knew they would be.

She moistened her lips. "What should I say?"

"Tell him to give me Victoria's location or you die. That if he comes near this house, you'll die."

To her credit she didn't flinch. "That won't matter."

"Just answer it!" he roared as he drew his weapon. He had to know where she was! He swallowed hard, fought the dizzying sensations clawing at his composure.

Tasha nodded reluctantly. When she reached for the receiver he moved closer, put his head next to hers so that he could hear the other end of the conversation, as well.

"Hello." Her voice sounded shaky.

He didn't give a damn. He just needed that location. He had allowed her to distract him last night and now they were one step ahead of him.

"North, are you all right?"

Male. Not Lucas.

"Yes," she said. "We're fine."

With those two words she'd just let the caller know that he was listening. She was no fool.

Maybe he was the fool.

"He wants to know where Victoria is," she said bluntly. "If you don't tell him he says he'll kill me. If you come near the house, he'll kill me."

"I understand. I can't give you that information because I don't have it," the man explained. "But I'll contact Lucas for further instructions. I'll call you back at this number in a few minutes. Stay calm, North. We've got your back."

Seth wondered if the man was stupid enough to believe he could stop him.

"Leberman is dead," she blurted as he snatched the receiver from her to hang it up. Seth didn't miss the other

man's response. "We know." He slammed the receiver
back into its cradle and glared at her.

"Don't do this, Seth. They'll kill you. When I told you
I thought you were worth saving, I meant it. Don't let this
happen. Leberman is gone. He was the one who caused
you all this pain. Let it go."

"Shut up." He didn't want to hear about how the woman
who called herself his mother really loved him and still
grieved for him. He didn't want to hear any of it.

"Please listen to me." She touched his arm. He jerked
away from her. Hurt glimmered in those brown eyes. A
ploy, he told himself. She wanted him to believe she cared.

No one cared if he lived or died.

He didn't even care. He existed for one purpose only.
For vengeance.

He dragged her from the room and down the hall. He
needed to set up surveillance around the perimeter. Lucas's men would be moving in for the kill, if they hadn't
already.

He hesitated outside the door to the guest room and
glanced inside. Victoria's house was always meticulously
neat. The box and its scattered contents on the bed didn't
fit. He moved in that direction to investigate. What he
found had him dropping down on the mattress for a closer
look.

Tasha eased onto the bed and picked up first one item
and then the next. The shuffling of photographs and papers echoed in the stark silence that followed.

His heart rate steadily increased as one alien sensation
after the other bombarded him.

"This is you," she murmured, pointing to a picture of
him as a small boy, James Colby kneeling beside him,
smiles beaming from both their faces.

"This, too."

She picked up picture after picture of little Jimmy Colby. His father showing him how to ride a bike. His mother playing in the sand on a beach with him. The whole family, all smiles, in front of the castle at Disney World.

He didn't remember any of it. It was like looking at pictures of strangers. But somehow the images affected him…confused him.

Then there were stuffed animals, a baseball with some famous player's autograph, tiny race cars…childish artwork. But none of it gripped his insides like the newspaper articles he looked at next. He scanned headline after headline. All focused on the massive search for one missing boy. He read the quotes from James and Victoria Colby. The pleas for the return of their son. The million-dollar reward they'd offered.

His hands started to shake and it was hard to see.

He scrubbed at his eyes and his hand came away wet. It had to be a trick…couldn't be real. Leberman had told him over and over…

Tasha peered up at him from the article she'd been reading, tears streaming down her cheeks. "Would people who didn't want you…who didn't love you…have done all this?"

He lunged to his feet, a new fury building inside him burning away the other sensations. It was meant to confuse him. All of it. This box had been left here to throw him off course and make him second-guess what he knew.

"Let's go."

"But Maverick's going to call back with word from Lucas," she protested as she got up, some of the yellowed-with-age clippings still in her hand.

"We're not waiting."

She retreated when he reached for her. "But how are you going to find her if you don't wait for the call?"

He grabbed Tasha by the arm and jerked her close, staring into those emotion-filled eyes with all the savage rage burning inside him, searing away the lingering remnants of those alien feelings he'd experienced only moments before. "If she loves me so damned much, she'll find me."

Chapter 38

They sat on the deck and enjoyed coffee, with the morning sun sparkling across the still water. Lucas knew without doubt that he could spend the rest of his life doing nothing but looking at Victoria. Making love with her had completed the bond he'd felt for her all these years. Had sealed his fate.

She'd been right when she said it was time he made an honest woman out of her. They'd laughed about it afterward. But it was no laughing matter. They were no longer young with a lifetime ahead of them. He wanted to share the rest of his years on this earth with her...like this.

But first he had to tell her the truth. He could not hold back that knowledge any longer.

"Victoria, I've made a decision of my own this morning," he announced with as much cheer as he could summon.

She set down her mug of warm coffee and peered across the table at him. "Oh, really. And what decision is that?" She smiled, and all those years of pain and suffering etched on her face disappeared.

God, how he hated to resurrect this part of her past.

But he had no choice.

Maverick had called. "He" wanted a face-to-face with Victoria. Or Tasha would die.

Lucas would ensure Tasha's safety, one way or another, even if it meant exchanging himself for her. There was no way he was letting this man anywhere near Victoria. But he couldn't make this move without Victoria's full understanding of what might happen in the course of protecting her. Her son might have to die.

"You were right last night," he said, delaying the inevitable. "You know I would have asked you to marry me long ago had I felt you were ready." Her little comment last night was her way of letting him know she was ready. Warmth spread through his chest. She wanted to be his wife. Whether he lived to see that happen or not, simply knowing gave him more joy than she could imagine.

"Lucas." She placed her hand on his. "I made you wait a very long time. I'm so thankful for your patience, but it's time now. Our time."

He nodded. "You're more right than you know. I have news."

She sat up a little straighter. "What news?"

"Leberman is dead." He'd learned this information hours earlier, but he'd waited until morning to tell her, not wanting to spoil their night. Now he was glad he had. At least this news would temper the rest.

Her breath caught, then she released it in a sigh filled with equal parts confusion and relief. "How?"

Now for the hard part. "The assassin he hired, or coerced into stalking you, killed him."

Her hand went to her chest. "My God. What does this

mean?" She shook her head. "Other than the obvious. I mean, you're sure it's Leberman. The bastard is really dead."

Lucas nodded. "It's him."

"But the assassin still poses a threat?" she guessed.

He nodded again. "He has his own ax to grind with you."

She frowned. "Should I know this man?"

Lucas took the hand she'd placed over his and held it firmly. "I want you to know up front that I've confirmed his identification through DNA. There is no question as to who he is. But you also have to understand that he's not the same. It's him, but…it isn't really. I don't know all the details just yet but I suspect brainwashing at the very least."

"You're scaring me, Lucas," she said softly.

He felt a fine tremor go through her. Saw the tension turn her posture more rigid, tighten the features of her face.

"There's no other way to tell you this, Victoria. This assassin is your son."

For several seconds she simply stared at him. Shock, disbelief, horror, all danced like frantic shadows across her face.

"That's impossible," she finally said, her voice as thin and fragile as handblown glass.

"It's difficult to comprehend, but it's true."

She blinked back the tears shining in her dark eyes. "Well, that's…insane. Why would my son want to kill me? Why would he be following Leberman's orders? The shirt…"

"Victoria." Lucas leaned forward, wrapped his other hand over hers as well. She started to shake…the shock, he knew. "He's been brainwashed. He's not the same. He doesn't understand what really happened."

Victoria stiffened, fury sent a flush up her neck and across her face. "What did that monster do to him?"

Her breathing became labored, and Lucas knew she was about to break down. He shoved out of his chair and moved beside her. "We don't know all the details yet."

She snatched her hand away. "How long have you known?"

"Not very long," he hedged.

"I want to see him." She pushed to her feet, knocking over her chair. "I want to see him now."

Lucas stood, reached for her, but she retreated too quickly. "You have to understand that he's still a danger to you."

"My own son wants to kill me," she lashed out. "Why is that? What did Leberman do to him? Tell me, Lucas!"

He dropped his hands to his sides. There was no point in trying to do this rationally. There was nothing rational about it. He couldn't spare her feelings. There was no lighter side…no saving grace to any of this.

"We only know that there are lots of scars. He doesn't appear to feel any kind of emotion. He killed Leberman last night." Lucas looked directly into her eyes, hoping he could reassure her as he told her the rest. "His intentions are to kill you next."

She closed her eyes as the import of those words rocked through her. Lucas's chest squeezed painfully. What he would give not to have to put her through this.

When she looked at him again, she said the last thing he wanted to hear. "Arrange a meeting." She squared her shoulders and struggled to put a stop to the visible shaking. "I want to see my son…even if it kills me."

Chapter 39

"You have to be reasonable, Victoria," Lucas argued.

"Reasonable?" She looked directly at him, those dark eyes clear and crackling with determination. "What's reasonable about any of this?"

Lucas wanted to throw up his hands. Wanted to hog-tie her and throw her over his shoulder and carry her away to safety. All reason had fled from her the moment he'd told her the truth about the assassin.

Lucas couldn't bring himself to consider this man bent on killing Victoria as her son. He supposed, to a degree, he was being irrational, as well. The only difference was he was trying to save her life.

"You've ordered my men to leave," he argued. "You want to just let this man—this killer, need I remind you—waltz in here and do whatever he pleases."

"That killer," she said pointedly, "is my child."

"Yes, I understand that he's your child," he half shouted, exasperated. "I understand it well."

She shook her head, tears welling in her eyes once

more. "You can't possibly. Lucas, I know you love me, but you can't possibly even fathom how this feels." She moved closer to him, her hands clasped together in front of her. "I carried him inside me for nine months…held him close to my heart as a baby, then taught him how to tie his shoes…how to brush his teeth properly. I tucked him into bed at night, read stories with him. He felt safe with me." A single teardrop slipped down her cheek. "And I let him down. I let that monster steal him from me and I couldn't save him. Can you honestly say that you…" She paused a moment to compose herself. "You can't know how that feels."

He pulled her into his arms, held on tight when she resisted. "You're right," he confessed softly. "I can't possibly know how it feels. But, dear God, I can't let him harm you. Can you understand that?"

She nodded. "I know it's because you love me. But I have to do this, Lucas. I have to. Because he's my son, and I love him."

He did understand that. But he would do this his way. She didn't have to know that his people had taken up sniper positions all around the cabin. He'd insisted the meeting take place on the deck just for that reason. Inside, his people couldn't put a bullet in the assassin's head. He suppressed a shudder at the too-vivid image that accompanied that thought.

Killing her son was the last thing he wanted to have to do, but he had ordered his men to trust their instincts. His Specialists would not shoot to kill unless it was absolutely necessary.

Back at the Colby Agency Ian and Simon had been put on alert. Victoria had insisted that they merely stand by. Neither of the men liked it, but would obey her orders, just as Lucas's would obey his.

He held the woman in his arms more firmly for a few seconds more, then drew back to look into her eyes. "As much as I hate to admit it, I do understand that you feel compelled to do this. But you must understand also that I will do whatever I have to in order to protect you."

She smiled faintly. "That's a given, Lucas." She took his hands in hers and held them close to her heart. "I only wish I could protect you, but you won't go, as I've asked you to. I'd rather you were safe from whatever is going to take place."

Asked? She'd demanded that he leave her here alone. She could forget that one. He gave her an answering smile. "Well, I guess we'll just have to face this together."

Tears glimmered in her eyes once more. "Then so be it."

He desperately hoped it wouldn't be the last thing they did together.

Seth braked to a stop at the entrance to the long drive that would take them to the cabin where Lucas and Victoria waited.

Tasha watched Seth survey their surroundings. The woods were dense, most of the brilliant fall foliage still clinging to their limbs. Vivid hues of orange and gold and rust against the varying shades of gray bark formed an ironically natural backdrop for the wholly unnatural scene about to play out.

Seth was intent on killing his mother. She knew his plan. Lucas, no doubt, had estimated what he had in mind, as well. Though they might sit here now and see nothing but the lovely forest landscape, danger lurked in every direction. Lucas's Specialists would have taken careful positions to protect their leader and the woman he loved.

"They're going to kill you, you know," Tasha murmured as much to herself as to him. He knew exactly what was going to happen and he didn't care. But she did…she cared far more than she should.

"Not before I accomplish my goal," he said without reservation. And she didn't doubt his certainty.

He intended to tell Victoria Colby what Leberman had done to him and then he fully intended to kill her.

There would be no happy ending.

Dread and fear and regret all churned in Tasha's stomach. Whatever happened this afternoon, no one would walk away untouched by the horror of Errol Leberman.

The bastard had won.

The SUV rolled forward, slowly making its way down the long, narrow dirt-and-gravel road that led to certain death.

Though Maverick had given her specific orders along with the time and place of the meeting when Seth finally allowed her to call him back, she had no intention of obeying those orders. He'd told her to stay out of the line of fire, not to get involved.

She knew what that meant. They had it covered. Every possible scenario had been run. Every precaution taken. As far as they were concerned, if anyone died today it would not be Victoria Colby or Lucas Camp. Tasha was to stay out of the way. Seth would be terminated if they couldn't control the situation. She didn't need anyone to spell it out for her.

Seth had to know this. He was far too smart to believe he would get away with what he had planned. Simply walking in and shooting Victoria wasn't going to happen. But something inside him had changed after he'd looked at those photographs and newspaper clippings. The rage was still there but it was different somehow.

He stopped in front of the cabin and turned off the engine. He took out his 9mm and faced her. "Slide over the console and get out on my side."

"Wait." She grabbed him by the shirtsleeve when he would have opened his door. "It's not too late to just drive away." She searched that icy gaze for any flicker of uncertainty and found none.

"It's been too late for eighteen years."

There was something in his voice…some emotion that she'd never heard before. "Seth, I don't want you to die."

For one fleeting instant she thought she'd reached him. He looked at her with an intensity that made her believe he felt something for her…something beyond the physical attraction.

"I'm already dead."

With that simple yet profound statement he got out of the vehicle and she had no choice but to follow. She blinked back the tears and cursed herself for loss of all professionalism. What the hell kind of field operative would she make if she couldn't keep it together any better than this?

His weapon resting against the back of her skull, she led the way around the cabin to the back deck, just as Lucas had ordered. Other than the occasional seagull and the lapping of water against the shoreline, absolute silence crushed in around them. She felt the weight of it directly on her chest, making each breath difficult.

When they rounded the rear corner of the cabin, the deck came into view.

Tasha tried to slow her step, but he urged her forward with the muzzle of his 9 mm. Victoria waited on the deck, Lucas at her side. Neither of them appeared armed.

As they moved up the steps, Tasha could see the devastation and the anticipation cluttering Victoria's weary face. She drank in the sight of her son as if he were the answer to her prayers rather than an assassin determined to end her life. And he was. She had likely prayed ceaselessly for his return. Did it have to end like this?

"Jimmy?" she offered, her expression so hopeful it made Tasha's heart ache to look at her.

Seth pushed Tasha aside, leaving nothing between him and Victoria except a six-foot span of thick-with-tension air and aged wooden deck.

"That's right," he said tightly. "Your long-lost son has returned."

His every feature was set in stone. His eyes as cold as ice as he stared at the woman who had given birth to him…who'd loved him and cared for him for the first seven years of his life. But he didn't remember that time… Leberman had erased it. Had tortured him until he forgot all else but the pain. Until he knew nothing but the lies.

"Don't do this, Seth," Tasha pleaded, praying somehow her voice would get through to him. The hand holding his weapon hung loosely at his side. If he lifted it, even a fraction, she was certain he would be terminated.

"Listen to her," Lucas urged. "Leberman is dead. Let the past die with him. You've got a chance for a new beginning here. We know he did this to you. We—"

Fury erupted across Seth's face and he aimed all that rage at Lucas then. "You don't know anything." He ripped open his shirt with his free hand, displaying the hideous scars like badges of honor. "You have no idea what I've endured. What *he* did to me." He turned back to Victoria. "What he paid others to do to me."

Victoria drew in a shuddering breath. "I would give anything to change that." Tears spilled past her lashes, and Tasha's heart squeezed so hard for her and this man who could not bear what life had done to him that she lost her breath.

"Please," Victoria urged, "please, let me help you."

Seth shook his head. "It's too late. I've waited a long time for this moment. To be able to look into your eyes and see the horror when you learned the truth...when you realized what your precious son had suffered because of your negligence. I wanted to be certain that you took that knowledge to hell with you. So watch closely."

At the same instant that he lifted his weapon Tasha suddenly understood what he intended to do.

She hurled her body at his. *"No-o-o-o-o!"*

The sharp *crack* of a high-powered rifle rent the air.

The impact knocked her off her feet.

Slammed her against the wooden deck.

She blinked at the sun, confused, numb.

Seth stared down at her...blocking the bright light like a sudden eclipse.

The weapon slipped from his fingers.

Frantic voices.

Hurried footsteps.

He dropped to his knees beside her. His lips moved... called her name.... His voice followed her into the darkness.

Chapter 40

There was hope.

Victoria sat very still in the private visitation room and recalled those moments after the gunshot rang out.

Tasha had realized his intentions and shoved him out of the line of fire. She'd taken the bullet intended for him.

Thankfully the result had merely been a shoulder injury, but it had required immediate surgery. She was fine now. It could have been so much worse. She and Victoria both had learned something about the men in their lives. Lucas, contrary to her specific orders, had stationed his people around the cabin. Blue Callahan had taken the shot which had been intended only to disarm the man wielding the handgun.

But he hadn't come there to kill Victoria, they now knew. He'd decided to destroy her in a completely different manner. She was to have acknowledged that her son was indeed alive and the extent of what he'd suffered, then she would witness his assassination, ordered by the man she loved. That was to have been her final punish-

ment, her destruction, for having allowed her son to fall
into Leberman's hands. He had assumed Lucas's orders
were to shoot to kill. She might never know precisely what
had altered his course...the discovery of the mementos
she'd left on the bed, possibly. The old newspaper clippings and keepsakes from his childhood. Perhaps fate
had been on her side for once.

Despite the turmoil of those frantic moments when
the gun had slipped from his hand and half a dozen Specialists had swarmed onto the deck, she had watched this
would-be assassin...her son...fall to his knees next to
Tasha. She'd seen the pained expression of helplessness
on his hard, unyielding face as he'd watched the blood
soak into Tasha's blouse.

That's when Victoria had known there was hope.

He wasn't completely without emotion...he could still
feel. He'd felt something at that moment. And some basic
human compassion had rendered him unable to execute
her or maybe he'd simply thought that watching him die
would be more devastating to her. She couldn't be sure.
Despite the horrors he'd suffered she was so thankful he
was alive...to have him back. As selfish as that was, she
couldn't help herself.

If only the doctors could get through to him. The team
of medical experts working on his case had insisted that
he could have no contact with anyone for a period of
thirty days while they evaluated his condition. Victoria
had waited impatiently for the time to pass. Tasha had
waited with similar anticipation.

The day had finally arrived.

Victoria, of course, being immediate family would
go first.

She didn't know what to expect. The doctors had
warned her that he was uncooperative, even violent at

times, but those moments had lessened in frequency the past couple of weeks. Despite his decision to allow one of Lucas's people to kill him in front of her, he wasn't considered suicidal, just determined to wield the ultimate blow. He refused medication, resisted hypnosis and outright defied their attempts to analyze him. The one thing he had done that even hinted at cooperation was to study the photo albums and other mementos Victoria provided. That was the only thing he really appeared to respond to. The doctors were amazed he even accepted the suggestion to view them. He'd adamantly refused to give them up since.

She couldn't help but smile. He'd definitely inherited his father's stubborn determination. Well, admittedly, he'd gotten some of that from her. Being exposed to the moments they had shared before he was kidnapped might not change anything, but maybe, just maybe, it would tear down that wall Leberman had erected. If Seth...Jimmy, remembered even one moment they'd spent together as a family, he would know without question how very much he'd been loved. Still was.

For that very reason, Victoria knew what she had to do. It had to be done today.

Seth stared beyond the bars that obscured his view from the window of his room. He watched the people moving about outside. It was colder now, forcing them to wear coats and hats. He touched the glass and wondered if he would ever be free again.

He didn't actually care about his freedom, but he did want to find Tasha. To see with his own eyes that she was all right. That bullet she'd taken had been intended for him. He could no longer deny that she felt something for him. Anyone who took a bullet for another person defi-

nitely cared. But no one would give him any significant
information, only that she had survived and was fine.
He banged his fist against the glass in futility. He hated
being trapped in this mental institution.

No matter how they prettied it up or how much it
cost to be here, that's what it was. A frown tugged at his
mouth. He didn't like the questions they asked him…the
way they made him remember too many details of the
past. He preferred to forget. But they just kept digging,
kept prodding for more. What the hell did it matter? He
was screwed up. It didn't take a whole damned team of
shrinks to figure that out. And until one month ago he
hadn't really given a damn.

But things were different now. He lived and breathed
for one thing, to see Tasha again.

Nothing else mattered.

Leberman was a ghost who only haunted him in his
dreams. The past couldn't hurt him anymore, except when
those mind excavators started their digging. He blocked
it out the rest of the time. He glanced at the table across
the room and the photo albums there.

She had sent those.

Victoria…his mother.

She wanted him to remember…like he had for that one
instant when Tasha had first shown him those newspaper clippings. A hundred memories had come flooding
into his head, overwhelming him. But he'd tried to push
them away, the same way he always had. It was easier
not to remember. But the knowledge that his parents had
searched for him had somehow changed something inside
him. Made it difficult to keep the memories at bay. Had
rendered him unable to execute his original plan. He'd
told himself that watching him die would wield much
more devastation, but he wasn't so sure of his motives

now. He simply hadn't been able to kill her. Hadn't been able to strike.

And now, *she* wouldn't go away.

The doctors said that she required daily briefings on his progress. That she was coming to see him today. The frown that had been annoying his mouth worked its way up and across his forehead. He wasn't sure he wanted to see her. What she'd shown him with her old photos confused him.

He heard the lock on his door being disengaged and he knew she was here. Lunch was over, and he didn't have any appointments this afternoon. It had to be her.

Two orderlies stepped into the room. The tallest one said to him when he turned around, "Okay, Mr. Colby, let's make this easy, shall we?"

He didn't like being referred to as Mr. Colby, but they all called him that. Like it would change who he really was. But then...he didn't even know who he was. Little Jimmy Colby had died in a cold, dark basement a long time ago. And Seth, the man he had become, was missing in action in a lot of ways. They'd even removed the tattoo that Leberman had used to mark him as a beast.

He allowed the two men to restrain his hands in front of him with transparent nylon bands. This place was too ritzy to use iron shackles, but the effect was the same. They led him to the visitation area. Not the one the rest of the residents used, but one especially for him since he was considered *dangerous*.

He didn't miss the relief on the two men's faces when they'd reached their destination.

"Behave yourself now," the tall one said as he opened the door. "We'll be waiting right outside."

Seth smiled at him, and every ounce of assurance

drained from the man's expression. Maybe he really was a monster. It definitely had its advantages.

Inside the room he hesitated a moment before turning to face his visitor. The subtle scent of her flowery perfume reminded him of her home. Her room had smelled that way. He hadn't been able to put the scent out of his mind the past few weeks.

"It's good to see you," she said, hoping to garner his attention.

He executed a slow, deliberate 180-degree turn, more to control his reaction than to intimidate her. He wasn't sure how he would respond to her presence. He was unsure of a lot of things lately. He'd been ready to die to hurt her, hadn't he? His brow creased into a frown. He didn't know anymore.

Forcing the disturbing thoughts away, his gaze settled on her. It felt strange to look at her and not feel the hatred that had been his constant companion for so long. He wasn't sure where it had gone. It was simply gone. Maybe it was the medication they sneaked into his food. He was reasonably certain that's what they were doing since he refused to take it. He'd eventually had to eat. They had known he would. Which provided the opportunity they needed.

She sat stiffly at the table provided. The bland room hadn't been designed for comfort. Only one barred window. A table with four chairs. Nothing else. All white, no pictures on the walls, no rug on the floor, plain old commercial-grade tan tile.

But she was anything but bland. She wore a pink suit that looked tailored for her. Her dark hair was up in its usual smooth bun. Her makeup, what little she wore, was applied expertly. She was a woman of means who wore her position in society proudly.

She was too strong to give up on him...or too stubborn. Seth hadn't decided which yet.

He approached the table and sat down, his scrutiny continuing as he observed her every response to his movements. She wasn't afraid...resigned maybe, but definitely not afraid. She looked troubled and he knew he was the reason.

"I want to know more about Tasha," he said, careful to keep the alien emotions he'd experienced of late out of his tone.

Victoria nodded. "She's fine. In fact, she's here to see you."

Anticipation surged through him, but he suppressed the urgency that welled up in his chest. "She wants to see me?"

"Yes. She's wanted to see you from the moment they released her from the hospital, but the doctors wouldn't allow you visitors until now."

He didn't like those damned doctors.

"I'd like to see her now." Anything Victoria Colby had to say to him could wait. He wanted to see Tasha. His heart kicked into a faster rhythm as his mind recalled the moments they had shared together. He tried to control how the memories affected him, but he couldn't manage the feat anymore.

"I'd like to spend a few moments with you first," Victoria said, dragging his attention back to her.

He had endured endless beatings and worse in the past to earn the right to a meal or a few hours' sleep, he supposed he could endure a few minutes of her company. Though he couldn't understand why she would want to see him. He'd spent a great deal of time thinking about killing her. She was well aware of that. And still she came to see him.

"The doctors have told me that you've experienced a few breakthrough memories about your life before…"

Before Leberman, she didn't say. He didn't like thinking about Leberman. "That's right." He resisted the urge to tap his foot as his agitation began to build. There was something about her demeanor now that made him uneasy. He couldn't quite put his finger on it…but something wasn't right.

"You must know, then, that your father and I loved you very much. We were a happy family."

The tears he expected to see in her eyes weren't there, just a dullness that made him curious to know what was going on inside her head.

"What do you want me to say to that?" The question came out bluntly. What did she expect from him? A sudden return to life the way it was before? Was he supposed to hug her and tell her that he loved her? He didn't know how to love. Leberman had made sure of that. Hell, he'd never even missed another human until Tasha.

Victoria looked away for a moment, then settled her gaze back on his. "I don't know what I expect you to say," she admitted, her fingers clasping the clutch purse she carried even tighter. "This is difficult for both of us."

She was upset. The doctors would be watching and analyzing his ability to interact with her. Shit. He'd never get out of here if he didn't do better. Did it matter? He thought of Tasha and decided it did.

"The photo albums have been useful," he offered, hoping to placate her.

Her whole expression seemed to brighten at his words. The reaction confused him. Increased that uneasiness twisting inside him.

"I've done a lot of thinking since I learned that you

were still alive," she said quietly. "And I've decided that you're right."

His instincts went on alert.

"If I had been a better mother I would have found you before your father came home that day. Then you wouldn't have slipped through the gate and hidden in the forest. I would have found you...before."

The doctors had told her the things he'd remembered. She had been playing with him in the backyard. She'd gone inside to answer the phone and he'd hidden in the bushes near the entry gate to the lake house property. The security measures had been to protect him from the water...and other things he'd been too young to understand. While she was looking for him in the backyard his father had come home. He'd sneaked out as the gate closed behind his father's car. He'd thought it would be so funny to hide in the woods. He and his mother had taken walks there before, he wasn't afraid.

But night had come too fast for her to find him. Then he'd gotten scared...had tried to find his way out...but he'd found Leberman instead. Leberman had had someone watching the house for just that moment. Under hypnosis, Seth had remembered another man but couldn't identify him.

"I should have watched you more carefully. I didn't protect you...it was my fault." She looked into his eyes, and the pain he saw there was hard to look at. "All of this was my fault. You're right to hate me. I should have protected you."

His apprehension escalated, making him increasingly uncomfortable. She didn't seem to want answers...she just wanted to talk...to say the words.

"I would have gladly traded places with you if I could have found you. But he was too elusive...too smart for me, so I failed. Now the decision is yours. Where do you want this to go, or do you want it to end here and now? I need to know how you feel. If you still wish me dead. I, for one, can't live another day with this guilt. With the not knowing."

He thought of the strong woman he'd watched for months, waiting until the time came. Leberman had wanted him to kill her as well as Lucas Camp. He'd planned for it from day one. But Seth hadn't been able to follow through...he'd decided to simply destroy her from the inside out. To make her suffer as he had. At least, he thought that's what he'd decided. She would see him die and that would be worse than death.

As he stared into her dull, hollow eyes, he knew he had accomplished that goal.

Oddly, it gave him no satisfaction.

All he'd ever seen of Victoria Colby was her strength... her stoicism no matter what was thrown her way. Where was that woman now?

"I've decided to give you the opportunity to have your vengeance."

He stilled, his instincts rushing to a higher state of alert.

"You realize, of course," she went on, "that they're watching us, so there won't be time for second thoughts or deliberation. But I have to know that I've done every-thing within my power to make the past up to you. If tak-ing my life will give you even one moment's peace, I'll gladly surrender it."

Before he could string together a response, she reached into her purse and withdrew a small-caliber handgun. A .32. She placed it on the table in front of him and said, "The decision is yours."

He stared at the gun for about three seconds then

looked directly at her. She was dead serious. Willing to do anything to give him peace, even if only for one fleeting moment. Could anyone really be that selfless? Could he possibly mean that much to her? His gaze dropped to the weapon once more. For his whole life a weapon had been the one thing he could rely on. The one thing he trusted. But now, staring at the cold, black steel, he felt nothing. No desire. No urgency.

He heard the scuffle of running feet in the corridor outside.

"They're coming," she warned.

He didn't know how the hell she'd gotten in this place with that weapon, but he had to hand it to her, she didn't make idle boasts. She was willing to die for him.

Two guards rushed into the room. He didn't move. Knew if he did that he'd get an injection that would put him out for about six hours. Like all his lessons, he'd learned that one the hard way.

The .32 was snatched off the table by one of the guards. "Mrs. Colby, we'll have to ask you to come with us now."

She looked confused…startled.

They needed more time.

Seth glared up at the burly guard and said, "We're not finished yet."

If the widening of the man's eyes was any indication, he didn't want to argue. "I'll need your purse," he said to Victoria. She handed it over. The guard glanced at Seth. "We'll be right outside with your orderlies."

Seth said nothing. There was no need.

For a couple of minutes after the guards left, he and Victoria simply looked at each other. He wasn't sure what he wanted to say and he imagined she felt the same way. But there was one thing he had to know. "Did you have that much faith in those few years we spent together to believe that I wouldn't take you up on your offer?"

She smiled sadly. "Yes, I did. But I had to know for sure."

He shook his head. There she was. The superwoman he'd watched from a distance. The woman who visited him every single day through the memories her photo albums evoked.

He exhaled a mighty breath. "I guess we have a long ways to go in a lot of respects."

"Does that mean we have a truce?" she asked, that hope springing to life in her eyes once more.

He stared at his bound hands for a moment and tried to think above all the lies and ugliness he'd been force-fed all those years. "Yeah." He met her gaze once more. "I guess it does."

She stood, seemingly satisfied. "I've taken enough of your time. I'll send in Tasha."

He wasn't sure he could let her go without saying more, but he wasn't even sure what he needed to say. "Wait." He grappled for the right words.

When she hesitated and turned back to him, he stood, towered over her by nearly a foot. But she didn't look intimidated, she just looked hopeful. That undying hope affected something in his chest. "I don't know where things will go from here. I don't know how to be what you probably want me to be." She shouldn't get her hopes up. He might never be able to live up to her expectations.

A tremulous smile peeked past the emotions cluttering her face. "For the record, I only want you to be happy." She laid her hand against his arm, a gesture of comfort. Remarkably, he didn't feel compelled to flinch. "I'll be back tomorrow."

He nodded, then watched her go.

His heart started to beat faster at the thought of seeing Tasha. He was so damned thankful that she was here.

The orderly came in, looking annoyed. Seth tensed. Were they taking him back now? Had someone decided he wasn't allowed to see Tasha?

"I'm going to let your hands loose," the orderly said gruffly, "but if you give us any trouble, they'll go back on. Got it?"

Seth nodded, relieved that they weren't taking him away. Victoria had to be behind this. She must have insisted they release his restraints. He could see her making that happen. Something like respect nudged at him. It was going to take time to get used to all these unfamiliar feelings.

When the orderly had exited the room, the door opened again. Tasha stepped inside. She looked great. But a whole month had passed. Her injury had obviously healed.

He started to shake, and he didn't understand the reaction…couldn't stop it. He had to look away. Didn't want her to see the weakness.

She moved in close to him, took his trembling hand. "Hey."

Despite the way his body shook and his gut clenched, he had to look at her, had to hold her. He pulled her into his arms, and his breath caught at the feel of her.

"They wouldn't tell me what I wanted to know," he managed to say without his voice quavering. "Wouldn't let me see you."

"It's okay," she murmured as she held him tight in her arms. "Everything's okay now."

They held each other that way for a long time. He couldn't say for sure just how long.

She finally pulled back far enough to press a soft kiss to his lips. "It's good to see you. I've missed you."

He cupped her face in his hands and tried to think of how to tell her what he was feeling but couldn't find the words. "It's good to see you," he echoed.

"Victoria says they're moving you to a different room now. You'll be able to have visitors every day."

He liked watching her lips move…liked the way she smelled. He wanted to taste her. "Will you come every day?"

She smiled and nodded. "If you want me to."

He tasted her lips and she kissed him back. "Yes," he whispered between kisses. "I want you to."

She kissed him again and he shivered. He wondered vaguely if the guards would come running if he stripped off her clothes and took her right here on the table.

Maybe he'd just see.

Epilogue

"I'll be ready in a moment!" Victoria called from the bedroom of their penthouse suite.

Lucas loosened his bow tie and pulled it free of his neck. The wedding was behind them. The champagne was on ice. And Victoria was getting "comfortable." He still shuddered when he thought of her taking that weapon into that clinic, but she'd been determined to do something to break the ice between her and her son. When Lucas had learned about her bold move he'd gone ballistic. But she'd insisted that she'd known going in how it would end.

He opened the French doors and stepped out onto the grand balcony. All the suites on the empress deck had balconies and he'd wanted the best for their honeymoon. The crisp December breeze sent a chill across his skin, but the knowledge that the woman in the other room was now his lawful wife kept him plenty warm.

If he squinted he could just make out the wedding party still waving from the pier as the ship moved farther and farther from shore. Every single member of the Colby Agency was there, as were a number of his Specialists.

A nice long cruise was in order.

He and Victoria deserved it.

Ian and Simon could take care of things at the agency.

Director Casey had Mission Recovery under control.

And Tasha would keep Jim company.

He still considered himself Seth, the name Leberman had given him long ago. He'd never had a social security number or driver's license. Leberman had provided the essentials he'd wanted him to possess to go along with any number of aliases as necessary. For all intents and purposes, the persona Seth had never existed on paper or in any other "legitimate" capacity. He tolerated Victoria's constant use of the name that had belonged to the boy he once was. He had a long way to go. The doctors weren't sure he would fully recover his early memories, but he would learn to cope with his newly developing emotions. His sessions had gone well enough that he was allowed to leave the clinic for weekends. All of which were spent with Tasha, except for Sunday brunch with Victoria, of course.

All in all, Lucas felt good about the way things had worked out. Leberman was dead, the evil bastard, and Victoria had her son back, for the most part anyway.

Tasha had given Lucas notice that she'd decided to join the Colby Agency rather than his team. Well, he couldn't fault her there. She wanted to be close to Jim. A job in research at the firm would keep her out of harm's way, as well. Making a life with Jim was going to take a lot of patience and understanding. Tasha was the right woman.

His cell phone rang, and Lucas fished it from his jacket pocket. He'd taken care to mute it during the service or risk facing Victoria's, as well as the minister's, wrath.

He smiled at the thought as he flipped open his phone. Victoria Colby-Camp. It had a hell of a nice ring to it.

"Camp," he said by way of greeting.

"I'm not interrupting anything, am I?"

Director Casey. "Not yet," Lucas warned. He glanced back into the room to see if Victoria had appeared.

"There might not be a better time for us to talk later."

"Now is fine," Lucas insisted. He knew his director wouldn't call unless it was important.

"I spoke with the doctor at the clinic this morning. Since they started hypnosis there hasn't been much real progress. According to his conclusions, Jim is still resisting, subconsciously he believes."

Lucas rubbed his forehead and considered the ramifications of that information. He'd asked Casey to personally look into the situation with Victoria's son since he couldn't do so without her knowledge. No one at the Colby Agency could know about his growing suspicions. It wasn't that he didn't trust Victoria, she simply had enough on her plate right now with sorting out the fledgling relationship with her son. She didn't need this added worry. But he was certain that there was, at the very least, someone in the agency who'd leaked information, quite possibly without realizing it. Leberman had known too much. According to Tasha, he had known who she was from the beginning. He'd known the security codes to both Victoria's properties. The very thought of a mole made him extremely nervous. Lucas had to be certain.

"We need to know how he got his information," Lucas said on a sigh, well aware that he was preaching to the choir. "With Leberman dead I guess we have no choice but to wait it out. See if Jim knows something. With the brainwashing technique Leberman used he could know all sorts of things and be completely oblivious to the information. Like the identity of the other man involved in his kidnapping eighteen years ago." Not to mention certain aspects of his neurological programming could be in sleep mode. God only knew what Leberman may have programmed him to do at some unknown future date. Just another reason why he needed Tasha by his side. But Casey was already well aware of those possibilities. He'd sought out an expert to work with Jim, but there were no guarantees he would learn anything.

"I agree. I'll keep you up to date," Casey assured him before ending the call.

Lucas dropped the phone back into his pocket and looked out over the water. Although there were still outstanding questions and concerns where Leberman was concerned, most especially with regards to the Colby Agency, life was good.

Scratch that, he amended, life was excellent.

"I'm ready, Lucas."

He turned in time to see his lovely bride exit the bedroom wearing the sexiest, most beautiful white silk negligee he'd ever laid eyes on.

The only thing he could imagine being more beautiful was her out of it.

"So am I," he murmured as he moved toward the woman he loved and their future together. *So am I.*

* * * * *

Dear Reader,

My favorite story of all time is the *Beauty and the Beast* fairy tale. I've used that theme in many of my books— the wounded hero, scarred by life, misjudged by society, bearing scars and disfigurements on the inside that match a harsh facade on the outside. There's so much potential for emotional depth and a rich love story because it's all about the hero's redemption. He must learn to love himself. And who better to teach him that difficult task than a heroine who is brave enough, smart enough, stubborn enough and kind enough to see beyond his ugly face or scars, his handicap or injury, or even just his gruff, beastly personality to the true heart and soul that lies within. It is the heroine's need for him and her courage to love him that redeem the beast.

That love for a *Beauty and the Beast* tale is why I'm so pleased to bring you Bryce Martin's story in *Forbidden Captor.* This physically and emotionally scarred soldier, big and gruff and far from handsome even before his injuries, has turned his warrior skills to bounty hunting. But when he is captured, tortured and held captive by the ruthless domestic terrorist he's after, he discovers the most important battle of his life—rescuing Tasiya Belov, a beautiful woman blackmailed into servitude. Forced to feed and care for all the prisoners at the remote island compound, Tasiya's heart goes out to the beast in his cell who listens to her troubles and cares that she is all alone. They risk their lives to be free—and they risk their hearts to find that happy ending to the fairy tale.

Happy reading!

Julie Miller

FORBIDDEN CAPTOR
Julie Miller

Prologue

St. Feodor, Lukinburg, November 4
9:07 p.m.

The chocolate-caramel torte was a delicious success. And an incredible mess.

But Anastasiya Belov didn't mind being elbow-deep in suds and dishwater, scraping the sticky topping from the pan. Not when her latest recipe had brought such a delighted smile to her father's face and earned her a hug even before she'd served him coffee.

Lukinburg, an eastern-European monarchy reformed after the disbandment of the Soviet Union, was a country beset by hard times. Even with her job cooking and cleaning for the minister of finance, Dimitri Mostek, she and her father, Anton, barely made ends meet.

But Anton, one of the senior accountants working for the ministry, had earned a bonus in his November paycheck. To celebrate his success, Tasiya had been extravagant with her market shopping and had prepared her father a feast far grander than anything she was allowed to fix for the Mosteks. Her father's smile had been worth the extra pound of butter and brown sugar.

"You look so like your mother when I see you in the kitchen like this."

Tasiya smiled and turned at the sound of her father's musical accent. His rolling *r*s and guttural consonants echoed in her own voice. "You mean hot and perspiring, even though there's snow on the ground outside?"

He brushed aside a strand of curly black hair that clung to her damp cheek. "I mean beautiful. Strong in spirit and body."

"I love you, Papa."

He leaned in and pressed a kiss to her forehead. "I love you, Tasiya. Now—" he stood straight and tall and clapped his hands "—is there more of that chocolate cake?"

Tasiya laughed. "It's a torte, Papa." She reached for a towel and dried her hands, then gave him a nudge back to the living room where he'd been reading the paper. "You go. Relax. I will bring you another slice and a fresh cup of coffee."

"You spoil me, daughter."

"You're the only one who'll let me. Now go."

As her father disappeared around the corner, Tasiya went to work. She twisted her long tresses into a bun and secured them with her metal hair clip. Then she set the coffeepot back on the stove to reheat while she prepared a second helping of dessert.

She was glad to do this for him, glad to bring a little happiness into their humdrum lives. There'd been far too little rejoicing in recent years. Not since King Aleksandr had ascended the throne. His solution to creating order and reviving a badly wounded economy had been to rule with a tight, cruel fist. Inflation was out of control. And while the royal family lived in a palace that showcased the elegance and wealth of the Lukinburg of old, basic supplies such as food and fuel couldn't be guaranteed to its citizens. Financial aid from foreign countries had been rejected time and again, and those who protested the king's strict policies and isolationist philosophy were often imprisoned, or else they mysteriously disappeared.

So Tasiya took joy in her father's success. She celebrated it as her own success because it was the only type of achievement she would ever be allowed.

After setting her mother's silver tray with a plate, fork and napkin, Tasiya reached for the coffeepot and—

Gunshots exploded in the living room. "Papa!"

"Tasiya!"

She ran to her father as the front door splintered and cracked around the lock and swung open. Four or five men dressed in black from head to toe stormed in, along with rifles and curses and a blast of snow and frigid air.

"What are you— Papa!"

She never reached him. One of the men grabbed her around the neck and shoved her back into the kitchen. "Stay back!"

Tasiya twisted to see around the man blocking the archway with his gun. Though her father struggled, Anton was no match for the three men who dragged him outside into the snow. "Papa!"

Not waiting to ask questions, Tasiya pulled the lid from the coffeepot, grabbed the handle and whirled around to sling the steaming liquid into the man's face. Even with a stocking mask on, the scalding coffee did the trick. He screamed in pain, lifted his hands to his face.

She scooted past him and dashed out the door in her slippered feet. "Where are you taking him? Papa!"

She leaped down the front steps and saw to her horror they weren't taking Anton anywhere. Instead, two of the men pushed her father down onto his knees in the middle of the street. The third man pulled a gun from his belt and placed the barrel against her father's forehead.

"No! Don't!"

Tasiya ran straight into the nightmarish scene. Snowflakes bit into her cheeks, and cold soaked into her feet. She shoved the gun aside and hugged her father's head to her breast.

"Don't hurt him!"

"Tasiya, no—"

"What do they want?"

"Isn't this a pretty picture?"

Tasiya recognized that voice. Smooth and arrogant, used to having its own way. She spun around as the fifth man approached, not dressed in black like the others, but wearing a finely cut suit and expensive wool coat. Keeping her hands on her father's shoulders, she stared at the familiar face in shock. But she didn't for one minute think this man would help.

"Minister Mostek." Her employer. Her father's supervisor. The man with the beautiful wife and three children and roving eye. "Why are you doing this?" she demanded. "What do you want?"

"Justice." He trailed the tip of one leather-gloved finger along her jaw and Tasiya flinched. His smile never reached those cold, beady eyes. "Your father has stolen from me."

"It was so little," Anton protested. "I only took enough—"

With a nod from Mostek, one of the so-called soldiers of the kingdom rammed the butt of his gun into her father's temple. Tasiya sank to her knees as he fell, cradling his bleeding head in her arms.

"Your bonus," she murmured. Not a reward for a job well done. But funds stolen from the coffers of men who would terrorize their own country in the name of order and line their own pockets while citizens starved. "Let him go," Tasiya pleaded, looking up at Mostek. "He's an old man. He's no threat to you. He was only trying to keep a roof over our heads and food on the table. You cannot punish a man for trying to survive."

Dimitri Mostek cared so little for her father's plight that he'd pulled a tiny cell phone from his pocket and placed a call. "We have him," he reported, his greedy eyes dropping to the beaded tips of her breasts, made rigid by the wintry air seeping through her blouse. "We will execute him and set an example for others like him who would put themselves before our cause."

Execute?

"No!" Tasiya bolted to her feet, not knowing where to place herself with three guns all aimed at her father. "Minister...Dimitri...please."

His black eyes glistened as she used his given name. He'd asked her to do that before. In the pantry one morning where he'd trapped her unloading groceries. In his son's bedroom when she'd been changing the sheets. One time he'd held on to her paycheck until she'd said his name. Each time she'd reminded him she was there to work, to perform menial tasks for his family, nothing more. But to save her father...

"Take me instead." Bold words for a woman of no value.

"Tasiya, no." Her father's weak voice whispered from the ground at her feet.

Mostek held up his hand. The guns lowered. "You would be killed in your father's place?"

The man she'd burned inside the apartment came charging down the steps. "You bitch!"

Tasiya whirled around and gasped at the raised hand swinging toward her face.

"No!" Mostek grabbed the man by the collar and shoved him into a snowbank. "Stand down."

"But she—"

"I said no." Mostek's deep, articulate order silenced the man. "No one touches her but me."

The man in the snow, nursing his scalded cheek and humilated pride, had shed his stocking cap. But it wasn't enough damage to keep Tasiya from recognizing the chief of security in Mostek's office. Her heart raced at the discovery. She glanced all around her. Did she know all these masked men?

Dimitri shrugged, straightened his coat and faced her with a smile that oozed a repugnant brand of charm. "So, Anastasiya. You would sacrifice yourself for your father?"

He seemed to doubt her loyalty to the only family she'd ever known, the only person she'd ever loved. "If it will spare his life."

Tasiya's deep breaths clouded the air around her as she waited for a response. She lowered her eyes, sensing Mostek's traditional beliefs that a woman shouldn't be allowed to address anyone, especially a man, above her station.

"Such a waste of beauty." She detected the same lustful hunger that had repulsed her when he'd offered to set her up as his mistress that day in the pantry.

"Yes. I'm here." Mostek's voice sharpened. He was talking into the phone now, though she could feel his gaze on her. "Anton's daughter has offered herself to me as a gift in exchange for his life. I would like to accept."

"No." Anton tugged at her skirt. He wavered as he pulled himself to a sitting position and clung to her arm. "She cooks and cleans for you, but she will not be your whore."

Mostek flicked his hand and the guns went up again. "Then you will die."

"Papa…"

Mostek spun away, arguing with the man on the phone. "I have been your loyal servant, carried out every secret…"

"These are very dangerous people, Tasiya." Anton reached for her hand. "I knew the risks when I embezzled their money."

She knelt beside him. "But the punishment does not fit the crime."

"These are terrorists, my love. They do not care who they hurt, only that their cause endures and is triumphant."

"And what is their cause?" A long-suppressed anger blended with her fear. "Who benefits from their so-called patriotism?"

"Do not question them."

Tasiya cupped her father's swollen face between her hands. She unbuttoned the cuff of her white cotton blouse and dabbed at the blood collecting in his eye. "You are a good man who has been loyal to king and country as long as I have known you. And how do they repay you? With threats and violence." She blinked back the tears that stung her own eyes. "You are all I have in this world. I will not let them hurt you."

"Tasiya—"

"It is done." Mostek stuffed his phone into his pocket

as he hooked his hand beneath her elbow and pulled her to her feet. Away from her father. "The arrangements have been made."

"What arrangements?"

Mostek nodded to the others. "Take him away."

"No—" Tasiya lunged for her father as two of the men grabbed him beneath his arms and dragged him toward a long black limousine adorned with two flags bearing the Lukinburg coat of arms.

Mostek jerked her arm in its socket, drawing her up against his chest. He moved his thin, shapeless lips against her ear. "In exchange for allowing your father to live, you are going to take a small journey for me."

Tasiya swallowed hard to keep the bile from scorching her throat. "Where am I going?"

"To America."

"America?" So big. So far away. The country that had given Crown Prince Nikolai asylum after speaking out against King Aleksandr at the United Nations. America—the country Aleksandr had called an empire-building bully. The country that would join the international movement to overthrow the Lukinburg government.

"My superior…" He seemed to find the word distasteful. Any man Dimitri Mostek feared and reviled must be very dangerous and powerful, indeed. "…believes you can be useful to our cause."

"I don't believe in your cause. There has to be a better way to find peace and prosperity for our people."

He smiled. She hated that loathsome sneer. "Your beliefs are irrelevant. I'm putting you on a plane to America where you will be delivered as a gift to some friends." Tasiya shriveled inside at the implication. "They will be warned not to touch you. *That*—" he kissed her temple, making her skin crawl "—will be *my* reward."

Tasiya pulled back as far as his unrelenting grip allowed. What else did she have of value, if not her body? "Then what am I to do in America?"

"What you do so well. Cook. Clean. Serve my friends as you have served me." He reached into his pocket and pulled out a squarish device that looked like a miniature version of his own phone. He pressed the gadget into her palm and curled her fingers around it. "And call me every day on this secure line to let me know exactly what they're doing."

"You're asking me to spy on the Americans?"

"I'm telling you what you must do to save your father's life."

Chapter 1

Devil's Fork Island, U.S.A., November 7
12:00 a.m.

"*Alpha-Bravo-Tango—Abort! Abort! Abort!*"

"*Negative!*"

Sergeant Bryce Martin defied the command crackling over his vest radio and slipped a large safety pin into the land-mine housing, holding it in place while he dismantled the trigger assembly. The charge was still there, but it could no longer be detonated by simple pressure.

Taking deep, steady breaths to counteract the racing fury of his pulse, he spared a moment to glance up at the women, children and old men huddled like live bait in the center of the rows of cultivated coca plants turned minefield.

Only three more to go and they could lead the hostages out through a safe zone. He had the mechanics down now. Though the jungle of San Ysidro was laced with these deadly contraptions, their design wasn't any more complicated than a hand grenade. After diagnosing and learning the procedure on the first one, he could neutralize each mine in just over a minute. He'd come this far, he'd finish the job. "I need three minutes, sir."

"I don't have three minutes to give you, Sarge." Colonel Murphy's signal was breaking up. His soldiers were on the move. "The damn setup's an ambush. You gave it your best shot, but you need to get the hell out of there. Cordero's men are lining up mortars. They're going to blow your position. I order you to abort. Powell's hijacked an evac chopper. We're buggin' out. Now!"

Bryce moved on to the next mine and dropped to his knees, his big hands surprisingly agile as he opened the trigger housing and slipped in another safety pin. He couldn't leave these innocent people behind at the mercy of a greedy dictator and his drug-funded army.

Not when he'd been so close to finding something meaningful in his life. Not when he'd been so close to caring.

He jimmied the housing apart and snipped the wire before risking a glance up at Maria. Some of the men in his Special Forces unit saw her as the village madam—older, plumper, past her prime. But he saw her as something special. A kind soul who looked beyond his scarred-up face and truck-size body to offer him comfort and friendship in a decidedly unfriendly country.

Her world-weary eyes had tears in them now as she shook her head.

Two minutes.

"Dammit, Martin—get your ass out of there. You've got incoming."

Bryce averted his ears to the telltale thump of mortar fire. Their fiery trails lit up the sky.

He couldn't tell the civilians to run.

He gripped his assault rifle and rose to his feet.

He couldn't save them. He couldn't save Maria.

"I'm sorry." He barely mouthed the words. He was already backing up.

"Sarge!"

He shouldn't have cared. Dammit. Why the hell did he have to care?

"Gracias." She blew him a kiss. "Be happy."

Bryce turned, ran. The mortars hit. The mines exploded. Smoke billowed in the air behind him and rushed upon his heels.

White-hot pain ripped through his legs and back, cutting through scars and skin and muscle and bone.

He flew through the air, knowing he'd been toasted long before he hit the ground.

Campbell and Blackhaw charged from their cover. He felt their hands on him, dragging him out of the fire and smoke and death.

Bryce twisted in his scratchy, lumpy bed, reliving the torturous pain, inside and out. Replaying the months of recovery that had tested even his considerable patience, unable to find a comfortable position that didn't make something itch or burn or ache.

A gunshot cracked through the night air. The sound jerked through him before Bryce went still. His eyes snapped open to hazy darkness. Not a remembered firefight. The real thing.

Dread made his body rigid, suffused him in sweat. God, no. He swung his legs off the cot and ran barefoot across the slimy cold stones of his cell. Over the rattle of his chains, he heard the hoots of laughter and triumph from outside in the courtyard.

Grasping the vertical bars of his cage, he hoisted himself up to look out. "Son of a bitch."

He dropped to his feet, turned his back to the wall and sank down on his haunches. He knew the wall was as cold and damp from the night air as the floor beneath his feet. But he barely felt it. He couldn't feel much of anything beyond rage at his captors.

This was worse than his nightmares.

The bastards had just executed an innocent man.

Devil's Fork Island, U.S.A., November 8
2:13 a.m.

Bryce stared at the soldier's bloody chest. "Kid?" God, had he ever been that young?

Cruel hands dragged him away from the dead man he'd scrambled into the slick underbrush with. Despite a flying tackle, he'd been too late to save him. Hell. He and his comrades from Big Sky Bounty Hunters had unknowingly brought the enemy with them in the first place.

Tailed. Like a bunch of amateurs. When they'd been trying to help. To warn their old unit of a terrorist attack.

Only, these were no terrorists. Not the foreign kind, at any rate.

The fight was on.

"Grab the big guy! Take him down!"

How many times had he heard that kind of threat?

Three men piled on, forcing him to the ground. He got his hands around the throat of a black-haired man, butted him in the head, kneed him where it counted and shoved him out of the way. Down to two. More wrestling than punching. Idiots. With all the mud and water they couldn't get a grip. His meaty fists were far more effective.

"Martin!" He heard Jacob Powell's voice, shouting his name. "Money's on you, big guy! Take 'em—"

A deep grunt silenced his cheering section. They were

outnumbered. Taken by surprise. Going down or neutralized one by one.

Bryce felt the bonds going around his wrists as they finally wised up and started beating on him. He pitched, kicked, pounded—and with a mighty effort, he lurched to his feet, hauling the two men up with him.

The tattoo of an upside-down burning flag swam across his vision before a new fist connected with his jaw, driving him back to his knees in the muddy marsh of North Carolina's Swamp Lejeune. But it was the telltale click of a military-issue Colt sliding a bullet into the firing chamber that finally stilled the fight in him. "Let me just shoot him like I did the other one."

The man with the curly black hair and the gun, the only man here who could match Bryce in stature, waited for the okay.

"No, Marcus! The ones out of uniform are not to be killed. You've enjoyed enough target practice for one day." Even with the steel barrel of the Colt pressing into the back of his skull, Bryce turned to get a good look at the scraggly beard and brown ponytail of the tall, well-armed man approaching him.

"Boone Fowler."

"I see my reputation precedes me."

Like a rat spreading the plague.

The weasly son of a bitch headed up the Montana Militia for a Free America. Fowler was the fanatic who'd broken out of prison four months ago with his loyal minions, regrouped his own private army and waged a personal vendetta against the men of Big Sky who had imprisoned him in the first place. He didn't care who he hurt or how he hurt them—only that he got his way.

Bryce breathed hard, tasting the blood in his mouth and ignoring pain in his side, keeping his enemy in sight.

Fowler doffed a distinctly unmilitary salute. "I want them alive. But I don't necessarily need them in one piece."

The man named Marcus needed no urging. He rammed the butt of his gun into Bryce's head, swirling pain around inside his skull.

Bryce struggled against the beating hands that bound his wrists and ankles and inflicted what damage they could.

He was still swinging until the moment his world went black.

Bryce swung at his attackers in his sleep, rattling iron chains, pinching his wrists and startling himself awake.

He sat bolt upright in the bed, orienting himself to surroundings illuminated only by the cold threads of moonlight shining in through the open grating at the small, high window.

Sweat trickled along his cheek and dripped onto the deep rise and fall of his naked chest. It pooled at the small of his back and soaked into the waistband of his jeans. With each breath, he inhaled the stale smells of mold and damp, the pungent odor of the straw ticking in the mattress beneath him, and the cool, salty tang of an ocean breeze. They were familiar smells by now, though not necessarily welcome ones.

Two dead now. Boone Fowler had promised to kill one man every day until he got what he wanted. Whatever the hell that was. They had to get out of this hell-hole.

As Bryce's eyes and mind adjusted to the here and now, he took note of the stone block walls. The surfaces had been worn smooth, the edges eroded unevenly by centuries of use. He noted the new steel bars and massive lock that kept him from leaving his six-by-eight cell.

His ankles chafed and the chain between them rat-

tled as he swung his legs off the side of the iron cot and
flattened his bare feet against the cold stone floor. This
fortress was solid as a tomb and sported all the archaic
comforts of a medieval dungeon.

Ignoring the scars of his life and the bruises from his
capture, he jerked his wrists out to the side, stretching
his arms as wide as the eighteen or so inches of chain
connecting them allowed. He squeezed his hands into
fists, swelling his mighty forearms and biceps until every
muscle shook with the effort to rip the restraints apart.
Though rust from age and the damp sea air colored the
chain and cuffs, each link held fast.

Releasing his breath after the feverish exertion, he
dropped his hands to his knees and watched a mouse
scurry from its cubbyhole in the corner up to the window
and disappear outside.

Lucky bastard.

Bryce was hungry and sore, isolated and trapped like
a caged bear on some uninhabited island he didn't recognize. His injuries were minimal—a puffy right eye, a cut
lip, bruised ribs and a gash on his right cheek that would
need stitches to heal pretty. Not that one pretty scar would
make much difference amongst the marks left by the fiery
car wreck that had killed his parents, and the shrapnel
wounds from that San Ysidran minefield that had ended
his official military career. But his injuries would never
heal if the beating and pointless questions he'd endured
that afternoon were going to become a daily ritual.

His three comrades from Big Sky Bounty Hunters, as
well as the thirteen Special Forces soldiers who'd survived
the ambush at the Marine Corps training base nicknamed
Swamp Lejeune, could be dead now or imprisoned in another barred room inside this ancient prison. And from
where he sat, he couldn't do a damn thing to help them.

Like he hadn't been able to help that kid last night.

"Hell," was all he said. The word echoed in the darkness.

Waking up hadn't made the nightmares go away.

"A gift for a job well-done, huh?"

"Yes, sir."

The man named Boone Fowler read the letter from the sealed envelope Tasiya had delivered from Dimitri Mostek. Though the two men had little in common in the looks department beyond their forty-something age, she sensed they'd been cut from the same arrogant, power-hungry cloth. Mr. Fowler was a good four or five inches taller than Dimitri's stocky build. His hair was a faded brown, long and pulled back into a ponytail. While Dimitri's short, black hair framed a pampered face, Fowler's face was marred by acne scars, outdoor living and a thin beard.

It was the calculating black eyes that made her think of the man who held her father prisoner. Like Mostek, Fowler's eyes were cold and hard. Full of suspicion. Quick to show blame and temper. Unused to reflecting patience or compassion.

Tasiya stood in the middle of Fowler's stucco-walled office, still clutching the carry-on bag she'd brought with her on the flight to New York and a place called Wilmington, North Carolina. The same bag she'd held on the long truck ride to a white, sandy coastline and the remote ferry that had brought her to this place.

Devil's Fork Island, the man had called it. He mentioned something about a conquistador stronghold, a sailor's prison and pirate hideaway.

But Tasiya hadn't been interested in the history of the place. She'd been thinking of that last glimpse of her injured father being dragged away from her and driven off to who knew where. She'd been thinking about how quickly Dimitri Mostek had put together a passport and traveling papers for her. Where he'd gotten the secure, high-tech phone that had been designed to dial only one number. His.

She'd been thinking that her father had taken money from some very dangerous people, and that it was her responsibility to make sure he didn't pay too high a price for that mistake.

Now she realized the men she'd been sent to spy on were equally dangerous.

And wouldn't take kindly to being spied upon, judging by the numerous security measures she'd seen thus far.

They'd been the only vehicle on the boat, and once it had docked, several armed men had materialized out of the tall, reedy grass on the banks to secure the ferry and tie camouflage tarps across the deck and wheelhouse. Clearly, there wasn't going to be a return trip to the mainland anytime soon.

The wind off the ocean had whipped her long skirt and coat about her legs. And though the sun was shining and the temperature was several degrees warmer than the frozen home she'd left behind, she'd shivered.

She'd been shaking by the time her short, skinny escort had wrapped his hard fingers around her upper arm to lead her into some trodden grass along what she now realized was an unmarked path. He paused at a tall, wire mesh fence, hidden in a line of scrubby trees at the top of the sandy incline.

The man pulled a walkie-talkie from his pocket and pressed a button. Another man's voice answered, demanding identification. Even with her limited English, she could tell they were speaking some type of code. Once approved, Tasiya heard a staticky hum from the fence that seemed to charge the air around it and stand the hairs on her arms on end. She started when the hum ended in an abrupt silence. With an "All clear," the man pulled her beside him through a gate. Then there was another call, and the hum resumed behind her. Tasiya realized they'd passed through some sort of electric security barrier.

Such extreme measures to keep people out. Not that she'd expected a friendly welcome. Not that she'd trust anyone who did make a friendly overture.

No one had welcomed her to America or Devil's Fork Island or Boone Fowler's office. No one had asked about her trip or whether she was tired or hungry. No one had said anything beyond, "Show me your passport," or "Get in," or "This way."

She had a feeling Boone Fowler was more used to barking orders than striking up conversations. Tasiya longed for a kind word, a bit of reassurance, a smile, to make her think she could pull this off. Because she had an equally strong feeling that—like Dimitri Mostek— Boone Fowler would have no qualms about taking retribution on anyone who crossed him.

"So we're not supposed to touch you?"

He tossed the letter onto the gray metal desk and looked up, raking his dismissive eyes up and down her figure. Tasiya kept her own gaze trained to the floor. "No, sir."

"That's not a problem for me. I don't do foreign trash." He stood and circled around the desk, stopping just in front of her. "But I do like having a woman at my beck and call."

Tasiya stared at the buttons on his black-and-red flannel shirt. "Minister Mostek said I should help you in any way I can."

"You a decent cook?"

She nodded, not out of ego, but of honesty. "That is how I make my living."

"Good. Anything would be better than that slop Bristoe's been serving us." Tasiya held her breath as his hand moved toward her chin, but he caught himself before making contact. He snapped his fingers instead. Her breath rushed out in a startled gasp and he snickered in his throat. Understanding the command to submit to his will, she steadied her nerves and tilted her eyes up to look into his. "I don't want any of that spicy foreign crud where you can't tell what it is you're eating. Plain cooking. Nothing fancy. Use the supplies we have on hand. Can you manage that?"

Just like Mostek. "Yes, sir."

"Marcus!"

She turned away as he shouted the order over the top of her head. An even bigger man opened the thick wooden door from the outside hallway. He had to stand six and a half feet tall, nearly a foot taller than she. He was built like an ox and seemed to share the same personal habits of a beast of burden. His slick, curly black hair and stained hands needed to meet a bar of soap. And the pool of yellowish-brown tobacco juice that swirled in front of his leering smile before he turned and spat his cud into a corner of the hallway nearly made her gag.

Quickly Tasiya closed her eyes and pictured an image of her father's kind, smiling face. The face of the gentle man who'd read her bedtime stories as a child, and talked about her mother so she wouldn't be afraid of the imaginary creature she'd thought lived beneath her bed.

She was calmer when she opened her eyes, but the big ox with the suggestive grin and large pistol strapped to his belt was still staring at her.

"I heard we had company," he drawled, strolling into the room. "I'm Marcus Smith, Mr. Fowler's newly promoted chief of security. 'Cause I'm so good at what I do. And your name, little lady?"

Little lady? She was five feet, seven inches tall. Of course, everyone must seem little compared to this brute. She fixed her gaze squarely in the center of his chest. "Anastasiya Belov."

"She's a gift from our benefactor for a job well-done," Fowler explained. "He's impressed that we were able to neutralize the strike force."

"I'm the one who's impressed." The man called Marcus Smith reached out and twined his thick, grubby fingers into the long curls of hair that fell across her left breast. "Nice. Prettiest damn thing I've seen in weeks."

Tasiya curled her toes inside her boots to keep from bolting.

But, surprisingly, Boone Fowler saved her the trouble. "Hands off, Marcus." He shoved the big man back a step. "She's not *that* kind of gift."

Tasiya winced at the pinpricks of pain that danced across her scalp before Marcus let go of her hair, but she refused to cry out. This was nothing. Her father might be suffering much worse than this. She could endure a few unwanted gropes for his sake.

But apparently Boone Fowler intended to follow his instructions to the letter. "The note says we're not to touch her. Our contact wants her in pristine condition for himself. And since his people are funding our operation, I don't want to jeopardize that relationship. Yet. We have business to attend to, anyway. Or have you forgotten our purpose?"

Marcus bowed his gaze like a chastized child. "I

haven't forgotten. I just thought maybe, since you seemed so pleased with my performance lately, that—"

"Keep it in your pants for a few days, okay? We'll use her to free up some manpower to increase security patrols and interrogations."

Keep it in your pants? Another strange Americanism. She might not understand the words, but she had no problem recognizing the lechery in Marcus Smith's eyes, or the blame she read there for being reprimanded by the boss.

"I'm sure you can find other ways to entertain yourself. After all, I intend to break every one of Cameron Murphy's team. I want them begging to do my bidding when we make that videotape and broadcast it."

Breaking someone seemed to have a reviving effect on Marcus Smith's mood. He was smiling as he looked up again. "Murphy's men have been pretty stubborn so far. But I like a challenge." He glanced down at Tasiya, giving his statement a double meaning. "I've got a few tricks up my sleeve to try, if need be. This old pirate hideout is proving to be a very resourceful place."

Fowler nodded, pleased with the answer that Tasiya couldn't quite understand. "I don't care how you get the job done. I just want results."

"You'll have them before we shoot the video next week."

Tricks? Video? Were these the sort of things she was supposed to report to Mostek?

She hadn't yet come up with an answer when Boone Fowler stepped beside her and demanded her attention. "I've got thirty men here who all need to be fed three square meals a day. When you're done with that, in the evening, we've got seventeen prisoners. You're to take them bread and water. Marcus will show you your room, the kitchen and larder, and the route you're to take when you feed the prisoners."

Three square meals versus bread and water? Compassion had her looking up into those cold, dark eyes. "Only one meal for the prisoners?"

Those dark eyes sneered. "Rule number one around here, Ms. Belov. *Never* question my orders."

"No, sir." Tasiya covered the unexpected flare of sympathy for someone besides her father by quickly lowering her gaze. "I just wanted to be clear on my duties."

"You're not stupid, are you?"

She had no trouble comprehending the insult. But she ignored it and made an excuse. "English is not my first language, sir. I only asked because I wanted to make sure I understood correctly. Three meals for your men. One meal for the prisoners."

"In between, you can clean my office and the latrine. But I don't want you in here without myself or a guard present. As a matter of fact, I don't want to see you anywhere but your room, the kitchen or making your rounds to the prisoners unless you have a guard and my permission." He bent his knees and brought his face level with hers. "Do you understand that?"

"Yes, sir."

"Then you're dismissed." He straightened and returned to his seat behind the desk.

Tasiya swallowed her anger and the urge to blurt out that he wasn't a god. And that if he was as smart as he seemed to think he was, he'd realize he had a traitor in his midst. Standing in his office. A black-haired sheep in wolf's clothing, to put a twist on one of those childhood stories her father had read to her.

Fowler was a lot like Dimitri Mostek. Full of himself and high on power. No qualms about being cruel and ma-

nipulative. The only thing lacking were the lusty over-
tures, and she had a sick feeling that Marcus Smith would
be adding that dimension to this living hell.

"This way, sugar," said Marcus, turning sideways in
the doorway instead of stepping aside, so that her shoulder had to brush against his chest as she exited into the
hallway.

Crinkling her nose at the whiff of stale tobacco and
sweat, Tasiya clutched her bag tight against her stomach
and hurried past him. She fixed an image of her father's
loving face firmly in her mind as she followed Marcus
Smith down a spiral staircase of worn, warped stone to
the doorless closet off the kitchen that would serve as her
home for the next few weeks.

Chapter 2

"Please, Minister," Tasiya whispered into the phone, glancing over her shoulder to make sure no one was eavesdropping on her call. She trimmed the wick on the kerosene lantern on her two-drawer dresser, dimming the light so as not to draw attention to her presence in the room.

By the end of the night, she vowed to at least find a blanket to hang across the arched opening so she could change her clothes without the curious eyes of Marcus Smith or anyone else ogling her. "I want to talk to my father. If he's not safe, I have no reason to do this for you."

"Anastasiya. Darling." Mostek's cultured voice tried to seduce her even across the ocean that separated them. "I like it so much better when you call me Dimitri."

Tasiya swallowed her gag reflex and her pride. "Please… Dimitri. Let me speak to my father."

"Very well." Tasiya drifted toward the corner of the twin-size bed that took up half the room. She sank onto the hard mattress, hugging her arm around her waist while he spoke to someone on his end of the line. But Dimitri still had a few more words for her. "That wasn't so difficult, was it, Anastasiya? I'm pleased you made it to your destination and are getting acquainted with the men you are working for."

She had no desire to get acquainted with anyone she'd met thus far, but didn't think it wise to share that information with Mostek. "No one complained about the dinner I prepared. In fact, I believe Mr. Fowler has ordered his men not to address me unless it is about my work."

"Good. Your father's well-being depends upon you doing your job there and then returning to be my mistress. I don't want you sullied by American hands."

"How can you—" Tasiya bit her tongue to keep the question to herself. It wasn't her place to understand how men like Mostek and Fowler could do business when they didn't like each other and trusted each other even less.

"How can I want you?" She let Dimitri run with the topic so she wouldn't have to explain her impetuous question. "Because you're a beautiful woman and I'm bored with my wife. I told you I could set you up in style in an apartment here in the city if you'll let me."

"What about my father?" She glanced at the clock beside the lantern, knowing she needed to cut the phone call short and get to her rounds delivering the prisoners' rations before anyone questioned her absence from the kitchen. "What will happen to him when I return?"

"I'll give you enough money that you can support him as well. But I don't want him living with you." She could visualize Mostek's vulgar sneer. "I'll require privacy for my visits."

Not exactly the motivation she needed to successfully pull off this charade.

"Here's Anton. Keep it short."

Tasiya shot to her feet and trained every aural cell in her ear to the precious sound of her father's voice.

"Tasiya?" He sounded tired.

"Papa?" This was what she needed to hear. "Are you all right? How is the cut on your head? Are you eating? Have they hurt you any more?"

"I'm fine, daughter. They cleaned the wound and put a bandage on it. But I'm worried about you. So far away. So—"

"I'm fine, Papa." He was being held by terrorists who wanted to use him as an example of how they dealt with anyone who dared oppose them. She wouldn't be a burden to him on top of that. "The work here is no different from at home. I cook and clean."

"But these men…" She could hear the fear in his tone. "Are you safe?"

She hurried to the open doorway and looked around the empty kitchen. For now, she could give him an honest answer. "I'm safe." But Marcus Smith had warned her to start her rounds by eight o'clock or he'd show up to escort her himself. It was nearly eight now. She had to go, even though she wanted nothing more than to cling to the sound of her father's voice. "I love you, Papa. We'll be together again soon, I promise."

"I love you."

Those three words would have to sustain her courage. Dimitri Mostek snatched the phone from her father's hand, ordered his men to take Anton back to his room and lock him in, and added a final threat.

"Your loyalty to your father is touching. I hope you will prove as loyal to me."

Tasiya felt as if Mostek had ripped her father from her arms again. But she squelched her fear with a deep breath and kept her voice calm. "I've done everything you've asked of me thus far. I won't disappoint you."

"It's imperative for your father's health that you don't. I'll expect a call from you tomorrow. I want to know everything the militia is doing, the status of their prisoners, anything you can tell me. I also want you to find an American television—"

"A television?" In this drafty old place whose only modern amenities seemed to be its security systems? She'd had to hand-pump the stove to make it work, while a small generator produced electricity for the refrigerator and freezer. He wanted too much. "Where will I—"

"Do not interrupt me again." Tasiya bit her tongue, lest he take his displeasure with her out on her father. "A radio or newspaper will do as well. I want to know what propaganda they are saying about Lukinburg, and what news they have of Prince Nikolai and Princess Veronika."

"I'm to spy on them, too?"

The two royal heirs had remained in the United States after speaking out against their father's inhumane policies in their homeland. Though branded a traitor by King Aleksandr and the Lukinburg press, Nikolai had apparently become the heroic darling of American women and politicians alike.

Providing news of the prince and princess to the king would no doubt bring some favorable reward to Dimitri. "I will try my best."

"You will do these things," he corrected. "Is that clear?"

"Yes."

"Such a good girl. Such a good, beautiful girl." The false charm bled back into his voice. "I'll be thinking of you tonight. In my dreams."

Tasiya cringed at the implication, but checked her response. "Goodbye."

She risked a rare, perverse pleasure in ending the call before he could answer. Hiding the phone inside her pillowcase, she glanced at the clock. Two minutes past eight. Marcus would come looking for her soon.

Her father's life depended on her carrying out Mostek's orders.

Her own life depended on her doing it without getting caught.

Ponderosa, Montana

"What do you mean they shot another one? Where the hell are my men?" The tall, black-haired man wheezed, trying to rouse himself from his bed.

"Easy, Colonel." Trevor Blackhaw braced his hand against the shoulder that wasn't bandaged and eased his boss at Big Sky Bounty Hunters back against the propped-up pillows. "You've been home from the hospital all of two hours. If Mia finds out we're in here talking business, she'll have my hide."

Mention of Cameron Murphy's wife, who had just stepped out of the bedroom to put Olivia, their four-year-old daughter to bed, seemed to ease his agitation. "I guess this means you had to cut your engagement celebration short?"

Trevor sank into the chair beside the bed. "Sierra understands. She might be free of the militia's influence now, but none of us will rest easy until Boone Fowler and his men are back in prison where they belong."

Cameron rubbed at the scruff of beard that had sprouted along his jaw in the days since barely surviving a chemical bomb attack by the Montana Militia for a Free America at a nearby mall. Though he'd suffered critical burns and some temporary damage to his lungs, there wasn't a damn thing wrong with his intellectual capabilities or leadership skills. "Tell me what we know."

Trevor picked up the grainy black-and-white photographs he'd brought in to show his boss. "An army search-and-rescue team found one deceased soldier down in Swamp Lejeune at the ambush site. Michael Clark," a fellow bounty hunter whose background in army intelligence made him an expert detective, "dates the second photo about a week after the initial capture. The army ID'd the victim as one of theirs, but it's too dark to get any kind of fix on the location."

"What about where the photos were processed?"

Trevor shook his head. "Clark's still trying to trace the source. It passed through a lot of hands before reaching us."

"And there's no way to track them from the ambush site?"

"Lombardi and Cook are in North Carolina now. But Lejeune training base covers thousands of acres over a variety of terrain. They found some heavy-vehicle tracks, but the trail went cold at the New River. Fowler's men could have choppered out, taken a boat, landed a seaplane. They could be camped out next door or halfway around the world."

Cameron crumpled the sheet and blanket inside his fist. "Fowler's on American soil, I guarantee it."

"Both his victims were military, both were part of the covert strike team that was running training ops for an intel incursion into Lukinburg. The executed prisoner photo was delivered in Washington, D.C., with Fowler's usual demand—if the UN insists on sending our men into Lukinburg, then he'll find a way to stop them."

"By killing off hostages one by one?" Cameron shook his head. "Terrorist tactics aren't going to change the government's mind."

Folding his long, olive-skinned fingers together, Trevor leaned forward. "He's probably sending a subtle message to you, too. What he's doing to these soldiers, he intends to do to your bounty hunters."

The bad blood between Cameron Murphy and Boone Fowler went back a long way. "Dammit, Blackhaw—Fowler murdered my sister for his cause. How many other innocent lives has he erased in the name of what he calls patriotism? He's taken potshots at every one of us—hit us where it hurts the most. Why can't we get this creep?"

"We will. Campbell, Powell, the sarge, Riley Watson, Brown and the others—we've all sworn to end this bastard's reign of terror. Fowler's the one who made this war personal. But we intend to finish it. I promise you that."

A painful breath rasped through Cameron's lungs. Though his dark eyes remained sharply focused, his battered body was fading toward much-needed sleep. "How are we gonna do that if we can't find him?"

"I've activated every contact we have around the country. There's a Special Forces unit waiting to assist us the minute we know anything. Don't think for one minute your men—the men we fought with down in San Ysidro and in Africa and the men you hand-picked to work for you now—are sitting in a cell somewhere twiddling their thumbs." Trevor tucked the graphic photos inside his jacket and stood. "If I know Sergeant Martin and the others, they'll find a way to contact us."

Cameron nodded. "Then let's be ready to roll."

Tasiya smoothed her palms down the length of her cream-colored sweater and steadied her nerves before slipping the elastic band of keys Marcus had given her around her wrist. Then she unlocked the wheels of her stainless steel cart and pushed it out of the kitchen into the breezeway that separated the refurbished quarters housing the militia members from the prison section of the compound.

She passed back through centuries of time as she unlocked a thick wooden door and entered the long passageway that housed the prisoners. In this part of the stronghold, little had been done to reclaim it from its colonial past. The uneven settling of the stones paving the floor created an uneven, repetitive clanking sound that chafed her nerves as her cart bounced over bumps and into ruts.

With no central heating and few covered windows, the chilly night air off the ocean drifted in and caught in the dark, dank corners. The breeze swirled her skirt around her knees. She'd brought one pair of denim jeans with her, which she suspected were going to become her new uniform if she couldn't shake the damp chill that permeated her skin.

Behind locked doors she could hear the hum of generators and other machinery, which she supposed had something to do with the island's alarm system. Driven more by survival than curiosity, she didn't test her keys in any door until she reached the rusted iron monstrosity Marcus Smith had shown her earlier. After unlatching a modern steel padlock, she scraped the dead bolt across its hinge. The door itself groaned from weight and age as she shoved it open and entered the prison proper.

Foul, musty air stung her nostrils and made her eyes water. It was inhumane to keep a man in these conditions, but then she supposed kindness and compassion weren't on Boone Fowler's list of virtues.

Besides the padlock she'd slipped into her pocket to keep from being trapped inside herself, the only visible hint of technology was the single electric wire that ran the length of the stone walls to illuminate a bare light-bulb every twenty feet or so. And she suspected that had more to do with security than with the prisoners' comfort.

Unintelligible snippets of conversation teased her ears and bounced along the walls, but the prisoners fell silent as she approached the steel bars that separated her from the men she was feeding. They all watched her with as-sessing, unfriendly eyes. Three soldiers in one cell. Four in another. Then three and three more.

They took the small loaves of bread and cups of water she poured for them with a variety of comments at see-ing a woman, and a few jeers as they mistook her for a member of Fowler's militia. But hunger quickly over-rode their defiance, and they sat down to eat with a piti-ful gusto that reminded her of some of the poor families she'd seen in Lukinburg.

Another key unlocked a second iron door. In this long, twisting catacomb, there were four isolated cells, each one separated from the other by thick stone walls and steel bars.

Here the men sat, bound by leg irons and wrist man-acles, one to each cell like condemned murderers. These men didn't wear uniforms like the others, but civilian clothing.

The first one had unusual blue-green eyes that looked right through her without blinking. She idly wondered if the blood on his torn shirt was his own or someone else's. He never moved until she had passed on by. The next one stood up when she approached. Despite the bruising and swelling around one eye, he was a handsome man. He nodded a silent thank-you, then watched her every move until she'd rounded the corner out of sight. The third was deep in his own thoughts. And pain, she suspected, noting a dozen or so cuts across his roughly shaved head. Tasiya quickly set the bread and cup of water just outside the bars on the floor in front of his cell and moved on.

When she turned the corner to the last, most isolated of all the chambers, Tasiya hesitated. The lightbulb here had burned out, leaving the only illumination to the bulb twenty feet behind her, and the moonlight that streamed in from what must be the cell itself.

Tasiya silently cursed her luck. She could either travel all the way back to the kitchen for a flashlight, or she could swallow her fear of the unknown enemy around the corner and follow the wall with her hand until it opened up onto the cell itself.

Weighing the options of retracing her steps through the dungeonlike chambers past sixteen prisoners versus checking on the welfare of one man made her decision a quick one. If she could face down the guns of Dimitri Mostek's men, she could certainly handle a shadowy passageway and an unarmed man who was locked safely behind bars.

The stones were smooth with age but sticky with moisture and dust as she trailed her fingers across them. Leaving her cart behind, Tasiya headed toward the shaft of moonlight. When she reached the end of the wall, she peeked around into the cell.

She caught a silent breath.

On the other side of those shiny steel bars stood the hardest-looking man she'd ever seen. He wore only a pair of jeans that hung loosely enough on his hips to reveal a strip of the white briefs that hugged his waist. He stood with his back to her, his arms reaching above his head. He was fiddling with something at the base of the window, doing something with the rusty iron brace at his wrist. He wasn't any taller than her father's six feet of height, but he was massive across his shoulders, arms and back. Twice as broad as her father. Muscled and formed in a way that reminded her of tanks and mountains.

He was all male from the short clip of his dark brown hair to the flexing curve of his powerful thighs and buttocks.

And even in the moonlight that mottled his skin, she could see he was horribly disfigured.

Raised, keloid scars formed a meshwork pattern from his waistband up to his left shoulder, where the dimpled terrain of a faded burn mark took over and disappeared over onto his chest, up the side of his neck and down to his elbow.

Tasiya pressed her fingers to her lips to stifle a gasp. Her stomach clenched and her heart turned over in compassion. My God, how this man had suffered.

To her horror, he froze at her nearly inaudible gasp. With precise deliberation, he lowered his arms and slowly turned.

Shrinking back against the cold stone wall opposite his cell, Tasiya stared. The front view was nearly as harsh as the back. She could see, now, that the shadows that dappled his skin weren't all tricks of the dim light, but from bruising, as well. The old burn injury covered nearly a quarter of his chest and one side of his neck and jaw. His chin was square and pronounced. One carved cheekbone was bloody with the slash of an open wound. And the swelling around his left eye distorted the shape of a face that would have been harsh and forbidding under any circumstances.

Without a word he took a step toward her. But when Tasiya, trapped in a circle of moonlight, flattened her back against the wall, he stopped. His mouth opened as if he wanted to say something, but he shrugged instead. Tasiya's gaze instantly darted to watch the fascinating ripple and subsequent control of all that muscle.

When she realized he'd stopped and was even retreating to the rear of his cell to alleviate her fear of him, Tasiya's breath seeped out on a deep, embarrassed sigh. This man knew he was frightening to look at, imposing to get close to. Others had cowered from him before.

What a lonely, terrible existence that must be.

Sensing some of his pain, Tasiya looked up into his face. The only thing not forbidding about the prisoner was his eyes. Enhanced by the glow of the moon, they were a cool, soothing shade of gray that reminded her of the quiet, wintry skies of her homeland.

And they meant her no harm.

Unlike the lechery she'd seen in Marcus's and Dimitri's eyes, the cold condescension she'd seen in Boone Fowler's expression, or the blank, preoccupied stares she'd seen from the other prisoners, this man was making a point of putting her at ease.

Responding to that unexpected civility, Tasiya summoned her courage and retrieved her cart. She wrapped the last small, crusty loaf, which couldn't be more than a snack to a man his size, in a napkin and poured some water into the last metal cup. Then she knelt down in front of the steel bars and laid the bread and water just in front of them, the way she'd been instructed.

When she heard the rattle of his chains as he moved to pick up his meal, she shot to her feet and backed well out of arm's reach. Compassion or not, he still made two of her, he was still a prisoner, and he still frightened her.

But in her haste to put distance between them, she'd

kicked the cup over and spilled the water. Tasiya watched the puddle quickly seep into the cracks between the stones on the floor.

She couldn't leave the man without water.

She glanced up at him. He was staring at her, with ever-watchful eyes, but he wasn't condemning her. He glanced down at the cup, and she knew what she had to do.

Shaking her head at her own skittishness, Tasiya picked up the pitcher of water from her cart. She had far greater things to fear from men far more handsome than this one. Good looks didn't make a hero. Scars didn't make an enemy.

This was her job. This was for her father.

"I am sorry," she whispered, picking up the cup and pouring him fresh water. "Here."

With a show of bravery, prompted by human compassion, she reached through the bars herself and held the cup out to him. He stared at it for a moment, as if he didn't understand the gesture. Long, silent moments passed. But she waited until his agile, nicked-up fingers closed around the cup. She quickly pulled away as he gently took it from her grasp.

"Thanks."

The deep-pitched voice startled her. The husky tone resonated in that big chest and washed over her like a warm caress.

Tasiya looked into those wintry gray eyes and felt the first human connection she'd known in the four days since Dimitri Mostek had kidnapped her father. She didn't know if making that connection with this beast of a man should be a comfort or an omen. But she sensed that when he looked at her, he saw *her*. Not the *foreign trash* hired to cook and clean and be forgotten. Not a blackmailed mistress-to-be. Not the tool of betrayal.

Her.

"You are welcome."

He retreated to his cot and sank onto the bare mattress to eat and drink.

Tasiya quickly replaced the pitcher and turned her cart to leave.

"I'm Bryce Martin," he said between big bites.

She stopped midstride. He wanted to make personal conversation with her? No one else, not even her employers, had. The idea was almost as disconcerting as the darkened hallway and the threats she'd received.

Turning back to his cell, she watched him take a long drink. The ripple of muscles along his throat fascinated her. How could one man be so much...man? The visible proof of all that physical and mental strength was daunting. She didn't need any female intuition to sense that Bryce Martin was a very dangerous man. And that she should be careful around him.

She quickly returned her gaze to gauge the trustworthiness of those assessing eyes. "I am Anastasiya Belov. Tasiya to most."

"Your accent's foreign, i'n't it?" His wasn't like any of the others she'd heard here in America yet, either. She detected a lazy articulation in his bass-deep drawl.

"I am from Lukinburg. In Europe." She wasn't revealing any secrets with that much information.

He stuffed the last bite of bread into his mouth and stood. She tilted her chin to keep those gray eyes in view, her heart rate doubling as his size and scars moved closer. His wrist chain grated across the bars as he thrust the empty cup between them.

The keys at her wrist jangled as Tasiya snatched the

cup and hugged it to her chest, dodging back a step to avoid contact. Bryce Martin scowled, as if her aversion to touching him neither pleased nor surprised him.

"Next time, Tasiya Belov," he warned, "be more careful 'bout stickin' your hand inside the monster's cage."

Chapter 3

The monster's cage?

Smooth move, Sarge. Had he really said that out loud to that woman? No wonder she'd high-tailed it out of here last night.

Bryce sat on the edge of his cot and twisted the crick from his neck. Squinting into the dust motes that filled the rays of morning sunshine, he wondered what kind of hell awaited him today.

Especially after he'd gotten an unexpected glimpse of heaven last night.

Tasiya Belov was a damn sight prettier than that scraggly Bristoe fella with the dirty hands and playground taunts who'd brought his bread and water the past seven nights. The insults and tough talk didn't faze him—Bristoe was a misguided kid trying to prove himself a man. But it sure was nice to finally get a taste of food that was clean and water that was fresh.

It was nicer to get a look at Tasiya.

Bryce rubbed at the skin chafing beneath his wrist

manacles and thought himself twelve kinds of fool. He should have come up with something decent to say to her, or kept his big mouth shut the way he usually did. Then, at least, he could have enjoyed the view a little longer. All that curly hair—blacker than the night around them—falling nearly to her waist. Skin that was as pale and pearlescent in the moonlight as her lashes were thick and dark. Lashes that surrounded wide, slightly tilted eyes the shade of rich, robust coffee.

Or maybe that was just the scent he got off her. Homey. Normal. Like his grandma's good cookin'. Far removed from any of the crap that was going on around here. Something about Tasiya's fairy-tale beauty and quiet ways had breached the cool reserve he wore like a suit of armor. He didn't allow himself to be attracted to many women. By age thirty-three, he'd wised up to that futility. But Tasiya Belov, with the exotic eyes and accent, had gotten to him before he could distance himself from a man's basic, male reaction to a beautiful woman.

So, of course he'd warned her off.

His chains jangled as he crawled onto the floor and squared off to do a set of push-ups. For years he'd used physical activity to dull the aches and longings and regrets of his life. What he couldn't burn out of his system this way, he tried to ignore.

Bryce knew he wasn't any great shakes to look at. The burn scars were old news; he'd had them since he was a kid, from the car accident that had killed his folks. The shrapnel scars that marked the end of his military career were more recent, more shocking to the unfamiliar eye. And the condition he was in now made his appearance even less appealing than usual.

It was a fact of his life. He was a big, scary-looking man. It made him a formidable enemy, a boon to his second career as a bounty hunter working for his former military commander, Cameron Murphy. He used his intimidating countenance to his advantage; few of the criminals he'd brought in expected the big guy to be so smart, or so good with his hands. And yeah, if it came down to it, he could outbust just about anybody in hand-to-hand combat.

He'd had years to learn to accept his fate. It shouldn't bother him.

But when Tasiya had looked at him with those wide, frightened eyes, he'd felt like a monster.

Yep, she'd had to muster up some real guts to hold out that cup of water. As if treatin' him like a human being was some kind of apology—like *she'd* done this to him. Or maybe it was defiance that had made her reach out to him. But what was she taking a stand against? Him? Boone Fowler? Her own fear?

And what the hell was a beautiful woman from Lukinburg, of all places, doing here on this godforsaken island? The Special Forces unit he and his buddies from Big Sky had been ambushed with had been secretly prepping for a covert surgical strike into Lukinburg. The UN wanted to oust their despotic king and restore democratic rule there. Bryce's former unit was supposed to be the first team in—to gather intel and remove a few key leaders.

So how had Boone Fowler's militia gotten wind of that attack when the team had been under a communication blackout for days?

He did one last push-up, shoving himself up and bracing his weight over his arms. An image of a willowy woman with frightened eyes blipped into his thoughts. Surely not. A Lukinburg spy on the militia's payroll? They'd never go for it. The whole point of Boone Fowler's life—beyond his quest for vengeance against Cameron

Murphy and the Big Sky team who'd put him in prison before his escape a few months back——was to cleanse America of any foreigners. And to keep Americans off foreign soil and out of foreign business.

So where did Tasiya fit in?

Dammit. He was thinking about her again. He was curious. Worried. *Swift one, Sarge.*

Bryce clapped his hands together as he pushed to his feet to do a round of squats. The noise startled some movement in the corner of his cell. He slowly sank to his haunches and smiled.

His little mouse friend was back, scoping out the nooks between the stones, scrounging for crumbs. Bryce's empty stomach growled right on cue.

"You're outta luck, buddy," he teased his furry roommate. They both were.

He was doing his best to stay in peak physical condition in case the opportunity for escape presented itself. But his insides felt as if they were rubbing together. A little extra food would go a long way to maintain his strength and keep his thinking sharp. If there were any crusts of bread around, he'd have gone after them himself.

Bryce stilled as the mouse scurried between the steel bars and disappeared into the darkness of the passageway beyond.

Smart mouse.

Crossing to the locked cell door, Bryce wrapped his fists around the cold, unyielding steel and pressed his forehead to the bars to peer into the shadows.

That's what he should be doing, searching this place.

But not for bread crumbs.

Let's replay this escape scenario again. He needed to get outside to get the lay of the place. Scoping out the location of the other prisoners and ascertaining a sense of schedules, the number of militiamen at the compound and security protocols could secure a way off the island. Bryce had no doubt they were somewhere off the eastern coastline of the U.S. They hadn't been transported by air, and after he regained consciousness on the boat they'd been tied up in, they'd traveled only a couple of hours. Not long enough to get them out of the country.

And it had to be the ocean. He recognized the smell of the salt in the air. In the still of the night he'd identified the pummeling of waves hitting land with a force too powerful to be a lake or river's edge.

But knowing he was on an island in the Atlantic was hardly enough information to mount an escape attempt. And if he couldn't get out of this hole to investigate for himself, then he needed to make a connection with someone who did have the freedom to move about the place.

Tasiya Belov.

A tight fist gripped his stomach and squeezed. He hated the idea of using her. But it made better sense than digging the mortar from around the bars at the window and climbing out into who knew what kind of situation.

He'd spotted the armload of keys around her wrist and suspected they could get him into nearly every place he needed to go. They could get him out of these chains, at any rate, and that would give him the ability to move about the compound with less chance of being detected.

That had been his first thought, grab the keys. But, short of using brute force against the woman—which wasn't his style—that wasn't gonna happen.

That left convincing her to befriend him, to run a few errands for him. Of course, he had no idea whether or not he could trust that she'd bring back the truth. Skittish as she seemed, she might run straight to Boone Fowler and tell him what the monster had asked of her.

Yeah, that'd go over real big in the escape-and-bring-these-murdering-bastards-to-justice department.

That left charming the woman.

A nearly impossible feat.

Long days out in the hills of the Missouri Ozarks where he'd grown up—hunting, fishing, camping—and quiet evenings spent on the porch with the grandparents who'd raised him didn't go a long way toward developing a man's sweet-talkin' ways.

Maybe one of the other bounty hunters, Aidan Campbell, Jacob Powell or Riley Watson—strike that, Craig O'Riley was the alias he'd been using when they were captured—were thinking along the same lines. They had the sweet words and the deceptive smiles and handsome faces he lacked. Hell, the way Powell ran his mouth sometimes, he could wear down a body's resistance, make a woman happy to concede to his will. And O'Riley was the master of undercover work. He could don a persona and make anyone—man or woman—believe every word he said.

So how was a former army sergeant who knew more about weapons and explosives than he knew about conversation and seduction supposed to get close enough to Tasiya Belov to gain her trust and enlist her help?

He wasn't.

He'd have to find another means of escape.

And he'd have to find it soon.

Bryce had been staring down the hallway long enough for the shadows to lighten and take shape. His cell was at the dead end of a passage that doubled back on itself. He knew that route led to a series of locked iron doors, one of which was the interrogation room—four stone walls that housed all the twisted toys of the Inquisition. From this vantage point, all he could see was an electrical wire and broken lightbulb tacked up between the stones.

But he could hear the enemy coming. Since they had the guns and he wore the chains, there was no need for stealth. Bryce backed up to the center of his cell and shook loose the muscles in his arms and legs, mentally bracing himself and prepping his body for the hours to come.

Marcus Smith and a pair of bully sidekicks lined up outside his door to pay him a visit.

"Ready to talk today, Sergeant?" Marcus spat his chaw through the bars on the floor next to Bryce's bare foot.

Bryce didn't shift his gaze from those icy blue eyes. Satisfying Smith's power-hungry need to control him wasn't on his to-do list. Smith was buttin' heads with a man who'd already endured the worst the world had to offer. His boys and toys couldn't break him.

Bryce's only response was the silent promise he made.

Ready to get what's coming to you? Because it will come. Maybe not today or tomorrow. But the days of the Montana Militia for a Free America are numbered.

Bryce and his fellow bounty hunters at Big Sky were damn well gonna see to it.

"Did you get a load of the big guy today?" Even with the buzz of other conversations in the room, Tasiya couldn't tune out Marcus Smith's booming voice. She couldn't ignore the lecherous fascination of his eyes, either. His cold blue gaze followed her as she moved from one table to the next to pour more coffee. Thank God she was out of arm's reach and he was busy regaling his men with stories. "Sits there and stares at you. Never says a word. Pisses me off."

"At least he doesn't get you off track with all his smart-ass remarks." Steve Bristoe, the skinny blond man who didn't seem to mind that Tasiya had replaced him in the kitchen, stuck a forkful of apple pie in his mouth and continued talking. "That Craig O'Riley is gonna say the wrong thing one of these days and I'm gonna really let him have it."

Marcus held up his mug, indicating he wanted her to return to his table for a refill. "Maybe it's time to execute another one of the soldiers. If physical force won't turn them, we'll have to find another way. We'll put one innocent life on each of their heads until we have those Big Sky bozos eating out of our hand."

Execution? Was that the kind of atrocity Dimitri Mostek and his unknown boss were financing here? Would he put a stop to the killing if she reported the militia's activities? Or would he applaud their work?

Tasiya swallowed the lump of dread in her throat and wiped all emotion from her face before stepping into Marcus's personal space. In fewer than forty-eight hours she'd already learned that Marcus Smith, with his yellow teeth and dirty hands, didn't think the no-touch rule applied to him. Unless Boone Fowler was around, of course. And since the militia leader preferred to take his meals in the privacy of his office instead of in the mess hall with his men...

A large, meaty palm attached itself to her backside. Tasiya nearly stumbled as Marcus pulled her even closer. "That's it, sugar," he said, as though his hand on her butt provided some sort of assistance in her duties. "Fill it all the way up."

Even when his words were seemingly innocent, or didn't quite make sense in her translation, his tone always made her feel dirty. The same way Dimitri had made her feel. This is what she'd sentenced herself to by agreeing to Dimitri's plan. A life in which she jumped at the touch of a man's hand, a life in which she turned off her emotions so as not to draw attention to herself and her discomfort, a life in which she would never know a man's kindness or love.

But, for her father, she would do this. He was all she'd ever had. For Anton Belov she would do anything.

"Thanks, sugar."

With the slightest of nods, Tasiya turned out of his grasp, unable to stop herself from wiping at the warm spot he'd left on the back of her jeans.

"Whoa, pretty thing, where you runnin' off to so fast?" His hand at her elbow stopped her escape.

"I have work to do in the kitchen."

This time, Steve Bristoe paused midchew to take note of the grubby hand on her sweater, then looked up at Marcus with a question in his eyes. He wanted to know how Marcus could get away with this infraction. But the black-haired giant was meaner and tougher than Bristoe could ever aspire to be. He was clearly the most feared man in this room. One look from Marcus, and Bristoe quickly turned his attention back to his dessert. With Marcus staking such a proprietary claim on her, there was no one in the room who would come to her defense.

Tasiya twisted against his grip, making an effort to defend herself. "There is food in the oven I must see to."

"Now you hold on a minute, sugar." The instant she saw how her struggles amused him, Tasiya forced herself to relax. Her quick concession to his will wiped away his grin. "I'm trying to pay you a compliment. I want you to clear these things from the table and bring me another piece of that delicious pie."

"There is no more pie."

His grip tightened, demanding she look at him. "I don't like that answer."

"It is the truth. You have eaten everything I prepared."

"Then prepare some more."

Tasiya shook her head. "But the time…" She pointed to the open kitchen door. "The bread I have baked for the prisoners will burn."

Marcus stood up. Towering over her, he bellowed his fetid breath in her face. "Who the hell cares about them?"

His commander did.

"Mr. Fowler's instructions were to feed them every night. To help them keep their strength—"

"Yeah, yeah, I know all that. He wants them alive, but they don't have to be healthy. You take care of all our needs first. And then you can feed whatever the hell you want to those traitors." He pinched her arm. "Are we clear on that?"

Tasiya bowed her head. "Yes."

He released her and threw his hands up in the air as if reprimanding her had taxed his patience. "Now get this mess cleaned up and don't defy me again."

For a moment Tasiya couldn't stem her temper or find her courage. She opened her mouth, but the right words wouldn't come.

It was a moment long enough for Marcus to shove his plate into her empty hand and swat her rump to speed her toward the kitchen. "Tomorrow night, know that I'm expecting two desserts."

She stumbled over her own feet in her hurry to put as much distance between her and Marcus Smith as possible. Temporarily beyond the sight of that big baboon, she dumped the dishes into the sink and ran cool water over a towel. Angry beyond words, feeling frustrated and helpless, she could do nothing more but silently curse Marcus and Dimitri Mostek. She was trapped by her love for her father in a completely horrible mess in which she had no one to rely on but herself.

Patting the towel across her flushed face and holding it against her nape beneath the French knot of her hair was the only comfort she could give herself, the only outlet for the feelings she couldn't express. She allowed herself five minutes of relative privacy. Time enough to shut off the ovens and let her temper cool along with the loaves of bread. Time enough to fix her emotionless mask back into place, pick up a plastic tub and return to the dining room to begin clearing the tables.

The smells of tobacco and liquor stung her nose as some of the men lit cigarettes and doctored their coffee from flasks in their pockets. A few headed out into the breezeway or checked the pistols at their sides and returned to their posts. Those remaining went back to trading stories, plotting strategies and ignoring her as she worked.

"Hey, listen to this, Marcus. We're on the radio." A short, stocky man she knew only as Ike shushed the room when he turned up the reporter's voice on his battery-powered radio.

"The nationwide manhunt continues for the eight prisoners who escaped from The Fortress prison in Montana where, like Alcatraz, escape was once thought to be impossible. The man believed to have spearheaded the prison break, Boone Fowler, the reputed leader of the Montana Militia for a Free America, is also sought as a suspect in a recent nerve gas incident at the Big Sky Galleria mall…"

"We're famous."

"Is the boss hearing this?"

"They'll never find us here."

"Shut up. I want to listen." Marcus silenced the men.

Tasiya began quietly stacking and clearing dishes from the tables to hide how intently, she, too, was listening to the American news report. "In other news, Crown Prince Nikolai of Lukinburg—at a speech in Kalispell, Montanta—spoke of his gratitude to the American government and its people for their support in helping to bring peace and prosperity back to his country."

After a crackle of applause, she heard the familiar, cultured voice of the man who would defy his king and father to save the country she loved from ruin. "Kalispell, Montana is quite delightful in November. It's almost as pretty and picturesque as Ryanavik Mountain in my nation, Lukinburg. Can you envision the same..."

Tasiya paused with a handful of silverware, frowning at the eloquent oratory. Ryanavik was the name of a lake outside St. Feodor, not a mountain. A native of her homeland would never make such a mistake in geography. Was Prince Nikolai taking poetic license to create an analogy pleasing to the Americans? She dropped the silverware into a mug and reached for the wad of paper napkins at the center of the table. But Lukinburg had so many beautiful mountains, why not—

"Turn that damn crap off!"

Boone Fowler stormed into the dining hall, picked up Ike's radio and hurled it across the room. It hit the stone wall and shattered, silencing Prince Nikolai and any protest from the men in the room.

Like the others, Tasiya froze. Her heart, thumping against the walls of her chest, was the only sound she could hear.

With the pinkie of his left hand, Fowler brushed aside a stringy lock of hair that had fallen across his forehead. But as calm and controlled as that tiny movement was, there was nothing soft or gentle about him as he paced the length of the room. "You men are getting weak and lax. Basking in your own glory. We are fighting for our country, not ourselves. Our campaign is not about our egos and making the news. This is about the truth that I have taught you again and again."

"America for Americans," Ike mumbled dutifully.

Fowler braced his hands at his hips and nodded, slowly turning to make eye contact with each man in the room. "America for Americans," he articulated through the clench of his jaw. "I've trained you all to be better men than this. I've trained you to believe in the cause as much as you believe in me."

He reached out and put a hand on Ike's shoulder. Tasiya, clutching the trash from the table to her chest to hide her own trembling hands, didn't for one second believe Fowler's contact was meant to be a comforting, fatherly gesture. Yet Ike looked up into his leader's black eyes as though receiving wisdom and reassurance from a saint. "I believe in you, sir."

Fowler nodded, then stepped away. "I've devised a plan we must follow to the letter. I've given you orders and I expect them to be obeyed. I haven't let you down yet, have I? I showed you the truth about how our government is betraying our citizens, I gave you something to fight for. Is there any room in that plan to bask in personal accomplishments?"

"No, sir." The timid responses echoed across the room.

Fowler turned. "Is there?"

"No, sir!" they answered with more force.

"America for Americans!" one man shouted. He repeated the slogan and others joined in. Soon they were clapping their hands and pounding on the tables. Tasiya never felt more isolated and unwelcome in the world than she did when the chant reached a feverish pitch.

But as a nervous sweat broke out across the back of her neck and chilled her spine, Boone Fowler seemed to relax. A smile sliced across his thin beard, though the satisfaction never warmed his eyes.

This impromptu rally for their patriotic cause was not unlike the protests in support of King Aleksandr in her own country. But if anyone dared voice a dissenting opinion against king or crowd, the state police would show up. Or else minions like Dimitri Mostek and his security force would pay a more private visit after the fact.

These men were afraid of their leader. And he'd used that fear to brainwash them into obeying him.

If this was democracy, it was truly a frightening thing.

"Marcus."

"Sir." Marcus jumped to Fowler's side.

The cheers began to fade and were replaced by excited chatter. Tasiya laid the napkins in the tub and tried to make as little noise as possible sliding the chairs back into place.

"I have the prisoners' speeches written for the video. I want an update on your progress with them today," Fowler ordered. "Report to my office in twenty minutes."

"Yes, sir."

Fowler turned to the hapless Ike who was already on his feet, with his shoulders back and his chin tipped up at attention. "I want you to go to the communications center and doublecheck the accuracy of the wire I just received."

"But Simmons is on duty, sir."

"Don't argue with me. I want your expertise to verify it."

"Yes, sir." Ike scooted out the door, pulling out a ring of keys as he disappeared into the breezeway.

"The rest of you—I want a complete sweep of the island. Check every inch of the security grid. I want to know if so much as a pelican has breached the perimeter today."

A chorus of "Yes, sir" and the scramble of feet and chairs left Tasiya standing alone at the center of the room.

"And you—" She flinched when Boone Fowler pointed straight at her, yanking her from anonymity into the spotlight. "Bring me coffee in my office. Black. And plenty of it."

"Yes, sir." She needed no excuse to linger. Propping the loaded tub on her hip, she turned and hurried out to the kitchen where she dumped out the dregs and started a fresh pot. But she could still hear Fowler talking to Marcus Smith.

"I need to know if any of the prisoners have made contact with anyone on the outside."

"Impossible, sir. The bounty hunters aren't even allowed contact with each other."

"Good. Now here's what I want you to do."

Apparently, the two men had left the room. Tasiya could hear nothing now but the silence of just how alone she was.

She glanced quickly at her watch. If she hurried, by the time the coffee was done brewing she could make her call to Dimitri about the executions and Prince Nikolai's speech, along with what she'd gathered about Boone Fowler escaping from prison and orchestrating some sort of terrorist attack in Montana. Hearing her father's voice would replenish her strength and give her the courage to venture into Fowler's office and face the man one on one.

Fifteen minutes later, Tasiya had to bite the inside of her lips to keep her nerves from screaming out as she carried a tray into Boone Fowler's upstairs office.

Dimitri had denied her the chance to speak to her father. Whether the excuse that Anton was asleep was the truth or a lie hardly mattered. She'd been denied the one thing that could sustain her through this hellish sentence of servitude. Now she was left to wonder and worry if her father was all right. Had Dimitri's men harmed him? Was he locked up the way those poor prisoners here on Devil's Fork Island were?

Dimitri's compliment on her ability to ferret out detailed information had done nothing to boost her morale. And she couldn't very well tell him how Marcus's unwanted advances angered her or how Boone Fowler's temper frightened her. If Dimitri learned that his prize mistress had been soiled in any way, he might take his disappointment out on her father.

So Tasiya's goal was to slip into Fowler's office, set the tray on his desk and disappear just as quickly as she came in.

But this just wasn't her night.

Fowler must have seen her reflection in the glass as he leaned against his office window and gazed out into the moonlit sky. "Pour for me."

Tasiya hesitated for a moment before setting the tray down next to a wrinkled sheet of paper that looked as if it had been crushed into a tight ball, then spread out flat and smoothed back into shape. She could do this. She'd fixed a full meal for thirty men and served them in two shifts without a mishap until Marcus Smith got her in his sights. Boone Fowler didn't care about such things, certainly not with her.

Drying her nervous palms on the legs of her jeans, Tasiya asked. "You said black?"

"Yes."

She picked up the mug and the steaming pot. As she poured, her gaze strayed to the words on the page that had been discarded, then reclaimed. It looked like some sort of press release. The wire he'd mentioned to Ike? Is this what had Fowler so upset?

"Cameron Murphy released from Montana hospital. Bounty hunter expected to make full, if lengthy, recovery. Timing critical."

Bounty hunter? Like Bryce Martin and the other three prisoners she'd heard the militiamen talking about?

Who was Cameron Murphy? The timing for what?

"Can you read that?"

Tasiya gasped, startled by Boone Fowler's voice behind her. She quickly set down the coffeepot and gripped the mug with both hands before she spilled something. But the warmth that seeped into her fingers couldn't dissipate the chill of being caught poking her nose in where it wasn't welcome.

She uttered the first lie she could think of. "It helps my English to read."

"You didn't answer my question." He breathed his suspicion against the back of her neck.

The coffee in the mug splashed up the sides as she started to shake. His brand of intimidation was even more frightening than Marcus's ranting threats. "I can read the words, but they do not all make sense."

She had to get out of here. She spun toward him. "Here's your coff—"

But he was already stepping around her. "Maybe if you stuck to your own—"

Her hands smacked against his chest. The coffee sloshed over her fingers, scalding them. Her grip popped open and the mug crashed to the floor, splintering on contact. The hot liquid splashed Fowler's jeans and spilled over his boots.

Tasiya gaped at the spreading stain, soaking into suede and denim. "I'm sorry. I'll get another cup. A towel." The man was too still. This was too dangerous. She looked up into the cold void of his eyes and knew she was in trouble. "I am sorry."

"You...stupid..." She tried to retreat, but her hips hit the desk. She turned, grabbed the paper napkin off the tray and squatted at his feet to sop up what she could. He never touched her, but his words were like a slap across the face. "Get up. Get away from me."

Tasiya lurched to her feet, but he cornered her against the desk, preventing her from doing the very thing he asked. "Please."

"Please what?" She squinted her eyes against the foul words he slung at her. "I don't owe you any favors. You're a clumsy foreigner poisoning the land I love. Your incompetence reminds me of every foul, stinking reason I have to do what I do." He snatched the napkin from her fingers. "Now get out of my face! Go! Get out!"

Shuffling to the side, Tasiya scooted away. As soon as she was clear of the desk, she turned and ran.

His threats chased her out the door. "That's right, you witch. Run. Run!"

"Hey, sugar. What's your hurry?"

She didn't bother sliding to a halt as Marcus Smith emerged at the top of the stairs in front of her. She shifted directions to run right past him. "Leave me alone."

But his bear-size paw latched on to her wrist and hauled her up to his level. "Now that ain't nice—"

"Don't touch me!"

Tasiya jerked her arm away. Her hand flew back and hit the wall, scraping knuckles against stone and shooting a jolt of pain straight up to her elbow.

The sharp ache cleared the fog of panic that had consumed her long enough to shove Marcus aside and dart down the spiral staircase.

"Hey—"

"Marcus!"

Boone Fowler's summons kept Marcus from pursuing her. But Tasiya didn't stop running until she reached the relative security of her tiny room off the kitchen. She unfurled the blanket she'd hung across the opening, sank onto her bed and hugged her pillow to her stomach. Burying her face in the pillow's muffling softness, she screamed until her throat was raw and her energy was spent.

She was less than a human being in this place. Without kindness. Without security. Without respect.

By the time she could think clearly again, she looked at the clock. It was going on eight o'clock. She had seventeen hungry prisoners to feed.

Men who'd been chained, caged, tortured, beaten. Men who might be executed on Marcus Smith's whim.

It was empathy, more than duty, compassion or even fear, that finally prompted her to rise to her feet and dry her eyes. Tasiya straightened her bed, repinned her hair and walked into the kitchen with a determined stride. She fixed an unsmiling mask on her lips and buried her emotions in the deepest hole she could find.

She was a prisoner, too.

Only, her chains were the greed and lust of powerful men. Her cage was the deal she'd made with the devil to save her father's life.

Chapter 4

Bryce's hands stopped their diligent work as he tipped his head to listen to the food cart clanking over the uneven stones in the passageway.

She was coming.

That better not be his pulse rate kickin' into a higher gear. Bryce's sigh of self-disgust ached against his tenderized rib muscles and stirred the plaster dust at the base of the window. He had to move past this fascination with the woman. He had to focus.

But he'd been thinking about Tasiya's visit all day long. He'd thought about that silky waterfall of raven-colored hair when Marcus and his thugs had him chained in the interrogation room, pointing out every antique torture device they could use on him before resorting to good old-fashioned fists. He'd thought about those dark, exotic eyes instead of reading the standard hostage script Marcus had pushed in front of his face.

Even now he could close his eyes and remember the

normal, out-of-place scents of cooking and coffee that had clung to her skin and clothes.

There was something racing through his veins he couldn't control. An excitement. Anticipation. It made him itchy inside his own skin.

Man, wasn't this a disturbing development?

It wasn't like this was a date. It was only dinner.

Hell, it was scarcely that.

When he heard Tasiya's cart round the corner, his years of training were the only thing to rouse Bryce's survival instincts enough to brush away the loose plaster at the window. He'd been digging with the iron brace around his wrist so he blew away the telltale bits that had collected there, too. Then he used his toes to cover his tracks by nudging the dust out of sight into the cracks in the floor.

He rolled the stiffness from his neck and turned to face the bars of his cage.

Escape.

He forced the word into his brain, forced the memories and reactions out of his system. He put himself firmly in the moment and completely focused on the task at hand.

His goal was to get her to take a message to one of the other bounty hunters. Powell or Campbell or O'Riley could strike up a conversation with her. They were smart enough to see that she might be the key to getting out of here, too.

If he could get her to take a message.

But Tasiya Belov wasn't in the mood for talking.

Bryce frowned. Something about her was different tonight. Not just the elegant way she'd swept all that hair up onto the back of her head. Not the jeans she wore that looked just as feminine against the willowy curves of her body as the conservative sweater and skirt she'd worn last night.

Nah, this was something in her posture. There was a brittleness to her carefully precise movements as she set aside the flashlight that had guided her here, wrapped the bread and poured a cup of water from her pitcher. He saw a blankness in her expression that he recognized from battlefields—from Maria, stranded in the middle of that San Ysidran minefield with mortar shells winging her way, bringing certain death.

Fear.

Helpless, paralyzing fear that could only be dealt with by denying the expression of *any* emotion.

Son of a bitch.

What had happened to her? Bryce drifted forward, forgetting for a moment that he might be the cause of that fear.

Tasiya froze. Her gaze careened from the cup she was setting on the floor to his feet inside the cell. Bryce stopped in his tracks.

He retreated, and she slowly stood and turned his way.

She wasn't making eye contact. Instead she stared at the middle of his chest. But he had a feeling she wasn't seeing the old scars or the new bruises.

She wasn't seeing him at all.

"You okay?" The deep, rusty sound of his voice startled him almost more than it startled her.

Tasiya blinked, and a spark of light and focus gave her eyes life as she raised her gaze to his. She hugged herself, rubbing her hands up and down her arms as if she'd just woken up from a troubling dream and didn't quite know where she was. "You do not say much, do you?"

Not an answer, but at least she was talking. "Nope."

"The other prisoners...say more."

"I reckon."

She tilted her head at an angle and squinted, drawing a fine line of confusion above the bridge of her nose. *"Reckon?* I do not know that word."

Maybe that's all this was. She was having a little trouble with the language, misunderstanding things, feeling isolated—homesick, even—by the frustrating process of learning to communicate in a foreign language.

And he thought he could draft her as a messenger?

That's when Bryce saw the knuckles of her right hand against her pale-blue sweater. The porcelain skin was swollen and discolored with darkening blotches of deep purple and violet.

The blood in Bryce's veins steamed. Her distance tonight wasn't about words at all. "Who hurt you?"

Tasiya glanced down at her hand, as if embarrassed or frightened that he had seen it. She quickly tucked the betraying appendage beneath her arm, out of sight. "I hit it against a wall."

She must have punched the wall pretty damn hard.

Or somebody had punched it for her.

A protective anger churned inside his stomach. It had always been this way for him. If somebody was hurtin' and he could help them… Well, hell, what else was a big brute like him good for?

His grandma had said that soft spot of his would always keep him human, no matter what the world threw at him. Seemed like it never caused him anything but trouble, though. It complicated things when they should be simple, like telling Tasiya to ask the other bounty hunters whether or not they were being beaten every day in the same interrogation room.

That alone should be enough of a clue to let them know his condition, a bit of the militia's routine and get them to start comparing notes about the prison's schedule and layout. Plus, it would get them to thinking about striking

up a relationship with Tasiya so that she might willingly—
or without knowing it—aid them in an escape attempt.

But this wasn't simple. A woman getting hurt while
he was around didn't sit right with him. Even chained up
in a damn cage, he couldn't bring himself to use Tasiya
the way he needed to.

Not when somebody else was already using her.

He'd have to move on to plan C or D, or whatever letter of the alphabet it took until he could find a way out of
this place with every bounty hunter and surviving Special
Forces soldier in one piece. Maybe he could devise a plan
that might even help Tasiya. He shook the thought out of
his head and tried to focus on his own mission again—
get the hell out of here and take down Boone Fowler and
his militia in the process. But it was too late. He'd already
passed into complicated territory.

Tasiya retreated to the far side of her cart as Bryce
crossed to the bars to pick up his bread and water. He
needed to eat and drink and send her on her way before he started thinking crazy things and making foolish promises.

But his grandma had known Bryce better than he knew
himself. He sat on his cot, demolished the bread in a few
bites. Then he washed it down with the water and said,
"You get into any kind of trouble, come see me and I'll
do what I can to help."

Bryce let the words fall into silence. They drifted
across the moonlit shadows to the woman whose eyes
gleamed like polished mahogany against the pallor of
her skin.

Their gazes locked through the ghostly moonlight—
hers, seeking, searching, disbelieving…his, merely stating a fact.

Finally Tasiya released a deep, perplexed sigh. She

smoothed her palms against the denim at her thighs, steeled her posture and walked up to the bars that separated them. That tiny line of confusion that added dimension to her beauty was back in place as she wrapped her fingers around the bars and leaned in. "Why would you want to help me, when your enemy shows you no mercy?"

Interesting. She wasn't interested in how a man in chains could help her, but *why* he'd want to. Bryce stayed put, respecting her caution, admiring her courage. "You my enemy?"

She considered the question for several moments. "I do not know. You do not feel like an enemy. But it is not wise to trust in this place."

"Nope." She was being smart. There wasn't a man in this compound who didn't have an ulterior motive, himself included. Hell, he hadn't yet figured out why she was here on the island. He licked the crumbs from his fingers and rose to his feet. After stuffing the napkin inside the mug, he held it out to her and explained, "Helpin' folks is what I do."

She wrapped her fingers around the mug, linking them together even though they never touched. "You have a funny way of speaking, Bryce Martin."

Like calling him by his first and last name wasn't an odd way to talk?

But her serene smile hit him like a punch to the solar plexus, and for a moment he forgot how to breathe, much less take offense. God, she was beautiful when she smiled. As though a light went on inside her and spilled over into his dark world.

Bringing a smile to her strained expression made him less self-conscious about his hillfolk drawl, less guarded about his fearsome appearance, less aware of the band of keys on her arm that were so easily within his reach.

But before Bryce could move past that awkward, adolescent rush of pleasure and take advantage of her trusting proximity, his stomach interrupted. A deep, low-pitched rumble protested being teased with a snack when it was looking for a full-course meal.

Tasiya's gaze dropped down his bare torso. Her cheeks heated with color. Bryce wished Marcus Smith hadn't taken his shirt so he and his men could jeer at his deformities. He should be able to hide himself so Tasiya didn't have to see the scars, didn't have to fear the bulk of him.

He should forget about her and her safety and her smile and grab the damn keys.

But Tasiya had taken the mug and backed beyond his reach before he could reconsider.

"You are still hungry, aren't you?"

Bryce shrugged, damning that soft spot inside for caring what happened to her and complicating his escape. "I'll live."

"A few bites of bread is not enough to sustain a man your size. It is not enough to help you heal from your injuries."

The rations they'd been feeding him weren't enough to sustain *her.* "I'll get by."

She stacked the mug on her cart. But Bryce was mistaken in thinking she'd been making polite conversation. "There is dried fruit in the pantry. I could add it to the bread I bake tomorrow—to give you vitamins, a more balanced diet. There are different grains that are more filling."

He eyed her bruised hand. She wanted to defy Boone Fowler's orders? "Don't do anything that's gonna get yourself into trouble."

She nodded as if he hadn't spoken. "I will bake this

bread tomorrow. For you and your comrades. To keep up your strength."

"No."

"You would help me if you could. I will help you."

"Don't do it," he warned, fearing repercussions beyond his control. "Fowler will know."

"Good night, Bryce Martin." She pushed her cart down the passageway.

"Forget about the bread. Watch your own back." Bryce yanked at the bars, wishing he could pull them apart and stop her. "Tasiya?"

But Tasiya Belov, her noisy cart and her surprising stubbornness had already disappeared around the corner.

"Papa?"

"Daughter, it is good to hear your voice."

Anton's weary sigh concerned her. "You sound tired."

"I am fine," he reassured her. "I think they give me something in my food to make me more docile."

Tasiya released the blanket that now covered her door and paced to the far corner of the room. She'd seen no one in the kitchen eavesdropping on her, but she wouldn't risk anyone overhearing the panic that sprang into her voice. "You are not cooperating with Dimitri's men?"

He dropped his voice to a whisper she could barely hear across the miles. "I cannot stand what he has done to you. Maybe we cannot stop his bullying ways, but I do not intend to make his rule over our lives an easy one."

"Papa..." Hadn't she promised to defy Boone Fowler's bread-and-water rations order for the prisoners? It wasn't much in the way of rebellion against the rules and oppression here, but it was one little stab at independence that might keep her from going completely mad. However, hearing that her injured father might be taking a similar stand against Dimitri Mostek worried her. She hugged an arm around her stomach, but found little comfort. "You must be careful."

She'd witnessed the penalty for not cooperating with a superior here. Verbal abuse. Humiliation. Even violence. She squeezed her eyes shut and remembered the horrible welts and bruising she'd seen last night on Bryce Martin's ribs. Though they'd all been tortured in one way or another, it seemed as though he was being punished more than the other prisoners. Isolated in the last cell. Kept in the dark. And perhaps because he was able to endure more abuse, Fowler's men inflicted more.

It pained her to see such a physically able man as Bryce being hurt that way. To think of her more fragile father enduring such cruelty… "Please do everything they say. Let me take the risks, Papa. I am young and strong. I can do this. Knowing you are safe is what gets me through each day."

"Is it really so awful there?"

"It is lonely." She bit her tongue to keep from blurting out how her encounters with Boone Fowler and Marcus Smith had alternately shamed and frightened her. Anton didn't need to worry about that. "But I am fine."

"Is there no one there you can talk to?"

You get into any kind of trouble, come see me and I'll do what I can to help.

Bryce Martin wasn't exactly what she'd call a confidant. But in the dark shadows of the night, when she'd felt vulnerable and alone, when she'd ached for a kind word—for hope—he'd noticed. He hadn't said much, but the depth of his voice had resonated across every shattered nerve, calming her, grounding her. He seemed solid as a mountain to cling to, yet just as forbidding.

There was a kindness to his perceptive gray eyes that had washed over her like a gentle spring shower. A sadness, too, as though the ugly marks on his body were etched even more deeply inside.

He'd called himself a monster at their first meeting, and she'd believed him. But last night she'd seen a glimpse of the heart within the beast. And that paradox, as much as the anticipation of speaking to her father, had given her the strength to survive one more day.

But how could she explain to her father that she was drawn to such a man, and still ask him not to worry?

"I am fine, Papa," she repeated. "Do not test Minister Mostek's patience. Please."

A self-satisfied laugh grated against her ear. "Excellent advice, my dear Anastasiya."

Her father had been taken away from her again. Determined not to give verbal vent to her frustrations, Tasiya began to pace, three steps this way, three steps back. "You did not let me say goodbye to him."

"You should not test my patience, either," Mostek warned. "You had your chance to talk. Now tell me what Fowler and his people are up to."

She shoved her fingers into the hair at her temple, massaging the twinge of a headache that had formed the instant Dimitri returned to the line. For a moment, she considered setting the phone back on the charger and disconnecting the call. For a moment. "They talk about a video they will make next week."

"Good. They are staying on schedule. My superior will be pleased."

"Minister…" Tasiya stopped her pacing, swallowed her pride and begged. "Dimitri. There is no place I can go here. I cannot leave Mr. Fowler and his men. I promise

I will still call you…but can't you let my father go free? Aren't I payment enough for his transgression?"

The silence on the telephone line worried her. When Dimitri began to speak, she worried even more. "My darling Anastasiya. While it pleases me to hear you offer yourself so freely, you must remember that this is not my decision alone. The man I work for does not overlook those who would cheat or deceive him. You should be counting your blessings that your father is still alive."

"But the king does not even know my father—"

"The *king*," he emphasized, "has put me in charge of this project and has granted me discretion to handle it as I see fit. I will not take the chance that you would seduce one of the American infidels in order to bring about your escape. By keeping Anton close to me, I'm confident you will keep the men there at a distance."

Tasiya quietly gnawed her lip until his outburst dissipated. "I have no intention of sleeping with any man here," she stated quietly. She had no intention of sleeping with Dimitri, either. But that was another trial she would deal with when—and if—she survived this one. "Will that be all? I must attend to my duties here before I am missed."

"Tell me again about this note you read in Boone Fowler's office that upset him. I do not want him to be distracted from his purpose, either."

Though the name Cameron Murphy meant nothing to her, apparently it had some significance for Dimitri. With the clock ticking toward eight o'clock and the bile rising in her throat at every slimy innuendo from Dimitri's lips, Tasiya answered his questions. She dutifully repeated his instructions for listening to tomorrow's American news reports, ignored the kiss he blew across the line and rang off.

* * *

Bryce stood on tiptoe in the darkness with his hand fisted around the bar at the window. He'd dug enough mortar from the base that he could twist it back and forth now, starting the painstaking process of loosening the bar from its upper mount. Removing one bar still wouldn't create a space large enough for him to crawl through to the outside, but the bar itself would give him a weapon, a tool.

The digging would go faster. He could pry himself out of these chains. He could defend himself if he got the opportunity to make a run for it.

It would give him the first advantage he'd had since getting tossed into this place.

He froze at the muffled sound of footsteps in the passageway. Ignoring the tender twinge that ached along the right side of his ribs, he breathed in deeply, silently— mentally and physically bracing himself for another visit from his captors.

Then he heard the distinct metallic clank and rattle of Tasiya's food cart bouncing across the paving stones.

Make that his second advantage.

The wary tension in Bryce's muscles eased at the familiar sound. His breath seeped out on a slow exhale and he dropped flat on his feet, brushing away and hiding the evidence of his handiwork as he turned to wait for her arrival. He was almost grinning with the keen anticipation of seeing her again. But a scratch at his whiskers on the unscarred half of his jaw gave him a sobering reminder that while her face might be a sight for weary eyes, his was not.

The rattle of metal cups and rhythmic thump and bump of the cart fell silent before she reached his cell. She'd stopped several feet away, near the turn in the passage-way. Or had she been stopped?

Bryce's senses buzzed on alert, listening for some other sound in the shadows. Items moved, shifting on the cart, as though someone was searching among the napkins and baskets. Son of a bitch. He clenched his hands into fists and crossed to the door of his cell, wishing he was a super hero so he could pull the bars apart and go help her.

"Tasiya?" he whispered, so softly that his voice was swallowed up by the shadows.

If Fowler or Smith or some other yahoo had stopped her…if they suspected she'd used their rations to feed more to the prisoners, that she was doing something kind for him…if they'd chosen a dark corner so far removed from the rest of the prison that no one could hear her scream …

He heard a soft gasp. The grind of metal. The tinkling shatter of delicate glass breaking. A word in another language he could only describe as a curse.

"Tasiya!" His voice boomed off the rock walls. Hell. Let Fowler's men make a connection between them. If she was getting into trouble, then it was *his* fault. They should punish *him*. "Tasiya?"

He peered into the darkness, unable to make sense of the moving shapes. And then a sharp pain pierced his retinas. He had to blink and turn away as an unexpected light flooded the hallway.

After so many days and nights in relative darkness, the artificial light reflected off the smooth stone walls, fill-ing the space in front of his cell with a cold, harsh glare.

But when the reassuring thump of the cart resumed, Bryce shaded his eyes with his hand and forced himself to look. It wasn't that bright, really, but it took several mo-

ments for his eyes to adjust before he focused in on Tasiya, wearing jeans and the long, cream-colored sweater
she'd worn the night of their first encounter. She appeared
to be alone, unharmed—and well beyond arm's reach.

Bryce's concern for her petered out on a resigned sigh.
He was still standing at the cell door. He'd been imagining the worst, frantic to get to her, to save her from
whatever had gotten its hands on her. But *he* was still the
monster she feared.

A little frisson of useless resentment fired through his
blood. He looked beyond her to the lone lightbulb, weakly
shining from its mount at the end of the passageway. He
purposely challenged the caution in her eyes by wrapping
his fingers around the bars and staying put.

"I thought someone was after you."

Loose black curls danced across her face as she turned
to glance over her shoulder, just now realizing how her
scuffling sounds in the darkness and the clumsiness of a
broken lightbulb might sound. She quickly turned back
to him and tucked one of those curls behind her ear. "I
am all right, Bryce Martin," she stated. "Even Mr. Fowler
would not begrudge me a light to illuminate my path."

Bryce continued to lean against the bars, and Tasiya
still kept her distance. But his resentment was gradually
replaced by acceptance. It had always been this way, and
Tasiya's misgivings about him weren't gonna go away
just because he seemed to be developing an overzealous
sense of protection where she was concerned.

She looked mighty pleased with herself over changing a lightbulb. And while that added bit of confidence
was a welcome change to the fear that had haunted her
expression last night, Bryce felt compelled to remind her
of the risk she had taken, and the danger she might be
in as a result.

"You ever think maybe they want to keep me in the dark?"

"Yes."

Startled by the bluntness of her reply, Bryce looked deep into her eyes. Hell. She was dead serious. She got the whole torture thing. Maybe she wasn't as naive about the dangers surrounding them here as he'd originally thought.

"Well," he released the bars and retreated, giving her the distance she needed, "it doesn't bother me none."

As soon as he moved, Tasiya began assembling his meal. "It should bother you. It is wrong for one man to have so much power over another. You have no shirt, no blanket, no shoes. They treat you as if you are…"

She pinched her lips together, searching for the right word. But Bryce could translate for her. "Not human?"

Her pitying gaze locked onto his and she nodded. She set his bread and water on the floor and backed away. Bryce rattled forward like the ghost of Jacob Marley in Dickens's *A Christmas Carol*, dragging his chains along with him. They were a visual and aural reminder of the burdens he carried through life, a reminder that Fowler and Smith—and even Tasiya, with her reluctance to get too close—saw him more as a monster than a man.

But it wasn't a topic he cared to discuss at the moment, despite the polite need to apologize he could see dancing through Tasiya's shifting feet and the stricken expression in her eyes. Pity was an emotion that had never done him any good. He'd rather deal with her fear, or have her ignore him altogether, than waste his limited emotional expertise trying to ease the guilt of someone who pitied the way he looked or was treated.

So, Bryce silently retrieved his meal and settled on his cot. He broke apart the crusty loaf and saw that, true to her word, Tasiya had added some wheat bran to the processed flour, and filled the inside with moist red and blue bits his nose quickly identified as cranberries and blueberries.

But even if he was done talkin', Tasiya had more to say. "In my country, they treat political prisoners this way. The king would break down his people's spirits so that they do not complain about poverty or the bullying police. We are not allowed to speak out or better ourselves unless we…" Her voice and gaze trailed away to a distant place, and Bryce wondered if she was remembering some event in particular or if this was a philosophical argument. "In Lukinburg I could not even have this conversation with you. If someone heard me say these things…"

"No one can hear us back here." On his short walks from his cell to the interrogation room and back, he hadn't passed any occupied rooms or cells, so there was no one around to eavesdrop. He'd heard the hum of generators through layers of walls and locked doors. But whatever they were running on all that power, it wasn't listening devices or video cameras. Security at this end of the compound, at any rate, was all iron and stone, without one high-tech doodad in sight. "Say what you want. I won't tell."

"Is that why they beat you?" she asked, in a soft, hesitant voice. "To get you to tell them things?"

"I won't tell," he reiterated, closing the subject. If he could keep Big Sky's secrets, he could keep hers, too.

He pressed his nose to the bread's soft interior and savored the rich aromas. His grandma would have served it slathered in butter or honey or both. But he didn't feel he'd been deprived of anything when he sank his teeth into the first delicious, crunchy, chewy bite. He moaned in his throat at the first real flavor that had enriched his life since he'd been taken prisoner.

He opened his eyes and sought Tasiya's gaze. This he could discuss. "You made this?"

She nodded and drifted closer to the bars that separated them. "I am a cook in my home country."

Bryce took another bite. "You're a damn good one."

"Thank you."

He had to look away and concentrate on the second half of his bread. If she smiled that prettily at one lame compliment from him, just think what she might do if a more charming man plied her with a bunch of the right words. Thoughts of escape, ever present in his consciousness, surged to the front of his mind. How would she respond if *he* could come up with the right words?

"Anybody give you any grief over doctorin' up the recipe?"

She wrapped her fingers around the bars and leaned closer. He could see they were long and dexterous fingers, blunt tipped and businesslike in their practical elegance. He could also see she hadn't quite gotten his question. "I am not sad to do this for you. I enjoy preparing food."

"No, I meant…" Bryce gave up on that line of discussion. "I appreciate you doin' it."

She rested her cheek against the steel bar and smiled again. "You like to eat?"

Two hundred forty pounds of muscle and bulk wasn't an obvious indication? "It's one of my favorite pastimes."

That line of confusion furrowed between her eyebrows.

Pastimes. Yeah, this was goin' real well. Communication was so not his area of expertise. He rubbed his palm over the scars and stubble of his jaw, searching for a simpler way to rephrase. "My grandma was an excellent cook. I enjoy it when I find food as good as hers."

"Your grandmother was a cook?" That seemed to interest her.

He nodded. "Not a professional. But we ate better than just about anybody in the Ozarks."

"The what?" He'd lost her again. "Oze...?"

Yeah, right. Try explaining the bastardization of a French Acadian word about a tribe of Native Americans to a woman who spoke whatever Russian dialect it was they spoke in Lukinburg.

Time to change the subject if he was ever going to get this messenger thing to work. He popped the last bite into his mouth and picked up his mug. "So what brings you to this place? Is there some kind of trouble at home you're trying to get away from? Can't be much better in this place. I know Fowler doesn't cotton much to foreigners."

"Cotton much?"

She shrugged, narrowing her eyes in a quizzical frown. Her stiff, self-conscious posture pulled her sweater taut and thrust the curve of one small breast between the bars. Of course, he had to notice that. Too damned observant for his own good. Look away, Sarge, he warned himself as his blood thickened and pooled behind his zipper as if she was dressed to seduce and that innocent movement had been some sort of intentional come-on.

Closing his eyes to break the spell she seemed to cast over him, Bryce stood up to get his common sense circulating again. "I wouldn't think he'd want a woman around here."

"He doesn't mind if I am serving him."

Bryce swallowed the last of his water in one long gulp, doubting if Boone Fowler made any distinction between a servant and a woman who was subservient to his needs. "So what does a gig like this pay?"

"Gig." The line between her eyes deepened. "I do not understand."

Shaking his head, Bryce turned away. He was getting as frustrated with the language barrier as she was. But, refusing to surrender just because a task was tough, he faced her again. "How much money does he pay you to work for him?"

"Money?"

"You know what money is, right?"

"I know." Her porcelain cheeks flushed with color. Her eyes were looking everywhere but at him now. "He does not pay me."

Since he doubted she shared Fowler's fanatical views on American isolationism, and she wasn't in it for the money, that left only a handful of reasons why Tasiya could be here—and none of them were good. Bryce moved imperceptibly closer. "Why *are* you here?"

The question had her so agitated she forgot about keeping her distance from him. "I am paying off a debt."

He slipped even closer. He could smell the scents of baked bread and spices that clung to her hair and clothes.

He could smell the fear on her, too.

"What do you owe Fowler? What the hell business does he have in Lukinburg?"

She snatched the mug from his grip and spun toward her cart. "I have to go."

Uh-uh.

"Tasiya." Bryce reached through the bars and grabbed her wrist.

She jumped at his touch, turned back and tugged and twisted for her freedom. "Let go!"

He wasn't hurting her, but he needed her to stay and answer the question. "Just hold your horses. Please."

Then, just as abruptly as a light switch flipping off, she

went still and dropped her gaze down to his belly button. Though there was such a determined lack of focus in her eyes that he was sure she wasn't looking at the abs or the bruises. It was a practiced pose of submission, as if she'd responded that way to a man's touch a dozen times before.

Ah, hell. He liked this response even less than her eagerness to get away from him.

Bryce's big hand easily spanned her arm beneath her sleeve. His sensitive fingers noted that her skin was as cool and velvety soft as it looked. And the pulse beating beneath his fingertips raced with a madness that belied her distant, aloof posture.

"Tasiya," he whispered, giving her arm a gentle nudge. "Look at me." Long, tense seconds passed before her shoulders lifted with a trembling sigh and she tipped her chin. Curling black tendrils fell away from her pale cheeks as she blinked her eyes into focus. "I'm not going to hurt you. I know it looks like I could, but I wouldn't do that."

She tried to latch on to something she saw in his eyes, but couldn't quite bring herself to make that leap of faith. However, her wide, unadorned lips moved with a succinct articulation that could be understood in any language. "I am not supposed to be touched."

Bryce instantly popped his grip open, releasing her. He took a step back, holding his hands up in apology. He imagined his questioning frown only added a fearsome quality to his concern. "Is that your rule or somebody else's? I just wanted you to finish the conversation. I wasn't puttin' the moves on you."

She understood *that* phrase well enough, judging by the sudden color that flushed her cheeks. But she didn't answer the question. She was suddenly too busy organizing the empty mugs and baskets on her cart and wheeling it around.

"I am sorry. The hour is late. I must clean up and get to bed. They require that I prepare breakfast quite early." Now that he'd let her go, she'd forced a brightness into her tone and pasted a taut smile on her mouth. But at least she had the guts to look him in the eye as she prattled on. "For Mr. Fowler's men, unfortunately. I am sorry to mention food when I know you are hungry. I will see what else I can bring you tomorrow. Perhaps a shirt and socks as well. It is cold here at night."

"Forget all that. Just do me a favor, will ya?"

Man, she was ready to bolt. He suspected years of polite good breeding and fear of drawing more attention to her obvious discomfort were the only things still keeping her here. "If I can."

"Check on my buddies for me. Jacob Powell. Craig O'Riley. Aidan Campbell. Tell 'em I'm okay—"

She frowned and looked straight at the puffy, fist-size bruise on his rib cage. "But you are not."

"Tell 'em I'm okay," he insisted. "Find out how they're doin'. Just tell 'em Sarge asked."

"Should I not tell them the truth?"

She could say whatever she wanted, just so long as she got one of them talking. "I've been hurt worse than this. Trust me."

Tasiya paused at those last two words, considering them, and then—though it didn't surprise him—dismissing them.

"Good night, Bryce Martin."

And then she was gone. A noisy, graceful wraith with ebony hair, a compassionate heart and a truckload of fear and distrust balanced on her narrow shoulders.

Bryce scrubbed his hand across his jaw, damning his

body's interest and his conscience's concern over her.
He'd been in this medieval island hell for over a week
now. He should be concentrating on nothing else but finding a means to escape, or a way to contact his colleagues
at Big Sky Bounty Hunters in Montana so they could
mount a rescue.

But no, he stood in the gloom of a cell made a little
more bearable by the unexpected kindness of a single
lightbulb, and inhaled the sweet, womanly smells that still
clung to his hand from where he'd touched her.

"Son of a bitch." Tasiya wasn't the only thing he'd
touched.

The sentimental aura vanished. Bryce blew out a disgusted sigh and called himself every sorry name in the
book. He'd had his hand on her keys...the keys to his
freedom. Forget about trying to communicate and using
her as a messenger. If he'd been thinking straight—if he'd
been thinking with his head instead of other, more easily distracted parts of his anatomy—he'd have snatched
them off her wrist.

But no, he was a dope with a soft spot who'd let an
opportunity to escape slip through his fingers. Literally.

With no one to blame but himself for the sentence of
another night in this cell, he returned to his tedious work
at the window. Tasiya Belov better get interested in conversing with one of the other men.

Because he was gettin' a mite too interested in these
late-night chats himself.

Chapter 5

"Mr. Fowler, you gotta hear this!"

Tasiya dodged out of the way as Ike rushed past her into Boone Fowler's office. Wearing headphones, wires and antennae, the short, squatty man reminded her of a trained chimp who'd been readied for a launch into outer space.

But Tasiya didn't laugh at the humorous picture Ike made as he set up an old military-emblemed box loaded with buttons and knobs on the edge of the desk. She hadn't allowed herself the luxury of laughter since her father had been taken hostage. And the only time she'd given in to so much as a smile had been late at night in the farthest corner of Boone Fowler's pirate-prison-turned-militia-camp. In the private shadows, where a quiet, battered man spoke in funny phrases, and where the kindness of his eyes offered a respite from the trials of her day.

As always, in the four days that had passed since the night she'd changed the lightbulb, when her thoughts turned to Bryce Martin, she felt combative urges of dread and anticipation.

She was saddened that he'd been so horribly disfigured, and a little afraid of whatever unknown events had scarred him so. He was hurt and cold and hungry, and she could do so little to help him. More than that, she felt guilty because she had to lie. He'd been so endearingly sweet, trying to carry on a real conversation with her, hinting at a grandmother he loved and an appreciation for simple pleasures. Even when she'd felt stupid and frustrated, not comprehending his American slang, he hadn't given up on trying to communicate with her.

But then everything had taken a personal turn. He wanted reasons why she was here, truths that could only get her or her father killed. She couldn't tell him about her double life as a slave and a spy. She couldn't be his friend. He couldn't be her confessor. Those desires were too dangerous to even contemplate.

But as much as she needed to keep her distance from that formidable strength, as much as she feared that his odd, deep-pitched voice could trick her into revealing more than she should, as much as she knew that trusting the wrong man—trusting any man—could be fatal, Tasiya still wanted to get closer to him.

Tightening her fists around the broom in her hands, she swept the dirt out of the cracks beside the office door. But she couldn't sweep aside the uncomfortable realization she'd made about herself.

When Bryce Martin had reached beyond the confines of his cell and touched her, she'd been startled. For a moment, that had been Dimitri Mostek's hand on her. Or Marcus Smith's. She'd been repulsed. Afraid.

But then the difference in his touch had registered. The surprising restraint of all that muscle power binding her wrist had stunned her. She'd known the oddest sensation of comfort. His grip, though unbreakable, had been as gentle as the cool refuge in his wintry eyes.

Tasiya closed her eyes and breathed deeply, remembering how she'd felt something seductive in the casual stroke of his thumb against her pulse. For a few brief moments, Tasiya Belov had been a real woman—with thoughts, choices, freedom, desire. And she'd wanted nothing more than to squeeze her way through those bars and be wrapped up by all of Bryce Martin—to sink into his warmth, to be surrounded by his strength, to be shielded by the deep understanding of life, danger and hardship that branded his skin.

"Should she be here, boss? This is business."

Blinking her eyes open at Ike's accusatory question, Tasiya quickly resumed her be-neither-seen-nor-heard posture. She swept the dirt into a dust pan and dumped it into the trash beside the desk. Then, picking up the trash can and gathering her cleaning supplies, she hurried to the door, intending to slip out and leave them to their secrets.

But Fowler snapped his fingers. "Foreigner. Wait."

Tasiya turned and dipped her chin, avoiding eye contact the way she'd learned he preferred after a week on Devil's Fork Island. "Yes, sir?"

He rose and circled his desk, crossing to take the trash can from her hand. "I want to inspect this before you leave, in case you're trying to steal anything."

Tasiya's feathers ruffled beneath her sweater. But she chewed the inside of her lip to keep her indignant response to herself. What could she possibly want to take away from this place? A rifle or pistol from the padlocked gun cabinet? Sure, she'd stand a real chance of breaking in and escaping against thirty armed militiamen. Was he worried she'd abscond with one of the hateful diatribes she'd seen him penning at his desk? Even if she wanted a souvenir, she couldn't take it. She could barely move the furniture to sweep beneath it without his ever-watchful devil eyes boring holes of suspicion into her back.

"I have taken nothing, sir," she stated calmly. "I really should get to the kitchen to begin preparations for dinner."

"You'll leave when I tell you to."

"Sir?" Ike urged. "The radio? It's broadcasting now."

"Put it on speaker," Fowler ordered. He stared down at her a few moments longer. "You can dust in here until I'm ready to dismiss you."

She'd done that before she'd swept. But she knew this was more about control than cleanliness. "As you wish."

"Exactly."

Leaving that word hanging in the air like the threat it was, Fowler carried the trash can back to his desk and had the gall to rifle through it. Inuring herself to the insult, Tasiya leaned her broom against the wall and pulled the dust rag from the pocket of her jeans. She went to work moving the heavy volumes of notebooks she now knew to be various maps from across the United States and dusted the clean shelf beneath them.

In the center of the room, Ike peeled off his earphones and reconnected a couple of wires. "I picked this up off an FBI comm-link first. But it's already on military bands, ham radio reports and Internet chatter. Network news will be picking it up soon."

Fowler grabbed a pencil and notepad to add to his copious notes. "Fill me in."

"News from Montana. Somebody tried to kidnap Veronika Petrov."

"Princess Veronika?" The name was out of Tasiya's mouth before she could stop it. Fair-haired Veronika Petrov was the darling of the Lukinburg people, although the king's daughter had been kept out of the spotlight, even presumably out of the country, for most of her life. "Is she all right?"

Fowler glared Tasiya back to her dusting without an answer. He turned to Ike. "You said *tried?*"

Tasiya moved the cloth across the books, but her attention was on Ike's response. "Her bodyguard was killed. But it seems some guy came out of nowhere and busted it up. He shot one of the perps outside a restaurant in Bozeman. Apparently, this good Samaritan stuffed her in his truck and took off even before the cops could get there."

Couldn't the man in the truck be the real kidnapper? A backup plan? Why would anyone attack the princess in the first place? Veronika had nothing to do with her father's politics back home, and nothing to do with her brother's rebellion here in the States.

From the corner of her eye, Tasiya saw Boone Fowler twisting the pencil between his fingers and thumb. "Let's hear it."

Ike turned a knob and the room filled with the sporadic, staticky sound of two men having an official-sounding conversation.

"…one man in custody. He's not talking. Claiming diplomatic immunity."

"And the two DOS?"

"We identified one man as her bodyguard. The other man dead on the scene fits the same description as our perp. Black hair, olive skin. No ID. But if he could talk, I bet he'd be spouting immunity in the same accent."

"So we think this is a Lukinburg plot?"

"Too soon to say. Aleksandr has a lot of enemies. Or it might be an attempt to silence the Crown Prince. Could be part of the nationalist movement—another one of those militia attacks."

"That son of a bitch." Tasiya dared a look at the growing fury in Boone Fowler's eyes. Was he condemning the authorities on the radio? The king? Prince Nikolai? "I would never use foreign trash to do our noble work."

"But that's good PR, right, boss?" Ike gestured toward the radio. "I mean, they know who we are if they're talking about us."

"Shut up."

From the radio came: "What about the guy who drove off with the princess?"

"Montana plates and a general description are all we got. Tall. Blond. Knew how to use a gun. Far as we can tell he's a local hero. Maybe an off-duty cop? We're combing—"

Fowler slammed a button on the radio, silencing the two men. "Local hero?" He crushed the pencil in his fist, spraying the shards across his desktop and the floor as he stalked across the room. "I'll bet Cameron Murphy has something to do with this."

Tasiya's attention quickly shifted gears. Cameron Murphy was the name on the memo that had ignited Fowler's temper a few days ago. Why would the militia be interested in the kidnapping of a foreign princess? Why was Cameron Murphy's name so upsetting to Boone Fowler?

And why was that connection of such interest to Dimitri? Tasiya's breathing went shallow with dread as she thought of her phone call to Minister Mostek tonight, and how he'd grill her when she told him about the radio report and Fowler's reaction to it.

Ike tenderly gathered his gear away from further abuse. "I thought Murphy was out of commission."

"He doesn't work alone, you idiot. That's why four of his men are in my…" Fowler's voice trailed off in intensity, but he countered with the pinpoint attack of his cold, black eyes. "Foreigner."

Tasiya jumped at the snap of his voice. But she buried her trembling inside as she slowly turned to face him. "Yes, sir?"

"Don't pretend you weren't eavesdropping. I dislike people who pretend to be stupid. But you know as well as I do that there is no way off this island. And if I thought there was any chance of you telling someone what you've heard around here, I'd be cutting out your tongue right now." He strolled up to her and pulled out a long, thin pocketknife. With the press of a button, a sharp, skinny blade popped open in front of her eyes.

Tasiya gasped and automatically retreated half a step before butting up against the bookshelf and discovering she had nowhere to go. Again he avoided touching her as if he found that contact as loathsome as she. But he had no qualms about twirling the knife blade into a tendril of her hair and playing with it so that it tickled her ear.

"I will not say anything," she lied, knowing Dimitri would be expecting her call.

"Oh, but you will." He flicked the knife from her hair and mimicked a slicing motion through the air in front of her throat before pointing it straight at the tip of her chin. "You'll tell *me* everything you know about Veronika Petrov."

Tasiya clenched her fingers around the shelf behind her to keep them from shaking with fear or striking out in anger. There wasn't much to tell about the princess. "She is a few years younger than me. Very beautiful in the pictures I've seen. Well liked in my country."

"Does she have any political enemies?"

"I do not think so. King Aleksandr does not allow women to be involved in politics."

Fowler laughed, but the sound grated along Tasiya's nerves. "Maybe the old bastard's smarter than I thought. What about personal enemies? Does she have some famous boyfriend she's dumped? She ever cause a scandal?"

"I've only seen Princess Veronika a few times in my life, in official royal portraits. She does not make public appearances. Mostly, she has been away at school. In Paris, I believe."

The knife point wavered back and forth, slowly searching for a target. "She doesn't like living at home?"

Tasiya swallowed hard and tried to focus her hatred on the knife, instead of risking the impotent fury she longed to glare into Fowler's eyes. "How would I know? I am a cook, not a confidante to the princess."

"Don't get uppity with me, foreigner." He pressed the knife into her chin and tilted her face up to his. "I don't tolerate back talk from my men. I won't tolerate it from you."

Tasiya gnawed the inside of her lip to keep from crying out as she waited helplessly for the blade to break through the skin and draw her blood. But then, just as she closed her eyes to brace for the pain, he lifted the blade. Maybe Fowler had remembered Dimitri's direct order to keep his "gift" in pristine condition, or perhaps he believed that just the threat of cutting her was intimidation enough.

"Now. Answer the question. The UN claims that Lukinburg is a country worth saving. But if it's really so hot, why doesn't the princess go home where she's safe?"

Tasiya swallowed her fear and contempt and answered as evenly as she could. "King Aleksandr has been very vocal about his children choosing to remain in this country and defy his rule. I am not sure he would welcome them home."

"So you think she staged her own kidnapping? Maybe to get Daddy's attention?"

"I do not know."

"You think the king was trying to force her home since she wouldn't go voluntarily?"

"Again, I do not know."

"What *do* you know?" He snorted in disgust and flipped the blade back into the knife. "Don't move."

Tasiya dared to do little more than breathe as Fowler strode back to the desk to pick up the notepad he'd tossed and to find a surviving pencil.

He gave Ike a command while he scribbled something on the pad. "Find out everything you can about the kidnapping attempt. I need to know who's behind it. Kidnapping the princess isn't on my agenda. If somebody's trying to interfere with my schedule or smear my name, I want to know about it. And get me an update on Cameron Murphy's condition."

"Yes, sir."

"Go." Fowler nodded toward the door. Ike wasted no time scooping up his gear and hurrying out in his waddling, bow-legged gait.

"Foreigner." He ripped the top page from the notepad and folded it in half. He held the paper out to her as he turned. "I want you to deliver a message to Marcus Smith for me."

Tasiya nodded. She tucked the note into her jeans and gathered her cleaning supplies, as anxious to be out of there as Ike had been. "Where will I find him?" she asked.

Please don't say his quarters. Marcus Smith was one of the few men who had his own private room at the compound. He'd invited her to visit more than once, but she'd always found an excuse to avoid spending any one-on-one time with the man. Groping hands in the mess hall she could grit her teeth and ignore because, with an audience, she knew he couldn't completely disregard his boss's order about keeping his hands to himself. But behind the privacy of a locked door, she'd be on her own. And Tasiya knew she'd have no ally to help stop the lecherous brute then.

"He's working in the interrogation room. In the prison wing." Fowler pointed toward her wrist. "Take your keys. You'll find him."

Ponderosa, Montana

Trevor Blackhaw sat in the communication bunker hidden beneath the Big Sky Bounty Hunter headquarters building and listened to the impatient man on the phone.

He swiped a weary hand through his long, black hair and couldn't help thinking how wonderful Sierra's fingers had been last night, tangled up in his hair and massaging his scalp before they drifted off to sleep in each other's arms. But the past several days had allowed them little time to savor their recent engagement.

He'd nearly lost her to the craziness surrounding Boone Fowler and the escaped prisoners, terrorist attacks and the unknown maniac behind it all whom they'd dubbed The Puppet Master. Trevor wasn't going to lose anybody else he cared about. He was going to get his team out of wherever the hell Boone Fowler had taken them and keep fighting until his world was safe again for the woman he loved.

However, this was a complication he hadn't expected.

Propping one boot up on the edge of the console, Trevor waited for a pause to reiterate his advice. "Joe, there's nothing we can do right now. I talked it over with Murphy. We both agree that the best thing you can do is just lay low for a few days until we can figure out how the kidnapping attempt is related to the UN resolution to invade Lukinburg—or if there even is a connection."

He could well imagine Joseph Brown pacing circles around his beloved black pickup truck—or whatever vehicle he'd gotten to replace it by now so he couldn't be found. "Whoa. You mean me and Princess Poor Little Rich Girl are going to be stuck alone together indefinitely? I'm a tracker, Blackhaw. Don't you have someone better suited for bodyguard detail?"

"You're the one who saved her pretty ass." Normally his colleague was all business, setting aside his emotions when it came to getting the job done and hauling in his bounty. But this evening Joe was so worked up that Trevor couldn't resist the tease.

"Yeah, well for as much trouble as she is, it's not all that pretty."

"So you've been lookin'?"

Joe's denial was both colorful and revealing. Interesting. So Joseph Brown, the born-again bachelor who'd sworn off women since a messy divorce, had the juice for the princess. "I just happened to be in Bozeman, following up on a rumor about a militia connection when those two guys jumped her."

"She was lucky you were there."

"Maybe."

Trevor had no doubt Veronika Petrov was in safe, capable hands. Instead of giving Joe any more grief over an apparently unexpected and unwelcome attraction, Trevor went back to business. "You got a safe place where you can take her?"

"I know a place. If she'll follow orders." Trevor could envision the scowl that matched Joe's voice. "I swear to God that woman's never met a man, child or animal she didn't want to meet and make friends with. I nearly lost her at a gas station. I sent her to the john and told her to come straight back to the truck. I knew we hadn't been followed, but after ten minutes, when she didn't show up, I went looking for her. I found her in the garage, talking to the mechanic."

"From what I hear, women aren't allowed a lot of freedom back in Lukinburg. Maybe she's just feelin' her oats here in the States, away from all those restrictions."

"Yeah? Well, my job would be a hell of a lot easier if she'd lock herself in the barn and stay put."

Trevor grinned. There was only one man on the team he knew could be more stubborn than Joseph Brown, but it sounded as if Joe was giving the Sarge a run for his money. "Good luck, buddy. Keep us posted, and if you need anything, call in."

Resigned to his princess-sitting duties, Joe eased into a more professional tone. "Will do. Hey—how's the colonel?"

"Beat-up and worn out, but in a better frame of mind now that he's at home with his family. He'd be a lot happier if we could hear some news about Sarge and the other hostages."

"We all would. Let me know if there's anything I can do at my end. You can reach me on this secure line."

"Just keep the princess safe. We'll bring our boys home. I promise."

"All right, Mr. Martin. Let's try again." The mock pleasantness in Marcus Smith's voice underscored the soft rustling sound of a piece of paper being unfolded. Again. He thrust the worn letter with the familiar scribbles in front of Bryce's face. "Read it."

The blockhead needed a shave and a breath mint, and

just wasn't getting the idea. Bryce looked beyond the page, beyond the ice-blue eyes, and stared at 6-12.

Smith nodded to the man on Bryce's right.

Damn, this was gettin' old.

The blow to his gut hit like an explosion in his side. Pain radiated outward in aftershocks that clipped the top of his thigh, his back and lungs before fading into one dull ache in the middle of his body.

Bryce concentrated on his breathing, taking slow, shallow breaths that would keep him conscious and cognizant without hyperventilating or putting any added pressure on the burning ache in his torso muscles. Wincing, he swallowed a curse. Oh, yeah, one or both of those bottom two ribs on his right side had cracked.

Pulling his gaze away from 6-12, as he'd dubbed the chipped, moldy stone—sixth row from the top of the wall, twelfth block over—that had been his point of focus for two weeks, he let his peripheral gaze sneak a peak at Bristoe and Hodges. Marcus Smith's two goons had switched to brass knuckles this week, probably because their own hands had taken a beating after so many days working out against his tough hide.

Bristoe hit like a girl, probably the only reason Bryce's left side was in better shape. Hodges had either boxed Golden Gloves or grown up on the street, though, because each blow was on the mark—the same mark—time and again. But Hodges's glass eye, probably the result of all that boxing experience, would give Bryce a maneuvering advantage—if he ever managed to free himself from these chains.

That was getting to be a big *if.* He was trussed up like a pig at the slaughterhouse, with his wrist chain suspended from a rusty *O*-ring in the ceiling. Bryce's feet touched the floor, easing the pressure on his chest and prevent-

ing suffocation. Marcus Smith knew his business. He
didn't want his prisoner to pass out or die during an interrogation—he just wanted him to experience lots and
lots of pain.

Try burying your parents when you were eight, your
grandparents when you were twenty-one. Try living
through second- and third-degree burns over half your
body, skin grafts, shrapnel wounds, startled gasps and
rude comments because you were an ugly son of a bitch.
Try living with loneliness nearly every day of your adult
life. Bryce knew more about pain than Marcus Smith ever
would. He could handle this interrogation.

He fisted his hands where they hung above his head,
then splayed his fingers and wiggled them to keep the
blood circulating through his arms. For a few seconds
he considered letting the tingling pinpricks of numbness
settle down into his wrists and forearms. Maybe if he lost
the sensation in his arms, he wouldn't notice the raw skin
chafing beneath the iron manacles.

Of course, if his arms went numb, he wouldn't be able
to keep subtly twisting the *O*-ring. Bristoe and Hodges
were good little soldiers who only took orders. And Smith
was so close to his boiling point that he hadn't noticed
the little crumblings of mortar dust that had snowed from
the ceiling every now and then—ever since Bryce's very
first day in the interrogation room.

Smith huffed with impatience, wadded up the letter
and chucked it at Bryce's head. Bryce ignored the pain-
less blow and spared little more than a blink when Smith
got up in his face and hollered. "Dammit, Martin, you
are gonna talk!"

Bryce sought out 6-12.

"Your buddies from Big Sky have already broken,"

Smith spat in his face. "They've read their letters. They're ready to make the tape."

Bryce doubted it.

Smith's meaty hands curled into fists at his sides. He let his hot breath wash over Bryce's face and tried to stare him down, waiting for some kind of reaction, anything he could jump on and use against Bryce. Bryce suspected that Marcus Smith would like nothing better than for the two of them to head outside and duke it out until only one of them was left standing. He was tempted to give Smith the satisfaction. But with who knew how many other militiamen to back up his enemy, Bryce doubted it would be a fair fight.

It was a good measure of the power Boone Fowler held over all his men that Smith reined in his pride and testosterone and stuck to their plan. As self-titled security chief, Smith was charged with *convincing* each of the Big Sky Bounty Hunters to read a letter on videotape. The tape would condemn the UN's resolution to send troops into Lukinburg, and apologize for any role they had played in interfering with the Montana Militia for a Free America—including imprisoning their leader and pursuing him as a criminal instead of honoring him as a patriot.

Fat chance.

Bryce kept his expression as craggy and unmoving as 6-12.

Marcus Smith stormed across the room. He picked up the wadded paper and spread it flat against his thigh before speaking again. "Tell me your name."

That he would do. "Bryce Martin."

"Who do you work for?"

Uh-uh. Rank and serial number were the only other information he'd share. And since Bryce was no longer military, he was done talking.

"Read this letter."

Old 6-12 was becoming a good friend.

"I can put you on the rack." Smith pointed to the rick-ety wooden structure whose antique pulleys would give out before Bryce did. "I'll put you in the stocks." At least Bryce would get the feeling back in his hands. "I'll whip you with that cat-o'-nine-tails on the wall." The guy talked too much.

"Read it!" Marcus commanded, striding back and waving the paper in Bryce's face. "You will answer my questions and you will read these words."

Bryce shifted his position, adjusting his arms and squinting as a shower of dust sprinkled over them.

Smith nodded. Bristoe's punch scraped the skin, but did little damage inside.

Bryce was finding 6-12 again when a metallic knock echoed through the room.

Scratching his fingers through his thick beard, Smith answered. "Enter." A key turned in the lock and the rusted iron door groaned on its hinges. "Well, well, well, what have we here?"

The insidious delight in Smith's voice was enough to prick Bryce's curiosity. But he fought the urge to look.

He didn't have to.

When the door opened into the room, he caught a whiff of home-cooked heaven. He knew it was Tasiya, even before she spoke. "Mr. Fowler asked me to deliver this message to you."

"Come on in, sugar. You'd better wait right here until I find out whether or not I need to send a reply." Smith swung the door open wide, giving Bryce a clear view of Tasiya's raven-dark curls piled at the back of her head, her creamy skin and dark eyes that widened and locked instantly on him.

Bryce's pulse rate tripped into a higher gear. He didn't want her here. She didn't need to see this place, didn't need to see him like this. A spot deep inside him, softer than the one Hodges had been working over, began to ache.

Though he tried like hell to concentrate on 6-12, he couldn't miss each dart of her eyes to every bruise, every bloody scrape, every lock and chain that held him in place.

She pressed her lips together around her hushed gasp. But that slightest of sounds seemed to fill the chamber's dank, heavy air and settle deep into Bryce's conscience. Marcus shifted his attention from the note and saw her distress. Even worse, those sick blue eyes saw the flinch of Bryce's reaction to her shock.

Go away. Bryce risked making contact and silently warned her with his eyes. This was not gonna be good.

Marcus Smith smiled. "You wanna watch me work?"

Shaking her head, Tasiya tore her gaze away from Bryce and stared at the buttons on Marcus's shirt. "I only came to deliver the message." Her bottom lip quivered before she drew it quickly between her teeth. "What are you doing to him?"

"Why don't you see for yourself." Marcus reached over her shoulder and pushed the door shut, trapping her. Bryce's blood caught fire and surged in his veins. He jerked against his chains, fighting to stay in control.

"No." Tasiya clawed at the iron ring behind her back, caught hold and opened the door. "My duties. I have dinner to prepare."

But Marcus's hand reached over her and slammed it shut with a dire inevitability that shook through her.

Bryce's fingers splayed, then fisted above his head, giving vent to his frustrated need to shield her from this nightmare. He watched her shut down her emotions like that night at his cell when she'd been terrified of something she feared more than him. Her body went still except for the quiver in her chin as she clenched her jaw too tight and put on a brave show. Bryce counted the raging heartbeats pounding in his ears as she averted her gaze and pretended she didn't mind Smith moving closer, tangling his beard with the curls at her forehead.

When the big bastard grinned at her discomfort, Bryce made his first mistake. "Let her go, Smith."

With his hand still braced on the door behind Tasiya's head, the big man slowly turned. He raised a bushy eyebrow in triumph. "So—your mouth works after all, eh, Sarge?"

"She doesn't need to see this."

"I think maybe she does."

Tasiya's panicked gaze flew up to Bryce's the instant Marcus turned his back on her. But Smith never stepped away, keeping her backed into the corner without enough room to open the door. Bryce drilled Smith's icy eyes. He didn't want to give the security chief any more of an advantage than he already had.

Smith flipped open the note she'd delivered, barely taking his focus off Bryce to read it. "I think we finally found the key to making him talk, boys."

Hodges's and Bristoe's rowdy taunts were nothing but white noise in the background. Bryce knew where the real threat in the room lay—and that threat was too damn close to Tasiya.

He swallowed his pride, his plan and the bitter taste of capitulation in his mouth. "Let her leave and I'll say whatever you want me to."

Smith gestured with Fowler's note, obviously a revised set of instructions from the head honcho. "Tell me about

Cameron Murphy. We left him for dead at the Galleria Mall. Is he still alive?"

"He was in the hospital when I left Montana."

"He still calling the shots at Big Sky?"

After two weeks in his solitary prison cell, Bryce had no clue about the status of affairs at Big Sky. He only knew his loyalties were with the colonel. "I still work for him."

"Not what I asked, Sarge." Smith clicked his tongue with a pitying reprimand. "Who's making the decisions for them now? Do they have the manpower to mount a rescue?"

Why don't you let me go and I'll ask. But the sarcastic response on the end of Bryce's tongue never came out. It wasn't his way. "Send Tasiya back to the kitchen first."

"She's fine where she is." Smith nodded once and Hodges nailed him in the ribs.

"No!" Tasiya cried out as Bryce swallowed a curse and fought to master the pain spiraling through him.

"Let her go." He ground out the words on the deepest breath he could manage.

"Are you gonna read this letter now? Like you mean it?"

"When she's gone."

Smith turned his face to the side and spat out his chew. It was the only respite Bryce got before his captor gave the order to attack.

"No!" Tasiya screamed as Hodges and Bristoe pummeled him with their fists. There was no disguising the terror on her face now. Bryce dodged and braced as best he could. He strained against his bonds, but without his hands, he made an easy punching bag.

Marcus Smith laughed, and Tasiya snatched at his arm, begging him to listen. "Make them stop!"

Bryce took an easy shot and kicked Bristoe in the gut. But while one man doubled over, the other rammed his brass knuckles into Bryce's exposed back, knocking him off his feet. He pulled against his chains and righted himself, but the fists kept coming.

"You are killing him!" Tasiya shouted. Instead of making a break for it while Smith watched the fight, the crazy woman shot forward, trying to help. "Stop it!"

Marcus grabbed her around the neck and shoved her up against the wall. "You watch, sugar."

"Let her go!" Bryce ignored the coppery tang of blood in his mouth. "I'll read it. I'll read the damn letter!"

Smith nuzzled his lips against Tasiya's ear, holding her by the chin and pinning her with his hip so she couldn't look away. "Listen to him. Now he wants to cooperate." He glanced over his shoulder at Bryce. "I don't care what you have to say now. My boys can have at ya until they get tired."

"Stop!" she cried.

Tears glistened in her eyes. And while they had no effect on Marcus Smith, they tore Bryce up a lot worse than Hodges's fists. "Tasiya!" *Close your eyes. Look away.* "Let her go!"

"So you can take a beating, but you can't stand to have the little lady watch it? Oh, man, this is rich," Smith laughed. He wrapped his arm around Tasiya's waist, pinning her arms and picked her up. Then he set her down in front of him, squeezing her chin and forcing her eyes toward Bryce. "The view's better from here."

"You son of a bitch!" A shower of dust rained down from the ceiling and stuck in the sweat and blood on Bryce's skin.

He saw a flash of Tasiya's straight, white teeth and suddenly glimpsed a rebellious spirit inside the demure cook he'd never have suspected. With a twist of her neck, she sank her teeth into Smith's hand.

The big man yelped, cursed and threw her across the room.

"Tasiya!"

She smacked into the wall and bounced off, landing on her hands and knees.

Bryce fisted his hands around the chain and pulled with all his might.

Smith followed her across the room, his hand raised to strike as she pushed herself to her feet.

"Tasiya!" Chips of mortar and stone crashed down from the ceiling as Bryce ripped out the *O*-ring. Before his bellowing voice faded away, he'd looped the chain around Smith's neck and jerked him away from Tasiya. He spun around, sticking Marcus in front of him to absorb the next blow from a startled Hodges. "Run!"

Dammit, she wasn't moving. He couldn't maintain the advantage for long. He shoved Smith into Bristoe and Hodges, knocking them into the rack and off their feet.

"Bryce Martin?"

"You can't help me." He grabbed her by the wrist and hustled her toward the door. "Just go."

"But—"

Angry hands yanked him away and slammed him into the wall, knocking the air out of his already tender lungs. "Please, dammit!" he wheezed. "Get out of here!"

"Please, dammit," Marcus mimicked.

Bryce summoned the strength to ram his fist into Marcus's mouth, drawing blood and shutting him up—and igniting his temper.

Smith wiped the blood from his lip, called him the devil and worse. And while his thugs held on, he hit Bryce low in the gut.

As Bryce's knees buckled, Bristoe and Hodges took him the rest of the way, pinning him stomach-down on the cold stone floor. A crack of sound that could only be the cat-o'-nine-tails snapped in the air. "You're done, Sarge. You don't have to say another word."

"No! Mr. Smith—please!"

But all of Smith's rage was focused on Bryce now, and Tasiya's presence was blessedly forgotten.

Bryce raised his head, warning her away with his eyes, apologizing for the stark terror he saw in hers. He could only mouth one word. *"Go."*

"I am so sorry." She backed into the door, fumbled in her hurry to find the handle. "I am so sorry."

She threw open the door and ran.

Bryce breathed an odd sense of relief that she was gone, that she'd been spared the hell that was about to claim him. He could endure this now that she was safe. He wouldn't add to the fear in her eyes.

Her footsteps and sobs faded as the whip hit his back, all nine of its claws ripping their way through his skin.

Chapter 6

"*Maria? Maria!*"

Bryce shivered at the fiery pain that burned through his feverish body. Maria was dead. Seventeen innocent civilians were dead because he hadn't been quick enough to save them.

There were too many mines. Too many damn mines.

And the mortar fire.

The command to retreat.

Ordered to save his own hide and let them die.

"*Sarge? You've got to pull through this. You're a fighter. I need you on my team.*"

Colonel Murphy's voice. He'd always obeyed that voice. But he couldn't do it. He didn't have the strength in him anymore.

He was in the hospital. Lying on his stomach with his face looking through a hole to the green linoleum tile on the floor beneath him. He'd been lying here for weeks while the doctors battled infections and waited for enough skin to grow back so they could stitch him together.

"You did your best, Sarge. We'll have another chance to get the bad guys. I promise."

Bryce nodded, but he didn't believe. Murphy was here. Powell and Trevor Blackhaw, too. Campbell. Brown. They'd all been in to see him.

He should rise to attention. Salute. But all he wanted to do was roll over and be done with the pain. He wanted to be done with giving a damn about things that could never be his.

He wanted to be done with living and losing.

"Bryce Martin."

They were taking away his career—nerve damage, loss of flexibility—an honorable discharge and a couple of medals? They were taking away the last thing he cared about, denying him the one place where it didn't matter where he'd come from or what he looked like.

"Keep fighting, Sarge."

"I can't."

It hurt too much. Inside and out. The pain burned through him. Cut him to the heart as easily as the shrapnel cut through his skin.

"Bryce Martin."

Something cool touched the back of his neck. Soft words he didn't understand murmured a gentle rhythm against his ear, scattering his bleak thoughts.

"No, sir," he answered with less strength. "Can't fight... No reason to..."

"Do it for yourself," the colonel ordered. "Do it for your men."

"No." It hurt too damn much.

"Shh."

Sweet relief traveled across his shoulders and down his back, giving him the first real comfort he'd known in weeks. The fever in him cooled along with each gentle touch, each hushed word. The anger in him abated.

"*Bryce Martin.*"

Bryce awoke without opening his eyes, slowly sifting his way through hazy layers of consciousness.

He frowned into his pillow. Why would the colonel call him by his first and last name?

"Shh." The cool balm settled at the back of his waist. "Rest easy. Shh."

His breathing eased at the tender command. He never knew Colonel Murphy had such a soft, sexy voice.

Bryce's eyes snapped open.

Murphy talked like a soldier. Nobody talked soft and sexy to Bryce Martin.

His muscles tensed with confusion as Bryce tried to sort through the images in his brain and place himself in his surroundings. Which were memories? What was feverish illusion? Where did the nightmares from his past end and his present reality begin?

A foggy mist of light and shadow told him nothing but that it was night. So he listened to the world around him—ocean waves splashing a rocky shore in the distance, a gentle trickle of water closer by. He sniffed the musty odor of damp ticking, and the more pungent smells of citrus and ointment.

Was he back in the hospital? Did that hushed, heavenly voice belong to a nurse?

"Are you awake, Bryce Martin?"

Trilled *r*s. Succinct articulation. The homey scents of yeast and spice.

An instant awareness cut through the shroud of fever, pain and confusion. *Hell.*

He wasn't in any army hospital.

Colonel Murphy wasn't whispering in his ear.

"Tasiya?" His voice was a ragged croak. He tried to get his arms underneath him, to push himself up. But his muscles were weak, wobbly.

And her hands were surprisingly strong against his shoulders. "Do not move. You should rest."

But he'd been whipped. As if he wasn't already hard enough to look at, she was sitting on the edge of his cot beside his prone body—in his cell—tending the wounds on his back. "You shouldn't be here."

She oughta leave. She oughta run as far away from him and his hell as her long legs would take her. He should make her leave. But her tender hands—the cloth and cool water and salve she used—felt so good against his skin.

"I am not leaving until I am finished. This is my fault."

How could Marcus Smith being a son of a bitch possibly be her fault? Bryce turned his head on the mattress to glimpse her from the corner of his eye. "You're not responsible. I had it comin' to me sooner or later. I'll be—"

"Do not tell me you have faced worse than this and survived." She leaned forward so he could look straight up into those stern brown eyes. "You are facing this because of me. You are hurt now because of me."

Such a sharp tongue. But he understood the difference between anger directed at him and a misguided woman being angry *for* him. Other people didn't stand up and fight for Bryce—especially a slender slip of a woman. The men he'd fought with and worked with watched his back, but no one defended him. Most figured he didn't need the help.

But Tasiya Belov was fired up—in her own reserved, ladylike way. If he had the strength, he'd smile and thank her for the uncustomary honor. But he needed to conserve whatever energy he had left. "Marcus Smith and his ego did this. Don't feel guilty."

"I did not know it would give him such pleasure to see you suffer." Bryce followed her precise, efficient movements as she rinsed the cloth in a basin of water made pink with his blood. When she faced him again, some of the fight had gone out of her. Her eyes seemed darker, sadder, full of regret. "If you were not such a gentleman, you would not be so hurt."

A gentleman? Was the translation between them that far off? "He used you to get to me. I shouldn't have let him."

Tasiya resumed her work without comment, folding the cloth and laying it over his triceps muscle. Some of the nerves there hadn't functioned since he was a kid, so he felt no sting from the lemony soap she used. But he could feel the light, sure pressure of her fingers as she doctored the laceration there, handling him like a baby instead of a man twice her size.

A woman's gentle touch was as foreign to him as the weakness that consumed his body. He'd lived a hard life, had never really done relationships. What he knew about women had to do with sex, generally the quick, no-strings-attached kind. He didn't even have buddies who were women. A few co-workers, but that was all business. Jacob Powell's fiancée had tried to talk to him a couple of times, and he appreciated the effort, but friendly banter was just awkward for him.

He knew his mama had loved him, but he'd been an unscarred, untested boy then. His grandma had loved him for the young man he'd become, but theirs had been a secluded life.

All this talking, all this tenderness from Tasiya was... perplexing. In the end, all Bryce could do was be who he was. "How long was I out?"

"You have not gone anywhere."

"I meant, how long have I been unconscious?"

"Oh." She pulled her hands away, clutching them to-gether in a self-conscious gesture. Bryce wished he could withdraw the question. He should have just shut up in-stead of making her self-conscious about the language barriers between them.

But Tasiya was made of sterner stuff. "Mr. Smith's men brought you here before dinner. You did not waken when I brought your food, so I…" She glanced over her shoulder at the steel bars that had separated them for so many nights. "I came in to help you. It is nearly three in the morning now."

He tried to roll onto his side, to at least hide the worst of his injuries from her. "You need your sleep. I'll be all right."

But her firm hands guided him back down. She squeezed some ointment from a tube across the tips of her fingers and dabbed it over the cuts, stubbornly refus-ing to be shielded from his ugliness. "There is no doctor here, but I know something about taking care of wounds like this. My father was once…"

Bryce waited expectantly to learn more about her, but she didn't complete the sentence. Reading the distant sor-row in her eyes, he didn't want her to. He knew Tasiya Belov was no stranger to hardship. That wasn't right. But Bryce didn't know how to make things right for her, how to make whatever scared her go away. He couldn't even get things right for himself.

"Tasiya?"

"I am almost finished." She rose and carried the cloth and basin out into the passageway. She set the items on the floor, and for the first time he noticed she'd sneaked in to see him without her noisy cart.

Sneaking couldn't be good for her safety.

"Finished with what?"

"Bathing you."

She meant cleaning the cuts and welts, of course. Then Bryce realized that he smelled a heck of a lot better than he had yesterday. His face and hands had been washed and he...

He clenched and released his muscles, all the way from his nose to his toes. He ignored the stabs of pain and took note of the breezy sensations in between. Lordy. *Now* he was wide awake. His jeans were unzipped and hanging low on his hips, his briefs pulled down just short of indecent. The dainty, practical miss from Lukinburg had been quite thorough in her washing. His skin heated up, but not with the fever from his open wounds.

A new kind of feeling that had nothing to do with pain, and everything to do with the thought of Tasiya putting her capable hands on his buttocks and other interesting places that hadn't been injured, charged his blood with a uniquely masculine burst of strength. Propping himself up on his elbows, Bryce managed to drop his legs over the side of the cot and push himself up to a sitting position.

The uneven floor swam before his eyes. "Whoa."

"What are you doing?"

Bryce laid his forehead in his palms and tried to shake off the dizziness. Metal scraped against metal, and hurried footsteps brought her back to him. He swayed into her hands, but they latched onto his arms and steadied him until the light-headedness passed and he could open his eyes.

"I must have lost more blood than I thought." Or he was still recovering from shock. He patted at her fingers and lifted his gaze to an eyeful of gently sloping breasts, rising and falling beneath her pale-blue sweater. She was long and lean and, oh, so feminine, making it damn near impossible for his pulse rate to regulate itself when she was this close. Wisely, he averted his eyes before giving in to the tempting urge to rest his head against her. "I'm okay."

The cot shifted slightly as the mattress took her weight beside him. He angled himself away from her, but didn't have the legs yet to put any more distance between her and his libido.

"I heard the men talking at dinner. Mr. Fowler said to give you a few days to heal before resuming interrogation. You must use that time to rest."

They were finally cutting him a break? That probably meant Smith and his goons would be loaded for bear when they got the okay to torture him some more. In the meantime, they'd no doubt be practicing their skills on one of the other hostages.

Bryce should use the uninterrupted time to plot a way out of here—a way to get them all out of here—the bounty hunters, the soldiers. Maybe even Tasiya, assuming she wanted to go.

Right now, though, he could barely manage to pull up his pants. A pinch of pain beneath the elastic told him how far down his injuries went, but he didn't plan on mooning the woman who'd been so foolishly kind to enter the cage with the monster and doctor him up.

Bryce flinched when Tasiya's fingers brushed against the small of his back. But whether she attributed the corresponding flood of goose bumps to pain or understood that his body just wasn't used to a woman's familiar touch, it didn't deter her from straightening the elastic and tugging up his jeans.

He drew the line, though, when she reached around to help him with his zipper. Bryce grasped her wrists and pushed them gently back into her own lap. Wounded or not, there was a thing or two about his male anatomy when he was around her she didn't need to see. "I can get it."

He tried not to be disappointed at how quickly she moved on to a new task—pouring him something that was too dark to be water out of her pitcher and unwrapping a crusty loaf of bread. "I saved you some food." She tore the loaf in two and cradled one end in her lap while she dipped the other into the cup. "It's cold now, but I made some broth to help you regain your strength."

Propping the cup between her knees, Tasiya cradled the soaked bread over her palm to catch the drippings. When she carried it to his mouth, Bryce had to stop her. "I'll get that, too."

Letting Tasiya feed him was just too suggestive for his peace of mind right now. How incredible would it be if her tender attentions were motivated by attraction instead of a guilty conscience? Bryce had lived long enough to know not to ask for the impossible. But his weakened body seemed to have no problem interpreting the touches and the talking and the delicious smells of food and cook as a personal invitation to be aroused.

He sank his teeth into the first rich bite of nutty bread and beef au jus before he realized just how far she'd gone to help him. His chewing slowed as he stared at his naked wrists. He swallowed before trying to gauge the motivation in her expression. "You unchained me."

"I put medicine on the welts around your wrists and ankles. You were already heavy enough to move. It was less awkward to bathe you once I removed them." She was either exceedingly practical or too naive for her own good.

"You should have put 'em back on," he suggested.

That tiny vertical line of confusion and doubt appeared

between her brows. "You will not run away from me, will you?"

She must not know how badly he was hurtin'. He eyed the keys around her wrist. She'd been cautious enough to secure the manacles in the passageway outside his cell, but then she'd been trusting enough to lock herself inside with the keys to his freedom within arm's reach.

"I wouldn't get you into trouble that way."

Yet.

But with that promise, she relaxed and smiled.

Bryce quickly stuffed another bite into his mouth, though the bread and broth had turned bitter. Maybe there *was* something he could do to earn her trust. He could take advantage of the pity she felt for him, the way it lowered her guard and made her believe he was some kind of victim or gentleman. Maybe he didn't need Powell or Campbell to sweet-talk her.

And while she worked off whatever penance she felt she owed him, he could slowly gain her trust. She'd answer his questions out of guilt. And if pity could make her unlock his chains tonight, then a growing bond would make it a piece of cake to steal those keys without resorting to force.

Problem was, he didn't want to leave her company, not just yet. And while he had no illusion of a happily-ever-after with any woman, he was human. He'd never known a woman's gentleness before. He'd never known how much he craved it.

He risked a glance into her dark, mysterious eyes and allowed himself one moment to dream. Would her hair be as silky to the touch as it looked? As rich and heavy in his hands as it was a feast to his eyes? What would her lips taste like? They were pink and full, with enough attitude to make them interesting—like sweet, tart raspberries ripe for the plucking. What would she feel like in his arms? Strong? Delicate? Would she melt in a puddle of shy femininity? Or would she be as practical and efficient and sure of herself as the woman who'd stripped him down and washed him from head to toe?

Bryce snatched the bread and cup from her lap and turned away, damning the useless needs that heated his blood and made him hungry for more than a batch of fried chicken and mashed potatoes. This wasn't a fairy tale, and he wasn't gonna be anybody's prince—not out of love or pity.

He just needed some time to heal. Then he needed to use her and not look back with longing or regret.

Tasiya wondered what dark thoughts had put such a scowl on Bryce Martin's harsh face. She swore that his beautiful gray eyes had sparked with desire, that they'd shared an inexplicable warmth and closeness in the cool, dim air of his quiet cell. But maybe it was only an apology she had read there. She'd had so little experience with men who made her feel anything, it was hard to be sure.

Perhaps her presence here embarrassed him. The men she knew liked to be strong. And with the exception of her father, they seemed to possess a brutal urge to show off their power and lord it over others.

But Bryce Martin had needed her. At least, he'd needed a nursemaid to help him before he risked infection, perhaps even death, in this forgotten cage in the middle of the ocean. Since he'd taken the horrific beating to protect her, Tasiya felt honor-bound to repay the favor by bringing him food, clothing and medicine and tending to his needs.

She could have left an hour ago, been less thorough in her caregiving. But conscious or awake, Bryce Martin was a calming presence. Well, *calming* might not be the right word. She moved her gaze past the raw strips of skin that had been peeled from his broad back and studied the intriguing stretch and flex of his bottom each time he moved to find a relatively comfortable position or to finish the rest of his late-night snack.

Tasiya smiled to herself at her surprisingly naughty thoughts. She'd learned he was muscular all over—warm to the touch, too—even on parts of his body that she rarely got to see on a man.

If she looked past the surface of his skin, past his square, craggy face, he was really quite a fine specimen of a man. Tasiya's smile quickly faded. She couldn't ignore the old scars or the new ones he would bear from this ordeal. And she couldn't ignore his face, because that would mean avoiding his eyes. There was such strength in his wintry irises. Such depth. Such beauty.

Those eyes, and these quiet moments together, had become as necessary to surviving her sentence here on Devil's Fork Island as keeping her secret from Boone Fowler was. That's where the calm feeling came from. Bryce Martin was a mighty mountain who could withstand the storm spinning around them. It was only natural to seek shelter beside him.

Even in his weakened condition, Bryce had a hearty appetite. In no time he'd polished off the bread and drunk the last of the broth and a cup of water. With a flattering thoroughness, he licked the last crumb and drop off his fingers and thumb. "I'll bet you could even make a brick taste good."

She liked the musical cadence of his voice, even if his words didn't make sense. "Why would you eat a brick? Is that an Americanism?"

"It's a compliment." He handed her the cup. "Good stuff."

"Thank you."

Unlike Fowler's men, Bryce didn't make fun of her ignorance or berate her when she couldn't quite grasp the intricacies of American slang. Maybe his funny accent, *hick,* she'd heard Marcus Smith say, helped him understand how difficult communication could be—and made him sympathetic to how lonely a soul could get when not allowed to express herself.

Tasiya carried the cup and pitcher into the passageway and picked up a man's shirt and the manacles she'd taken off his body.

Whatever verbal shortcomings Bryce lacked, there was little that his eyes missed or failed to communicate. She felt him watching her as she draped the heavy chains over her arm and sorted through her keys. When she dropped them to the floor, she sensed the shift in his focus. As she stooped to retrieve them, his gray eyes stared at the keys with an intensity that had matched his silent warning to her in the interrogation room. When he lifted his gaze to where the door stood ajar, Tasiya quickly rose and pushed it shut.

He was thinking of escape, wasn't he? Debating whether or not to take advantage of her visit. Maybe she was wrong to trust Bryce too quickly. Wasn't freedom every prisoner's dream?

If she could be free—if she could free her father—wouldn't she be willing to take advantage of Bryce?

But freedom wasn't an option for her. Even survival didn't look all that promising if she managed to allow one of the prisoners out of his cell.

Surely Bryce was too injured to try anything. And as cruel as it seemed, once she put him back in his chains, he'd be even less likely to try to bolt. She truly didn't think he would harm her—his actions and his eyes had told her that. But if Fowler and Smith found out what she'd done tonight, *they* would have no qualms about punishing her.

Tasiya slipped the keys deep into the pocket of her jeans, just in case she was wrong about Bryce Martin. "I do not know if Mr. Fowler only sent me to make things worse for you, or if it truly was important for him to find out about this Cameron Murphy who upsets him so."

Bryce didn't seem put off or surprised by her own subtle interrogation. "Maybe both."

"Why does he hate him?"

"Colonel Murphy—the man I work for—put him in prison once. We intend to do it again."

The chains weighed heavily in her arms. Neither one of them needed to explain that thus far, the only person who'd successfully captured anyone else was the man Bryce and his friends were after. "What did Boone Fowler do?"

"Killed Murphy's sister. Plus a bunch of other innocent people. He masterminded a plot to escape from a Montana prison, orchestrated more terrorist attacks in the name of patriotism, killed two innocent soldiers and stuffed the rest of us into this hellhole to be used as pawns in whatever scheme he's planning next."

Tasiya clutched the shirt that Fowler had insisted would be treatment enough for the wounded prisoner. Why waste first-aid supplies when he could simply hide the wounds from the camera? Let the guy sleep it off for a few days, Fowler had ordered—if he could stand and talk, they could find him.

But she wasn't used to hearing such bile in Bryce's voice. The man he'd described wasn't all that different from Dimitri Mostek and King Aleksandr. The emotions

Bryce revealed weren't all that different from the resentments and frustrations locked up inside her.

Not for the first time since coming to America, she battled with her conscience. How could she allow men like Bryce to suffer so that her father wouldn't have to?

She crushed the faded cotton in her fists. Maybe it was only a rationalization to ease her guilt, but she *was* helping him. She couldn't set him free, but without her help, he and his friends would surely starve. Without her help, he might not recover from his beating.

It was enough of an excuse to fix a polite smile on her face and walk back to the cot.

"Let us not talk about him anymore. Here." She shook out the khaki shirt—the biggest one she could find. "It is clean. You need something to protect your wounds."

She helped him into it, easing it slowly over his back and shoulders. Even that much effort seemed to tax his strength. He rested his elbows on his knees and leaned heavily against them. Tasiya breathed a little easier about him attempting an escape.

She held out the chains next. "I must put these back on you. I do not want anyone to question how you removed them." But his skin was still so raw; it hurt her just to look at it. "Perhaps only the wrists."

He pushed himself upright and spread his feet apart on the floor. "Better do 'em both. I don't want Fowler or Smith suspicious about you…bein' kind to me." Tasiya reluctantly snapped the manacles around his wrists, then knelt in front of him to lock his ankles together. "You better head on back to wherever you're bunkin' out, too. I don't want anyone to come lookin' for you and find you here."

But Tasiya didn't want to leave just yet. "No one comes into the kitchen where I sleep. And the sentries are posted outside the building at night. Unless I make too much noise and wake someone…"

Despite her hesitancy to trust and her guilt at deceiving him, Tasiya didn't want to be anywhere else. Though she could never tell him why, he understood the things she was feeling. Cocooned by the night, in this remote corner of the compound, she'd found a soul mate. So Tasiya gave herself another job to delay her departure. Rising in front of him, she reached out and helped him button his shirt. "Tell me about your Oh-sark."

Bryce's big fingers stopped on the button above where she had paused. He lifted his face, and their gazes locked together.

Maybe she'd found something else, as well.

Tasiya was sinking, deep and fast, into the gunmetal depths that seemed so like home to her. The heat from his body seeped into her hands and she felt herself leaning. Or perhaps he'd inched closer. His gaze dropped to her mouth, and her lips parted as the breath inside her swelled with anticipation. He caressed her lips with his eyes, awakening every female instinct inside her with the raw desire stamped in his features.

She was struck by the bold notion of closing the gap between them and pressing her lips to his. She wanted to crawl into his lap and burrow inside him, to soak up his heat and be sheltered by all that strength. She wanted to kiss him. To be kissed by a man as wild and rugged as the snow-capped mountains of her homeland. She wanted to be taken from her world of vicious words and violence and simply be a woman that a man wanted—the way Bryce Martin's eyes said he wanted her.

She curled her fingers into a handful of shirt and skin, and let her eyes drift shut. Just one kiss…

But Bryce had a saner notion in mind.

She blinked her eyes open as he pried her hands from his chest and pushed her away.

"It's Ozarks," he stated, emphasizing the *z* and the *s*.

"What are Ozarks?" she asked, carefully mimicking the word. She wondered if she should be feeling grateful rather than disappointed that Bryce had kept her from making a fool of herself. And she'd been afraid of trusting him!

"It's a place." Tasiya sat down beside him as he rolled up his sleeves. "Ancient mountains, worn down to rugged hills and exposed rock. In southern Missouri and northern Arkansas."

Those were states she knew from her studies. Gradually she began to relax. The more he talked, the more she reminded herself of why she'd been drawn to him in the first place. "They look like your Rocky Mountains, then? I have seen them in pictures."

"Nope. The Ozarks are green."

"What makes them green?"

"Water."

"We have many beautiful lakes outside our capital, St. Feodor. Where does your water come from?"

The tension seemed to be easing from Bryce, too, as he talked about his home. He leaned forward over his knees again, away from her. But it seemed to be a posture that gave him some relief rather than an intentional snub. "Rivers. Man-made lakes. Natural springs. There's a lot of underground water there. A lot of caves carved out by water."

"The foliage there must be very lush."

"Yep."

Behind his back she smiled at his funny word. "Are there flowers? Grass?"

"Trees mostly. Lots of 'em everywhere you look. Oak,

maple, elm, locust. With lots of good cedar. It smells fresh and clean out in the woods."

Not much like this place, in other words. "Green is the only color of your Ozarks?"

"Nope. On the hillside, if you look close among the taller, darker trunks, in the spring you'll catch a glimpse of white or pink flowers. Those are the dogwood trees. In the fall, all the leaves change colors. Bright red. Gold. Orange."

The subtle longing in his deep-pitched voice spoke to the kindred soul inside her, as though he knew what she needed more than she knew herself. She shouldn't fantasize about passionate kisses. This strange, budding friendship was already more than she could ask for. "Your Ozarks sound very beautiful."

"Yep."

"I should like to get permission to see it one day. Where do you get a travel voucher in your country?"

"You don't have to get permission. You just go. The United States isn't like this place." He shrugged, then winced as if the gesture had caused him considerable pain. Tasiya found herself holding her breath along with him until he slowly exhaled and could speak again. "You can go wherever you want, whenever you want to."

He didn't have to register travel dates with the Ministry of Security? Report in at the local town hall upon his arrival? "You did not need travel papers to go from Missouri to Montana?"

He shook his head. "I needed a change of scenery so I up and went. That's where the job was."

"Even a woman could do this?"

He huffed a sound that might have been a laugh and angled his head to look at her. "Hell, yeah."

"Incredible."

Her father had told her similar stories about his childhood, how he remembered taking drives to visit his grandparents in the country. Sometimes they enjoyed themselves so much that on the spur of the moment they would decide to stay the night—or a whole weekend. But that was before the reign of Aleksandr Petrov and the restrictions on travel she had always known.

Curious at how casually Bryce talked about moving from place to place, Tasiya tucked one leg beneath her and scooted closer. "Tell me more about your country. The Grand Canyon. And New York City."

"Ain't you talked out yet?" He'd spent what little strength he had left, no doubt.

"The men here ignore me as if I do not exist except to serve them. I hear no 'Good morning.' No 'Good night.' No 'How are you feeling?' No one else tells me what a beautiful country you have."

"That ain't right." He turned away and stared out into the passageway. "But talkin' i'n't my best thing."

Tasiya frowned, unseen behind his back. Did he honestly have no idea of the effect he had on her?

On impulse, she leaned forward and kissed his cheek. "You do it beautifully, Bryce Martin."

She fished her keys from her pocket and headed for the door, hoping she didn't look as startled by that little kiss as he did. The urge to offer him a kindness—to thank him for his solace—didn't surprise her. The fact that she wanted to offer him so much more than a peck on his whiskered cheek did.

As she reluctantly locked the steel bars behind her and gathered her things, the rattle of chains diverted her attention.

Bryce wobbled on his feet, bracing one hand against the wall for balance. But he was standing.

"'Night, Tasiya Belov."

She nearly burst into tears at his sweet chivalry, knowing that this wounded giant had truly listened to her, despite his pain. A forbidden bond had been forged between them this night, inside this horrid prison where they were both held captive.

They'd traded comfort for comfort, strength for strength.

And for the first time since that fateful night in Lukinburg when terrorists had shattered her world, Tasiya had hope.

"Good night, Bryce Martin."

Chapter 7

Tasiya clutched the collar of her jacket together and huddled against the mist blowing off the water.

Devil's Fork Island was small enough that, from the port between the old stone fortress and the newer fiberglass docks, she could see the two long inlets that formed the trident shape giving the island its name. But the island was large enough that when the ferry chugged around the tip of the westernmost peninsula, the jetty and dock blocked it from view.

The landscape where she'd stopped to breathe in fresh air and remind herself what the sun looked like was wild and barren of animal life except for the large sea birds that fed and nested along the shoreline. And while the prison compound stood like a weary, yet unbending sentinel on the windward side of the island, here, along the half-mile path, Tasiya felt as if she might be standing in the middle of an unspoiled nature preserve. If she closed her eyes and tipped her face to the warmth of the sun, she could almost imagine what it was like to be free.

But the strident hum of the electronic security fence rebooting around the perimeter was a harsh reminder that she wasn't free. Maybe she'd never truly been free. Growing up in the increasing oppression of Lukinburg society, she hadn't been allowed to continue beyond basic schooling to become a chef. She couldn't travel from place to place—wherever she wanted, whenever she wanted, the way Bryce had described living in America—without being documented at a checkpoint. Not even to visit her mother's and grandparents' graves in the countryside outside St. Feodor. All she could do was work a menial job or become a man's mistress.

His victim or his slave.

Shaking with a suppressed anger that blotted out the November chill, Tasiya opened her eyes and looked around. There wasn't a guard in sight, and a quick check of her watch said she still had ten minutes before she had to report back to the kitchen.

Such a generous privilege, she noted with sarcasm. After fifteen days of reliable work, Boone Fowler had granted her permission to walk down to the docks unescorted to deliver a list of supplies she needed from two men heading to the mainland. But he'd given her a strict time limit on her freedom, and reminded her that there was no way on or off the island without being detected. How were time limits and restrictions any different from the life waiting for her back in Lukinburg?

Seized by a rebellious urge after twenty-seven years of being the dutiful citizen who knew her place, Tasiya left the path and hiked up a shallow slope to the edge of a rocky drop-off overlooking the island's western shore. In vain, she peered along the horizon, seeking some sign of the beautiful, free America Bryce had described. But there was no land, no civilization. The stormy gray Atlantic sluiced over the rocks below, then ebbed and rolled into waves that seemed to throw themselves against the matching sky in the distance.

Not that she'd have any chance of reaching the mainland on her own. She couldn't swim that far. The island's ferry and two speed boats were heavily guarded. And since she hadn't seen any sails or heard heavy engines or sounding buoys since she'd arrived, she guessed they weren't on any shipping lane where she'd have a chance of flagging down a passing tourist or tradesman for help.

Tasiya grasped the corkscrew tendril the wind plastered against her cheek and tucked it behind her ear. There was no sense depressing herself by noting how far she was from America proper, or how much farther she was from Lukinburg and her father.

Her only ally was the battered giant locked in solitary confinement.

The kindness and resolute determination beneath Bryce Martin's gruff manner and harsh exterior had awakened something deep inside her. An urge to fight back, to do more than resign herself to a life of servitude and discontent. And while she would not jeopardize her father's life, she wouldn't sit idly by and let Bryce be slowly tortured to death, either. Above all, she would not let Boone Fowler and Marcus Smith break the big man's spirit.

Letting her attention slide back to her immediate surroundings, Tasiya began forming a modest plan. The foliage on Devil's Fork Island had all been beaten down to a sandy color, including the sturdy, thigh-high grass that clung to the gritty soil and rippled in the breeze like an extension of the sea itself.

Reminded of the reeds that grew around Lake Ryanavik, she reached down and plucked a blade. The whole shaft, from tip to roots easily came loose in her hand. She rolled the three-foot stalk between her palms and tried to snap it in two. A satisfied smile curved her lips. With the daily beating it took from the elements, of course it grew to bend and not break. It was fibrous and strong, yet pliant to the touch—perfect for basketweaving.

One of Tasiya's most useful homemaking skills was making do with whatever she had on hand. With an island full of this unique grass, she could make a basket to carry the bread and water to the prisoners, instead of pushing that noisy metal cart and worrying that she was waking every militiaman and shouting her presence everywhere she went. With a basket, she could move quietly through the passageways and worry less about paying a late-night visit to her friend in the last cell.

The five minutes she had left before Fowler sent a guard after her wasn't much time. But the grass came away easily in her hands, and if she couldn't gather enough now, she could make up an excuse to come outside again to finish her work.

Or…she spotted a clearing at the bottom of the rise close to the beach where bundles of the grass had already been uprooted and cast aside.

Shifting the grass she'd already collected into one hand, she made her way down along the edge of the drop-off, carefully avoiding the slippery rocks and a certain tumble. Like walking through molasses, the sandy ground sucked her boots into its grip, forcing her to shorten her stride and push off at every step. She was breathing hard by the time she reached the clearing.

As she hit the flatter ground, she idly wondered why Fowler's men would create such a muddy mess. The grass surrounding the turned-up soil had been trodden and destroyed. Perhaps it had something to do with the security system. Or maybe it was nothing more than a place to bury their trash. Tasiya herself had come up with the idea of burning any leftover garbage she couldn't use in the wood heating stove at night. Perhaps such a practical idea was beneath Boone Fowler's grandiose scope. Certainly, Steve Bristoe wasn't bright enough to think of such a thing for himself.

Grinning at the idea of having outsmarted her captors, and reminding herself that coming back late would make her just as foolish, Tasiya quickly gathered the bundles of discarded grass and laid them in her arms.

Beneath the last bundle, the first real shot of color she'd seen in the landscape caught her eye. Dark green and russet brown. A leaf, perhaps? But how could an autumn leaf of such a rich hue bury itself in the sand on Devil's Fork Island?

Squatting down to investigate, Tasiya saw that the mottled colors weren't natural, but a pattern on a tiny corner of cloth sticking up from the ground. She shifted the grass to one arm to pick up the material, but it was stuck. She dug away some of the wet, sandy soil on either side, wrapped all five fingers around it and gave it a good tug.

About six inches of mud-caked cloth ripped up through the soil. Enough for her to recognize a camouflage pattern. Tasiya frowned. The soldiers who'd been captured along with Bryce and the other bounty hunters wore uniforms of this material.

Why would someone bury a uniform?

With a new sense of urgency and half-formed revelation of fear, Tasiya dropped the bundles and used both hands to pull. Mud and gravity worked against her, but with a determined heave she pushed with her legs and yanked until the ground gave way.

Tasiya flew back and landed on her bottom. But she

hardly noticed the discomfort of mud and water soaking through her jeans.

She could only shiver and stare.

She'd unearthed a man's cold, dead hand.

Biting her lip to keep from screaming out loud, she scrambled to her feet. But mud and panic and the heels on her boots kept her from finding her footing, and she slipped. Windmilling her arms and fighting for balance, she stumbled backward. Between leather soles and slick rocks she went down hard on her hands and knees.

Allowing nothing more than a gasp of pain, she planted her feet, stood, then cried out in shock as her knees and shoulders were zapped with a jolt of electricity.

Tasiya collapsed to the ground, shaking. But she was less concerned about her body's temporary paralysis than she was about the sudden, loud, blaring alarm she'd triggered when she hit the invisible security fence.

"Oh, God. Oh, God," she whispered, her tongue tasting like copper in her mouth.

Each howl of the alarm grated along her nerves like a vicious shout in her ear. But she could feel herself breathing again. And though the feeling hadn't returned to the tips of her fingers and toes, her larger muscles were beginning to work. The sight of that stiff, crumpled hand sticking up through the ground warned her of what she must do.

That dead man would be her if she was discovered here.

Pulling herself up to her hands and knees, Tasiya crawled across the rocks like a drunken woman. But with every inch, she gained speed, clarity, control.

She could hear Fowler's men shouting in the distance now. She gave her fingers no choice but to cooperate as she pushed the hand back into its resting place and scooped the sand and soil back over it. Booted feet were tromping through the grass now, closing in on her position. She was running out of time to hide her discovery.

Tasiya lurched to her feet, grabbed one of the sheafs of grass, swept it across the sand to cover her tracks, then tossed it over the exposed fingertips. Snatching up the remaining bundles, she scrambled up the hillside.

For the few seconds she climbed, she debated whether it was smarter to run and put distance between her and the body, or whether running would only make her look suspicious. But the decision became a moot point as she cleared the rise and was greeted by voices shouting "Halt!" and the black steel barrels of three rifles pointed straight at her.

Tasiya cast her eyes to the ground and froze.

"What are you doing out here?" Steve Bristoe, the skinny blond man who'd been so inept in the kitchen, seemed much more sure of himself on guard duty.

She bit down on the hateful resentment shouting inside her. Bristoe was one of the men who'd beaten Bryce and held him down while Marcus whipped him. Her lungs swelled painfully in her chest as she tried to calm her breathing and keep her head. "I went for a walk. I was gathering grasses to weave a basket and I fell. I am sorry about the alarm."

Bristoe nodded to the other two men. "Walk the perimeter to make sure she's the only thing to set it off."

As the other two hurried in opposite directions to do his bidding, Bristoe nudged the tip of his rifle through the grass in her arms. Apparently satisfied that she hadn't run off with the militia's silver, he shouldered his weapon.

"Basketweaving?" he asked skeptically.

Tasiya nodded. "The kitchen supplies are limited. I thought I could help by making some items myself."

He might have withdrawn his weapon, but he wasn't letting her go. Wrapping his bony fingers around her upper arm, he jerked her into step beside him. "Whatever smokes your shorts."

Tasiya glanced up. She had no idea what that meant. But as long as he was taking her away from the unmarked grave, she wasn't going to ask any questions.

"Wait here."

Tasiya was well aware of the temperature as she stood outside Boone Fowler's office in her wet clothes. The blustery draft swirling up the spiral staircase raised goose bumps along her skin and made her teeth chatter. But it was nothing like the coldhearted chill of Boone Fowler's voice as Steve Bristoe knocked and pushed open the door to report how the cook had taken herself for a walk, and accidentally tripped the alarm when she fell.

When Fowler's response didn't match the report, Tasiya realized he was holding two conversations—one with Bristoe, and one on his cell phone. As had become her habit of late, when the militiamen talked, she went quiet as a mouse and listened.

"…more money, for one thing. You can't expect me to get the results you're after in only two weeks. I have too many new recruits. Training isn't cheap."

Tasiya hugged her arms around her middle and tried to rub some warmth into her body without drowning out the terse posturing in Fowler's voice.

"You don't worry about what I have on video. It will be very persuasive, I promise you." Dimitri would no doubt want to know about this conversation. "When the time is right, you'll get your money's worth, I promise you.

Just what kind of message did Fowler want to send?

Did his method of *persuasion* have anything to do with the dead man?

"Uh-uh, pal. You don't screw with *my* timing. Was it your idea to kidnap the princess?" Tasiya turned her ear to the doorway, wishing she could hear who was on the other end of that line. She wondered if that person was as displeased as Fowler seemed to be. "The whole world's lookin' for her, and I don't need that kind of scrutiny." He paused. "No. No one has any idea where we are. Now why would I tell you? That'd be one more person I'd have to trust." She huddled tighter within herself at the evil in Fowler's laugh. "Not any more than you trust me. Good. I'm glad we understand each other."

He snapped his fingers, and Tasiya quickly stepped away from the door when she heard Bristoe headed her way. But Fowler's voice still carried into the hall. "I'll expect a deposit in my account tomorrow. The usual amount." With an insincere friendliness he added, "Always a pleasure."

Tasiya pressed her back against the cold stone wall and closed her eyes, breathing a sigh of relief that she'd gathered information without getting caught. At some point Dimitri would hear whatever news he wanted to hear from her and hopefully release her father. Though the thought of returning to Lukinburg and beginning her sentence as Dimitri's mistress was growing more unappealing by the minute.

"I didn't know you were into mud wrestling, sugar."

Snapping open her eyes, Tasiya looked straight up into Marcus Smith's leering smile. The leisurely stroll of his gaze along her sticky clothes sickened her as if he'd groped each clinging curve with his meaty hands.

"He'll see you now." Steve Bristoe's startling grip on her arm was almost a welcome relief.

But Marcus pointed a finger and shook his head. "Hands off, Bristoe." He wagged his finger, and the younger man let go. "The little lady's not to be touched."

Every bruise on Tasiya's body, whether from the rocks this morning or Smith's hand at her throat last night, throbbed in protest at the hypocritical order. She might not be familiar with American customs, but she was painfully familiar with the lustful need to punish and control shining in Smith's yellowed, solicitous smile. He wasn't being gallant, he was staking his unwelcome claim on her.

"Bristoe!" Fowler yelled from his office. "You're wasting my time."

Smith nodded over his shoulder. "Go back to your post. As security chief, I'll take care of her."

Screaming *no!* would do her little good. Bristoe was already jogging toward the stairs, clearly intimidated by the bullying ox.

"After you." Marcus Smith moved close enough for her to smell the sweat clinging to his clothes, close enough for his stale, tobacco-steeped breath to wash over her face. But he didn't touch her. He didn't have to. She understood the mockery in his defense of her. She understood the threat of retribution somewhere down the line if she ever dared speak out against him or interfere with his treatment of the prisoners again. "Move it, sugar."

With a dutiful nod, Tasiya slipped past him and entered Boone Fowler's office. Smith followed right behind her, making sure she walked right up to where Fowler perched on the edge of his desk.

The militia leader patted the folded-up cell phone beside him on his left. "I had to tell my colleague we were running a drill." His calculating black eyes bored into hers. "What happened, foreigner?"

Tasiya fixed her eyes on the scruffy tip of his faded

beard. "I was returning from the dock when I decided to take a walk. I have been inside for many days. I needed fresh air. The ground was uneven and I fell. I am sorry."

On Fowler's right side lay a black-handled pistol. His men weren't the only ones who had gone on alert when the alarm sounded. *"You* decided to take a walk? *You* needed fresh air?"

As soon as he saw her gaze dart to the gun, his hand snaked out. Before she could draw her next breath, he had the barrel of it shoved up beneath her chin. Using the gun, he tipped her face up to his and demanded that, for once, she look him in the eye. "First I had to discipline Marcus for putting his hands on you, after you tried to come on to him."

Was that Marcus's version of what had happened in the interrogation room? She could almost feel that yellowed smirk leering behind her. Tasiya's stomach clenched into knots since the gun allowed her no other outlet for her rage and frustration.

"And now you're setting off alarms? Do you want me to think you're deliberately trying to sabotage my work?"

Tasiya bit her tongue on the lie she must keep and swallowed her pride. "I am only one woman. How could I possibly hurt you or any of your men?"

Fowler considered her response for a moment. She held his gaze, daring him to believe her. Either the direct approach had appeased him or he was tired of dealing with someone he'd labeled inferior. Shrugging aside the life or death moment, he removed the gun and got up to lock it inside the gun cabinet that framed the wall behind his desk. Growing shamefully accustomed to spying by now, she took note of where he stashed the key in his top drawer.

When he strolled back to face her, she quickly averted

her eyes so he wouldn't know what she'd seen. "Just so long as you remember that, foreigner. You have no power over me. No one does. Not even our illustrious government. Gift or not, understand that I will do whatever's necessary to keep it that way."

Even kill a man and hide him in an unmarked grave?

"I understand." More than he knew.

"Now go get cleaned up before you touch my food. Marcus, you're with me. I want to start recording tomorrow."

The woman needed to talk.

Bryce sat on his cot, eating the broth-soaked bread and cheese Tasiya had brought, and watched her pace off the length of his cell as she recounted the events of her day. Mostly, he watched the soft folds of her skirt catch around her long, strong thighs and tease the curve of each shapely calf. Three steps one way hinted at the womanly shape beneath her drapey clothes. Three steps back, and he caught a glimpse of creamy skin.

Though his stamina and flexibility had been severely compromised by the whipping, he noted that he must be regaining some of his strength. How else could he account for his body's healthy response to the mental debate of whether he liked the view better coming or going?

Certain parts of his anatomy didn't seem to care that he was supposed to be recuperating. Every precise movement of that articulate mouth, every careless bounce of those midnight curls, every spark that glittered in those exotic eyes triggered an answering pulse beat in his veins. The night air coming off the water was cool, but his temperature seemed to rise another degree with each detail he noticed about her. And judging by the rising heat pooling behind his zipper, he was noticing a lot more than he should.

Coming or going didn't matter. He drained half the cup of water she'd poured and wished it was icy cold. No matter how he looked at Tasiya Belov, there was something to like.

And if she'd shown any interest in him beyond the need of a sounding board, Bryce might have forgotten his plan for tonight.

He had only a few days of solitude, with minimal supervision from the militia, to make something happen. And whether she knew it or not, Tasiya was going to help.

"I think if I was a man, he would have shot me." Tasiya had finally stopped. She stood at the window, hugging her arms around herself and staring up at the waning moon.

Bryce stopped chewing. He scrambled for the emotional detachment he'd been practicing all day, choking the bread past the lump of rancor in his throat. "He pulled a gun on you?"

His voice sounded remarkably calm, considering the damage he wanted to do to the man who'd threatened her.

Her slim shoulders lifted with a deep breath. "He held it to me right here." She faced him and pointed to the deadly target beneath her chin. "He has three rifles and several pistols in the cabinet in his office. One day it's a knife, now a gun. For a man who cannot stand to put his hands on me, he seems to have a very—" Bryce gritted his teeth as she searched for a word he was pretty damn sure he didn't want to hear "—disturbing...way of making contact."

When had Fowler pulled a knife on her?

Screw emotional detachment.

Finding out where a cache of weapons was located barely registered through the impotent fury firing in

Bryce's veins. He set aside his last bite and pushed himself to his feet, forgetting for a moment that Bryce Martin on full charge could be a pretty terrifying thing as well. "Did he hurt you?"

"No." Tasiya flinched. Her eyes widened like saucers. Their focus darted from corner to corner of his tiny cell, no doubt taking note of the fact that he stood between her and the door.

No, Fowler didn't hurt me? Or no, don't come any closer, you big brute?

Bryce curled his toes into the floor and fisted his hands to keep his protective anger in check. He turned to the side to let her know she could pass by without fearing him, that she could leave at any time. He had to show her with his body that she didn't need to fear him since he knew that *reassuring* wasn't an expression his face could make. "I'm sorry."

Tasiya's brow furrowed as she searched for something in his craggy features. He couldn't tell what she saw until she spoke. "You startled me is all. You are not like Boone Fowler. The man has no heart. He cares about causes, not people. I am the one who is sorry if I made you... uncomfortable."

"Hell, you can't hurt me."

Her eyes were touched with some of that pity he'd planned to take advantage of. But the tight set of her mouth and the flush of color on her cheeks made her look as if she was mad enough to spit. "Just because you can withstand pain does not mean it should be inflicted upon you."

Tasiya's succinct words chipped away at that brittle shell of self-protection he wore like armor around his heart. She was defending him the way his grandparents used to, back when kids had teased him on the playground or a girl had reneged on a prom date when she got a better offer.

It just meant she had a kind heart, he reminded himself. She was a good person, nothing more, nothing less. But her insistence touched him. The fact she took a couple of steps toward him meant even more.

Still, he had to remember *he* was the protector here, not her. "He's got no right to treat you that way."

"He thinks because I am a woman, because I come from another country, that I am too stupid to know what he is doing. He does not believe I have the courage to defy him."

Defy? Bryce didn't like the sound of that. That was his job. "Maybe you'd best not—"

"I will show him." She was hugging herself again, rubbing her hands up and down her arms to dispel excess energy or warm herself. His own hands itched to do that for her, but he suspected keeping his distance right now would do a lot more to calm her than touching her would. "I am smarter than he knows. I bring the prisoners extra food and inventory the supplies so he does not know they are missing. I have found out secrets about this island."

"What secrets?"

"There is a body buried here. On the western shore at the edge of the grass. One of the soldiers."

The kid they'd executed two weeks ago. Hell, she'd seen that?

"I wondered what happened to him. I saw him the night he was…murdered. Damn." Bryce squeezed his eyes shut, unable and unwilling to forget the ominous crack of a single gunshot and the sight of that lifeless body being recorded by a laughing cameraman.

The subtle scents of yeast and shampoo teased his nose just before he felt a tug on his shirt. Bryce blinked his eyes open to find Tasiya straightening the open placket. About a size too small, the shirt wouldn't button without rubbing the cloth across the cuts on his back, so he'd let it hang open.

But that didn't stop her from tucking it together and smoothing it across his skin. What? Did she think he was gonna catch cold now? It wasn't a hug or a smile, but her matter-of-fact attentions eased some of the pain and anger inside him. "I would think your army would want to punish Mr. Fowler for that."

"They'd love to kick his ass." So would he. "Honey, you gotta watch talkin' back to Boone Fowler. Don't give him any excuse to hurt you."

Bryce shivered, whether from the stroke of her fingers or the realization that he'd just crossed a very dangerous line, he couldn't tell. *Honey?* Where the hell had that come from? But Tasiya didn't seem to notice. Maybe she didn't understand the significance of the word—or what her gentle touches were doing to his efforts to keep his distance from her.

Her hands were on his neck now, straightening his collar. "Do not worry. My rebellion is silent. I know my place. A woman cannot speak out against a man. My word would not be good in court. But I will—"

"Your place?" He wrapped his fingers around her wrists and pulled her hands away. Touching her soft skin sent him one step farther across that line, but Bryce wasn't paying attention to the warning signals. "Where does Fowler get off treatin' you like some kind of second-class citizen? Why couldn't you testify in court?"

She shrugged as if she'd uttered something that was common knowledge and he was a dolt for not knowing it. "I am a woman."

"Men and women have equal rights here in the United

States. Your word's as good as any man's. A damn sight better than Fowler's, I'm guessin'." A new understanding dawned. "That why you don't always look me in the eye? 'Cause I'm a man and you're a woman?"

Automatically her dark eyes shuttered and her gaze dropped to the middle of his chest. She pulled her hands away and held herself in a subservient posture that busted at that soft spot inside him. "Should I not be so bold with you?"

"Hey." He nudged her beneath the chin, splaying his tanned, roughened fingers against her paler, velvety skin, finally touching her the way he'd wanted to. Her eyes glittered like polished mahogany when he tilted her face up to his, and the night air warmed up a good ten degrees between them. "I know I ain't handsome, but I like a person to look me in the face when they talk to me."

"Your face isn't..." Her forehead crinkled in mute apology and the right words tried to form on her lips. *Oh, no, woman. Don't tell me it ain't ugly.* A lie now would spoil the tenuous bond he felt with her. "You have very beautiful eyes. The color reminds me of the mountains and the robust winters in my homeland. I feel...safe...when I look into your eyes."

Though the words were a little too poetic for his taste, her soft, melodic voice sounded genuine. She hadn't called him handsome, hadn't said anything remotely provocative. But Bryce felt the admission deep beneath the scars that had hardened him inside and out.

"Thanks." He pressed a chaste kiss to that frown mark on her forehead, resting his lips there for a moment until he felt the tension in her relax. Then he pulled away. "That might be the best compliment I ever had."

Bryce's voice sounded deep and growly in his own ears. But he was standin' a might too close to her clean smells and amused smile to retain much objectivity about where they were, who he was and what he had to do.

Right now Bryce wanted only one thing. And the drowsy sigh in Tasiya's throat said that maybe she wanted it, too.

He slipped his hand beneath the ebony fall of hair behind her ear, cupping the back of her head and tangling himself in the silky weight of springy curls that caught around his fingers and teased his palm. The curious way she focused on his mouth made him hungry to taste her.

Go slow, he warned himself, dipping his head. Their eyes met for one hesitant moment, asking permission, granting it. And then he touched his lips to hers.

She was warm and soft and pliant beneath him.

And Bryce thought he'd gone to heaven.

It was just a little kiss at first. He was every bit as mindful of his size and scars and not wanting to frighten her as he'd been with that modest kiss to her forehead. He'd suspected she hadn't had much experience—as controlled as her life had been, as old-world and ladylike as she behaved—why else would she even consider him a candidate to strike up a friendship with?

But then Tasiya inhaled a stuttered breath. Her lips parted and she braced her palms against the center of his chest.

"Kiss me like I was an American woman," she murmured against his mouth, brushing her lips across his in a tiny sampler of kisses.

"Tasiya…honey…" He met each kiss with a grateful one of his own. He touched his tongue to the fullest part of her lip and traced the rim. She tasted so good. He'd bet she tasted even better along the smooth, damp warmth inside her mouth. He swallowed hard, reining in his desire. "In this country we're equals, remember? If you want something, or you want me to stop, just say so."

"Don't stop." She almost whimpered with the protest. "I don't know how, but I want…more."

She caught his bottom lip between hers and suckled, sending a jolt of pure energy straight to his groin. This was a woman who didn't know how to kiss? If she ever figured out what she was doing, he'd be in serious trouble.

Bryce curled his left hand into a fist at his side to keep himself from grabbing her, plunging his tongue inside and taking everything she was offering. As far as he could tell, the woman was a natural talent. But if she was looking for a man to teach her the seductive intricacies and delights of kissing, then his normal bull-in-the-china-shop technique probably wouldn't get the job done.

Yeah, he'd had sex. But cuddling? Kissing? Tender foreplay? They just weren't in his dossier of experience with women.

And this one—strong and innocent and eager to explore—got into his blood and fired him up. He wanted more, too. Soon. Now. But he was too big, too strong, too damn lonesome for the physical acceptance she offered. He'd scare her off for sure if he gave in to the flashfire of hungry need that was burning him up from the inside out.

In his condition, *slow* should be about all he could do, right?

Slow, slow, sl—

"Bryce Martin," she gasped. Her hot breath fanned across his cheek in an urgent plea. She moaned low in her throat, curled her fingers into his shirt, kneaded his skin and demanded he give her what she wanted. "Please."

Not slow.

Who was he kidding? He had to be the man he was. Bryce tunneled all ten fingers into her hair, forcing her

head back into the basket of his hands so he could plun-
der her mouth. He thrust his tongue inside, finding hers,
touching the tip, twirling them together. He snatched up
handfuls of that liquid midnight hair and let the heavy
tendrils sweep across his bare forearms, teasing him with
dozens and dozens of tiny caresses.

He wanted to feel that hair brushing his naked chest.
He wanted to see it fanned across a pristine white pillow
while he went down on top of her.

"Tasiya." He groaned her name into the silk at her
temple, fighting for a deep breath to erase the images of
sex and Tasiya and explosive heat that consumed him. He
kissed her again, unable to resist her seeking lips.

She wanted more? He wanted everything.

He slid his fingers down through the length of her hair
and discovered the silk didn't end until he reached her
waist. He splayed his fingers at the small of her back and
tried to pull her closer. "Touch me."

Wherever, however she wanted. He needed her to be
feeling at least half of this crazy madness that was steaming out of his ears.

But her hands and arms were wedged between them,
keeping them apart. Her fingers tangled in the canvas of
his shirt, pulling it across a gash near his shoulder blade.
He winced. She apologized.

"I do not know where—"

"I'm fine." He reassured her with a kiss.

She trailed her fingers down the center of his chest,
eliciting a groan of pleasure she mistook for another injury. "I am sorry."

"No, honey. Don't stop." He kissed her again, desper-
ate to reclaim her when she snatched her hands away.
He could feel his energy ebbing as his frustration grew.
But other forces were winging through his body now—

adrenaline, desire—giving him a new source of strength and purpose.

She tapped at his shoulders, tugged at one sleeve, looking for purchase but afraid to touch. "I do not want to hurt y—"

"I won't break. I promise."

He took her arms and looped them around his neck. In the same fluid motion, he snugged his hands at her waist and walked into her, pressing their bodies together from chest to knee. Her breasts pillowed against him. He slipped his hands inside her sweater and ran his palms across her cool, smooth back. She wound her arms tighter, sparking a delicious friction between the pebbled tips of her breasts and the wall of his chest as she pulled herself up into his greedy kiss. Equals? Hell. He was playing catch-up.

She couldn't hurt him. Not when it felt this good, this right to hold her in his arms. The only way she could hurt him now was to come to her senses and end the kiss.

Senses. Ah, damn. A nagging voice that had been with him a lot longer than this hunger for Tasiya reminded him of his mission. He tried to ignore the instincts that had been trained into him from the first day he'd enlisted in the army. The same creed he lived by now as a bounty hunter. *The mission comes first. Your men are depending on you.*

Bryce forgot all about even pretending he knew how to finesse a woman. Bracing a hand against the stones, he drove her back against the wall and wedged his thigh between hers in a desperate effort to ease the ache in every pore that had been ignited, and could only be assuaged by touching Tasiya—by absorbing her into his skin, his muscle, his heart.

She scraped her palms across the short hair at his nape

and hummed in her throat as if the needy, coarse action somehow thrilled her. "Bryce Martin," she gasped as he shamelessly rubbed himself against her womanly heat. "I have never—"

He stole her breath with another kiss. He didn't want to talk. He just wanted her. He wanted to feel normal. He wanted to feel her passion. He wanted to pretend that this was real, that she'd be kissing him anywhere on the planet right now—not just in this desperate, hidden corner of the night where two solitary souls had no one else to turn to.

But the voice was insistent. *You gotta do it, Sarge. Forget how good this feels, how bad you want this. Think. Do this before your strength gives out.*

"Whoa." What did she say? *I have never?* Did she mean—?

Get a grip on reality, Sarge.

"Whoa." He whispered the word more firmly against her mouth, drawing on sheer will to turn his lips away from temptation. But burying his nose in the clean scent of her hair wasn't much better for gathering his composure.

"Whoa." He planted both feet flat on the ground and pulled his body away from hers, praying the damp ocean breeze would chill the air between them and cool him off fast.

"What is *Whoa?*" she asked on a breath as raspy and uneven as his own.

Bryce couldn't pull away entirely. He wasn't strong enough to do it. Not yet. His back ached, but there was something inside him hurtin' even more. So he rested his forehead against hers, looking down into those beautiful eyes and kiss-swollen lips as he awkwardly straightened the clothes he'd nearly torn from her back. The stones were too hard, too cold for her tender skin. He pulled her

away from the wall and retreated a step himself, finally
letting go. He looked her straight in the eye. "It means
we should stop. We can't do this here. I can't do this to
you. Take a good look at my face, Tasiya. You don't want
to do this with me."

She frowned at his crude speech. He didn't mean to reject her or hurt her. He just wanted her to wise up. Devil's
Fork Island was too dangerous a place for either one of
them to be distracted by false hopes or fairy-tale kisses.

She smoothed her hair as best she could after his hands
had had their way with it. "I have never been kissed like
that before."

Join the club. But Bryce knew she was talking about
being inexperienced when it came to getting hot and
heavy with any man. "I shouldn't have—"

"Shh." Despite the innocence of her body, she smiled
like a siren as she pressed gentle fingers over his sensitized lips. "Do not spoil it with an apology. I knew who
you were when I kissed you. I looked into your eyes and
knew that I would be safe. I am not sorry it happened."

As stunned by her acceptance as he'd been by her enthusiastic, untutored response, Bryce could only turn and
stare as she crossed to the cot and picked up his chains.
"But it is late. I must go. You need your rest."

He held out his wrists and let her snap them shut
around him, transforming him from a man into a prisoner again.

But when she was done, she took the sting away by
blessing him with a gorgeous smile. "Good night, Bryce
Martin."

He couldn't help himself. This was as hard a goodbye
as any he'd faced in his life. Without touching her in any
other way, he bent his head and stole one more quick kiss.

She wisely backed out and pulled the door shut before he could steal another.

With a definitive click, the steel bars locked into place. And after one last, searching look, she picked up her things and walked away.

"'Night," he called after her, watching her every step of the way until the last flip of her skirt disappeared around the corner.

I am not sorry. Hell. She would be soon enough.

Every good, hopeful feeling she'd spawned inside him withered. Bryce cursed himself and turned away from the bars.

He pulled out the band of keys he'd stolen from her and unlocked the manacles from his wrists.

Chapter 8

Tasiya wasn't sure how it had happened—how thank-yous and comforts had escalated so quickly into a kiss that left her still shaky on her feet as she negotiated the shadowy passageways of the prison wing.

Clutching the water pitcher in the crook of her arm, she stuffed Bryce's napkin into his metal cup and freed her hand to trail her fingertips along the slick, cold stones. That was all it took to recall how feverish she'd felt, pressed between the wall and Bryce's hard body.

His needy hands in her hair and on the bare skin of her arms and back had been as sensuous as the raspy tickle of a cat's tongue and as hungry as a ravenous lion. His mouth had been gentle at first, then most insistent. Then he'd driven her absolutely mad with the need to learn how he elicited every tingle, every shaft of heat inside her. She'd been thrilled to discover that touching him, kissing him, striving to give him the same pleasure in return only intensified the experience for her.

She curled her fingers into her palms and hastened

past the corridors leading to the other prison cells, hoping the aftershocks of those last few minutes in Bryce's cell would dissipate before she reached the breezeway and ran the chance of bumping into one of the sentries posted outside.

But her breasts still felt heavy, and prickly at the tips. The intensity of Bryce's need, and the power of her own body's unexpected response, had frightened her at first. Then she couldn't seem to get enough of the way he made her feel. Ultimately she'd been left feeling mysteriously incomplete when he had recluctantly but, oh, so sweetly ended the kiss.

Though it had angered her at first for Bryce to claim that she was kissing him just because she wanted to be with someone, she'd quickly seen through his self-effacing lecture. He was worried that he'd frightened her or had taken advantage. He didn't believe anyone could see through his scars to the good man he was inside. That a woman, that *she* could want him.

Dimitri Mostek, with his handsome face and politic charm, had tried time and again to force a kiss, to seduce her. But though he'd said pretty things and offered her gifts, she'd never felt anything but revulsion for the man. She'd never once been tempted to offer him her trust or her body.

Bryce Martin, a wounded ogre of a man with kind eyes and a unique way with words, had nothing to give but his time and his patience. He spoke of things that made her dream of freedom from men like Mostek and Fowler and Marcus Smith, that made her feel better about who she was and the woman she could become. He listened when she talked. He cared that she was hurt and scared and alone.

And he kissed like…well, Tasiya had little to compare

it to. But there was something raw and honest and very basic about Bryce Martin's embrace. That immense physical strength, tempered by his determination to be gentle, then refined into desire in its purest form and focused on her, was enough to make any woman feel as if she was the sexiest, most beautiful woman on earth.

Dimitri Mostek's lust made her feel dirty and small. Bryce Martin's attentions empowered her with confidence and strength.

It was well past midnight now, but Tasiya felt renewed as she passed by the locked iron doors of the interrogation room, the communication center, and who knew what other secret places a man like Boone Fowler might hide. She was too keyed up to sleep, and more inspired than ever to, in some small way, put a crimp in the militia's plans.

She would work for a while on the basket she'd started that afternoon—the one that would allow her to creep about the prison wing and visit Bryce without being detected. She'd also start planning exactly what she wanted to say to Dimitri Mostek when she called him that evening.

Relating the argument over money she'd heard between Fowler and his mysterious partner should clue in Dimitri that the Americans he and his superior were funding were not so loyal as he would hope. They expected the militia to stop Prince Nikolai's speeches and stop the UN from invading Lukinburg and taking away their power.

Instead, the militia was murdering soldiers, torturing men who weren't even in the military, and demanding money from another source. Perhaps that would be enough to convince Dimitri that Boone Fowler was a much bigger liability than her father could ever be, and would shift his attention to the American traitor and let the petty embezzler who'd only wanted to feed his daughter go free.

She wasn't holding her breath that Dimitri would agree to such a thing. But it couldn't hurt to ask. According to Bryce, women in America could ask for anything they wanted—and she was in America, wasn't she?

A serene smile of satisfaction curled her lips as she closed the iron door that shut off the prison wing behind her. The dreadful weight of it creaked into place, and her smile quickly faded. She was no better than Fowler or Dimitri each night she locked this door behind her.

Her silent rebellion and pushy American questions meant little as she closed off Bryce and the other prisoners in their dismal time warp of eighteenth-century barbarism. But what could she do, short of setting them free and sentencing her father and most likely herself to certain death?

Tasiya's entire sense of hope seemed to be closed up on the other side of that door, as well. On this side of the iron barrier, there was no Bryce. She had no friend. There were only watchful eyes and suspicion and loneliness.

For two seconds she considered leaving the door unlocked, to give Bryce and his comrades some chance at escape, to give her an imaginary connection to the men inside. But, ultimately, Tasiya was a practical woman. Nurturing her own kinship to Bryce and the prisoners would only put them at greater risk. If Marcus Smith and his security team found the door open, there would no doubt be a price to pay. And after witnessing the price literally extracted from Bryce's hide for her defiance in the interrogation room, she would not put them at risk again.

Tasiya reached for her keys to open the padlock so she could slip it through the hasp and secure the dead bolt in place before the guard's inspection at dawn. She frowned. Her wrist was empty. "Where…?"

She quickly checked the other arm, refusing to acknowledge the panic that lit a fuse inside her. "What have I done?"

She set the pitcher and cup on the floor and shoved the sleeves up past her elbows. Nothing. She slid her sweater back into place the same way Bryce had done after… A funny little glitch of a memory tried to tell her something.

The fuse shifted direction inside her and raced straight toward her heart.

"He wouldn't." She checked her pockets, the pitcher, the cup. She pushed open the door and retraced her steps across the floor. But she would have heard the keys hitting the stones, wouldn't she?

"He didn't take them," she whispered out loud, needing to hear the reassurance herself.

Her breath came in quick, nervous gasps. She peered into the shadows, beyond the glare from the harsh bulbs, desperately looking for the shiny glint of her missing keys. "I dropped them somewhere, that's all."

One of the men might notice the jingling at her wrist had fallen silent. They'd see the locked padlock on the open door and come looking for her. Without her keys, she couldn't get into the pantry to prepare any meals. By their 7:00 a.m. breakfast call, the militia would certainly notice that.

The fuse inside her hit its mark and caught fire. Finding those keys was her only option for survival.

After tucking the pitcher and cup into a hidden corner, she raced back through the corridor. She spared a glance for the sleeping soldiers and curious stare of the handsome, green-eyed bounty hunter who rose to his feet as she checked the floor outside his cell.

"You're out kind of late, aren't you?" he asked in a croaky voice that might have something to do with the ligature marks around his neck. "Something goin' on? You understand me, don't you? You okay?"

For the briefest of moments, Tasiya wanted to ask him if he'd seen his friend, Bryce Martin. But she had a horrible feeling his answer might be yes. She clamped her mouth shut around the question, shook her head and ran down the next corridor.

"Hey, I appreciate the extra rations." But the compliment fell into an empty hallway as she continued her frenzied search.

There were no keys. No hint of anything modern along her path. She didn't want to think that Bryce had used...

But the last place she'd had them was to enter his cell and free him from his manacles and leg irons. Then she'd slipped them onto her wrist. They'd talked and... "No."

Anger hastened her steps, warring with the panic inside her. She whipped around the last corner. The light behind her cast a shadow, blocking what little moonlight streamed into the corridor.

"Bryce Martin?" she called in a heated whisper. She stumbled up to the bars. *No. No, no.* She grasped the steel in her fists and stared into the empty cell.

"No!" She pounded one of the bars with the heel of her palm, then turned and peered into the passageway. "How could you?"

The one man she'd cared about in this place—the one man she'd thought cared about her—had stolen her keys and escaped.

"Where would you go?" she muttered aloud, already moving back toward the solitary light she'd brought him so that he wouldn't be alone in the dark. Ha! He *was* a beast. He didn't give a damn about her consideration for him. She was a stupid, lonely woman who'd been easy prey for his kind words and abundant strength. He saw that she felt something for him, that she wanted to trust him—and he'd taken advantage.

Tasiya sulked around the corner as resentment gave way to disgust at her own naiveté. She intended to find Bryce and get her keys back, then let him suffer the consequences for leaving his cell. She peered into every shadow. Peeked under doors for any sign of movement.

But *consequences* was a dangerous word on Devil's Fork Island. Memories of a man being beaten until he fell unconscious, a man having his long hair shaved with a rough blade to purposely leave cuts and scars—a young soldier buried in an unmarked grave in the middle of nowhere—clarified every emotion into stark, wary fear.

It hurt that Bryce had used her. But she could understand. Freedom, as he'd taught her, was a precious thing. She'd never known it was worth fighting for. But Bryce had never forgotten.

"Where are you?" Her words bounced along the stone walls and were swallowed up by the breezy mist.

If Bryce made it all the way outside, the sentries would catch him. Even if he was stealthy enough to avoid capture, he'd eventually hit the perimeter fence. The electric shock would set off the alarm and incapacitate him. Every man would be awake and armed. And he'd be paralyzed while they hunted him down.

Suddenly Tasiya was every bit as afraid for Bryce's safety as she'd been upset with him for using her. She quickened her pace, sharpened her ears to any sound, and doubled her efforts to find him. She still wanted to throttle him, but she'd do it once he was safely back inside his cell, out of harm's way, beyond Boone Fowler's reach.

She heard a thump and turned toward it. "Bryce Martin?"

Tasiya hurried down the corridor, drawn to the sound. "Bryce Mart—!"

Rough hands grabbed her from behind and dragged her into a darkened room.

Tasiya's scream rang in her ears, muted by the large hand that covered her mouth. She twisted and kicked, but the hands wouldn't let go. A steel band cinched around her waist, trapping her arms and lifting her clear off the floor before a force, like a large truck, flattened her against the wall.

"Hush." A nearly inaudible warning brushed against her ear, and Tasiya went completely still, save for the shallow, sucking gasps that thrust her chest and stomach against a now-familiar immovable object.

Tasiya recognized Bryce by size, smell and the sound of his voice just as Ike waddled past the open door, oblivious to the statuelike couple in the shadows mere inches away. Over the bulk of Bryce's shoulder she saw that Ike carried a crumpled sheet of paper in his fist and muttered to himself between yawns. Because he had his headphones on, he thankfully hadn't heard her calling out. But she would have run right into him if she'd continued on her frantic path.

Eons seemed to pass before she felt Bryce's deep breath push against her chest. The prison had fallen silent now, except for the endless drone of hidden machinery that she normally tuned out as background noise.

He removed the muzzle of his hand and let her slide down onto her feet. "I thought you said there were no sentries inside."

His voice, barely a whisper, was as sharply articulate

as she'd ever heard it. She matched his volume, if not his tone. "Ike is in charge of communications. Normally, once I lock the door at night, no one comes into this wing until morning. I do not know why he is here."

"He must be sendin' a message. Somethin's goin' down."

She didn't know what direction *down* would be in a one-story building. Only the crumbling lookout tower that housed Boone Fowler's office and bedroom had a set of stairs. But as naive as she'd been about Bryce's intentions with her earlier, she didn't presume to understand him now.

"You must return to your cell," she pleaded. "If anyone finds you, you will be punished."

His fingers hovered close to her temple, as if he wanted to touch her. Instead he clamped his fingers into a fist and released her with a sharp, heated curse. "Not yet. I gotta get the layout of this place. I need to know my options."

Tasiya shivered as he crossed to the door and peeked into the corridor. She hugged her arms across her stomach, unsure whether the sudden chill was part of the close call they'd had, or the fact that she missed Bryce's abundant heat. As her eyes adjusted to the darkness, she could see a screwdriver poking up from Bryce's hip pocket. He'd stolen that instead of a knife or gun?

But a look around the room revealed there were no weapons to be had. It appeared to be little more than a storage facility, with scattered maintenance supplies and crates of spare parts she couldn't identify. "What is this place?"

Bryce spun around and slipped into the shadows. She could hear him quietly moving things. "Where's the communications room?" he asked. "You know what kind of setup they have?"

Setup she didn't understand. But going to the room where they knew at least one of the militiamen would be waiting for them was clear enough.

"Please. Give me my keys and go back to your cell." She followed the sound of him working across the room. "I will not tell anyone you got out or that you have stolen anything. I promise."

"I'm guessin' all this stuff's stolen. Or bought off the black market. But they'd need a lot of money to do that. Most of it's military issue."

Military? Tasiya picked up something that looked suspiciously like a microchip. It certainly wasn't native to the prison's antique decor. She scanned the room. While she couldn't identify most of the items, their markings—like the radio set Ike had carried into Fowler's office—were all painted in camouflage patterns or labeled with military codes. "Are they planning an invasion?"

It was a rhetorical question, but Bryce answered anyway. "They call themselves a militia. A group of citizens who train to be soldiers. Believe me, Boone Fowler's lookin' for a battle to fight."

"Against you?"

"He made Big Sky Bounty Hunters his enemy when he broke out of prison and started killin' people. He may call it patriotism, but he's just a murderin' thug. Whatever ideals he once had have been perverted into a lust for power."

Like Dimitri Mostek and his superior. Men who used glory of the homeland as an excuse to wield their corrupt authority over Lukinburg citizens. Very dangerous men. Not the sort that one man—even Bryce Martin—could take on, on their own.

"Please." Tasiya circled the crates and touched Bryce's arm. She knew how to put her feelings aside in order to keep someone safe. "You must go back to your cell. I do not want you to be found here."

He stopped his search for a moment and looked over the jut of his shoulder at her. His eyes glittered in the darkness. "You know what a son of a bitch is?"

She'd heard the phrase more than once since she'd been here, and only knew it to be a curse. "No."

"You're lookin' at one." He shrugged his arm away from her and went back to work. "You shouldn't be worryin' about me. I don't deserve it."

"Why? Because you made me think I was special when, in reality, I was merely a tool for your escape?"

He froze for an instant, and even through the dim light from the hall she could see the sadness on his face. But then he shrugged it off and reached for another crate. "Yeah. Somethin' like that."

She could scarcely overpower him, so she had to rely on reasoning with him—or guilting him back to safety. "So you will go to your cell now?"

He didn't answer.

His big fingers moved with surprising agility as he sorted through items and filled his pockets—small metal disks that looked like bottle caps, needle-nosed pliers and a spool of white cord that reminded her of the island grass. "You know if this Ike uses radio waves or a satellite connection? Is he hooked up to a computer? Use a cell phone?"

She was quite certain she didn't know any of those things. When it became clear that Bryce was going to finish the task he'd started before he made any attempt to do as she asked, Tasiya decided that providing some kind of information might speed the process. "I think they monitor military or law enforcement channels. They knew that someone had tried to kidnap Princess Veronika in Montana, even before it was on the news from the networks."

Bryce's hands stopped. She felt his wintry gaze on her in the darkness. "Veronika Petrov? She all right?"

"A man saved her. Now the two of them have disappeared."

"The militia have anythin' to do with it?" He set aside one crate and rifled through the contents of the next one.

"I do not believe so. Mr. Fowler seemed quite angry that the attempt had been made." She didn't mention the knife he'd pressed to her chin as though he'd blamed *her* for the incident. "He said it did not fit with his plan and would bring more scrutiny to him. He wants publicity, but I do not think he is ready for it. Not until the videos are made."

Bryce stopped. "What do you know about videotapes?"

"Only that he will start filming them tomorrow."

The outline of Bryce's shoulders sagged. "Damn. I thought I'd have more time."

"More time for what?" Tasiya reached across the crate and laid her fingers across the back of his hand. A shiver of goose bumps rose across his skin and she wondered if this might finally be the way to persuade him. "Please, you need your rest. I do not think your body will withstand any more punishment. And if you are caught, they will surely—"

He jerked his hand away. "I need to get to that communication room. See if I can get a message out."

"Not while Ike is there." She clutched at his sleeve and tried to keep him from doing such a crazy thing. "He wears a gun. They all do. He will shoot you."

But stopping Bryce was like standing in front of a moving train. He easily slipped from her grip and headed to the door.

"Bryce, no!" Tasiya dashed around the crates and hurried after him. But he stopped unexpectedly in the doorway, and she plowed right into the middle of his back.

He didn't cry out, but she could see the flinch in his posture, she could hear his fingernails grating across the stones as he squeezed his fists around the door frame.

She pressed her fingers to her lips to stifle her own gasp, but couldn't stop the sting of tears burning her eyes. Lord, how she must have hurt him. His skin would still be raw, his nerves on fire. She backed away, not fearing his wrath but aware of her own ineptitude at causing him such pain. "I am so sorry."

His shoulders heaved in slow, deep breaths. He dropped his chin against his chest, but he didn't seem to be able to move. Tasiya slipped beneath his arm and gently pushed at his stomach, nudging him back into the storage room, out of sight from Ike or anyone else who might walk past while he was in such a vulnerable state.

He released the frame, leaned his weight on her shoulder and let her guide him back into the shadows. "You're right. Maybe I'm not up to this yet."

With her hands still at his waist, offering what support she could, she looked up into the taut lines of his face. "Please. I will get medicine. Ice. A blanket. Whatever it takes to make you feel better. But you must stop this madness and go back to your cell."

"All right." He nodded, but she knew it was too soon to breathe a sigh of relief. "On one condition."

"What? Anything."

He took her hands and pulled her into the darkest corner where she could only imagine the expression on his face. But his voice was deep and strong with his husky request. "Forgive me for kissin' you."

"There is nothing to forgive." She answered the question too quickly and tried to leave, but Bryce's grip didn't budge.

"There is, and we both know it."

Tasiya wanted him to forget that humiliating embrace. Obviously, it had meant something different to her than it had to him. She ducked her head to stare at the black space where she knew his chest would be. "I know now you did not want to. That it was only a trick to distract me. I understand why you did it."

"I'm up here, honey." He slipped his callused fingers beneath her chin and tilted her face up to his. "You be mad at me all you want. Hate me, if that's what you feel. But I never want you to be afraid to look me in the eye and tell me the truth."

The warmth of his fingertips and his fierce words quickly took her back to the strength she'd felt before realizing he'd stolen her keys. But wasn't that just an illusion? Did Bryce Martin really care? She lifted her chin away from his touch but gamely held her head high. "I do not hate you. I am embarrassed to be so—what is the American word?—gullible? You must think me very foolish to throw myself at you like that."

"No." His hands closed around her shoulders, his fingers kneading her flesh with a little bit of that controlled desperation she'd found so seductive earlier. "You didn't read the signals wrong. I wanted that kiss more than my next breath. I wanted *you*. I still do." He released her and she could see the silhouette of his fingers splayed out to either side as if she was arresting him for touching her. "But this can't be about what *I* want. I got a job to do. My men are dependin' on me. Maybe you were, too, and I screwed that up. I'm sorry. I'm sorry I hurt you."

"Apology accepted. Now can we go?"

"Slap my face or somethin'. Call me whatever they call a pig in your country."

"I will not hurt you," she vowed, shocked at the notion after seeing so much violence in her life already. "And you are not the son of the bitch. It is no crime to help your friends or do your duty. I do the same thing when I bring you extra rations and care for your wounds. I am only sorry that I confused our comradeship with something more."

"What's goin' on between you and me is a hell of a lot more than comradeship."

"There is nothing going on between us," she insisted, confused to hear him claim he had some kind of feelings for her. "We are two lonely people caught in a terrible situation. Do not worry about it."

"How many men you ever kiss like that before?"

She shook her head. They needed to leave. "Forget it."

He grabbed her by the elbow as she tried to hurry past. He bent his head and whispered in her ear. "I've *never* kissed anyone like that."

Tasiya stopped in her tracks, feeling his breath like a caress that stirred her hair, hearing his ragged words like some kind of promise. She turned her head. His mouth was right there in front of her eyes. A rugged, sensuous line that had shown her kindness and passion, that had made her feel powerful inside and weak in the knees. "What are you saying?"

She watched his lips and waited for his words. But Bryce Martin had his own way of communicating with her. He tugged on her arm, tunneled his fingers into her hair and dipped his head to cover her mouth with his own.

Electricity arced instantly between them, making Tasiya catch her breath. He tongued the seam of her lips and she opened for him, helpless in the face of his unfiltered

need. The tug of an emotion too powerful to acknowledge squeezed her heart and filled her with the desire to
heal the hurts and distrusts and misunderstandings between them.

She lifted her hands up to frame his face, less aware of
the rigid scars at the surface than of the flex of muscle and
the pounding pulse beating underneath. Bryce's quick,
deep breaths fanned across her cheek as his mouth moved
against hers. This kiss was quick, fiery and all too brief.

With a groan from the cavern of his chest, Bryce lifted
his mouth. With his passion-hooded eyes looking deep
into hers, he pulled her hand from his jaw and slipped
something hard and cold into her palm.

His nostrils flared as he worked to regain control of
his breathing. Tasiya was too shaken by her own eager
response to move away, but she understood the gift as
he curled her fingers over her keys and held her fist in
his larger one.

"A gesture of good faith."

Tasiya nodded her thanks, unable to speak. She was
too busy trying to regulate the pulse still pounding in her
ears and decode all the emotions she'd felt in that kiss.

Bryce stroked his fingers through her hair, the only
place he touched her now. Maybe he was straightening
the tangles from his clutching hands, but Tasiya sensed
it was more of a petting, a soothing, an apology. Though
which of them needed more comforting right now she
couldn't tell.

"You're gonna get hurt if you get involved with me,
Tasiya, and that'd kill me. I don't know what you've seen
in me these past weeks, but I'm grateful. I will always
treasure our time together—even if it was all inside this
crazy place."

This was goodbye? How could that be? How could he

show her such need and concern one moment, then say such a fatalistic farewell in the next breath? "Bryce—"

But the man finally had something to say, and he wanted her to listen. "I gotta do my job. But I'll find a way to do it without you. So you don't get hurt again. By me, or anyone else. I can live with loneliness and I can live with anger. But I can't live with knowin' I hurt you."

He tucked her hair behind her ear, lingering in the long strands as if savoring a forgotten memory. But then he let her go and grabbed her hand. "C'mon. You can lock me up, and I promise I'll never mess with your head again."

"Mess with my head?" Was that part of caring or escaping?

He grinned at their latest communication snafu, but she noted the smile never reached his eyes.

"Let's go." He pulled her alongside him, keeping her out of sight as he paused in the doorway and checked for any visitors. With the light from the passageway to highlight his craggy features, it was easy to read his austere expression. He was all business now, and she should be thankful. But Tasiya missed the tender, passionate man she'd seen glimpses of tonight.

She believed, now, that he really cared about her on some level. As a friend, an innocent caught up in a dangerous game of survival, a woman he was attracted to. How else could a man be so protective yet feel so guilty? How could he kiss her as if she was a precious, beautiful treasure and then turn around and ask to be forgiven for wanting her in such a deeply personal way? She couldn't help but admire him for his loyalty to his friends and his devotion to freedom and justice.

Why hadn't any other woman seen through all his scars to the good heart he had inside?

Pressing a finger to his lips in the universal sign for

quiet, Bryce led her out into the hall. Darting from shadow to shadow, alcove to alcove, he guided her through the twisting halls.

"Where are the other prisoners kept?" he whispered as they crept through the passageway.

She pointed down the darkened corridors as they passed. "The soldiers are there. Your friends, there." She curled her free hand over his grasp on her and asked. "You are not going to try to see them tonight, are you?"

He shook his head. "I promised I'd go back. Besides, I need some time to think of a plan. I do need to make contact with them somehow. Before the tapes are made tomorrow."

They reached the last lightbulb and turned the corner. If he would do this for her, then she would repay the favor. "I will take a message to your friends for you."

"No. It's too dangerous."

He stopped in his tracks, tugging her off balance. But his hand was there to steady her. "You've already done more than you should to help us. It's probably best if you steer clear of me from now on. I have a feelin' things are gonna get pretty rough before this is over."

Steer clear sounded like never see him again. And she couldn't do that. She was falling in love with the man, and he was in danger. Nothing might ever come of her growing feelings, but Tasiya Belov was every bit the fighter Bryce Martin was.

She wasn't the same woman who'd first come to Devil's Fork Island, cowed and afraid of a country she didn't know or understand. She'd made a deal with a real devil to save her father's life. But she wouldn't sink to Dimitri Mostek's level and trade one's life and misery for another's.

Bryce seemed to think that was the end of the discussion. After she unlocked the cell door, he stepped inside and pulled it shut himself. Tasiya watched him pull the chains from between his mattress and cot and refill the hiding place with the items he'd stolen from the supply room.

She rested her forehead against one of the bars and watched the expression on his face turn grim and resolute as he snapped the manacles around his wrists and ankles. Though her bonds were less tangible than steel and iron, Tasiya understood his driving need to escape and to ensure the safety of the people he cared about. She even suspected she was one of them now.

"Can you really find a way to escape and free your comrades if you are out of your cell at night?"

The question seemed to take him aback. His gray eyes searched hers before he stepped closer. "I think so. But I promise I won't take advantage of you again."

This wasn't about *his* promises. "Can you stop the militia from killing anyone else?"

"I dunno." He came even closer, until only the steel bars and the memory of that goodbye kiss lay between them. "That's a tall order unless I can find a way to contact my boss in Montana and let him know where we are so he can send reinforcements. Otherwise, it'd be a pretty bloody battle to get out of here. It would help, too, if I knew where I was telling him to go."

Tasiya didn't hesitate for a moment. "Devil's Fork Island. It takes the ferry two hours from the North Carolina coast to get here. Does that help?"

His beautiful eyes narrowed. "What are you doin', Tasiya?"

She could feel the heat of his body through the barrier between them, almost as if there was an invisible link channeling his energy into hers. She curled her fingers around his where they hugged the bars and was rewarded when he shifted his grip to link their hands together. "Tomorrow night I will bring you my keys. I will help you and your friends escape."

Chapter 9

"Why is Boone Fowler demanding more money?"

Tasiya listened to Dimitri Mostek's accusatory voice and wondered why she didn't fear it so much anymore. "He says training new militia soldiers is expensive."

"He's not pocketing any of that money himself?"

Thrusting her fingers through the hair at her temple, Tasiya resumed her pacing. "How would I know what he does with your superior's money? He makes me clean his toilet and burn his garbage. He does not show me his bank account."

"Are you taking a tone with me, Anastasiya? I will not tolerate disrespect from a woman."

She stopped at the blanket that was her door and bit down on her retort. Another marvel of American life she'd learned was that she could lose her temper; she could have a different opinion and not be punished for it the way she would be back home. At least, Bryce Martin had accepted her in all her moods—from fear to anger to an awakening passion he did not believe she could feel for him. After tasting such a gift, it was difficult to remember the sub-servient mandate for women in Lukinburg society.

She lowered her voice and moved the phone closer to her mouth. "No. Of course, not. I meant no disrespect. Things have been very stressful here today, that is all."

Seemingly appeased by her quieter tone, Dimitri returned to the business of spying. "What things?"

Tasiya fingered the nearly completed basket on her bed, anxious to take it on her rounds tonight and get started on her dubious role as a double agent. She wanted to collect more grass to braid ropes and build the sides of the basket even higher, but with a handle and large, shallow base already, it would fulfill her need for a silent means to carry goods to and from the prisoners.

"Today Mr. Fowler began videotaping the soldiers he captured." She closed her eyes, but could not forget the terrible images she'd seen from the breezeway. "He marches them into the courtyard in chains and forces them to read letters he has written for them. Behind the camera there are men with guns aimed at the prisoners."

"It is an effective means of propaganda."

It was a cruel and dangerous practice. To the soldiers' credit, none of them had read their letters with any conviction. Nor did any of them make an effort to hide the injuries they'd received during their capture and imprisonment. If Boone Fowler thought the tapes would convince anyone that his ideas had merit, he was mistaken. But it had still twisted her stomach to see those strong, proud men denouncing the UN's planned invasion of Lukinburg, saying it would harm her people instead of help them. And then they read that their own lives would be forfeit if the militia's demands were not met.

Thankfully, Mother Nature had been their ally. "The salt air apparently is not good for the equipment," she explained. "Everything is damp here. There were some technical problems. A man was sent to the mainland for new batteries and cables. They will resume filming tomorrow. I overheard Mr. Fowler telling his security chief that they will send the tapes to the media the day after that."

"Good. I am tired of Boone Fowler dragging his feet. My superior is beginning to question his loyalty." Tonight she found Dimitri's lecherous laugh more annoying than intimidating. "And it keeps you away from my bed that much longer."

Tasiya pulled the keys from the pocket of her skirt and slipped them onto her wrist. She wanted to tell Dimitri that Boone Fowler was loyal to no one but himself, and that the hundreds of thousands of dollars he'd claimed to have spent on the Montana Militia for a Free America wasn't a sound investment.

She also wanted to tell him that she would never willingly go to his bed. But somehow she didn't think willingness made any difference to Dimitri.

Swallowing her distaste for the man, she made her usual nightly request. "May I speak to my father?"

"Keep it short," Dimitri warned. "As you are always reminding me, you cannot neglect your duties for too long, or Fowler's men will become suspicious."

Tasiya didn't respond until she heard Anton's voice. "Tasiya?"

"Papa." An instant warmth swept through her like one of her father's bear hugs. "How are Mostek's men treating you?"

"I am fine, daughter. Well fed, but hungry for the sound of your voice. Are you well?"

"Papa." Tasiya peeked through the blanket at her door to make sure no one could overhear. Then she ducked her head and spoke with an unmistakable urgency. "Can you speak freely?"

There was a short pause. "For the moment. What is wrong?"

"Do not be afraid for me. I have met a man here. No matter what Dimitri preaches about American infidels, I intend to help him however I can."

"You are helping the militia?" His shocked concern only reinforced her resolve.

"No. They are no different than Mostek and his bullies. I am speaking of one of the prisoners. Bryce Martin is his name."

"Is this Bryce Martin a good man?" He sounded less disappointed, though still cautious, with a touch of fatherly concern thrown in.

Tasiya smiled. Her voice softened as she sank onto the bed. "Yes, Papa. He is a very good man."

"He is special to you?"

More than she was ready to admit. She simply answered the truth. "He is my friend."

His long, weary sigh tore through her heart. "Then you must help him. Do not turn a blind eye to your captors the way our country has turned a blind eye for far too long to the king and his regime."

She'd never heard her father make any kind of political statement before. His words both worried and inspired her. "I will be as careful as I can, Papa. I do not want my actions here to harm you."

"I am a sixty-five-year-old man, daughter of mine. I have lived a full life. From the day your mother died in childbirth, I knew you would always be a special gift to me. Nothing you do could ever—" His startled catch of breath made her think Mostek or his guards had returned to eavesdrop. But Anton continued. "I raised you to be a good person. I have always been proud of you, and I will always love you with all my heart. No matter what happens, know that."

That sounded ominous. "Papa? What are you saying?"

He waited a deliberate moment. Long enough for her to hear Dimitri in the background. "You've talked long enough, Belov. Say goodbye to your daughter."

"I am not finished."

"What?" Dimitri snapped.

He was talking back? Tasiya shot to her feet. "Papa, no. Give him the phone. We will talk again tomorrow."

She heard the clicking rasp of metal against metal, and the distinctive sound of a bullet sliding into the firing chamber of a gun. "Now, Belov."

"Papa!" She'd screamed the word too loudly. Tasiya slapped her fingers over her mouth. Someone had surely heard her. She needed to disconnect the line now, and hide the phone before someone came to investigate. But she was so afraid it would be the last time she heard her father's beloved voice that she couldn't let go. "Papa, please," she begged on a ragged whisper. "Do as he says. I love you."

"I love you, too, daughter." Tears leaked through her tightly closed eyes. She prayed his defiance wouldn't cost him his life. "My highest regards to your friend."

The line went dead. Tasiya's breath rushed out on a painful gasp. "Papa?"

Had there been a gunshot after the disconnect?

Out of habit, she stashed the phone in its hiding place inside her pillow. But Tasiya could barely think, much less move. She was numb from the heart out. How much more of this could she take?

She laid her head in her hands and let the tears fall. But for only a minute. There was little allowance for tears in this place. She wiped her eyes with the back of her hand and sniffed through her stuffy sinuses.

"What did you mean, Papa? My highest regards to your friend."

He didn't know Bryce Martin. He'd been trying to tell her something. That he approved of her having feelings for a man he'd never met? Or was it code for something else? Was his rebellion against Dimitri an echo of her defiance against Boone Fowler? Maybe it was his way of giving her his blessing to side with the prisoners instead of the captors she'd been spying on.

"Be safe, Papa," she prayed. She slipped the basket handle over her arm, calmed her outward appearance with a steadying breath and forced one foot in front of the other.

She just hoped that hadn't been another man she cared about trying to say goodbye.

"If I hit you, I get to kiss the pretty lady."

Bryce perched on the edge of his cot and aimed the crumb of stale bread at his mouse buddy snuffling around in the corner.

He'd created his own version of Bull, the damn dumbest game ever, devised by his former platoon mate and buddy at Big Sky, Jacob Powell. Powell knew a lot about bull, to Bryce's way of thinking. But the guy's mouthy sense of humor grew on a fella after a while. His chatter filled a lot of the silences Bryce was known for. Powell's daredevil ways had caused Bryce more than one headache over the years, but he had to give the guy his props. He knew how to make even the dreariest of nights pass by a little quicker.

And this one was goin' way too slow.

Tasiya was running late tonight. Or maybe he was just more anxious than usual to see her.

With the steady, chilling rain falling outside, blotting out the moon and stars and muffling the sounds of sentry movement, it was impossible to keep track of the time. He'd had all day to think about what crazy notion she'd get into her head after her vow to help him escape. As much as he appreciated her promise, as much as he could use her help, it had been tearin' him up inside, worrying that she'd gotten caught where she shouldn't be. Maybe tossed into a cell herself. *Interrogated* by Marcus Smith.

Or something unspeakably worse.

"C'mon, mousie." He had to get rid of those waking morbid thoughts that haunted him every bit as much as his nightmares. "Ready, aim…" He closed one eye and chucked the bread.

Normally the game involved a dart board, a stupid dare and a lot of macho bravado. Hit the bull's-eye and everything was cool—miss and you had to pay up.

"Damn." He was payin' up tonight.

Now he had no excuse, lame or otherwise, to put his hands on Tasiya. It was tough to swallow, though he knew it was for the best. The sparks flyin' between them were definitely more than comradeship. But it wasn't a romance. It wasn't goin' nowhere—relationships with him never did. This was some gratitude-turned-attraction thing that had gotten out of hand because of these crazy circumstances. Shared danger, close quarters, lonely nights—they could play with a person's mind and make him or her think things were real that weren't.

In the real world a woman as kind and gorgeous and resourceful as Tasiya would be beatin' handsome, sociable—normal—men off with a stick. Away from all this, she'd see him for the scarred slow-talkin' hick he was, and move on to somethin' better.

Nah, it was just as well that he'd lost the bull game. It was harder to concentrate on business when Tasiya was around. And the hard truth of it was that, outside these bars, business was all he was good at. He was just askin' for trouble if he couldn't remember that. Better to distance himself now, so that soft spot inside him wouldn't be payin' an even heavier price later.

At least his mouse buddy would get some dinner. The mouse stuffed the crumb into his twitching cheek, climbed up the wall and disappeared through the window to dine al fresco in the rain. Bryce and his roommate were gettin' to be regular pals now. Maybe he could tie a note around the mouse's neck and teach it to swim. He hadn't come up with any other brainstorms yet on how he could contact Colonel Murphy at Big Sky to put together a rescue.

"Bryce Martin."

Bryce jumped inside his skin at the hushed call of Tasiya's voice. How the hell…? When was the last time anybody had gotten the drop on him? Just went to prove how his useless feelings for her were messin' with his head. But, showing no outward sign of being startled, Bryce set aside the little do-it-yourself project he'd been tinkering with and rose to meet her.

"Evenin'." This little exercise in control was good for him. It'd help keep him centered and focused on the job instead of the woman. He turned toward the ribbons of light and shadow in the passageway and saw why she'd been able to sneak up on him without a peep. "Where's your cart?"

Though she'd visited him late at night without the clanking metal monstrosity, she'd always used it to deliver dinner rations to the prisoners. Bryce squeezed the chain between his wrists in uneasy fists. That wasn't the only thing different tonight.

There was a jerky awkwardness to her normally capable hands as she unlocked the cage, without prepping his bread and water first. "Too noisy. I make basket."

Her broken English was another clue that something was wrong. His gaze slid to the woven grass basket on the floor, then back up to her red-rimmed eyes. An unwise need to make whatever was wrong right for her again simmered in his veins. "Tasiya?"

She knelt in front of him to unhook his leg irons, and he jerked the chain between his wrists, battling the urge to pull her back to her feet. "Honey, talk to me."

Dammit. No *honeys*. No touching. He could keep her safer, do her more good, if he focused on the job, not her. But she was pressin' her lips together so hard, Bryce worried she might bite through them. "What happened?"

She had difficulty getting the key to fit his wrist manacles. But before he could help, she'd yanked them off and dropped them where she stood. Then she fisted her hands in the front of his shirt and tugged him forward, burying her nose in the open collar at his neck. "Hold me, please. Just…hold me."

Jeez, Louise. Her cheek was cold as an ice cube against his chest. And if that stuttery hesitation was a sob, he was in real trouble. "Tasiya?"

And then he felt the heated moisture singeing his collarbone. Hell. She was cryin.'

So much for keepin' his distance.

Bryce closed his arms around her and gathered her as close as he dared without crushing her. He dipped his nose into the silky crown of her hair and rocked her back and forth, soothing her the best way he knew how.

"Hush, honey," he whispered, absorbing her distress through every fiber in his body. "Nothin's this bad, is it?"

Her hands slipped beneath his shirt, headed around his waist. His skin caught fire at the frantic touches, and he didn't think he'd even mind if she accidentally grasped the welts on his back. But with something like a curse in her throat, she pulled her hands back between their bodies and snuggled impossibly closer.

Damn. Boone Fowler had pulled another gun on her. Marcus Smith had put his hands on her. Bryce rubbed big, frictional circles up and down her spine, as much for his own comfort as hers, as his imagination took off and pictured a dozen ugly things that could have gone wrong in this place.

"Don't stop talkin' now. Did somebody hurt you? You gotta tell me what happened."

"My father. I think…" Her noisy sniffle was followed by a quiet sob that vibrated through her entire body and made mush of any effort at emotional detachment. "He might be dead."

His hands stilled their massage. "You never mentioned your daddy before."

"I heard a gun on the phone. He was trying to tell me something." Gun? Phone? Father? This nuthouse had just added a new dimension of craziness. "There is a chance he is all right. But I have no way of knowing until tomorrow night."

He went with the flow of conversation, still not quite sure of the problem. "What's tomorrow night?"

Instead of answering, she crushed his collar in her fingers and turned her nose into the crook between his neck and shoulder. He had a feelin' if he wasn't so beat up, she'd be huggin' him good and tight. He reckoned her consideration of his injuries was a good sign. That meant she was thinkin' clearly. Or it could just mean she was thinkin' about pullin' away.

Bryce wasn't ready for that yet.

He backed up until his thighs hit the edge of the cot. Then he sat down and pulled her between his legs into his lap. "C'mon, honey. Tell me what this is all about." He smoothed aside the curls that stuck to her damp skin and palmed her cheek, letting his fingers massage her nape, holding her as close as she was willin' to be. "You know you want to. I've never met a woman who enjoyed talkin' as much as you do."

She made a sound that was half sniffle, half laugh, and the music of it eased Bryce's worry a fraction. She pushed herself up in his lap and threw her arms around his neck. *Now* she was holdin' on. "How can you have such a big heart after everything that has been done to you? I do not think I can be so strong."

He was less aware of the pinches of pain on his upper back than of the supple hip wedged squarely against his groin. Who was he kiddin'? With Tasiya in his arms, sayin' sweet things and squeezin' up against him like she didn't want to be anywhere else, Bryce finally admitted he'd made the supreme tactical error.

He'd let his guard down. He'd started to care.

He would put his life on the line for this woman. He'd give her whatever she needed or wanted from him.

Anything.

Despite the fact his heart was gonna get ripped up one way or another, he couldn't help the way he felt about her.

She might give him a couple of weeks out of gratitude, like Maria had back in San Ysidro. But then she'd go home to Lukinburg and forget all about the beast who'd befriended her. More likely, she'd reject him once she got a good, hard look at him in the outside world. Or she'd die in this damn hole. No. Hell, no. That option he wouldn't allow.

Leanirg back enough to put some space between them, Bryce studied the cautious faith shining in her eyes and then captured her mouth in a quick, sweet kiss. He wasn't sure if that was for her benefit or his own. But it startled some healthy color back into her cheeks and sealed his silent vow to keep her safe.

"We're as strong as we need to be, Tasiya. My grandpa used to tell me that when I was growin' up. You'll find whatever you need inside you."

"That's how I got through losin' my folks when I was a kid." He shoved up his left sleeve. "A lot of these scars come from that. My colonel reminded me of my strength and helped me get through months in the hospital, after a minefield exploded on me."

"The rest of the scars?"

He nodded.

"You found the strength to stand up to the beatings here, too," she whispered.

"Yep."

That answer earned the glimmer of a smile. "And you think I have such a spirit inside me?"

"I know you do." He picked her up off his lap and set her on the cot beside him. Then he reached for her keys. "May I?"

She quickly pulled them from her wrist and handed them over in an extraordinary gesture of trust he didn't intend to betray again. "Where are you going?"

"Not far." Bryce checked the passageway, then unlocked the door and picked up her basket. He poured a cup of water, dabbed the corner of a napkin in it and sat beside her to wipe away the crystallized tears that had dried on her cheeks. "Now, tell me about your daddy."

He pushed the cup into her hands and watched her take a drink before answering. She stared down into the water, and Bryce wondered if she was searching for words or doin' the I'm-not-good-enough-to-look-you-in-the-eye routine again. "You will think less of me."

He nudged her gaze back up to eye level. "Try me."

She handed him the cup and insisted he drink and eat first. He knew it was a stall, but he gave her the time she needed. He was licking the crumbs from his fingers before she spoke again. "Several nights ago you asked me why I was here. In America."

"You said you were workin' off a debt."

"It is not *my* debt."

He picked up the crude radio he'd been working on and started to tinker with it. He was pretty much to the point where all he needed was a power source to activate it, but his hands needed the distraction to keep from reachin' for her again. "I know you're not here voluntarily. What does Fowler have on you?"

Tasiya hesitated, watching him wire a battery port behind the walkie-talkie transceiver that would hopefully allow him to send and receive messages, at least over a short distance. He could see her curiosity about his work, but she didn't ask. "*I* am the payment. From a man in my country. I am the militia's reward for capturing you."

Bryce nearly snapped the plastic housing in two. "Reward?"

No wonder Smith couldn't keep his grubby paws off her. The security chief thought she was some kind of toy who'd been sent for him to play with. But Fowler preached ethnic and nationalistic purity. He wouldn't allow Tasiya to prostitute herself with his men. But then, he had the marks on his back to prove that Smith didn't always follow orders.

Oh, man, he was practically shaking with anger and self-loathing. "You mean you're only here because we were too damn careless and got ourselves captured?"

He jumped when her fingers brushed across the back of his tight, white knuckles. But like he'd told her, she was stronger than she gave herself credit for. When he would have pulled away, she laced their fingers together. Needing the tender reassurance more than he could have imagined, he turned his hand, holding hers, palm to palm.

"The only reason my father is alive—" her whisper was muted by the dulling heaviness of the rain "—is that you are here. If men like you were not fighting for your beliefs about freedom, he would have been shot dead in the street in front of our house."

Bryce's guilt over her being used abated as she revealed the unfortunate kindred spirit they shared. Like him, she was no stranger to tragedy.

Sensing his newfound calm, Tasiya continued. "This man—his name is Dimitri Mostek."

"I know that name."

"He is our minister of finance. He is in the news sometimes." He'd more likely read the name in a few intel reports. Suspected terrorist? Foreign crime syndicate? Tasiya spelled it out. "Dimitri is holding my father prisoner. My father is an accountant. He took some money from Dimitri—we were so poor." She shrugged it off as if the poverty didn't matter. But her devotion to her father was clear. "To spare my father's life, I agreed to work for Boone Fowler. I have been spying for Dimitri and the man he works for, telling him everything Fowler and his men say or do. I have a special phone to call every night and make a report."

"Why would someone in Lukinburg—"

"They are funding the militia."

Bryce turned and saw the truth shining in her coffee-colored eyes. "Terrorists in your country are paying Boone Fowler to commit acts of terror here in the U.S.?"

"They are hoping Mr. Fowler can keep UN troops out of Lukinburg. Dimitri and his people are very powerful and very rich. They would like to keep it that way."

Snatching the napkin in her lap and wadding it up, Bryce rose and put away the cup and pitcher in the sturdy basket she'd brought, waiting on her the way she'd taken care of him for so many nights. "And they stuck you in the middle of all this?"

"I volunteered."

"You were coerced."

The frown between her eyes told him she didn't get the word. "They didn't give you any choice," he explained.

"I could have let Dimitri kill my father. He wants me to become his mistress, and would have let Papa go if I had agreed to that. When I return to Lukinburg, that will be the condition for Papa's freedom."

"This just gets better and better."

"It is not a good—"

He put up a hand to stop her confusion. "Sarcasm. I mean it doesn't sound like it could get much worse."

But it could. Ah, hell. He could read it in her tightly pressed lips. "There is someone else more powerful, a man even Dimitri fears. *He* is the one who ordered me to spy here."

Bryce squeezed his fist around the basket's handle as he set it on the cot beside her. Was she talking about The Puppet Master? The ultimate terrorist who'd masterminded prison escapes, sabotaged trains, organized kidnappings and murders? The man whose unknown identity kept him more than one step ahead of military authorities and a team of bounty hunters who wanted him behind bars? "Who does Mostek report to?"

"I do not know his name. It is only an angry voice I have overheard on the phone. He speaks our native language. King Aleksandr, perhaps?"

It wouldn't be the first time Big Sky had suspected the king of being The Puppet Master.

But there wasn't a hell of a lot he could do with this information from here. Bryce had to get back to thoughts of escape and the reason Tasiya had started this confession in the first place. Moving the basket to his lap, he sat beside her again. "So what happened during your phone call tonight?"

She took a deep breath and matched his gaze. "I was telling my father I intended to help you and the other prisoners. He gave me his blessing, I believe—Dimitri does not know what we were discussing," she reassured him, "Papa was speaking in code.

"Dimitri wanted Papa to hang up. But he wouldn't and…" Her eyes squeezed shut, and Bryce almost reached for her before the tears started again. But she forced them open and he stayed put. "I heard the sound of a gun—the clicking, not an actual shot."

"He loaded a bullet into the firing chamber."

She nodded. How sad that she recognized that lethal sound. "And then we were disconnected. I do not know if he shot Papa."

Bryce breathed a little easier now that he understood what had upset her. He couldn't tell her everything would be okay, but he did know a thing or two about the criminal mind and how thugs like Dimitri Mostek worked.

"I'm guessin' your daddy's in one piece. If Mostek still needs intel from you, he's gotta give you a reason to call him. You're too far away for him to control you in any other way besides your love for your daddy."

"Do you really believe that Papa is all right?" She turned her whole body to face him, and her hopeful energy did silly things to his testosterone level. Yep, he was the big man. He'd made the lady feel better.

And there he was, reachin' for her again. With the tip of a finger, he smoothed aside a tendril that had fallen across her forehead. "He's just tryin' to scare you, honey."

She raised one eyebrow. "He succeeded."

Was that a sad stab at humor? Yep, she was gonna be okay. She was still too close to make it easy to keep his hormones in check, but he pulled his hand back to the basket, where he traced his fingers around the rim. "So your daddy said to go for it, hmm?"

"If that means go to work for you, yes. I am ready." She pulled a big clip from her pocket and twisted all that hair up into a loose bun she secured at the back of her head. "What do we need to do tonight?"

He liked that, too. A woman who knew how to get down to business. "I need a battery or some electricity to power the radio I pieced together."

She picked up the mesh of gerry-rigged parts he'd been working on, seeming to admire his handiwork. "What about the wires that connect the lights in the passageway?"

"They'd blink." He'd already considered that option himself. "I need someplace a little more private to tap into, or an independent power source, so I don't alert anyone."

"What else?"

"Some recon would be nice." He didn't wait for her to question the unfamiliar word. "I need to find out where they store their ammunition. Get my hands on some explosives. I've got parts to build a bomb, but not the main ingredient."

"What would you blow up?"

"The generator. Whatever powers the perimeter alarms."

"I can look for these things, too." She handed him the radio in exchange for the basket. "I can carry things in here without being detected. If you need something like this for your work, too, I can make more."

Bryce held on to his side of the basket as a glimmer of familiarity tried to turn itself into inspiration. "You made this?"

She nodded. "The grass grows like weeds on this island. I think it is the only thing that can stand up to the wind and salt air. I braid it into rope and then weave—"

"Cord grass." He snapped to his feet, startling her. Yes sir, a good soldier's training always made the difference when a man's back was against the wall. "That's what it's called. Cord grass." He picked up Tasiya in his arms and spun her around like he'd just earned shore leave. "Hallelujah, woman, you just gave me the idea of how to let Big Sky know where we are." He planted a kiss on her before letting her slide down to her feet. "We're gonna do this thing."

She clutched at his shoulders, blushing at his excitement, sharing it. "You are like a little boy. The grass is good?"

"The grass is everything. I recognize it from my army training days. You said we were close to North Carolina. That's Ft. Bragg and Camp Lejeune Marine Base. We used to use these abandoned islands off the coast to practice blowin' things up."

He let her go and paced to the window. He needed a little of that cool rain to splash in on him after feelin' Tasiya's body pressed so close to his—their thighs tangled together, her breasts rubbing against him, her soft lips answering beneath his. Just like that, he was primed to celebrate their first real possibility of success in the most elemental way a man and woman could. *That* was hardly what he needed to be thinkin' about right now.

"I wonder if anyone else would remember it."

"If you could show the grass on your video—"

"Exactly." He swiped his hand over his scarred, scruffy jaw and turned to face her. Hell. Even with the distance between them, and the reminder of what he must look like to her, his body was still on fire for her. Didn't matter. "You think you can convince Marcus Smith to tie me up in some of your rope instead of usin' the chains when he puts me on camera?"

"I will try. I could make the excuse of your injuries. Tomorrow at breakfast, I will speak to him. If he does not agree, I can trade—"

"Whoa, whoa, whoa. Don't give him anything."

Major reality check. Bryce didn't want her to be makin' deals with any man. He sure as hell didn't want her to be beholden to Marcus Smith. Another reason why he should never have let his feelings for Tasiya get personal.

"Do you think he will listen to *you?*" she challenged. She was right. And she knew it. "There is no other way, and we are running out of time. I will get you your rope, and I will take care of Marcus Smith. Tonight we will do your recon."

Her calm sense of acceptance as she hid her things beneath the cot and slid the keys onto her wrist put him to shame. Tasiya Belov knew as much about duty as any soldier he'd served with. He cared about her and he owed her. If she got out of this alive, he wouldn't ask for anything more. He'd do his duty by her. That was all she really needed from him.

"Where's this Mostek holdin' your daddy?"

That quizzical frown reappeared. "There are hidden apartments in the Ministry of Finance Building in St. Feodor. Dimitri showed me."

"Do you wanna be his mistress? I mean—" this was killin' him "—you have any feelings for this guy?"

"Hatred. I used to fear him but..." A sigh of understanding replaced the frown. "I will do anything for my father. Even strike a bargain with Marcus Smith. Papa is all I have."

Bryce crossed the cell and framed her face in his hands. "He's not all you have." Damn it, he was gonna say it. "When we escape from this place, I want you to come with us."

"But my father—"

"I will find him. I will take him from Mostek and bring him home, back to you, wherever you two wanna be. Findin' people and puttin' 'em where they belong is what I do."

Her eyes searched his. Maybe she questioned his offer, maybe she simply didn't believe it. "You would do that for me?"

He'd go to hell and back for this woman. But all he answered was, "Yep."

Apparently, it was enough. She nodded. "Then I will come with you."

Chapter 10

The communication center was crowded with more types of equipment than Tasiya could identify, much less operate. But Bryce seemed right at home, turning machines on and off, monitoring transmissions, taking things apart. Meanwhile, she'd been assigned lookout duty while he read diagrams and borrowed the necessary items to complete his short-range radio and construct something he called a jamming device.

Tasiya hovered by the iron door, keeping one eye on the passageway through the crack they'd left open and one eye on the big man at the console in the center of the room. On first meeting Bryce, with his shocking appearance and muscular physique, one would think this soldier-turned-bounty-hunter's specialty would be anything involving brute force. But Tasiya had learned that patience and observation, dexterous hands and a vast knowledge of all things technical were the tools of his trade. Bryce Martin was as at home with his gadgets and machinery as she was in her kitchen.

She'd also learned that his brutishness was only skin deep. Beneath the scars lay kindness, compassion and the biggest heart she'd ever known a man to possess. A woman could do far worse than to have Bryce Martin care for her.

"Son of a bitch." Bryce's muttered curse pulled Tasiya out of her thoughts.

She was learning to recognize that grim look that hardened his handsome eyes. "What is it?"

He put up his hand to wave off her concern. "Stay put."

But she had already slipped across the room to look over his shoulder at the video camera's tiny view screen. Tasiya gasped, pressing her fingers to her lips to mute her shock at the cruel pictures. "Oh, my God."

"Honey, don't look." He reached for her hand.

Tasiya held on to his long, strong fingers like they were an anchor. Even when she turned her head, the voice speaking over the picture—Boone Fowler's voice—couldn't erase the image of a young soldier kneeling on the ground and being shot in the back of the head. "I will kill one man every day—until our demands are met. Americans should stay in America. Our government should put America first."

"How horrible." Bryce rubbed his thumb back and forth across her knuckles, instilling warmth when she felt none. "That is how I imagined my father—"

"No." He turned off the picture, and turned to capture her hand between both of his. "If Mostek's the kind of man I think he is, he wouldn't have the guts to pull the trigger himself. Your daddy's fine. I can feel it in my bones he's okay."

Tasiya smiled at the utter seriousness on Bryce's upturned face. She rested her palm against his disfigured jaw and brushed her thumb across his lips, coaxing a smile. "What do your bones know about a simple old man who eats too much cake and dozes off every evening before he finishes his newspaper?"

The smile was slow in coming, but it was there. "You make a mean cake, do you?"

There was nothing mean about her cooking. "My cakes are very sweet."

That unexpected glimpse of boyish joy she'd seen earlier that night reappeared. "I imagine anything you touch is mighty sweet."

The look in Bryce's eyes filled her with a curious heat. She'd picked up on many colloquialisms the past few weeks, but with English, there always seemed to be more to learn. But Bryce was smiling, and her fear for her father was once again under control, so she...

Bryce stopped smiling.

"What—"

"Hush." He put a finger to his lips and stood. Every cell in her body went on rigid alert, matching his wary posture. Pulling her along behind him, he hurried to the door, peeked outside, then pushed her flat against the wall beside him. "We got company."

Over the pounding of her pulse in her ears, Tasiya could hear the footsteps now, matched by the off-key singing in the passageway. Marcus Smith.

What was he doing here in the middle of the night?

"He must have pulled graveyard duty after pissin' off Fowler." Bryce answered her unspoken question. He hadn't expected an extra patrol tonight, either. Taking a deep, calming breath, he reached into his pocket and pulled out a steel bar. Like the ones in his cell. What did he intend to do with that? "Don't move."

He gave her hand a quick squeeze, then inched toward the door.

Tasiya held her breath. *Walk on by.* She willed the command through a telepathic wish. *Walk on by.*

She could hear Marcus grumbling now, mimicking Boone Fowler from the sound of it. "You've delayed the entire operation with your temper. If the man can't stand up, we can't broadcast. Bring him in. Let me look at him." He was coming for Bryce! Heading down the twisting path to Bryce's cell! "You've got sixteen other prisoners—who's gonna miss one who doesn't talk, anyway?"

He wouldn't find them in the communication room. But when he discovered Bryce's cell was empty, he'd set off every alarm in the camp to track him down. "What are we going to do?"

Bryce held the bar up like a weapon now. Attacking Marcus would surely wake the other guards. And a steel bar stood little chance against the pistol and hunting knife she knew Marcus wore on his belt. Tasiya clutched at Bryce's shoulder. "You must get back to your cell."

"Just how do you suggest I do that?"

Marcus paused, and she heard a stinging splat of sound. Tobacco juice. The nasty habit soured her stomach. How she'd love to clean up... Her gaze fell on the napkins and pitcher in her basket. Could she do that? Did she dare?

Marcus was singing again. Tasiya grabbed her basket.

"'Roll me o-ver, in the clo-ver.'"

"Tas—" She was out the door before Bryce could stop her. She felt rather than heard his curse and ignored it. He couldn't help her with this.

"'Roll me over, lay me down...' Hey, sugar."

Tasiya propped the iron door open, blocking Marcus's view into the communications room but forcing Bryce back into the shadows to stay hidden. It wasn't hard to act flustered when the stinky ox practically drooled at the sight of her. "Mr. Smith."

She strolled on past him, and he had to turn his back to the door to keep her in sight. "Whatchya doing over here this late at night, sugar?"

With a steadying breath and a silent prayer that she could pull this off, Tasiya faced him. "I finished delivering the bread to the prisoners. Some of them are very chatty," she added as an excuse. None of them were, but Marcus didn't know that.

She retreated another couple of steps, drawing the black-haired giant farther from the door. If she could get him to follow her around the corner, Bryce could slip out into the passageway undetected and return to his cell before he was discovered missing.

"I heard a noise." She remembered her deferring ways the militiamen liked so much, and ducked her head to focus on the tobacco stain at the center of Marcus's chest. "I unlocked the room to check. Should I not have done so?"

Marcus took the bait and drifted closer. "And here I thought you were lookin' for me, sugar. Now I find you're just trying to take over my job."

"No." He reached for a tendril of her hair and turned the corner with her when she backed away. "Please do not touch."

Run, Bryce.

"Fowler's not here to make us mind our manners." Tasiya clasped the basket to her chest, keeping it between her and Marcus. He braced his hands on the wall on either side of her head and leaned in until the basket pushed into her stomach. "You know, I nearly lost my job over you and the big guy. But if Martin says everything he's supposed to in the morning, Fowler will see that my methods work. Some men need a harder hand."

No man needed to be tortured so cruelly. But her time with Dimitri Mostek had taught her how to mask her emotions. She feigned ignorance. "The big guy?"

"Yeah, the ugly dude we beat the crap out of. Fowler says I can't have any more fun with him. But who the hell's gonna notice if that face is more beat up than usual, eh?"

Tasiya nearly choked on her anger at his crude laugh at Bryce's expense. She hoped Bryce couldn't hear any of this. Her palms were sweating at what she must do, but ironically, Marcus's callous comments infused her with a protective strength that made it easy to turn off both her nerves and her gag reflex. "I have an idea about the big guy that might help you regain favor with Mr. Fowler."

His tongue circled his lips in the middle of his bushy black beard. "I'm listening."

Tasiya unwound one of the cord grass braids from the basket's handle. "When you film him for the camera, so he does not appear to be more abused than he is, you should tie him up with this rope instead of so many chains. You will appear more humane."

Marcus pushed away from the wall. "He's too big a risk."

Had he figured out she was a diversion? When he turned back toward Bryce's position, Tasiya did the first thing she could think of. Reaching for Marcus's belt, she pulled out his knife and cut a swath of rope off her basket.

"What are you—"

"The rope is very strong." He spun around, snatching at the sheath on his belt as if she'd attacked him. Tasiya dropped the knife into the basket and set it on the floor. She held the rope up, taut between her hands. "I will show you."

"You want to tie me up?" His burst of temper turned into an amused grin. He twirled his finger through the rope and tugged her a step closer. "I didn't know you were into S&M, sugar."

Though she didn't understand the term, anything Marcus Smith seemed so intrigued with would no doubt disgust her. She released the rope he now held and backed away. "You can tie my hands, then."

"Now this is gettin' interesting."

Please be gone, Bryce Martin. Please be safe.

Tasiya held out her hands, and with no urging, Marcus looped the rope around her wrists. He pinched her skin in the knots he made, and pulled the grass tight.

"You see?" She strained at her bonds, pretending the panic that quivered across her lips wasn't real. "Very strong."

"God, you're a stupid woman," he laughed as he pushed her back against the wall and nuzzled the side of her neck. Nausea bloomed in her stomach. "But you're too damn pretty to resist."

"Mr. Smith." She inhaled a frightened breath and his gaze went straight to the heave of her bosom. "You are not supposed to touch me."

"Get real, sugar." He palmed the side of her waist, squeezed her breast.

Tasiya shoved her bound hands against his chest. "No!"

"You're waiting for me in a private corner? You ask me to tie you up?"

"I wanted to show you the rope." *Bryce? Bryce!*

Marcus's foul breath washed over her face just before he took her mouth in a bitter-tasting kiss. Tasiya's stomach churned.

"Smith!" Boone Fowler's voice crackled over the walkie-talkie strapped to Marcus's belt. "Get your butt back to my office now."

Marcus stopped grinding his mouth over hers and he cursed. "Go to the prison. Back to my office. I wish he'd make up his mind."

"Smith. Get on the walkie-talkie and answer me. Ike says the new camera isn't working. Bring the old one from the comm room. We'll switch out batteries and make sure it works before we release one of the prisoners."

Retrieve the camera from the communications room? No!

Marcus shoved her into the wall as he pushed away. He held up a warning finger as he pulled out his walkie-talkie. "Not one peep out of you when I press this button. I don't want him to know we've been together."

Together had such a horrible connotation when he said it. "Will you use the ropes in the video?"

"Smith!"

"All right. We'll tie his hands. But the leg irons stay."

Tasiya discovered she could smile without feeling anything. "My lips are sealed."

Marcus pushed a button on the walkie-talkie and answered. "I'm coming, Mr. Fowler. I'll bring the camera."

Smith strode around the corner to the communications room. Tasiya faded into the shadows, praying she'd given Bryce enough time to get back to his cell. When she heard the key twist in the lock of the iron door, she didn't know if he'd been sealed in or if he was in the clear.

But as soon as she heard Marcus Smith treading back toward the breezeway, she picked up her basket and hurried toward Bryce's cell. *Please be there. Please.*

"Bryce Martin?" She ran up to the bars and exhaled

such a relieved sigh it left her light-headed. "Thank God. Thank God you are safe."

He stood inside, putting on his chains. As soon as he saw the grass rope on her wrists, he reached through the bars. "What the hell?"

His chains scraped against the bars as he untied her, and Tasiya tried to hush him. "Someone will hear you."

But there was no stopping Bryce. "What did he do to you? Are you hurt?"

There was a desperation in his fingertips as he touched her cheek, cupped her neck, smoothed her hair. She wiped the taste of Marcus Smith from her mouth with the back of her hand, and Bryce's thumb was instantly there, brushing across her lips, stamping his care and concern there. Finally Tasiya latched on to his hands to stop his frantic inspection. "I am all right. I have been very successful. Marcus will use the ropes on you tomorrow."

He shook his head. "I hated what you were doing. Every minute of it. But you're a damn smart woman."

With that he palmed the nape of her neck and pulled her in for his kiss. It was wild and frantic, their bodies pressed against the bars, their faces meeting in between. Tasiya linked her hand behind his neck and parted her lips to drink in the deliciously potent taste of him. It was an assurance of lives spared, a prayer for future cautions, a joining of two souls who'd learned more about trust and survival in the past few weeks than they'd known their entire lives.

When Bryce pulled away, they both clung to the bars to catch their breaths. A wry smile softened the harsh lines of his face. "You'll never go down without a fight, will you?"

The admiration in his eyes filled her with pride. "I have a very good teacher."

His wry grin quickly faded. "You better get back to your room before someone misses you."

Tasiya picked up her basket and tucked the rope inside. "Good night, Bryce Martin."

"Watch your back."

She glanced over her shoulder. "I cannot see my—"

"Stay safe." That, she understood.

"I forgot." She handed him Marcus Smith's knife from her basket. "You, too."

Bryce took the knife and reached out for one last touch of her hair. "Damn smart woman."

Bryce took his time tying up the boots Boone Fowler had returned to him while Bristoe and Hodges stood watch outside his cell. Sure, stooping over to work around his leg irons pulled at the scabs just starting to form on his back and put pressure on his cracked rib. But he was more interested in stalling for time.

He didn't want to appear too eager to become a movie star.

The morning had dawned, red and overcast, with the biting threat of more rain on the wind. Everything inside Bryce's cell was damp, including the mattress ticking and the green camo jacket he'd buttoned over the khaki shirt that didn't quite fit. He knew these little amenities had nothing to do with a sudden attack of conscience over a prisoner freezin' his nuts off in a cell with an open window. They wanted to hide the marks of his abuse. Pretty him up for the camera.

Ha! There wasn't nothin' pretty about Bryce Martin and what he was planning to do to the militia.

"Move it, Martin." Hodges seemed a little out of his element, without his brass knuckles or permission to use Bryce as a punching bag. He paced back and forth in the passageway, checking his watch. "Mr. Fowler wants to get you on video before the storm hits."

Bristoe had his rifle looped over his shoulder and looked as if he was taxing every brain cell tying and testing knots in the cord grass rope Tasiya had given Marcus Smith. "You're sure this'll hold the big guy?"

Hodges snatched it out of the kid's hands and shook it loose. "If Smith says to use it, we use it." He gestured through the bars. "You ready, Martin?"

Bryce nodded, still refraining from striking up any kind of conversation with his tormentors. They didn't seem to expect it, and he wasn't about to offer. Hodges ordered him to the back wall of the cell as he unlocked the door, and Bristoe held him at gunpoint while the older man bound Bryce's wrists. Once he was secured, Hodges pulled out a folded piece of stationery and his pistol.

He poked the gun into Bryce's gut, grinning at the grunt of pain that was impossible to hide. "You give me any trouble, big man, and I'll shoot you where you stand. Got that?"

Bryce nodded.

"Good." He pushed the paper into Bryce's hands and shoved him into the passageway. Bryce gritted his teeth around his curse and breathed in deeply to control the waves of pain undulating across his back. "Now you be a good boy and read what Mr. Fowler wrote for you, exactly the way he said it, and we'll let you come back to your room for some more beauty sleep."

"Beauty sleep?" Bristoe laughed, pulling the door shut behind them. "That's a good one."

Hodges and Bristoe laughed, and Bryce began the long walk outside.

They passed through the familiar twists and turns, past

the interrogation room and the communications center, past the blank corridors that led to other prison cells, past the room that housed the generators. Bristoe slipped aside a dead bolt and pushed open a solid iron door that led onto an open, porchlike walkway paved in stone.

Bryce squinted as he saw direct outdoor light for the first time in three weeks. Even with the clouds hanging overhead, the muted sun seemed harsh to eyes that had grown accustomed to functioning in shadows and darkness. This must be the breezeway Tasiya had mentioned—and that screen door at the opposite end would lead into the kitchen, mess hall and militia quarters.

"Wait here." Hodges tapped him in the gut with the pistol again, and Bryce winced, caught off guard because he'd been too busy searching for Tasiya on the other side of that screen door.

With Bristoe's gun fixed on Bryce, Hodges hopped down the two steps that led into the courtyard and hurried over to exchange words with Boone Fowler and the short, squatty man behind the camera. Beyond the crumbling stone wall at the far edge of the yard, Bryce could see the golden cord grass whipping back and forth in the wind blown ahead by the coming storm. Somebody at Big Sky had to remember the hours they'd spent cartin' heavy equipment across these rocky, sand-soaked islands, then clearin' it all away so they could use 'em for target practice.

Making a cut sign across his neck, Fowler dismissed the hostage being filmed ahead of Bryce. Jacob Powell, of the crazy games and annoying charm, strode into view. Flanked by two militiamen, Powell was doing his own version of creating chaos and making life difficult for the militia. He was talkin'.

Bryce studied the ground and battled the urge to grin.

"I don't know, I think I got the whole Tom Cruise thing workin'. You know, with the teeth and the hair." Despite a hoarse voice, Powell was speaking in code as he walked up the steps and passed by, and Bryce was paying attention. "I got it all over Craig O'Riley. He doesn't have the profile for camera work like I do." Riley had a broken nose? "And he's not pullin' off that Lex Luthor look at all." Shaved head? "You know, what one gal thinks is sexy—"

"Shut up."

So, with Bryce temporarily sidelined, Riley Watson had become the guinea pig du jour for torture and neglect. Powell had indicated that he was healthy enough to put up a good fight, but Riley was hurtin'. Bryce would have to keep that in mind if he got a chance—correction, make that *when* he got the chance to make their rescue happen.

While Powell jabbered on, Bryce communicated the best way *he* knew how. He lifted his hands and rubbed at his wrists to let Powell know he was onto somethin' with the cord grass. Then he looked him straight in those clever green eyes and prayed his buddy could still read his silences.

"I'm ready for my close-up, Mr. DeMille." Powell winked, telling Bryce he understood that somethin' was goin' down. "Oh, yeah, I'm ready for that."

"I said shut up."

"Shutting up now."

One of the guards poked Powell between the shoulder blades with his rifle, and the three of them disappeared behind the iron door.

Showtime.

At Hodges's nod, Fowler looked across the uneven paving stones and inspected Bryce. The militia leader scanned him from head to toe, no doubt checking to see if he could play the part of a meek convert to Fowler's ideology.

But Bryce's effort to maintain a blank, downcast expression got sidetracked by the sound of Tasiya's voice. "I must return to the kitchen to wash up the breakfast dishes. Enjoy your coffee."

A door had opened up in the hall just on the other side of the screen. Bryce could see her backing into the hallway. She'd gone back to her jeans, which did as fine a job showing off her long, lean legs as any other damn thing she wore. A familiar longing tripped through his veins, suffusing him with the need to move, to go to her and wrap himself around her and shield her from the hellish games of this place.

She spared Bryce a quick glance through the screen, just enough to let him know she knew he was there, but not long enough for anyone else to pick up the connection. She made a motion with her hand down at her side— signin' somethin' maybe—but Bryce didn't catch it. And then she had company and there was no chance to repeat the message.

"I only wanted to see that you kept your word," she said through the open door. "Thank you."

"Anything for you, sugar." Marcus Smith materialized in the doorway, holding a mug of coffee. He stared down at the top of Tasiya's cowed head with a sick smile that heated Bryce's blood from the tender need to protect to the surprisingly violent desire to put that leering bastard out of commission.

"I must go."

Smith picked up a strand of Tasiya's hair and rubbed it between his fingers, holdin' on tight enough that she had to turn her head to keep it from pullin' at her scalp when she tried to leave. "Don't run off on my account, sugar. I think you and I have more to discuss."

"Later. I promise. I have to go." By the time she pried her hair loose and tried to move away, Bryce's toes were curlin' inside his boots, anxious to get to her and run interference.

That son of a bitch. Though Tasiya politely excused herself, Smith moved out right behind her. Bryce's hands fisted around Fowler's letter. A vein pounded in his jaw. *Why the hell didn't somebody stop him?*

With an all-important message to send on video, Bryce couldn't risk taking down Bristoe and the two guards who stood between him and the door. But his fists weren't the only weapon he possessed. "Should he be doin' that?"

The fact that he'd spoken startled Bristoe into answerin'. "What?"

Bryce nodded toward the screen door. "Him and that girl."

The kid wasn't slick enough to let it go. "Who? Smith?"

He said the name loud enough that Marcus stopped and turned. Thankfully, Tasiya trotted straight on out of sight, into the kitchen where she could grab a meat cleaver to keep Smith's hands off her. He hoped.

But Marcus wasn't near the fool Steve Bristoe was. His icy blue eyes met Bryce's through the screen. A silent message was exchanged between them. Boundaries were challenged. Paybacks were set.

Smith took a drink of coffee, then wiped his mouth

with the back of his hand. "Sweet on the little lady, are ya, big guy?"

Bryce didn't answer the taunt. His attention had been drawn to something more worth his time. That's what Tasiya had tried to tell him with her hand signals. A C and a 4. He'd taught her a list of items to look for in their nightly searches. And his gutsy lady had delivered.

Inside Smith's quarters were rows upon rows of boxes, all marked with distinct military signage. The security chief bunked in the munitions room, complete with shells, ammo clips, rifles—and two neatly marked boxes of C-4. Plastique explosive.

As if sensing the open door was an invitation for Bryce to challenge him, Smith pushed it shut and locked it with a key. Then he walked right up to the screen and dangled the key like a golden apple in front of Bryce. "Don't get any ideas, hick. About anything. Or anybody."

Then he stuffed the key into his pocket and turned to follow Tasiya. Bryce's need to stomp Smith's sorry hide poured adrenaline into his muscles and deepened his breathing. He strained against the rope at his wrists. But he had to bide his time. He didn't have the upper hand. Yet. He'd only make things worse for Tasiya if he tried to help her now and got incapacitated or killed. If he was gone, she'd have no one. No hope of escape. No future.

In the end, he could do nothing but pray that Tasiya knew how to use that meat cleaver.

"Your turn, big man." Hodges motioned him down the stairs and Bryce fell into step in front of Bristoe's gun.

This had better work. For Tasiya's sake as much as anyone else's on the team.

After a few preliminary instructions from Fowler,

Bryce faced the camera. He ignored the two guns pointed at him, positioned his hands on the paper and started to read. "The Montana Militia for a Free America has never forgotten the beliefs set down in the Declaration of Independence. But our government has…"

Ponderosa, Montana

"What do the three fingers mean? Is he pointing to something?"

"The other hostages all wore chains. Why is Sarge different?"

"Has he ever said that many words all at once?"

"He's telling us something." Trevor Blackhaw hit the pause button and stared at the image recorded from that afternoon's special news report.

Bryce Martin, an immovable rock of a man, with a deceptive package of brains inside all that brawn, stared back from the TV suspended from the ceiling. He looked a little more battered than usual—from the swollen cut on his cheek to the distinct ligature marks beneath the crude rope that bound his wrists.

Every available member of Big Sky Bounty Hunters had gathered in the command center secretly located beneath the ranch lodge that served as their headquarters building. Their boss, Cameron Murphy, sat at the head of the conference table, with the portable oxygen tank that he still carried to appease his wife's concerns but rarely used anymore, on the floor beside him. "What do we know, people?" he demanded, expecting some answers.

Anthony Lombardi leaned back in his chair, drumming his fingers against the table. "I can't get a fix on any landmarks besides the stone wall behind him. There's no topography to look at. With the sun covered up like that, it's hard to get a fix on the time of day. Pretty windy there, though."

Owen Cook had his laptop open, clicking through information the average computer hacker could never gain access to. "I plotted the cloud movement over the six minutes he's on camera. They're moving at storm speed. According to U.S. Navy weather reports, the only storms of that size in the past week have been over the eastern seaboard. That fits in with the general area of their capture."

"Assuming this video was made in the last week," Murphy noted.

"It's recent." Interrogation was Trevor's area of expertise. "They've been missing three weeks. It takes a while to coerce a hostage, especially a hardhead like Sarge, into saying what you want him to. Fowler needed time to either force him to submit or find the bargaining chip that would make the hostage turn."

Michael Clark looked up from the observations he'd jotted on his notepad. "Sergeant Martin doesn't believe a word he's saying. You can see it in his eyes, and that succinct articulation doesn't come naturally to him. The three fingers are definitely a clue. Looks like a trident to me. Could be the number three. Third? Triple?"

"So we can place him somewhere on the eastern seaboard," Murphy summarized. Timing was critical. According to the first few minutes of the hostage video, a prisoner would be killed every day that the United Nations didn't withdraw its plans to invade Lukinburg and overthrow King Aleksandr's corrupt rule. They had fewer than twelve hours until day two and the next murder. "That narrows it down to a couple thousand square miles. Please tell me we can do better than that."

Trevor nodded. "You'd think of any of the prisoners,

they'd have Sarge locked down tight. That rope has to mean something. Can you blow up that part of the picture?"

Cook typed and clicked on his computer, magnifying the braided rope around Bryce's wrists. "Coming up... now."

To a man they groaned and cursed and shook their heads.

"I recognize that from basic training."

"Cord grass."

"Devil's Fork Island."

Bingo.

Murphy braced his hands at the edge of the table and stood. "Get that FBI botanist on the horn and verify the species of grass and its exact location. There are several islands in that area. Call Major Hayes with Special Forces at Ft. Bragg and get us some backup. He owes me one. Take whatever you need and get yourselves booked on a flight out of here tonight. I want Boone Fowler back in a Montana prison."

As he snapped orders, his men went to work.

He stopped Trevor with a hand on his arm. "I'm not in any condition to travel yet." It was evident how much he hated to say it, but, "I'd only slow us down. I want you to take lead on this."

"Yes, sir."

"And Trev?"

"Yes?"

"Bring my men home."

Chapter 11

Trevor Blackhaw's voice crackled over the homemade radio in Bryce's cell. "I knew you'd have something rigged up, Sarge. Sorry it took us so long to find you."

Blackhaw and the rest of Big Sky, except for the colonel, were fewer than twenty miles away, camped out on the mainland and waiting to make their move. "I'm just glad this is finally gonna happen."

"We'll have the chemical agent on hand in twenty-four hours. You take out the perimeter alarm and we'll be there tomorrow night with the gas masks. The storms should subside by then, so we'll be able to get on the island undetected. If we can pull this off, we'll keep casualties to a minimum. We are not going to lose another man."

"Amen to that."

The rescue plan was far from simple, but Bryce had faith that his friends could pull it off. As long as he could get his part accomplished as their point man on the inside. At midnight tomorrow, Trevor Blackhaw and a group of bounty hunters would sneak onto the island and deliver gas masks for all the hostages. After a signal flare warned the prisoners to suit up, a Special Forces unit would drop a chemical agent that would knock out every living thing that breathed the nontoxic gas. With Fowler and his men sleepin' like babies, Big Sky and company could come in and round up the militia with far less danger of confrontation and a far better chance of getting everyone out alive.

"You'll get word to the others?"

"Will do." Bryce reached across the cot to take Tasiya's hand. She'd been listening to the hushed conversation as carefully as he had. And though he suspected she hadn't understood all the military jargon, he had no doubt she was ready to do her part. "I've found a pretty good friend here who can help us."

"Someone you trust?"

Tasiya's eyes widened in expectation of Bryce's answer.

"Yes." With that one all-encompassing word, she smiled, lighting up the gloomy cell and Bryce's lonely world. "Blackhaw, I've got another request."

"Name it."

"That friend—we need to take her with us when we go."

"Her?" He'd expected that kind of curiosity from Powell, Blackhaw and the gang. The teasing inflection, the hint-hint, tell-me-more tone.

But Bryce couldn't brag about what wasn't his, and he didn't want anything to come between him and Tasiya during this precious time they did have together. So he overlooked the I've-met-someone-amazing speech, and stuck to business. "She works as a servant here. But she's basically a hostage herself. I want her to be safe."

It wasn't every day that Bryce Martin talked about a

woman, but Blackhaw took the hint. "No problem. We'll get her a mask, too."

Tasiya tugged on Bryce's hand and whispered. "Remember, the militia cannot know I helped you, or that I have left with you. Even in prison, they will have contacts. If word gets back to Dimitri that I have betrayed him, then Papa..."

She didn't have to explain how her father's life would be forfeit. Bryce moved the radio to his lap and pulled her to his side, wrapping his arm around her strong, slender shoulders and pressing a kiss to her hair. "You hear that, Blackhaw? We have to make it look like she's been killed so there won't be any repercussions on her family back in Lukinburg."

"We've done some witness-protection-program work. We could pull off something like that." He paused in that unflappable way of his, and considered their options. "There are some herbs I know—a recipe from my Cherokee grandfather—that can slow down the breathing and heart rate enough to fake death, unless you've got some medical equipment there to detect a trace pulse."

"The only thing high-tech around here is the security grid." He hugged Tasiya tighter. "Is it safe to take?"

"My ancestors used it on vision quests. Your friend might have some funky dreams, but she should come out of it okay. I'll have a vial for her when she picks up the masks."

"Understood. And Blackhaw?"

"Yeah, Sarge?"

"Thanks."

"Are you kidding? Of course *you* had to do it the hard way, but you've given us the means to finally bring in Fowler and his men. If I never bring in another bounty, knowing we put that bastard away will be worth it."

"Amen. Martin out."

As Bryce dismantled the radio and hid the parts alongside his chains beneath the mattress again, he noticed that Tasiya seemed unusually quiet. She still put up her hair and cleaned up any trace of her visit the way she had each night before their recon missions. But quiet wasn't Tasiya's way—not with him.

"You all right?"

He barely touched her shoulder and she flinched away. She loaded her basket, unlocked the cell door and carried her things out into the passageway. For a minute he thought she wasn't going to answer him. And when she turned to face him, her eyes were so big, so sad, that he made a promise he wasn't a hundred percent sure he could keep.

"We're gonna get out of here. You're gonna be safe."

"Tonight, we get the C-4. Yes?"

"Yeah. I'll need it to knock out the generators tomorrow night so Blackhaw can get inside the perimeter and deliver the gas masks." Was that what she was worried about? "An explosion will create enough of a diversion that you should be able to slip out and meet him and get back without anybody missin' you. There should be plenty of time before things die down for you to take those herbs and fake your death."

"So the explosives are imperative to your mission."

"*Our* mission." He slipped the stolen knife into his boot and followed her to the door. "You ready to play lookout?"

Without any guards in the locked-down prison wing at night, Bryce had discovered he could pretty much have the run of the place. But getting into the militia's wing through the open breezeway was gonna be damn tricky, with sentries patrolling the grounds and Marcus Smith sleeping in the very room where Bryce needed to be.

"I will get it from Marcus Smith's room," she announced.

That's what she was stewin' about? Absolutely not. No way. "I'll go. It's too risky."

"It is my freedom, too." She was choosin' now to be stubborn?

"What if he puts his hands on you again?"

"Then he will put his hands on me. It must be done."

Hell. That's what she was worried about. *His* reaction. She knew he didn't want her in that kind of danger. Knew he'd fight her on this.

She pressed her palm squarely in the middle of his chest and shut him up when he opened his mouth to argue. "Do not think for one moment that his stinking breath and his foul fingers and bullying strength mean anything to me. Dimitri Mostek smells better, but he is no different beneath his skin." Her fingers curled into the front of his jacket. "Sometimes I think my beauty is a curse, that no man will ever look inside me to see who I am, what I dream about, what I need."

That sort of prejudice sounded achingly familiar. Maybe better than anybody he understood what she was sayin'. "Yeah. Sometimes it's hard to get past what a person looks like on the outside."

She slipped her hand up to cup the scarred side of his jaw. "*You* see inside me, Bryce Martin. For that I will always be grateful."

Yep. Just what he wanted, gratitude from the woman. Sucker. He pulled her hand down and tried to break away from any connection to pity or gratitude. "Yeah, well, we'd better get started if we're gonna do this. And just for the record, I hate it."

But she twisted her hand and latched on to his wrist.

He'd wanted her to talk, right? She wasn't done speakin' her piece. "I see inside you, too."

What the hell did that mean? What sort of dreams and wants and needs did she think she knew about him?

Maybe the most private secret of all. The one he'd never be able to share with her. How pathetic. If she'd sensed everything he felt about her...

Tasiya dropped her basket to the floor and reached for him. She framed his face between her hands and rose up on tiptoe to kiss him. His body lurched in an instantaneous, hungry response, and his hands automatically went to her waist. His pride was a little slower to catch up and deepen the sweet kiss.

But when her arms wound around his neck, her hands skimmed and clutched against his hair, and she moaned that needy whimper in her throat, Bryce snaked his arms around her and lifted her clear off the floor. He palmed her butt and grabbed a fistful of her sweater. He swept his tongue into her hot, honey-sweet mouth and took everything she offered. His blood caught fire and his heart pounded in his chest. If he could have consumed her on the spot he would have.

This was some friggin' goodbye, and he wasn't ready for it. He didn't want to let her go. He didn't want to lose her. Ever. Not to Marcus Smith, not to Dimitri Mostek, not even to the promise of the freedom she so richly deserved.

But when she pulled away, when she brushed her shaky fingertips across his sensitized lips and smiled that serene smile of gratitude, he let her go.

He set her back on her feet and looked away from her eyes only long enough to see the keys she pressed into his hand. "Give me fifteen or twenty minutes. Then come find me. I will be able to get in, but—"

"I'll make sure you get out."

If that was the only promise she wanted from him, he'd keep it. Or die trying.

Bryce watched her walk away. He held on to her hand, her fingertips, her gaze, for as along as he could. And then she was gone.

This plan stunk. Life stunk. Love stunk.

But, damn it all, it was the only way.

Every time the thunder smacked against the sky, Tasiya jumped inside her skin. The storm outside was a blessing of sorts: the clouds blotted out any natural light; the rain and wind and angry waves muffled any suspicious sounds and kept the sentries huddled at their posts with their chins tucked in.

But she couldn't help making a fatalistic analogy about nature's fury and the retribution that would be unleashed if their escape plan failed. If *she* failed Bryce Martin.

Lightning flashed outside, spotlighting for one eerie moment the walls lined with deadly weapons and ammunition that surrounded her. Knives, guns, bullets, explosives. But the most dangerous thing in the room stood at the table beside his cot, pouring her a shot of whiskey she didn't want.

Tasiya gripped the edge of the shelf behind her as the answering thunder echoed down around her ears. She wished she could think of a convincing reason for Marcus to open the door again, so she'd feel a little less like a helpless mouse caught in a trap, waiting for the slavering cat to spring upon her. But the wind off the breezeway had blown it shut, and the puddle of water already staining the doorway gave her no argument against Marcus's claim that it would continue to rain in through the screen door until the storm subsided.

"Here you go, sugar." He crossed the room through a path between stacked crates and handed her a dingy glass half-full of a potent amber liquid. She had to hold it in both hands to keep herself from shoving him out of her personal space. He clinked their glasses together, showing his yellow teeth in a suggestive grin. "Bottoms up."

Unlike her conversations with Bryce, where he patiently answered every question she had about the peculiarities of the English language, Tasiya didn't care that she didn't understand the significance of Marcus's words. He tipped his head back and emptied his glass in a single gulp. Then he wiped his lips and licked the residue off his fingers.

"Good stuff. Now, when you talk about *repaying* me for helping out your ugly friend, what exactly am I lookin' forward to?" He frowned, nodding toward her untouched glass. "Drink up."

She'd hoped to spot a potted plant she could pour hers into, but the militiamen had no such amenities. With Marcus standing close enough to smell the liquor on his breath and showing no signs of moving until she did as he asked, Tasiya had no choice but to raise the glass to her lips. Her eyes watered as the bitter liquid burned all the way down her throat.

"Oh, my." She hoped that light-headed feeling was due to the huge gasp of air she'd taken and not the immediate effects of the alcohol.

"Smooth stuff, huh?"

Not exactly the description she would have used. But the horrid taste gave her an idea. She held up her glass. "Perhaps it gets better the more I drink. May I have another?"

"Happy to oblige." He took her glass and returned to the table. With his back turned, Tasiya quickly went to work. "My old man used to work at a distillery down in Tennessee. Best thing he ever did for me was introduce me to the fine taste of whiskey. I went into the family business, too. But then I discovered I had a higher calling—one that paid better, too."

Tasiya had positioned herself next to the boxes of C-4. She'd already managed to unhook the latch on the top box while Marcus had dug through his duffel bag for the whiskey and glasses. Now that he was consumed with his favorite topic and pouring her another drink, she could reach inside and move the paper-wrapped explosives into her basket. One brick would suffice, Bryce had said. Done. Two would be even better.

But Marcus was turning around. The second brick would have to wait. Tasiya covered the C-4 in her basket with a dish towel and pretended an interest in the guns on the shelf above her. "Do you know how to use all of these weapons?"

"Of course I do." He walked up right behind her, making no effort to hide his arousal as he pressed against her bottom, trapping her between the shelf and his body. Tasiya closed her eyes and cringed, wishing she could walk through walls. "I'm an expert on firing things. That's why Fowler recruited me."

Tasiya didn't have to grasp the language to understand the lecherous undertones in Marcus's words. She should have told Bryce five minutes. She might not last fifteen minutes with this man.

She shuddered with the next clap of thunder and pushed away from the shelves, hating Marcus's groan of satisfaction as she couldn't avoid rubbing against him. "But there are so many different kinds." She circled to the opposite side of the room, hoping to turn his attention away from the explosives and the basket. He set down their drinks and followed her. "What about this one?" She picked up a black steel rifle that was surprisingly heavy. The metal felt unnaturally cold, the weight of it, lethal. "What do you use one like this for?"

"Sometimes a man needs a big gun to make him stronger than his opponent." He reached over her shoulder and plucked the rifle from her grasp. This time, she wisely scooted aside as he replaced it on the shelf. But she didn't get far enough, fast enough. He snatched her wrist and pulled her back beside him. His overgrown beard tangled with her hair. "Sugar, are you here to talk or to give me some action? 'Cause I guarantee you, talking isn't the payoff I had in mind."

He nuzzled her ear. Tasiya's breath lodged in her throat. "I thought I would bake you something special. Do you like cake? Pie? Cookies?"

He laughed and licked his way down her neck. "You're the sugar I want."

Tasiya tried to slide away but his hands locked around her hips. She wedged her arms between them and pushed. "What about Mr. Fowler?"

His mouth hovered over hers as he unhooked the snap of her jeans. "He's asleep. I won't tell if you won't."

Lightning flashed, giving her a frightening glimpse of his stained teeth and lustful intent.

"No." She couldn't take his groping hands and foul scent any longer. "No!"

Tasiya stomped down on the instep of his foot and shoved with every bit of strength in her. Marcus stumbled back a step and knocked over a crate. Tasiya didn't waste any time dashing across the room to grab her basket and run for the door. "I am your cook! Not your prostitute!"

Marcus knocked over another crate as he pushed himself upright and propelled himself after her.

"Uh-uh, sugar. *No* is not an option once you get me goin' like this. *You* came to me. You will be whatever the hell I tell you to be."

He grabbed her arm, jerked it in its socket as he swung her around. Thunder shook through the walls as Tasiya screamed. She slammed into a stack of crates and sent them flying before toppling into the midst of them. Ignoring the bruising jolt to her bones, she scrambled to her feet. She'd lost the basket! But as she knocked her shin on a crate, stumbling to retrieve it, she knew it was already too late.

She froze. The basket and its scattered contents were strewn on the floor between them, with the brick of C-4 sitting like a traitorous alarm beacon right on top.

"You thieving bitch."

Marcus's fist hit her square in the cheek, knocking her to the floor and swirling the room around inside her head. Waves of agony radiated through her jaw and skull. She was too dizzy to even steady herself on her hands and knees.

Marcus grabbed a handful of hair and yanked her upright. The zillion pinpricks of pain erupting across her scalp cleared her vision long enough to see the pistol he pulled from his belt and jammed to the center of her forehead.

"Don't touch you, huh? I will touch you any damn way I want!"

Thunder crashed through the room. The door sailed open. The rain poured in.

But it wasn't the storm.

"Tasiya!" A monster charged in from the darkness and plowed into Marcus.

Tasiya collapsed and crawled out of the way as Bryce knocked Marcus Smith clear across the room. They smashed into the shelves and hit the floor as an avalanche of heavy crates and weapons cascaded over their heads.

"Bryce!" Her screams were drowned out by the beating of the wind and the rain.

She learned that a fist hitting muscle made a terrible sound. A fist hitting bone sounded even worse. Boxes broke. Marcus cursed.

The rain through the screen door soaked her sweater and weighted her hair. But the hug of cold water clinging to her skin reminded her of the world outside this room. Though she wavered on her feet, Tasiya mustered the sense to close the door. With the cacophony of the storm, the fight might not be heard, but a man walking by might see.

"Bryce," she whispered, desperate to help but not knowing how. "Please. Please."

Like two leviathans, the men rose through the flood of knives and guns and splintered wood. Marcus had his hands on Bryce's throat now. His pistol had disappeared. Tasiya wanted to retrieve it, but in a sea of weapons, which was his? Which was loaded?

Marcus found his footing first and rammed Bryce against the broken wall. Tasiya flinched at the momentary grimace that contorted Bryce's face. His back! The wounds on his back!

But Bryce pounded on Marcus's arms, loosening his stranglehold. He pounded again, driving Marcus to his knees.

"Run, Tasiya!" Bryce growled.

Marcus clipped him around the ankles and dragged him to the floor. With a sickening sense of déjà vu, Tasiya was suddenly back in that interrogation room. Bryce was putting his life on the line. Again. For her.

This time she would listen.

She grabbed the basket, along with the C-4, and stumbled toward the door. But one last look at her hero stopped her cold.

"Bryce!"

Marcus had found his gun. He was on his knees over the man she loved. Blood spewed from his ugly mouth as he squeezed the trigger. "Die, you big bastard."

"You first."

Marcus jerked. His eyes wide like saucers. Bryce shoved his hand into Marcus's gut, and Tasiya realized he'd stabbed him. With a twist of Marcus's own hunting knife, Bryce finished the job.

The gun fell from Marcus's grip. His oversize body went limp. Bryce pushed him aside as the big ox fell dead.

"Bryce?"

He was shaking as he climbed to his feet and Tasiya ran to him. She wrapped her arms around his waist and braced him with her strength as he pressed his lips into her hair and hugged her close. "I had to bust the damn lock open. You didn't have a key that fit. I heard you scream."

She could feel the sticky warmth of blood soaking through the back of his cold, wet jacket and knew that his wounds had been reopened in the fight. She'd been just as frightened for him as he'd been for her. "It is all right now. I am safe."

With a steadfast determination, he pushed her away. His ragged breathing warned her that the fight had sapped most of his strength. "We're not safe. Somebody might have heard."

"But the storm—"

"I won't risk it. Back-up's not comin' till midnight tomorrow. We're still on our own." He turned her toward the door. "Go back to my cell. I need to clean up this mess and hide the body. Go. Now."

She planted her feet. "I will help. It will go faster if we work together. Then we can both leave."

For once his overblown sense of chivalry took a backseat to practicality. He reached out and brushed his gentle fingers across her cheek. Tasiya winced at the swelling there. Regret colored his voice. "I was too late, wasn't I?"

"I am alive, Bryce Martin," she whispered. "I believe you were right on time."

Chapter 12

For the second time in his life, Bryce awoke to find a beautiful woman gently tending his wounds.

This time he wasn't whacked out of his head with pain and anguish. He knew where he was and, thanks to the spicy, wholesome smell that wafted beside him on the cot, he knew who was with him.

He rolled onto his side and looked up into Tasiya's dark, exotic eyes. "Evenin.'"

It was about ten o'clock, he guessed, judging by the first stars dotting the sky outside his window. Melancholy and anticipation battled to dictate his mood. In just a few hours he'd be on his way to freedom—but his time with Tasiya would be over.

With her typical devotion to practicality, Tasiya urged him back onto his stomach to finish doctoring his shoulder. "Some of your cuts look infected. I wish I had an antibiotic to give you."

What, no 'Good evening, Bryce Martin'? He was growing used to the trills and musical articulation of his first and last name together. Her soft accent made it sound as meaningful a declaration of trust and caring as any words he'd heard from a woman.

She was probably nervous or preoccupied about her tasks tonight. Or still fearful that someone would discover Marcus Smith's body in the unused prison cell where he'd stashed him.

Deciding she was done taking care of him, Bryce pushed aside her protests and sat up next to her on the edge of the cot. He took the cloth and ointment from her hands and set them on the floor beside the food she'd brought.

"The medics can pump me full of antibiotics once we get off this island tonight," he reassured her. He hiked up his jeans and turned to prop one knee on the cot so he could face her and take her hands in his. "From the sound of things, I'm more worried about Craig O'Riley's injuries."

"When I gave him your message to be ready at midnight, he said he would be strong. He will be greatly motivated to 'kick butt,' he says." Bryce grinned at her endearing recitation of words that didn't fit a literal translation. "Your friend, Jacob Powell and Mr. Campbell, said they would be there to help him."

Tasiya looked down to where her smaller hands joined his in his lap. Her fair skin glistened in the dim shadows against his darker fingers. The differences in color and size created an evocative contrast of male and female, yesterday and tomorrow, despair and hope—and just how intrinsically linked and delicately balanced they each could be.

Bryce turned her hands so he could stroke the racing beat of her pulse at her wrists. Somethin' was eatin' her up from the inside out. "You worried about your daddy?"

She shook her head, stirring the long fall of hair that only partially hid the swollen purple bruise on her cheek. "No more than usual," she admitted.

"You afraid of what's gonna happen tonight? I promise you, Blackhaw's a stickler for details. Nobody's gonna get hurt. I'll whisk you outta here before Boone Fowler knows what hit him. I'll see you all the way back to Montana or New York City or Lukinburg, if that's where you wanna go."

Tasiya stiffened. Her eyes darted up to his. "You think I want to go back to Dimitri?"

"When you're free, you have the right to choose wherever you want to be." Bryce swallowed hard. Maybe this was the part she was dreading. He knew he'd been avoiding the inevitable. "I know you're probably feelin' grateful for me helpin' you out, or listenin' to ya talk, or thinkin' we're a team or whatever. But don't feel like you have to choose me or Montana when we get out. You don't owe me a thing. I don't want you to think you're tradin' one kind of blackmail for another. I wouldn't be any better than Fowler or Smith, then. I promised you freedom. And I'm a man of my word."

Even in the semidarkness, he could see the color flooding her cheeks. She pulled her hands away and stood, pacing clear to the steel bars before she turned and fired away. "I swear to God, Bryce Martin, if you were not injured, I would slap your face."

Huh! Maybe his looks weren't the only reason he'd never had a decent relationship with a woman. He threw up his hands. "Then what the hell's buggin' ya, honey?"

She twisted her lips together, struggling to contain somethin' that was too much for her to bear. "I have learned more about freedom inside this prison cell than

I ever knew existed in my own country. You've taught me that I have value in this world. That I can make choices."

"Yep."

Her breath emptied out in a hushed sigh. "I choose you, Bryce Martin."

He squashed down the surge of boyish joy and lifelong hope that licked its way through his veins. "Honey, I'm just one man. You'll meet others on the outside. Better-lookin' ones. Ones who know what to say to a lady." He rose and paced to the window, scrubbing his hand over his bristly jaw and starin' up into the sky. He couldn't look her in the eye and say this, couldn't see her sweet face and send her to another man. "You're a beautiful woman, with a kind heart and a stubborn streak a mile wide. You're smart. Gutsy. There'll be plenty of other men for you to choose from."

"Like Marcus Smith?"

"No." Bryce fisted his hands around the bars at the window. "I'm talkin' about good men. Ones who'll treat ya with respect. You can choose any one of 'em. Or no one, if that's what you want."

He flinched when he felt her cool hands on his shoulders. "I choose you."

Bryce turned around. He lost his resolve to keep his distance in the sirenlike call of her innocent smile. He brushed aside the hair at her temple and gently cupped her jaw, smoothing his thumb across her velvety cheek. "I might look pretty good to you right now, honey, but that's just 'cause I'm the only man here."

She leaned her cheek into his fingers and kissed the palm of his hand. "The first night I met you, you frightened me. I thought you were a monster."

Yep, he got a lot of that.

But she took away the sting of reality with her next

words. "Since that night I have seen into your beautiful eyes. I have seen into your heart." She spread her fingers across the left side of his chest. "There is no monster in you. I do not believe there are better men than you out there."

Bryce covered her hand with his own, holding her gentle acceptance against his beating heart. "That's sweet of you to say, honey, but—"

"Make love to me, Bryce Martin. I may not live through this night. I may be forced to return to Lukinburg and give myself to Dimitri Mostek in order to save my father."

Make love? His body lurched in shameless response at the mere suggestion. The blood seemed to rush from his extremities and pool behind his groin.

But he listened to everything she said and shook his head. "I won't let anything happen to you."

"You cannot promise that. As well as you mean, you cannot know that something will not go wrong." She dug her fingertips into his skin, pleading by her touch as well as her voice. "I want one night with a man whose hands do not make me feel dirty. Whose words inspire me with hope instead of fear. I want to know what it is like to be loved by a man who cares about the woman I am inside. If this is to be my last night in America, or on this earth, I want my memories to be of you."

He was already on fire for her. But to ask this, to give him this... "You don't know what you're sayin' to me, honey."

"You told me that, in America, a woman may ask for what she wants. I want you to make love to me. I want... you."

"I want you, too, honey. More than my next breath. It hurts sometimes to think how much you mean to me."

"Then it is settled." Ever practical and efficient, Tasiya's hands went to the hem of her sweater and she pulled it up. "I will try not to hurt you."

Damn. All that creamy skin and a plain lace bra that clung to pert, ripe breasts. He wanted to laugh at the irony of her promise, but his breath seemed to catch in his throat. "I should be sayin' that to you."

He tried to be a gentleman. He tried to look away. But he was a man. And he loved her. And his hands were drawn to that skin like a magnet. He skimmed her flanks, caught the weight of her breasts in his palms, moaned along with her, then joined her hands on the sweater, pulling it off over her head and tossing it aside.

Her hair cascaded down and she shook it loose, filling the air with her scents and covering her shoulders and breasts in a cloud of ebony silk. "If I do something wrong, you will tell me?"

Screw being a gentleman. This might be *his* last night on the planet. His last night with Tasiya. He wasn't a strong enough man to walk away from somethin' they both wanted.

"You're beautiful." His voice came out as a husky growl and she blushed. Bryce gathered her into his arms, binding them together skin to skin. Her curves fit snugly against his harder planes, and the twin buds that pearled at the tips of her breasts branded him with a searing heat.

She was supple and cool to the touch, yet he thought he might burn up with need for her. This was no slow fuse, no time-released detonation. He'd been primed to make love to this woman from the first moment she'd shown him tenderness, that first night they'd touched through the bars of his cage and an electric current had sparked between them.

Her hands rested on his biceps while her gaze darted

back and forth across his chest. Seein' his scars? Havin' second thoughts?

"I do not know where to begin."

"You put your hands on me wherever you want. Ask for whatever you want. Tell me no if you've had enough or I scare you in any way." He nudged her beneath the chin. "And you look me in the eye."

She skidded her hands across his shoulders and clasped them together behind his neck. "I am not afraid of you, Bryce Martin. I was only admiring how strong you are. How very—" the frown appeared between her brows "—not like a woman you are."

Bryce laughed and kissed her frown away. "Honey, you're gonna discover there's not much like a woman about me anywhere."

And then he was kissing her, drinking in the generous gift she offered, giving her everything there was in him. He skimmed his hands along her spine down to her bottom and lifted her up into his rising heat. He swept his hands into her hair, scooted the straps off her shoulders as he came back down. He pressed his lips to the delicate point of her collarbone, supped at the straining swell of her breast. He swirled his tongue around one distended nipple, wetting it through the lace.

Tasiya gasped. "I… You…"

Speechless. Bryce grinned.

Her fingers latched on to his head and took his mouth to the other breast. He toyed with it, teasing it through the lace, making her hips squirm against his. And when he didn't think *he* could take any more of those whimpers of pleasure that hummed in her throat, he unhooked her bra and let it join the sweater. A shiver of goose bumps pricked across her wet skin and Bryce eased the shock by taking her into his mouth. She was delicate and sweet and more responsive than he could have imagined.

This was a crappy place to make love to a beautiful woman, but when she threw her head back and arched into his mouth, Bryce thought he was in paradise.

"I want you, Tasiya," he whispered against her breast. "Any way you want." He kissed the thrumming pulse at her throat. "Now." He suckled her bottom lip, caught her stuttered breath in a kiss. "Tell me now if you want me to stop."

"No." She planed her hands across his chest, flicked across a flat male nipple, and he groaned. "You like that, too?"

"Yes. Oh, yes."

A quick study, she kissed the spot, then ran her tongue around it. Bryce's arms convulsed around her at the sweet agony of her innocent touches. "Honey, I won't last much longer if you keep doin' that."

She raised her mouth for a kiss and her fingers dropped to the snap of his jeans. "I do not want to wait. Now, Bryce Martin. Please."

Bryce needed no further encouragement. With the frenzy of last chances and moments stolen out of time, they stripped off their remaining clothes. Bryce laid them over the cot to make a relatively clean bed for them. Then he reached for Tasiya's bottom and picked her up, stretching her warm, moist heat against him. He sat down with her straddling his lap and the evidence of his desire butting against her thigh.

For one precious moment, she tore her mouth from his and looked down with a little bit of awe and worry in her eyes. "You are so…big."

Bryce caught her face between his hands and laughed. It was a tender, intimate sound shared in the darkness.

"You know, ninety-nine men out of a hundred would take that as a compliment. But I don't want you to worry. Nature has a way of making things…fit…the way they should." He kissed her then, deeply, reverently, stirring things inside him that had nothing to do with sex. "But if I hurt you or scare you in any way, I will never forgive myself. I can still stop."

"I said I was not afraid of you, Bryce Martin. Not of your scars, not of this."

Bryce forgot to breathe when Tasiya wrapped her hand around him.

Unable to help himself, he thrust into her curious grip. He leaned his forehead against hers and willed enough patience into his system to wait until he knew she was ready.

But Tasiya Belov had had a taste of freedom. She knew how to ask for what she wanted "Oh, Bryce. Please be inside me…now…"

With no answer but a kiss, Bryce lifted her. She held her breath as he sheathed himself inside her. She gasped against his neck and dug her fingers into his shoulders when he pushed through her barrier, and then he felt her relax. She sank down around him, took him deeper and deeper. She hugged him tight and he hugged her tighter. Mouth to mouth, chest to chest, sex to sex.

Her glorious hair was their only cloak as they rocked together and fell into a rhythm that transcended any differences in language or culture. Tasiya gave him her body and trust. Bryce gave her his heart.

Their joined mouths muffled their cries of passion and pleasure, and in the deepest corner of a solitary prison cell on a forgotten island, their lonely spirits finally soared free. Tasiya whispered his name as the tremors of her release broke through her and around him. "Bryce Martin. Bryce Martin. Thank you. Thank you."

He poured himself into her, stunned by the humbling power of his release. Then he gathered her into his arms and lay down beside her on the cot, keeping her warm with the blanket of his body until she drifted off to sleep.

Bryce Martin had been to hell and back more than once in his life. But tonight was the first time he'd been to heaven.

Even with her ears covered, the explosion was deafening.

But Tasiya didn't wait for her nerves to settle or her courage to falter. Bryce and his friends were counting on her. And she had no intention of letting them down.

She darted through the shadows, unseen in the sudden darkness illuminated only by hastily drawn flashlights and the flames from the generator room where Bryce had set the charges. Her footsteps were silent beneath the shouts of men and the slap of the ocean against the shore. She clambered over the stone wall at the edge of the courtyard, then took off at a dead run through the sea of cord grass and sand.

Her body was still tingly and replete from making love with Bryce, her mind on a euphoric high. The parts of her that were slightly tender from the newly discovered intimacy had nothing to complain about. He'd given her everything she wanted and more.

And it hadn't been a fluke, a one-time gift that would nurture and sustain her if her life turned dark again. Bryce's frenzied need and gentle touch had set a bar by which all men would be forever judged in her life. He'd awakened her later in the night and, without a word, he'd rolled her onto her back and made love to her all over again, communicating all she needed to know with every loving touch of his hands, mouth and body.

Bryce had been patient when she'd needed him to be; he'd been eager when she'd needed that, too. He'd been tender and thorough and demanding enough to make her heart sing with the worth and power of the woman she'd become in Bryce's arms.

That confidence gave her strength now as she slowed her pace and picked her way closer to the rocky drop-off where she'd discovered the dead soldier's body. Gruesome as it was, it was the only landmark she was sure she could find in the middle of the night that would be far enough away from the docks to avoid detection.

Trevor Blackhaw found her first, shushing her startled gasp with a finger to his lips before pulling her down to a crouch beside him in the sand. "Tasiya Belov?"

She nodded. Bryce's description of his bounty hunter friend had left out the intense blue color of his eyes. But she recognized the straight black hair and angular features that clearly reflected his Cherokee heritage.

"You are Bryce Martin's friend?"

"Trevor Blackhaw."

She should have breathed easier at the two rafts and twenty or so soldiers and bounty hunters hiding on the beach. But the weapons they carried and the funny, green-lensed telescopes they wore on their heads—night-vision goggles, Trevor explained—made Tasiya feel as if she was caught up in the middle of an invasion.

An army of prisoners inside, an army of rescuers outside. A frantic militia caught in the middle, dashing about the compound like ants scattering from a crushed ant hill. One lone woman, caught in the middle of it all didn't seem to stand a chance of surviving.

Oh, how she longed to be back at Bryce's side, in Bryce's arms. A single word in his gruff, loving voice would have bolstered her flagging courage.

But the clock was ticking. Once Bryce took out the generators that powered the perimeter alarm and security lights, he'd told her she'd have about twenty minutes, tops, to retrieve the gas masks and get them to the prisoners before returning to her room and drinking the herb mixture that would fake her death.

Trevor Blackhaw's instructions were as clear and concise as Bryce's had been. He looped the duffel bag with the masks over her shoulder and pushed a small vial into her hands. "We shoot the flare in fifteen. You'll have about a minute more after that before the gas hits. Give it another ten minutes for the wind to disperse it before you drink that."

"Fifteen. One. Ten," she repeated.

"You'll be out for several hours. But from what I hear, the sarge plans to take good care of you." Trevor smiled. "Is Sergeant Martin hangin' tough?"

Tasiya frowned at the question. Didn't he know? "Bryce Martin is very tough, though he is very gentle with me. He will get us all safely home."

Trevor's grin widened as he sensed something amusing that she didn't get. "Yes, ma'am. That sounds like the sarge to me."

Several minutes later Tasiya was panting for breath as she handed Bryce his gas mask through the bars of his cell. It was impossible to keep her gaze from drifting over to the cot where they'd made love, or to keep the blush of heat from staining her cheeks.

Bryce reached through the bars and touched her cheek. Those wintry gray eyes looked deeply into hers. "I know. Tonight will always be special to me, too."

On impulse, Tasiya pulled herself up on tiptoe and kissed him, square on the mouth, telling him in a few short heartbeats how much he meant to her. "Thank you for everything, Bryce Martin. Be safe."

And then she had to go.

"I'll be there when you wake up, Tasiya," he promised. "I will always be there for you."

"We are under attack," Tasiya shouted into the phone, playing her part just the way Bryce had told her. She'd already said goodbye to her father, promised him that she would be all right. No matter what he heard, she asked him to have faith in her American friend. She paced back and forth in her tiny room off the kitchen. She only had a minute or so until midnight, a minute or so to convince Dimitri Mostek that she was about to be killed. "There are many soldiers on the island. Americans. There was an explosion. Everyone is running. There are guns."

"The Americans have attacked the island? That is not supposed to happen. Where is Boone Fowler? When did it begin?"

"I do not know. I only know I am afraid." She picked up her gas mask off her bed and glanced at the clock—11:59 p.m. A minute away from starting a whole new life. "Tell Papa that my friend sends him a hug and his highest regards, as well." She paused for a bit of dramatic emphasis. "If I do not see you again, give Papa my love."

"What friend are you talking about? I said you were not to be touched! You must come home. You belong to me. To me!"

Stick it to yourself, Dimitri, she wanted to say.

"Tell Papa I love him. Give him my message." Hopefully, Anton would remember their secret code. He might not understand the details, but it should clue him in enough to know she was up to something, and not to believe everything he heard—like the news that his daughter had been killed in a raid against the militia compound on Devil's Fork Island. "I must go."

"Anastasiya!" Dimitri shouted. "Anastasiya!"

The sky turned red outside her window and Tasiya hung up the phone.

Tasiya's lungs filled with a breath of air that felt free and unfettered. The chaos outside her window was merely background noise to the song of hope dancing in her heart. Soon it would all be over and she would be free. Then she could find out if Bryce Martin had been telling her the truth—that he could rescue her father from Lukinburg—and that she could choose any man she wanted in America.

She hoped she could find the right way to tell him that she'd chosen him.

As the clock flipped over to midnight, Tasiya pulled the gas mask on over her face. She patted the jeans pocket where she'd slipped the vial of the knock-out draught Trevor Blackhaw had given her and sat on the edge of her bed to wait.

But her satisfaction over finally beating Dimitri at the intimidation game and her enervating hopes for the future had distracted her a moment too long to warn her of the voice in the kitchen.

"Smith! Smith! Where the hell are you?" She shot to her feet at the bellow of Boone Fowler's voice. She ran to the window, but the bars blocked any escape. She spun around, but her sparse room offered her no place to hide. It was hot inside the mask, hard to see and hear, but there was no mistaking the approach of footsteps or the angry, hateful, damning voice of retribution. "I swear to God, Smith, if you are with that foreigner..."

A fisted hand ripped the blanket off her door frame.

Tasiya backed into a corner. Found. Trapped. Denied her chance at freedom.

Boone Fowler's calculating black eyes drilled her across the tiny room. He held a gun in his hand, but it was the fanatical gleam in those eyes that scared her more. His absolute hatred for all things foreign seeped into her skin and turned her blood to ice. He made her want to shrivel up. Automatically she bowed her head.

"What the hell is going on here?"

She made a futile lunge for the door, but Fowler ignored the no-touch rule. With a surprisingly agile move for a man his size, he shoved her onto the bed and ripped the mask off her head, plucking several strands of hair with it.

He shook the mask in her face. "What have you done to me? You turned Marcus against me, and now this?"

A vinegary scent stung Tasiya's nose. She felt light-headed. "Marcus Smith is dead." She tried to protest, tried to hurt Fowler in any way she could. But she was powerless. Just like she'd always been. Before Devil's Fork Island. Before Bryce Martin. "Smith attacked me. We killed him."

"We? Who's in this with you? Who's helping you?" Her lungs felt heavy; she couldn't catch her breath. Boone Fowler's pock-marked face swirled in front of her. "What's this?" He picked up something on the bed beside her. The phone. The chain that bound her to Dimitri. He grabbed her by the collar of her sweater and shook her, but it only spun her vision out of focus. "Who have you been calling? What have you done to me, you damn foreigner?"

Tasiya sagged. Fowler's grip was the only thing holding her upright.

"What's wrong with you?" Fowler coughed.

He tossed her onto the bed and ran to the window to

look outside. "They're all dying. That's what I smelled. Some kind of gas." Fowler pounded on the bars at the window. "No. No!" He slipped her mask on over his head and took a deep breath. "You won't take me out like this, Murphy. Nobody does this to me!"

The last words she heard were Fowler's. "That's right, foreigner. You die. It'll be the most useful thing you've ever done for me."

The last thoughts she had were of Bryce. He would come for her. He'd promised. She would be safe.

Chapter 13

"Tasiya!"

Where the hell was she?

Bryce flipped over the mattress in her room in an impossible attempt to find her underneath. He stormed back into the kitchen and tossed open drawers. He smashed his foot through the locked pantry door and searched for her there. The refrigerator, the mess hall, Fowler's office. He'd covered every inch of this compound from prison cell to latrine. She was gone.

How the hell could Tasiya be gone?

"Damn it!" Bryce rammed his fist through a cabinet door, heedless of the pain.

"We just have to get the bad guys, Sarge. We don't have to kill their furniture." Jacob Powell had stopped by the kitchen door, leading a handcuffed Steve Bristoe toward the courtyard where Big Sky and the Special Forces unit were rounding up the militiamen once they'd regained consciousness. They all had a one-way ticket to prison in Montana.

"Not funny, Powell. She's missing."

"Well, have you looked—"

"I've looked everywhere. She's supposed to be unconscious in her room, waiting for me to pick her up. She's gone."

"Let me get rid of this scumbag and I'll help you look. Have you checked the docks?"

"Just once."

Powell nodded. "I'll check again."

Trevor Blackhaw walked in as Powell and Bristoe left. "We've got another problem, Sarge."

His Native American friend wore the responsibility of leadership well, and Bryce had to admire how Blackhaw and the rest of the Big Sky team had homed in on Bryce's clues. They tracked them down, put together a flawless plan and recaptured the militia.

But as far as Bryce was concerned, there was no other problem besides the fact that the woman he loved and had sworn to protect was missing. "Can't somebody else deal with it?"

"You're our man on the inside, Sarge. You know this place better than anybody." Apparently, not well enough if he could lose track of a willowy brunette hell-bent on obtaining her freedom. Blackhaw thumbed over his shoulder toward the breezeway. "We've rounded up enough supplies and weaponry to man a small invasion. I've accounted for the thirty militia members you reported, including the body of Marcus Smith."

Bryce couldn't concentrate on what he was saying. "So you came for thirty men, you got thirty men."

"Thirty men plus their leader." Every muscle in Bryce's body clenched with dread. "I've got no sign of Boone Fowler anywhere. And one of the speedboats is missing."

No Tasiya. No Fowler.

"That son of a bitch." A desperate sort of helpless anger squeezed his heart. "He took her."

"That's what I figured. Fowler's got the girl and he's using her as a hostage to escape."

Bryce's heart was bleedin' out. "We have to find her. And fast."

Because from everything Tasiya had said, according to Boone Fowler, the only good foreigner was a dead one.

"I can't. I can't do this." Tasiya refused to cry in front of Boone Fowler, but she was sobbing inside.

After recovering from the nontoxic sleeping gas, she'd awakened into a real nightmare. Those weren't Bryce's loving arms that had held her when she came to, but the vicious bond of Boone Fowler's controlling grip.

He'd spirited her away on a boat to a hidden cove in the middle of the night. He'd taken her phone line to Dimitri Mostek and called him, telling him the traitorous Trojan Horse he'd sent to his camp had been discovered. In the crudest of terms, he told Dimitri that his foreign tramp had seduced his chief of security and several prisoners, as well. Enraged, Dimitri had threatened to kill her father—he had no use for a defiled woman. But Tasiya had pleaded with Fowler to take her life instead.

And that's when she'd seen the true depth of Boone Fowler's madness. He'd caressed her bruised cheek with the barrel of his gun and answered, "Done."

But she was denied the quick execution she'd prayed for.

She became a tool again. Dehumanized. Expendable.

He'd driven her all the way to Montana. She'd finally gotten to see the mountains. But there was no beauty for her in their snow-capped granite peaks—only the visual reminder, everywhere, of Bryce Martin's beautiful gray

eyes; his craggy, eloquent, wonderful face; his unflinch-
ing, immeasurate strength.

Boone Fowler had brought her here to destroy all that.

For her father's life, she had to walk into Big Sky headquarters and kill them all.

"Get out of the truck." Fowler pointed the pistol at her
head and Tasiya climbed out into the snow. The bite of
the wind was less sharp here than it had been on Devil's
Fork Island, but the air itself was colder. Tasiya could
barely feel it through the layers of rage and despair and
guilt she wore. "The building's less than a mile over that
rise. I can watch the fireworks from here. Start walking."
He caught the door when she would have closed it. "And
remember, fail me and your father dies."

The fireworks. Right. A sick, deadly version of the
American Independence Day lights and colors and con-
cussive sounds Bryce had once told her about.

The fireworks that would go off the instant she released
her thumb from the arming trigger attached to the bomb
Fowler had strapped around her waist.

A bleary-eyed Bryce opened the door to the most beautiful sight in the entire world. "Tasiya!"

Relief and love and a joy so profound it made him
giddy shook through him as he ran to pick her up and
never let her go again. "I was so worried about you. We've
been lookin' all across the country for you. Anybody
Fowler knows, anywhere he's been. Did he hurt you?
How'd you get away?"

"No."

A blip of static tempered his joy at seeing her after
nearly three days of constant searching and fearing he'd
never see her again. "No, what?"

She braced her hand against his chest and stared at it.

Downcast eyes, tightly compressed lips and skin beyond pale stopped him in his tracks. Ah, hell. "Please do not touch me."

For the briefest of moments, Bryce thought maybe she'd come all this way to tell him they couldn't be together, that, as he'd predicted, she'd found another man. She'd chosen someone better. Or she was goin' home. Goin' back to that place that kept her beautiful spirit under its thumb.

But just as quickly, he nixed those thoughts. Somethin' wasn't right. Despite the quivering protest of her lips, he slipped a finger beneath her chin and nudged her gaze up to his. "You promised you were always gonna look me in the eye."

Crap. The fear was back. And somethin' more. What was she tryin' to say?

"I…it is good to see you Bryce Martin."

Cameron Murphy limped up to the doorway on his cane and introduced himself. "So you're the pretty lady who's got Sarge tied up in knots. Invite her in and get her out of the cold." His voice sounded like an order, but he was smiling. "I appreciate all your help in getting my men home safely. Welcome to Montana."

Then Trevor Blackhaw was behind him. Jacob Powell and the others all gathered round. But every friendly welcome, every thank-you, every invitation to join them only seemed to make that lip quiver more.

Finally the words burst from her lips. "I cannot do this." Tears flooded her eyes and spilled down her pale cheeks. "I love you too much, Bryce Martin. My father and I will die, but I cannot kill you."

I love you too much?

But she gave him no opportunity to question whether he'd understood her right. He would have swept her into his arms and kissed her right there in front of God and the colonel, but Tasiya shook her head, urging him back with a single look.

She unbuttoned the front of her coat and pulled it open.

"That lousy son of a bitch."

Bricks of C-4, wired to detonate, were strapped around Tasiya's middle. She wore enough of them to bring down the entire two-story building and collapse the secret rooms underneath.

"Boone Fowler did this to you."

Tasiya nodded. "He has sent me here to kill you all."

Bryce paced the command center like a caged tiger while Owen Cook read the intelligence report that said UN forces had launched a covert strike into Lukinburg. Political hostages were being freed, corrupt officials were being taken into custody, and an all-points search for King Aleksandr Petrov—the man believed to be behind the kidnapping attempt of his own daughter and the funding of Fowler's militia—was underway.

Murphy's wife, Mia, had taken Tasiya aside to help her freshen up or whatever it was that women did when they went off together for a quiet talk. Mia had been a well-trained bounty hunter long before becoming Cameron Murphy's wife and partner, so she had a working knowledge of explosives and dealing with hostage victims. Tasiya was in good hands, but she wasn't safe.

In the meantime, Colonel Murphy had summoned the bounty hunters together to discuss their options. As far as Bryce was concerned, there were no options. "Just let me take the damn thing off her."

Trevor Blackhaw was a steadier presence at the moment. "You sure you can disarm it without killing her or yourself?"

"Do you see anyone else around here who can?"

"Nobody's questioning your skills, Sarge. But there's a little objectivity missing here."

Screw objectivity. Bryce wanted Tasiya to be safe. He wanted her in his arms. He wanted to tell her how much he loved her and that he would move heaven and earth to make things right for her in this world. They'd find her father. They'd get Boone Fowler. He'd teach her everything he knew about loving her, and then, together, they'd learn some more.

Colonel Murphy tapped his cane against the table to get their attention. "We can use this as an opportunity to put Fowler right where we want him."

"Nobody's using Tasiya," Bryce insisted. "Ever again."

Theoretically, the plan Murphy outlined made sense. Fowler's hot button was Cameron Murphy and Big Sky. They could use that to their advantage to get Fowler to make a mistake. "He wants us dead? Let's oblige him. We all have safe houses across the country. We could evacuate Big Sky, then blow the place to smithereens. If he thinks we're all gone, he'll make a move."

Riley Watson, also known as Craig O'Riley and a dozen other aliases, leaned forward. His body was still recovering from the injuries he'd received while incarcerated, but there wasn't a thing wrong with that crackerjack mind of his. "When Fowler took us prisoner, he told me he had no use for hippies and shaved my head, he's seen me with a lot of hair and none at all. I believe I can alter my appearance enough that I could stay in the area without him recognizing me. As far as Fowler's concerned I'll be presumed dead like the rest of you."

Murphy nodded. "You could infiltrate the militia itself. Since we just put twenty-nine of his men back into prison, he'll be looking for new recruits."

"We'll bring him down from the inside."

Bryce scraped his hand across his jaw. "I want Boone Fowler dead or in prison as much as any man here. But I will not let you use Tasiya to do it."

A hushed sigh turned his attention to the two women who'd just joined them. Tasiya wore the same game smile she'd used when they'd been plotting their escape from Devil's Fork Island.

"What if I volunteer?"

"Talk to me, Bryce Martin."

Tasiya looked down to the top of Bryce's well-shaped head as he knelt in front of her, diligently working to remove the armed vest she wore without setting off the bomb. She sat in a chair in the middle of a secluded room with reinforced walls.

Everyone else she'd met today, the good men of Big Sky, were bustling around, packing things, carrying them into a secret tunnel that led into the mountains. From there they would go their separate ways, undetected, and hide out until Riley Watson contacted them. Once the vest was removed, she hoped she and Bryce would escape through that tunnel together.

She stroked her fingers through Bryce's short, crisp hair, urging him to look at her. She thought she'd be more frightened than this, sitting with her numb thumb taped to the trigger of a bomb. But Bryce was with her. His agile fingers seemed to know exactly what to do. His quiet strength provided an emotional rock to latch on to.

But she needed to hear his voice. Like those quiet nights inside his cell. His voice had given her hope. He'd instilled her with pride. He'd allowed her to dream and he'd made her feel safe. But most of all he'd made her feel special. She mattered to Bryce Martin. Until Bryce, she'd never believed she would matter to any man except her father.

His big shoulders shrugged, apparently healing now since the movement didn't seem to cause him undue pain. "Whaddya wanna talk about?"

"Anything. If it will not distract you from your work."

"Nah, honey." He lifted his wintry eyes to hers. "You're easy to talk to."

Tasiya smiled at the compliment. "Tell me more about your Ozarks."

He resumed his work. "The fishin's great there. The lakes and rivers are full of bass and catfish." He picked up the trigger and pulled the tape off her thumb, his nod telling her it was now safe to release it. He paused a moment to rub the circulation back into her hand. "You know how to cook a catfish? Breaded? Deep-fried? Or smoked on the grill?"

"I can cook fish. Why is it called a cat fish?"

He touched his callused fingertip to either side of her mouth. "'Cause it's got whiskers."

He reached for a pair of surgical-looking scissors and began to cut through the vest's webbed material. "I inherited my grandpa's cabin in the hills near Table Rock Lake. It's built of logs, but it's not really a cabin. It's got three bedrooms and a basement, and a porch that goes clear across the front that has a view of nothin' but trees and water."

"It sounds beautiful."

"You should come see it sometime. You could sleep in a real bed. I'd love to make love to you on a set of clean sheets and see what you could whip up in the kitchen." Tasiya caught her breath. She dug her fingers into his shoulder. Was that an invitation?

"No whipping. Please." She hesitated to hope, in case

she'd misunderstood. "You want me to come to your home in Missouri?"

"I'll teach ya how to fish. Your daddy, too."

"Papa?" What did Bryce know about Anton?

Bryce clipped through the bottom of the vest, then set aside the scissors. He took her hands and pulled her to her feet. "We've gotten word that the troops have taken over the Ministry of Finance Building in St. Feodor. Apparently, your daddy wasn't the only hostage being held there. There are several of Lukinburg citizens in military custody now, en route to a base in Germany. I asked Powell to get us some names."

"Papa is coming to America?" Tasiya jumped onto her tiptoes and reached for Bryce.

"Whoa, whoa." He caught her by the wrists and urged her to remain still until he had the vest removed. But she danced inside her boots, waiting impatiently for him to explain. "If that's what he wants. I've got a spare room in Missouri he could bunk in."

Tasiya curled her fingers into the front of Bryce's shirt and pretended she was strong enough to shake him. "Bryce Martin, you must speak in English. What are you saying to me?"

In answer, he smiled. Then he palmed the back of her head and kissed her. It was a quick, hot, soul-stealing kiss that left her shaking. "You understand that, honey?"

And then he left her. He took the vest and his tools and left her.

Before her knees gave way, Tasiya sank into the chair. Understand what? She needed a dictionary. Fast.

Tasiya flinched against Bryce as he counted down. "Four, three, two, one." The explosion's report jarred the air around them. Even at this distance, hidden more than a mile away in the abandoned miner's shack Bryce had used as a lookout point, he could see the satisfying evidence of his handiwork. The vehicles they'd left in the garage had caught fire, and splinters were still rainin' down and kickin' up a cloud of snow and debris that engulfed the air where the Big Sky building used to be.

"Like clockwork." Bryce turned off the cell phone he'd used to remote-trigger the explosion and slipped it into his pocket. "We are all now unofficially dead."

"I'm not going to miss that building as much as I thought." Colonel Murphy lowered his binoculars and shook Bryce's hand. "Nice job, Sarge." He nodded to Tasiya. "Miss Belov. Couldn't have done it without you."

Tasiya seemed surprised to be included in the congratulations. "You are welcome, Mr. Murphy. Good luck with your plan."

"Thanks." He snugged his arm around his wife and headed for the shack's door. "Men? Watch your backs. Lie low. I'll see you later."

With a friendly cacophony of handshakes and back slaps and goodbyes, the others left, taking off in different directions, each heading for his own safe house. Riley Watson was headed back to Ponderosa to assume a new cover, while Trevor Blackhaw was headed for Idaho. Soon Jacob Powell was the only man left, and he was sharing an animated conversation on his cell phone.

"You're sure about that? I'll pass along the good news. Oh, yeah, babe. That's right. You'll be the first thing on my list tonight."

He was grinnin' like the Cheshire Cat when he disconnected and pocketed his phone. He was waitin' for Bryce to ask. "What?"

"I just heard from Isabella." Powell's fiancée was a Secret Service agent with some definite D.C. connections.

"She's accessed a list of freed Lukinburg hostage names. Does Anton Belov ring a bell?"

"Papa?" Tasiya's face lit up. Her smile brightened the entire dingy shack. "Papa is free?"

Powell grinned. "Yes, ma'am."

"Thank you. Thank you."

She looped her arms around Powell's neck, and for one unguarded moment, Bryce had the urge to punch his buddy in the nose. But the stab of jealousy quickly vanished. Hell, if he could get his grandparents or his parents back, he'd be huggin' on Powell, too.

Besides, Tasiya shared the love. She released Powell and walked right into Bryce's arms, wrapping her arms around his waist and hugging him. Tight. He hugged her right back.

"Oh, Bryce, that is such wonderful news."

"Yep, honey. Nobody's holdin' anything over you now." He pressed a kiss to her temple. "You are finally and officially a free woman."

She leaned back against the circle of his arms and lifted those beautiful, star-kissed eyes to his. A shimmer of tears glistened against their dark color, and Bryce's thumb was there to wipe away the first one when it spilled over. "*You* have made me free, Bryce Martin. Not just from blackmail and evil men. But in my heart and in my dreams."

"Tasiya—"

She pressed a finger against his lips to silence him. "Earlier this afternoon you said something to me. Sometimes, because of my language, I miss something. I want to be sure I completely understand."

"Just talk to me. I'll answer."

Tasiya smiled. "I love you. And I think that you love me, too. But when you invited me to your home—"

"I meant for forever."

"Forever?"

"If that's what you want." He framed her face between his big hands and tunneled his fingers into her hair. "It's what I want. I love you, Tasiya Belov."

Damn. He'd said it. Out loud.

And it felt right. It didn't hurt.

Not when she smiled at him like that.

Not when she wrapped her arms around his neck and kissed him. Like he was a man. Not a monster. Like she loved him. Like she'd love him forever.

Bryce buried his hands in her hair. "Will you marry me, Tasiya? Will you come see the Ozarks with me?"

"I will go to the Ozarks, or stay in the mountains, or even go back to that horrible prison—as long as I can be with you, Bryce Martin."

"So is that a yes?"

She grinned and articulated her lips around one sweet word. "Yep."

Bryce scooped her up in his arms and twirled her around.

Powell cleared his throat. "Well, um, yes. I'll just be going. I have a fiancée at home who needs kissing."

"Good idea." Bryce opened the door.

"I could stay, though, big guy, if you need me for backup?"

"Go away, Powell." Without releasing Tasiya, Bryce shoved his friend's face out the door and shut it behind him. "I've got my own woman to kiss."

He pulled her up into his arms and covered her lips with his own.

No matter how tough—or easy—the job was, Bryce Martin was the man to get it done.

* * * * *